CLOVEN

Little has changed in the picturesque village of Cold Firton, where evil has thrived unhindered for centuries. In 1830 a surly Tomos Richards and his crippled sister Siân travel towards London only to be beset by danger and treachery. Siân mistakenly arrives at Tripp's Cottage Northamptonshire, where cholera has just taken hold and strangers are viewed with suspicion. Present day and Ivan Browning arrives at Tripp's Cottage. Now, as a foot-and-mouth epidemic begins Ivan begins to experience ghostly pleas for help.

Please note: *This book contains material which may not be suitable to all our readers.*

CLOVEN

CLOVEN

by

Sally Spedding

Magna Large Print Books
Long Preston, North Yorkshire,
BD23 4ND, England.

British Library Cataloguing in Publication Data.

Spedding, Sally
    Cloven.

    A catalogue record of this book is
    available from the British Library

    ISBN 0-7505-2019-1

First published in Great Britain in 2002 by Macmillan
an imprint of Pan Macmillan Ltd.

Published in Large Print 2003 by arrangement with
Macmillan Publishers Limited

Magna Large Print is an imprint of Library Magna Books Ltd.

Printed and bound in Great Britain by
T.J. (International) Ltd., Cornwall, PL28 8RW

For my parents, David and Dulcie Wolff.

Grateful thanks to all at Macmillan,
especially to my editor Peter Lavery.
Also, to my agent Judith Murdoch for
her wisdom and encouragement.

I am a pilgrim here
An alien on my way.

Dafydd Jones, drover, from Caeo

The night wind whispers in my ear,
The moon shines in my face;
A burden still of chilling fear,
I find in every place.

John Clare, from 'To Mary'

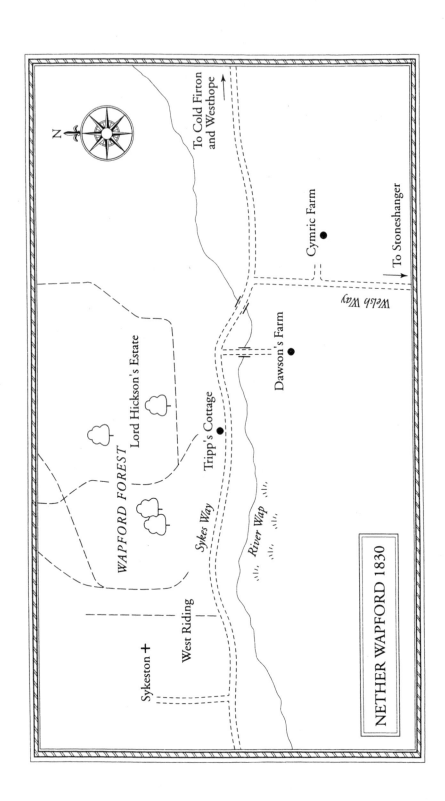

NETHER WAPFORD 1830

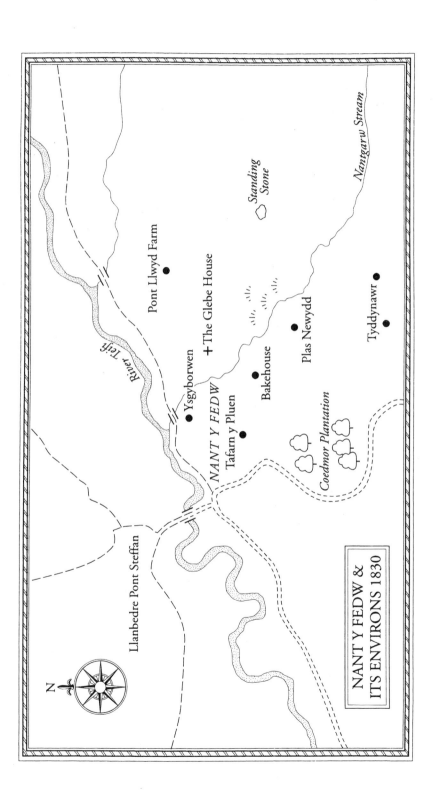

NANT Y FEDW &
ITS ENVIRONS 1830

N

River Teifi

Nantgarw Stream

Standing Stone

Pont Llwyd Farm

+ The Glebe House

Ysgyborwen

NANT Y FEDW

Tafarn y Pluen

Bakehouse

Plas Newydd

Tyddynawr

Coedmor Plantation

Llanbedre Pont Steffan

Prologue

It is 15 March 1830, the feast day of St Louise of Marillac, foundress of the Sisters of Charity, and the fourth day of the cholera. A day so white-cold with frost that even the venerable oaks seem hung with shrouds, and the three men who gather kindling wood stop to blow hot breath on their red hands...

A deathly silence surrounds them – for the birds have followed the barking muntjacs to the farthest edge of the forest, sensing sure danger to come – while the underwood is laid tight and firm, one branch across the other, until by noon the pyre is complete. Twice its makers' height, this black pyramid of intricate weave stands pierced by a stake of elm which is slower to burn. But by morning, nothing will remain of it save for a smear of powdery grey ash amongst the leaves, and the last dying echoes of some old Welsh drover's hymn:

> Arglwydd arwain fi'n Dy law
> N'ad fi grwydro yma a thraw
>
> Perein wyf ar daith
> A'm ffordd yn faith a phell
>
> Perein wy'n byd
> Ac alltud ar fy hynt.

15

One

The VW Golf hit seventy. Too fast for an unmarked road, and Ivan Browning knew it, but not fast enough to get him through that bloody scary stretch between the two farms, Wiseman's and Small Copse, the latter charred and eyeless black against the sky like the unending hedgerow and the fifty oak trees he'd first counted out in the daylight.

That had been back in July – just after he'd moved from Islington into south Northampton-shire, and gratefully accepted his appointment as a Lifelong Learning tutor in pottery – when he'd done a practice run to Cold Firton village hall along that same three-mile stretch, when his car was lit between the trees' thick shadows by the high midsummer sun.

Now, in late November, these same oaks hung pale and ghostly, their branches snaking white against the sunken moon, looming closer, hogging the windscreen it seemed, hogging his mind, until suddenly he saw double headlights veering round the bend in front of him.

He braked, heard the lurch of pots and all his other gear in the boot as he heaved his car halfway up on to the verge. His mind flashed back to that terrible night almost a year ago: a wet London street and a thirteen-year-old girl dying in his arms. After that he'd sworn never to

16

drive again and yet here he was, facing fresh punishment, possibly death, as if what he'd endured since then hadn't been enough.

'Jesus. Shit.' His pulse was working overtime, thud-thud-thud in his neck. The lunatic was in either a Saab or a Vectra he first thought, but as the thing drew near Ivan could make out more clearly the bulk of a 4x4 taking up the whole width of the road. There was nowhere else for him to go. He was a sitting fucking duck. On impact, his wing mirror screeched from its moorings, then came a long butting graze along the sills which locked his seat belt tight.

Afterwards came a silent blackness, except for his racing heart, as the other vehicle's tail lights vanished. Ivan turned the ignition key, expecting to hear the familiar burr that would take him away from that deadly place, but the engine had died.

Suddenly – from nowhere – he sensed a wetness on his right hand. Not blood or sweat but the warm spittle of a mouth, leechlike, seemingly drawing out bit by bit the last dregs of his courage. Was it Vicky? Vicky Walker? For that had been the poor dead girl's name. In his mind he saw her face once more – her mouth twisted in a rictus of pain and terror. Those white lips moaning 'Mum? Dad? Where are you?' bringing her ebbing breath cold against his cheek, until there was nothing left.

He screamed inwardly, unlocked his seat belt with frantic fingers, then baled out of the car. He could feel the long wet grass on his jeans, but it was the smell of the dead hare caught under the

17

wheel arch which finally turned his stomach and made him run like a man possessed towards the first lights of Cold Firton village.

He arrived there cursing that he'd left his keys back in the car, his fags and lighter still on the seat, his mobile in the glove box. He was sweating as if it was still that hot day back in July, his shirt sticking to his skin under his old leather jacket. But a residual fear kept him moving, first towards the only phone box, whose door was sealed up, then along by the high graveyard wall – harmless enough in daylight but now rearing up darkly as if defending at all costs its army of silent inhabitants.

The closest dwellings with telegraph wires connected to them, were three cottages joined as a terrace and almost smothered by a single steep thatch. Ivan rang the doorbell on the nearest one. No reply. He tried the next, letting the spaniel-head knocker rap out his urgency. Again, silence.

'Doesn't anyone live in this godforsaken place?' he muttered, charging round to the last cottage, number three, where a faint light glowed beyond the front door's glass panel. Having pressed the grumbling bell, he saw a shadow grow more definite as it slowly advanced until the door opened on the cottage's occupant standing behind a safety chain.

She was seriously old and her tiny colourless eyes peered at him as if he were her first visitor of the year.

'Yes? What is it?'

'Sorry to trouble you, but please may I use your phone, or would you ring this number for me?'

He fumbled for his RAC callout card and showed it to her. 'It's freephone, so you won't have to pay.'

Her surprisingly huge bony hand took the card and closed the door on him. While she was gone, Ivan's curious gaze scoured the rest of Cold Firton for any signs of life. There was nothing but the odd slit of light between curtains in the new executive development lying some distance away on the opposite side of the road.

The village hall lay a mile away up Church Street, amidst the council house outskirts – purpose-built for those cut off from civilization by distance and the lack of public transport. Tonight's would have been his eighth pottery class out of ten and normally he'd be there by now, hauling out the folding tables from under the stage, getting everything ready for a prompt seven-thirty start. But that was all down the pan now, plus his planned session when most of his students would have been underglaze-painting the items that now lay locked in his car boot.

He knew these good folk wouldn't have thought to bring along anything else to do, so would be sitting there gossiping instead. He never minded their chat while working, as long as by the end of the course all of his ladies possessed two glazed and finished items to take home with them – the objective as demanded by his line manager.

Ivan was shivering now. The evening chill had cooled his earlier sweat and now seeped into his bones. He could hear a dog somewhere, and the complaints of distant sheep infiltrated the deadly quiet. Whatever the old girl was up to, it was taking far too long. He pressed the bell again, hard this time, wanting only to get his car sorted and to retrieve something of the evening.

'Any news?' he shouted into the letter box. 'Don't worry if it's a hassle.'

Again he waited, and watched the moon rise between the trees and the church tower: a cold hard disc of light in a night that would surely plummet below freezing before it was finished.

Suddenly, as before, headlights illuminated the whole narrow street, but this time coming in from the Cold Firton road. Some four-wheel drive with a lot of chrome round the sills, it came to a swift halt. Ivan heard the thud of car doors and saw two darkened figures coming towards him. He stared again in alarm at the vehicle, wondering if it was the same one that had just nearly killed him.

'May I ask what you're doing bothering my mother at this time of an evening?' A heavily built man, in his mid fifties, Ivan guessed, pushed past him with door key at the ready. 'She's scared enough living here all on her own, can't you see that?'

The woman who accompanied him left a trail of expensive perfume in her wake. Ivan noticed her equally expensive camel-hair coat and headscarf, the immaculate wellingtons.

'My car's stranded back there, and I can't get it restarted,' he said to her back. 'Some idiot seemed hell-bent on driving me off the bloody road, the public phone's kaput and this was the only place I could seem to get an answer...Your mother's still got my RAC card,' he added futilely.

The big man let himself into the cottage and the woman followed. Total darkness now outside, the sound of muffled voices from within. Ivan stood cursing the delay, noticing Pam Barker's car nudging its way down from the Friar's Walk development. He tried to attract her attention by waving, but she wasn't even looking in his direction as she turned right up the hill towards the village hall.

'My name is Ivan Browning,' he shouted at the cottage. 'I'm supposed to be taking the pottery class tonight.' He heard the chain being secured again, then a gap appeared as the door was opened and beery breath met his nose.

'I don't care if you're the man in the bloody moon, squire. You've no business frightening a vulnerable old lady like that. Now sod off.' He handed back the RAC card and slammed the door.

'Well, if she's so bloody frightened, why aren't you looking after her?' Ivan muttered, as anger took him quickly up the hill past more bleak, lightless farms and those executive homes which seemed set too far back for him to try now. He decided it was best if he just got himself to the village hall where maybe, in between their gossiping, someone could help him.

The evening air seemed to steady his nerves as he reached the brow of the hill, but all the same that unpleasant meeting had disturbed him. Why was that old girl so wary in Cold Firton – such a quaint olde English village – that she had to phone up her son to protect her? And yet, he had to confess that when he'd first spotted it marked on his Ordnance map, its name had left a distinctly bleak impression.

And bloody cold it was here too. A dense, clinging cold without the usual bracing winds coursing across those high Northamptonshire fields. It was as if the night was being slowly frozen, in order to preserve its unknown secrets for all eternity.

The village hall car park was half full as usual – mostly people-carriers and small hatches, all with new registration plates. Money wasn't a problem for most of the local inhabitants and, according to his students' registration cards, there was no one claiming benefit. However, the council estate further up the hill was another matter, and he'd undergone two meetings already with his line manager on how to widen access and prevent what they called a class bias prevailing.

But that seemed the least of his problems now. He had to get help to recover his abandoned car, and fast. The new security light caught him by surprise as he climbed the short flight of slippery steps to the entrance. Inside, the equally bright vestibule was stickered with news of local events, plus instructions on how to use the latest gas heater, and a terse warning not to put sanitary materials down the WC.

It was then that Ivan noticed a dull red blemish on the top of his right hand. A ripple of alarm passed through him as he recalled that weird sensation in the car, still so fresh in his mind. He stared at the ring-shaped mark and the tiny hollows which defined the edge nearest his thumb, then, holding his breath, warily touched the spot. It lay like an oasis of heat on his otherwise cool skin.

What the fuck? He frantically rubbed his hand on his jeans to erase the thing. However, the more he tried the hotter and redder it grew.

From inside the main hall, Ivan could hear Joan Beddowes's guffaw followed by Pam Barker's high sustained cackle, the clatter of tools and the scraping of chairs on the wood floor. They were obviously doing fine, not needing him at all it seemed. He opened the door in bad humour: a man come down in the world, and realizing he was still falling.

'Hello, ladies. Sorry I'm late. Bit of a car problem on the way here, but I'll get your pots back to you next week. They'll still be ready by Christmas, that's a promise.'

The class stopped talking and looked up for a moment but because their dishevelled tutor didn't volunteer any more information about his mishap, soon resumed their chatter as if he didn't exist. All except one – Gill Bunnett, whose curious gaze stayed fixed on him as he scanned what they'd all begun working on without him. They'd obviously helped themselves to clay from the store cupboard, for he noticed one leaning coil pot after another, while Mrs Allen's had already collapsed and lay in a sorry heap on her board.

Damn, it had been the next session's plan to show them the correct method of continuous coiling with careful joining and awareness of balance, but how could he stop them now?

23

He signalled to the neat grey-haired woman wearing dungarees and a lumberjack shirt.

'Gill, can I have a quick word?'

In a trice she was out of her seat and washing her hands in the small kitchenette. He followed her.

'What went wrong? You're never usually late.' She snatched a paper towel from the dispenser.

Ivan watched the red-brown water swirl away as he explained to her what had happened to him between those two lonely farms. Gill, who seemed common sense personified, and above all someone he could trust, stayed pensive throughout.

'Hold on,' she said at last, before going back to retrieve her bag from under her worktable. 'I'll talk to my brother – Tom Coles, over in Westhope.' She returned, punching numbers on her mobile and, after a brief exchange, agreed to meet him by Ivan's car.

'You've saved my life, Gill. Thanks.' He poured himself a cup of tap water and downed it in one go.

'Well, you could be waiting for assistance half the night stuck out here.' She slotted her phone back in its case and reached for her jacket while Ivan returned to the hall to make fresh apologies to his class, only too aware that their latest conversation was centred around a forthcoming Christmas shopping trip to Milton Keynes and so he was largely speaking to himself.

The night's dense and eerie stillness hit him again like a fist, but once ensconced in Gill's new Focus, with Radio 4 faintly filtering through to break the silence, he began to pull himself together.

'That's where I tried for help first. At number three.' He pointed out the end cottage, now all dark. 'Not very pleasant or helpful, specially after the heavy mob turned up.'

She gave him a quick sideways glance. 'I'm not surprised. That's old Ma Oakley's place. You wouldn't think a little husk like that could ever have produced those three sons of hers. Thugs with plenty of folding dough, I'm afraid.' His driver obviously knew the road well and judged perfectly the unlit bend out of the village. 'The mafia of Cold Firton, we call them. Best not to get involved with that lot.'

Ivan was beginning to get a mental picture, and it wasn't one likely to feature in any *Quaint Northamptonshire Villages* brochure to attract the cream-tea brigade.

'Tell me,' he began. 'That stretch of road where my car seized up – it's so bloody weird, like... I don't know–'

'Like something bad's happened there, d'you mean?' She slowed as a van approached too fast, its headlights undipped for too long. Ivan paused, giving her a moment to recover her nerve, wondering why she'd said that.

'Yeah, could be... But before I left the car I felt this really odd sensation on my hand, as if someone was sucking for my blood.' He shivered involuntarily as he touched the spot again and, incredibly, it still felt warm even though the rest of his hand was cold. 'I know that sounds mad, Gill, but please don't spread it around. I don't

25

want people thinking I'm some kind of weirdo.'

'Course I won't, but it's funny you've mentioned it.' She seemed quite unfazed by his revelation. 'When Dr Rook and his wife called in for tea last summer she took me off into the kitchen and showed me a place on her arm where she'd experienced exactly the same thing.'

'And?' Ivan's eyes were fixed ahead in the dark, though not recognizing any of the trees.

'Well, Lord above, if there wasn't a reddish ring just above her elbow. Mind you, she's very pale-skinned so it certainly showed.'

'Has this ever happened to anyone else round here, d'you know?' Ivan asked, aware of being slowly, inexorably drawn into something he couldn't quite fathom. Also aware now that, surely, the dead Vicky Walker couldn't be anything to do with it. Or could she?

But Gill Bunnett hadn't time to answer. There was a man with a torch standing on the verge by a white estate car. Where Ivan's own car had been, surely to God. But where the hell was it?

Ivan stared through the windscreen, too numb with shock to speak as she slowed down.

'Good old Tom.' Spoken affectionately. 'We're twins, you know. He came out first.'

'Great.' Ivan's stomach felt hollow.

'Where is it, then? Where's your car?'

'You tell me.'

She pulled over and parked in front of the old Astra, as Ivan, panicking, thought of all his students' pots, Gill's included. And the turntables, the tools, his mobile. All the paraphernalia of his enforced new life. Probably damaged beyond

26

repair, just like himself – and that schoolgirl's still-grieving family...

He jumped out and took in Tom Coles's stale aftershave, the whiff of an old car engine, then the ominously empty space where his Golf should have been.

'Can see where your tyres were, though,' the other man said after the introductions. He trawled his torch over the damp verge. 'So it was obviously here.' He gave his sister a strangely knowing look, then got out his mobile, dialled the police and passed it over to Ivan to report his apparent loss. For a split second Ivan hesitated. Even though he'd been cleared of responsibility for the teenager's death, the case had spawned a lot of unwelcome publicity. Mention of his name might still be a problem, even out here in the backwoods.

Brother and sister watched the younger man's face growing more disheartened as his short conversation ended.

'They can't come out till tomorrow afternoon.' He pressed End and handed the phone back. 'Said sorry but they're fully stretched.'

'By that time' – Tom Coles again passed his torch beam over the tyre tracks – 'these could have bloody vanished. For starters the riding school uses this verge every day, and you can bet your life whoever's lifted your car will be back to remove all traces.'

Ivan felt sick with frustration. It was already half past eight and his class had half an hour to run. If he didn't show up before the end, one of them might tattle to the Adult Education office and he'd end up losing his pay when, at this moment in his impecunious life, every single pound counted.

'I'll run you back straightaway,' offered Gill Bunnett, 'and why don't you' – she nudged her brother – 'just have a bit of a look round? You never know, there may be some clue along the road here.'

As if in answer, Tom Coles trained his torch on to the bleak outline of Wiseman's Farm and its one tall chimney reaching into the sky. An upstairs light suddenly went out.

'I'll go try in there. For fuck's sake, we all know about *them*, don't we? I can pretend to them I'm looking for Fly. That dog of ours is always running off.'

Ivan noticed Gill's expression change. Now she gripped her twin's arm. 'No, you mustn't, Tom. Promise me you'll keep away from that place.'

'Don't be daft, woman. We've got to get to the bottom of this.' He turned to Ivan. 'What's happened to you is the last bloody straw, you poor sod. I'll give Gill a buzz tomorrow to let her know how I got on, OK?' He dug in his donkey-jacket pocket for his pipe, and jabbed it between his teeth without lighting it, then climbed into the Astra and reversed off the verge, moving along slowly until his headlights lit up the darkened farm's newly installed gate.

No music, no attendant babble. The car radio remained silent this time, as Gill Bunnett drove Ivan back towards Cold Firton. Her normally pleasant open face seemed tense, her hands

28

looked unusually stiff on the wheel. For a while, neither spoke.

'He's never listened to me,' she said at last, bleakly. 'Tom's got a heart of gold, but he always knows best.'

'So what did he mean, the last bloody straw?' Ivan still felt uncomfortable that he'd not tried to discourage the man's mission, but things were getting more out of his control, and those words of Coles's now seemed too full of foreboding.

'Everybody round here knows about the Oakleys, but everybody's scared of them.' Gill pulled over to let a motorbike go by.

'Scared of what?' Ivan noticed the moon had ballooned into a huge orb, and the trees below it had grown yet more oppressive.

'Wiseman's Farm is a den of iniquity, and always has been. But those Oakleys are very clever, oh yes. Just like the Dawsons who live over your way. There's never quite enough proof for any criminal charges to be brought against any of them – not that the cops round here are up to much anyway. No wonder people are getting hold of guns to protect themselves.'

'You're kidding? So what do they actually get up to?'

'You mean the Oakleys?'

'Yeah.'

'Well, just as the Dawsons kept cattle, so the Oakleys used to breed Texel sheep. But local people knew that was just a cover, and that nothing much ever went to market. So, now, it's still lots of fingers in lots of rotten pies. You name it, they've done it: receiving stolen goods, assault, intimidation. But there's been talk of much bigger stuff. *Real* money.'

'You mean drugs?'

Gill nodded.

'Even the old girl?'

His companion snorted. 'You bet. She was the mastermind behind their new ventures before the old marbles started going. They just use her now to keep that cottage warm. They're a hard bloody lot.'

'If they're doing that well, why nick my car?'

'Old habits die hard, I suppose.'

Gill Bunnett didn't drive into the village hall car park, instead she stopped on the kerb of Middle View Rise and kept the engine running.

'Look, it's ten to, now. You just go in and check the hall gets locked up OK – Margaret will give you the key. Then, if you make your way along here to number six, there'll be a meal and a bed for you. Or, if Bob doesn't need the car tonight, would you rather I run you back to Nether Wapford?'

Ivan shook his head. He'd had enough running around for one night, and the prospect of a Pot Noodle plus Mars Bar then a mattress that felt like the surface of the moon was no match for her offer.

'Great. Thanks. See you in a few minutes.' His long legs bounded away into the dark, until the wretched sudden glare of the security light showed that all but one of the cars had gone.

The main door of the hall was still open, and he prayed that the Polo still left outside was Margaret Allen's. He heard the WC flush and the woman emerged, smoothing down her skirt.

'I hung on for you,' she said pointedly, switching off the heaters and most of the lights. 'I don't think their hearts were really in it tonight. They were waiting for their pots to decorate.'

'Of course,' Ivan conceded wearily. 'And, like I said before, I'm really sorry.'

The little woman sniffed. 'Mr Rigby was *never* late, and he used to come over from Daventry.'

'Good for him.' Ivan noticed someone had thoughtfully wiped a clay table with the only tea towel. He ran some water into the washing-up bowl to let it soak. She passed him the door key and left without more ado.

Five minutes later, Ivan was walking along Middle View Rise, aware of the tiny neon-like strip of M1 traffic in the far distance and, as he neared Gill Bunnett's house, he felt once more the chill of that strange place touch every nerve, every fibre of his being, and finally settle on his heart.

They're as black as Dai Twp's beard, except for their terrible eyes which burn like old culm in the grate. I can hear the men yelling as the herd breaks towards me. I feel dead already. The hedge is too high and newly laid, no trees or hole to hide in... Hell's in their hooves and to them I'm no more than earth. I hear my bones break like old plates at the Tafarn, and the pain is of dying and I'll never know the end of it. Never...

'Eat up, girl. Your brother'll be here soon.'

Siân stared at the slab of bread whose burnt

31

oats stood up from its surface like rabbit droppings. Then her head slumped, suddenly full of the sleep her recent nightmare had stolen. Her nose hit the table hard.

A slap stung her ears. The fourteen-year-old tried to stand as, in protest, her mother snatched the crust and crammed it into her own mouth. 'A lodger you are to be sure, Siân Richards, and in my book never to be anything else.'

Her daughter watched crumbs fall from those tight dry lips that had not uttered one word of affection to her either before or after her accident. And gazed at those washed-out eyes, like the pools in the lane. Not like those of her father, Geraint Richards, which were deep and dark. But what was the use thinking that? What use was anything? He wouldn't be back from his job as a caster with the Dowlais ironworks till summer at least, and she missed him more than her old life itself.

'Dribbling again, are you?' The woman rubbed Siân's chin with her apron. 'The Lord knows how I try. The Lord knows.'

Then Siân suddenly froze.

Her brother had arrived – and something was going on. It was as if his shadow reached her from the door, bringing in a draught of icy air. Next came his voice, so like their father's she could pretend it was him, but for the smell. Her brother's boots were green with dung and his clothes reeked like ox skin.

'She'll need a coat, Mam.' Tomos went over to the range and plucked a trotter from the cold broth. He let the greasy stock drip down his front as he sucked, then returned the trotter to the pot. His mother, Mair Richards, watched from the stairs as if he were a stranger. Two years away from the Plas Newydd hearth and having his own herds had changed him. He licked his lips with a huge red tongue as Siân listened to her mother's silence, except for her opening and shutting of cupboard doors.

'*Why a coat? For me? He's never bothered before whether I freeze or burn.*'

The request had also thrown Mair Richards into confusion, and the girl wondered what her mother could possibly find for her. She saw Tomos open the small cupboard set below the room's one main beam and unearth a sliver of cheese edged with mould. He dropped it to the floor and trod it into a mess. Then he sniffed.

'Something's pissed itself in here, and I'm telling you straight, it's not me.'

He bent down and lifted the hem of Siân's skirt. 'Hey, I'm not putting up with her stinking like the drains.'

'You'll have to. I'm finished with her.' The forty-eight-year-old woman held up her husband's coat: the best *brethyn cartref*, patched and mended, still creased from lying in the honeymoon chest. 'You don't deserve it, mind.' Her mother laid it over Siân's back. It felt the warmest thing in that miserable hovel and for a moment their eyes met. Eyes looking from as far apart as other worlds yet, for a moment, Siân imagined a tiny smile stretched her mother's lips.

'Now you're to make no bother for your brother, since he's good enough to take you.'

33

'*Take me where? Where am I going?*' The girl's face searched from one to the other.

'You tell her.'

'No.'

Siân banged her fists on the table in frustration.

'Temper, temper.' Tomos glared down at her, his face filling with blood. Worse, when he pressed his wide-brimmed hat down on his head, it made him look devilish. Siân shivered.

'You're going to a hospital – in London.' Her mother raised her onto a chair and pushed both arms into the sleeves.

'*Hospital?*' Siân shook her dark curls and began to struggle.

'It's to see someone your Da knew when he was a boy.'

'*No, no, no!*'

'Well there's gratitude, you little incubus.' Tomos had learnt that word from his father-in-law, the vicar Meurig Jones, to whom Wales was a land overrun by Merlin's spawn. Besides, he liked the sound of it. Siân pushed and kicked him with her one whole leg, but she was no match for both mother and son.

'It's your Da who wants this,' Mair Richards said. 'D'you think our Tomos here'd be bothering otherwise at this time of year?'

The coat made her feel as though she'd been caught in the mire – heavy, pulling Siân down, making her itch. Yet it was his, her dad's, still bearing his smell, with even a grey hair still stuck to the front. She plucked it away and hid it deep in a pocket, and promised she'd never be parted from this garment till they met again.

'*Haiptrw ho!*' Tomos suddenly bellowed, rising up and promptly knocking his hat off against the beam. His curse filled the room. Since living at Pont Llwyd Farm he'd lost the knack of stooping – lost what little grace he'd had. He squatted down, hauled his sister onto his shoulder and made for the door.

Two untrimmed horses stood waiting. One a chestnut Welsh Mountain, the other a cob black as anthracite. Mair Richards watched them from inside her shawl, her face unmoving. She stayed to see her daughter hoisted into the saddle – and, when they'd moved off towards his herd, a small tear grew and froze in her eye.

I'm thinking she looks as old as Mamgu, our granny. Is that what I've done to her? Look at her standing there, wound round in black like a spindle. And why doesn't she wave? Or move, even, to keep up with us a few paces? I know why: she's glad to see the back of me and my ways. But you wait, you wait, I'll be coming back with proper legs. Someone who can speak and sing, not just make noises no one understands. I'm telling you. All of you.

Heavens above, there's Dewi Jenkins and Huw Davies waiting. Oh no, anyone else but Huw. He's really staring at me, and I know what he's thinking. He's getting something out of his pocket. It looks like a stone. I grip Collen's mane tighter, in case she startles, but he's coming over, smiling.

'Good luck, Siân.' He hands me a cooked potato. 'You might need this.' His fingers are cold, one of them badly cut from the forestry. I know I'm blushing: I can feel it spread like fire over my face. 'It's not much,

sorry,' he says, but inside the tater, just peeping out, is a halfpenny. Brand new.

I can hear his friend laugh, but that doesn't matter. Nothing matters except that Huw Davies's beautiful blue eyes are on mine.

'Give it here.' Tomos was suddenly alongside her. 'You've no need of that.' He flung Huw's offering into the hedge and slapped the chestnut's rump. Huw shouted and tried to run after Siân but, as the trot grew faster past Plas Newydd's neglected fields, he was soon just a small speck in the distance, his farewells lost to the wind.

Brother and sister soon reached the Glebe House where the new Mrs Richards and her father stood by the gate, their black hair almost interlocking in the breeze.

Like two crows. Siân thought. It was as if there were a burial taking place, for neither spoke, not even to Tomos. She hated her brother more than ever and when, with a dull ache, she realized Huw hadn't reappeared, she looked to where Wern Common sloped up to the standing stone, Maen Lefn, sharp against the sky. Its strange needle-like form seemed to move with the clouds; below it, on the soft mound, was where in the old days she'd sit with Eirwen Pugh and exchange precious secrets. Now her best friend had gone, suddenly moved south to the valleys, giving no reason why, taking such secrets with her.

Siân's eyes filled up with tears. She could again feel that summer grass under her feet, as vividly as anything before or since, the orange lichen

36

lodged in the boulders' cracks, the unfinished carving – *H D loves* – just above the turf line. Huw had promised he'd complete it by her birthday in May.

Then she heard hooves thrumming on the hard earth by Pont Llwyd Farm. Tomos, joined by two other men, was corralling his store cattle by his newly constructed gate. Their shouts shocked the church's ravens into the graveyard trees and set the dogs in a frenzy of barking.

Ben, a black-and-fawn Welsh Hound, was mad as a moth, but persistent on the heels of strays. Bigger, quicker than either of the two corgis, Tomos had trained him from a pup after Flint had died. Flint, her dog, the one who'd licked her face and stayed beside her in the terrifying dark those three long years ago.

Siân saw one of the men kick Ben quiet; Ben now threw his head back and howled as he cowered near the barn.

Tomos leapt from the cob and floored the man, sending his hat into a bush of weeds and his nose in another direction. Siân gasped. She'd not seen so much blood since her own injuries, and, smelling it, the cob took off towards Esgairwen, stirrups flapping, its tail high as a mast. The cattle drove was already an hour late, and now Tomos was charging at her as if his lungs would burst.

'Give me the mare, quick.' He pulled his sister to the ground and hammered his heels into the pony's sides. Siân dragged herself up against a fence post, realizing with a thudding heart that the bullocks were too close, confused, and climbing each other near the gate. It would only take another fright to send them her way – again.

'*Ben,*' she mouthed, '*come here.*' But the dog was still licking its bruises, while just the two Cardiganshire corgis yapped at the heels of the unruly herd.

Suddenly the winter sun vanished, and a huge shape towered over her. Droplets of blood the colour of elderberries fell onto her coat. She recognized Marcus Webb, one of the Tafarn gang, and when his filthy hand moved from his face, she could see his nose skewered to the right, with the bone jutting through the skin.

'A curse on you all,' he muttered. 'And if I was to untie the gate and clap my hands just the once, that lot of runts would be gone from here like the damned.' He gathered phlegm in his throat and spat it into her hair. 'You and your brother can rot in hell. Make sure you tell him.'

Two

Ivan had slept like a log and now, in the Bunnetts' pristine guest bathroom, he symbolically sluiced away the previous day's anxieties from his shoulders – but not quite. He was concerned about Gill's brother having possibly put himself at risk, and what, if anything, had transpired at that seemingly notorious farm.

Later, downstairs, despite the comforting aroma of bacon wafting into the dining room from the kitchen, and Bob Bunnett's cheerful good wishes as he left for work, Ivan's anxiety remained.

Gill brought in a fresh pot of tea and set it down. She also handed Ivan Valerie Rook's phone number, written on a Post-it note.

'I thought you might like to get in touch with her to compare notes about your strange experiences,' she added.

'Thanks. I certainly will.'

Ivan then slotted the piece of paper into his wallet.

'Be interesting to see if Tom's discovered anything as well,' she said, dispensing milk into his cup from a little jug she herself had made in her class. She, too, was obviously tense, doing her best to not let it show. 'Trouble is, the Oakleys have got such a huge place there – over two hundred acres – so it's not difficult to get rid of stuff.'

Ivan chewed his bacon thoughtfully, now

feeling definite that something wasn't quite right about any of this, even in daylight, and he felt a brief flutter of fear in that cosy room with its glowing stove and bright tablecloth.

'Can't you just give him a ring, see if he's OK – if he's any the wiser?' He asked this in such a way as not to alarm her.

She checked her watch with the wall clock.

'Could do, I suppose. He's normally around till half eight. Not at his best first thing, though, my brother.' When she'd dialled, she kept her fingers crossed. 'Jane? Gill here. Sorry it's a bit early, but is Tom around?'

Ivan watched as a frown formed on his hostess's face while her sister-in-law carried on talking. Then Gill replaced the receiver without saying a word.

'What's wrong? He's OK, isn't he?' Ivan demanded. The young man's cheeks burned with alarm and guilt at a worst-imagined scenario.

'No, but he's gone off to work much earlier than usual, apparently, as he'd got no sleep.'

Gill sat down and stared into her teacup. It was Ivan who attended to the toaster as the smell of burning bread wafted from the kitchen.

'Look, Gill, this is all my bloody fault, and I'll sort it now. I'll get a taxi into town, see the cops, and go from there. No, don't move. You and Tom have done enough.' He cleared up his breakfast things, then went into the hallway and ordered a Pronto cab from Stoneshanger.

Fifteen minutes later, after he'd helped load the dishwasher, it arrived.

'I'm sorry, Ivan.' Gill's eyes hovered on the

plain black vehicle waiting at the garden gate, then quickly looked away. 'We've got to live here. People from outside don't seem to understand that, but there it is. I've probably told you too much already.' She closed the door with a quiet finality, and he gave his instructions to the driver whose battered cap rested just below his eyebrows.

'Westhope, please. I need the garage there.' And, during an uneventful journey, Ivan regaled the middle-aged man with the previous night's events.

'Well, what with all the raping and pillaging, this was once quite a place, you know. Only now it's all ramming and shunting,' the driver elaborated.

'Ramming and shunting? What d'you mean?' The dreary November fields rolled by them, speckled by dirty sheep.

'With ramming, the bastards go for your wheel. Least damage to their own old crocks, see. Then they pick up a nice fat cheque to buy a new car, thanks very much. Shunting's different, though.' The driver slowed down to skirt round a girl on a big brown horse. 'That's when they either tailgate you off the tarmac, or–' he paused, half looking round as if what he was about to say was significant – 'they come at you full beam, specially on roads like these, hogging your side, so the only thing you can do is to start climbing.' He indicated the thickly overgrown verge. 'Normally you'd stay put, till help came along, but here, Christ, you'd be watching till the fucking blackbirds come up, and freeze to

41

fucking death. So what do you do if you ain't got a mobile handy, eh?' He shot the question like a bullet.

'Christ knows,' said Ivan, wishing the man would take a breather from all this doom and gloom.

'You'd take up your bed and walk, son, leave the vehicle unattended. Problem is, when *it* then goes walkies it's your word against some local with pals in the right places.'

'If you say so,' his passenger muttered bleakly, recalling how after that Hopcraft Street nemesis his city technology college's governors had tried to pin the girl's death squarely on him, insisting that, no, there'd been nothing wrong with their minibus – its service record was impeccable. Yet, returning from a Hans Coper ceramics exhibition at the Design Centre with a party of rowdy fifth-formers in the back, the brakes had failed when a young schoolgirl had suddenly stepped off the kerb without looking.

Since then he'd followed a succession of nightmare days, sleepless nights, and – until he'd gone ex-directory – strange random calls, calls which on occasions were worse for him than the tragedy itself, slowly ripping him apart.

His colleagues had constantly urged him to leave on the grounds of ill-health, but he damned well wasn't sick. He'd just needed a fair hearing from the management fat cats. But not one of them, not even his girlfriend, Tania, in the IT and Business Studies department, had suggested he'd have any sort of future there. So, with universal chants of counselling and self-restructuring filling his head he, Ivan Browning, aged thirty-two, with a salary to match plus the London Weighting, had resigned his post on St Patrick's Day.

He could have gone back to Northern Ireland, to Downwellan where his parents still lived in reasonable comfort, or hung on in the Barton Road flat as an external examiner for various Boards in Design Technology, but his one trusted mate, Noel Parr, who worked for the British Library and had introduced him to John Clare's poetry, had been endlessly extolling the virtues of that poet's native county. Northamptonshire. Still close to London, relatively cheap, and ideal for downtiming, Parr had reckoned.

Now Ivan wasn't so sure...

The cab had reached Westhope, a village even smaller than Cold Firton, dominated by a two-pump garage and a craft gallery where once the old forge had been. But pottery and a possible marketing outlet were now the last things on Ivan's mind.

'Can you hang on for two minutes?' he asked the driver. 'I'll need to get back to the cop shop in Stoneshanger straight afterwards.'

'Be my guest.'

Ivan ached for his cigarettes and watched enviously as the man produced a tin of Holborn and a packet of Rizlas from a crowded glove box.

'What with the railways all fucked up round here, I'm hardly rushed off my feet.'

George Pike & Sons' garage was set back from the road by a forecourt of uneven slabs darkened by oil and similar substances. Ivan walked into the gloomy service bay and opened a door marked CUSTOMERS ONLY.

A young lad in greasy overalls was busy hanging up sets of car keys onto a row of hooks behind the counter.

'Does someone called Tom Coles work here?' Ivan asked him.

The boy turned round, his almost colourless eyes surprisingly large and protruding. Ivan wondered if he was ill or, worse, on something.

'Why you askin'?'

His inquisitor really wanted to say *mind your own bloody business*, but he tried to keep his cool.

'I'm a friend of his sister's, and he helped me out last night. Just wanted to say thanks while I was passing, that's all.'

The boy looked out at the waiting taxi and suspected this was a lie.

'Public's not allowed to speak to me dad's employees during workin' hours.'

He's got that off pat, Ivan thought, realizing that total honesty might now be best.

'It *is* important, please...'

'Wass yer name then?' Another obstacle, and Ivan wondered what his fare was costing now, with the cab engine still running.

'Browning.'

The son slouched away through an adjoining door and, after less than a minute, returned.

''E's never heard of you – 'sides, Tom says he's busy.' With that, the boy went over to the wall phone, lifted the receiver, and, with an even stranger expression on his face, began dialling.

'Thanks for trying.' But Ivan was choked. *What the fuck was going on here?* Why did Coles suddenly want nothing to do with him? For a moment, he was tempted to call in again at Middle View Rise, but there was the insurance and God knows what else to organize first.

During a tobacco-scented journey back to Stoneshanger, made all the more hazardous by drain-clearance vehicles, various road works and traffic lights that seemed to have sprung up overnight, the driver chit-chatted about the malaise of the county's rat-runs and the number of new homes mushrooming on even greenfield sites.

Ivan waited until a pause in the man's musings made it possible to ask one particular question.

'Have you ever heard anything of the Oakleys in Cold Firton?' he ventured. 'I believe they've got a place called Wiseman's Farm.'

The man shook his head, almost too slowly, his passenger thought.

'Nope, can't say I have. Why?'

'Oh, nothing really. Someone at my class just happened to mention them. No big deal.' His voice faded as his unease grew.

'You a teacher, then?' The man obviously wished to change the subject.

'Sort of. Not classroom any more, thank God,' he said firmly, though he wasn't entirely convincing. 'Just people who *want* to be there, which is half the battle.'

'Yeah. S'pose it is.'

The taxi finally pulled in by an ironstone building with an archway separating the police station from the Lifelong Learning block and the adjoining courthouse. The driver held out a large mottled hand.

'Twenty-two quid to you, sire.' That sum brought a smile to the man's lips but Ivan's heart sank. He gritted his teeth as he extracted a twenty and a fiver from his wallet, but when it looked like the guy was about to keep the change he leant back through his window.

'Sorry, but I'm skint. D'you mind? Three quid's three quid – it's a lot to me at the moment.'

Instantly, the driver's persona changed. He growled something obscene under his breath, then: 'And how the fuck do I keep going with the likes of you tight-arses, eh? You teachers are all the bloody same.' The three coins he passed over were still hot from his hand. As Ivan checked that they weren't foreign before pocketing them, the cab revved up and whipped away as if the devil were on its tail.

It was only while heading for the police station entrance that Ivan suddenly made two alarming connections. The taxi driver now seemed the spitting image of the boor he'd met outside the old girl's cottage in Cold Firton. And Gill Bunnett, for some reason, had been none too happy to see him arrive outside her house.

'I see our own John Oakley wheeled you in,' observed the desk sergeant drily, stacking two files over to one side to make more room in front of him. 'I'm Sergeant Bryce. What can I do for you?' He picked up his pen. Pale grey eyes took in the younger man's disbelief, his obvious

46

frustration at not being sure where to start. But, once he'd given his name, the ballpoint started scribbling.

By the time Ivan had finished his story and made a written statement, a search of the immediate area in Cold Firton was confirmed for three o'clock that afternoon, and a genuine-sounding apology given for not having attended to him the previous evening.

'We had an incident over at Turwell, otherwise you'd have seen us earlier, and there's also been something tricky up at Radby End. Can't be everywhere, I'm afraid, sir, and now that rural crime's on the up and up, and police stations are closing left, right and centre, it leaves people like yourself more vulnerable than ever. Still, we do our best. Now then,' Bryce began a new page of his pad, 'were there any witnesses to the incident?'

'Witnesses?' The word still had a grimly hollow ring to it since that London night when all twelve of his pupils had deliberately denied seeing the dark-clad figure step into his path without giving him a chance to brake or swerve. After that below-the-belt betrayal just to keep themselves out of the limelight, he'd felt unable to teach them any longer in the way professional status demanded, and they'd been moved off his timetable. 'You mean to the shunting, as our friend Mr Oakley so aptly called it? No.' Only the lowering trees and that poor dead hare. 'But, like I said, Mrs Bunnett and her brother, Mr Coles, saw how my car had just vanished. I don't really want to involve them in this any more, if possible.'

At the second mention of Tom Coles's name, the policeman's mouth tightened, forming tiny grooves above his top lip. Ivan tried not to read too much into this almost imperceptible reaction, and continued, 'You see, she comes to one of my classes, and if she cries off now I'm down to seven. After that, who knows? As far as her brother's concerned, one night without sleep's enough, isn't it? He said he was going to try at Wiseman's Farm, so I reckon someone there must have given him a hard time.'

The sergeant kept his eyes on his pad, but his writing came to a stop.

'You don't know if that's what happened, Mr Browning, and you can't go round making assumptions, but I certainly agree we don't need to bother either Mrs Bunnett or Mr Coles any further at this stage. To be honest with you,' Bryce continued pointedly, leaning towards him, 'our particular pool's getting far too small for some of the fish we've acquired round here. Time we pulled a few of them out... Now then,' his tone lightened, 'can I get you a cup of tea?' It was clearly by way of consolation but, just then, his desk phone rang.

Ivan thanked him, said he'd got to arrange another car for himself and get a mobile sorted ASAP and all being well he'd be at the incident site at 3 p.m. He left the desk sergeant looking older and paler as he took the call. News of something grim was clearly coming through, and as he left, trying to gauge what the sergeant's quiet responses referred to, Ivan prayed to whatever god might be out there that it was

48

nothing to do with Gill Bunnett or her suddenly elusive twin brother.

Having also thanked this same god for Reedman Insurance Brokers' freephone number, Ivan telephoned them from the Lamb and Flag pub entrance, and spoke to a guy called Chris who assured him a replacement car from Turner's Garage would be outside the fire station at two-thirty. As for the mobile, his fags and everything in the boot, they'd have to be itemized, costed and a cheque sent to him personally.

With a new packet of Marlboros at the ready, Ivan then settled down in the smoking corner of the lounge bar, surrounded by early prints depicting Stoneshanger's racecourse, and with his half of bitter and a cheese roll in front of him. This had cost exactly the three quid that Oakley had so kindly allowed him to keep.

While he jotted down a list of things to do, on a scrap of invoice paper, Ivan noticed the girl who'd served him in the bar was occasionally glancing his way. She was certainly very pretty. Dark, where Tania was fair, slim where his former girlfriend had been curvily well-built. Tania's name still lurked in his address book, but just a name, nothing more...

Now this attractive girl was looking at him again, and coming over.

'Everything all right?' she asked, as if she actually cared.

'Fine, thanks,' he lied, having just written down Valerie Rook's name, the one Gill Bunnett had mentioned, with a question mark alongside.

'One of our chefs is ill, so it's a bit of a 'mare with food at the moment. Good job there's no racing on.' She cleared away some stray glasses and wiped over the bar.

'You been working here long?' he asked, killing his cigarette stub.

'Only two weeks,' she volunteered brightly. 'Just temping till my college course starts in January.'

'What's that, then?' Ivan found himself more than mildly curious.

'Garden Design. Part-time, mind – just for the first year. It's all Charlie Dimmock's fault.' She laughed, then turned to greet two women in Barbours, who were perching themselves on bar stools.

Ivan checked his watch. He still had time to call on his line manager to explain about the lost pottery work and ceramic materials and warn her of a possible fall-off in attendance within his class. Also to press their marketing team to advertise two more courses in other nearby villages for the start of the spring term. Recent events had shown that to put all his eggs in that particular Cold Firton basket was not such a good idea. But first he had to leave the pub knowing who this girl was.

'I'm Ivan Browning,' he announced over the head of the two women drinkers. 'I've got a pottery over in Nether Wapford. I'm new here.'

The girl looked up from the till, smiling. 'And I'm Jo. Hope to see you around.'

'Great.'

Buoyed up by this seemingly promising exchange, Ivan called in at the post office, bought

50

a thank-you card featuring a scene by some local artist, and sent it off to Gill Bunnett. Next, he made his way to the fire station via the bank. However, when he saw that the fuel gauge of his replacement car read empty, his mood soon changed.

'Sod this,' he muttered to himself as the man who'd delivered it pushed down the squeaky aerial. And, to add insult to injury, it was a basic model Saxo with as much power as a kid's pedal car. 'Do I have to push it to a bloody garage to get petrol, or what?' he asked.

'Sorry, mate, that's how we get 'em back from the customer. It's up to the next driver to sort it, otherwise we'd be on the skids filling all these buggers up each time.' The man handed him the keys, then eased himself into a bigger, smarter new Xsara which had just pulled up. 'Unleaded, remember, and you might have to check her oil.' Then he was gone, with a colleague at the wheel.

'And the rest.' Ivan manoeuvred his tall frame into the tiny space, and felt for the throttle, disconcertingly like a pea under his boot. Although the windscreen was filthy, at least the engine obliged. Sticking to third gear, he managed to reach a garage at the end of Cobbling Street.

Predictably, oil and screen wash were also dangerously low and as he settled up he wondered how long his latest kiln-load of casserole dishes would take to sell, in order to replenish his ever-shrinking savings.

He arrived on the dot for his meeting with the

police on that lonely stretch of the Cold Firton road. It was three o'clock, with the thick grey light already beginning to fade, the great knotty oaks swaying overhead as they'd done for centuries. He felt nervous enough just waiting there, as if some new imbecile might come ploughing into him from around that bend, and when, in his rear-view mirror, he could see a mass of horses and female riders jostling together along the distant verge, heading his way, a familiar surge of panic filled his chest. Should he bale out of there, or sit tight? Surely there wasn't enough room for them all on that relatively narrow strip of grass?

Suddenly, to his huge relief, a lurid yellow-and-blue-chequered police Land Rover crawled alongside the horses making them filter single file along the road. Thus they passed him, defecating and whinnying, but at least controlled. The last two girls looked down through his window and gave him a wave.

'Detective Constable Philip Marsh and this is Constable Brian Whitrow, Stoneshanger CID.' Marsh, the younger of the two officers shook hands with Ivan and the three of them then re-enacted the whole incident, pacing along the distance to the bend, examining the now well-trodden grass, and kneeling to find any trace of a shattered wing mirror or any hare's blood on the road itself.

'Absolutely nothing. Someone's cleaned up here good and proper.' Marsh sniffed his finger. 'Real little housewives.' He sniffed again. 'This is bleach, what say you?' He and Whitrow knelt down again, lifting the overhanging grass to reveal where mud and other leavings had gathered. A Chewit wrapper, a knot of old rope, nothing which had anything to do with Tuesday night.

They finally stood up, their eyes turning towards the Oakley chimney, then to each other.

'D'you know, we can't even get a bloody search warrant for that place,' Whitrow muttered to himself, 'but will we scare them off by being here, I ask myself, or make things even worse.'

'Hell, they're probably taking a peek at us right now – then will get themselves hidden away nice and cosy somewhere. Christ knows they've got enough room to hide a bloody army in there.' Marsh continued staring at the farm.

'Have you been inside that place before?' asked Ivan, coming round to look, while avoiding the horse shit.

'Worth double figures,' muttered Whitrow. 'But you've got to hand it to them, they're bright. No one ever answers the door. Zilch. And we can't go breaking and entering – got no proof of anything. Nor can we stop them going about their daily business. The law loves them: she's their fucking mistress.' He gave a sick little laugh, then got out his two-way and pulled up the aerial. 'Milly to Funfair 2. It's fifteen-twenty and we're going to sniff round Wiseman's. Over.'

Marsh turned to Ivan. 'Stay here in the Land Rover till we get back. You can make a note of any number plates travelling either way, but no eye contact, OK? And let's just hope those two pretty bow-wows of theirs have had their lunch.' The

DC disappeared through the gateway.

Ivan duly locked himself into the vehicle and waited. His pulse was throbbing, his mouth dry, though the only signs of life outside the car were an elderly man on a bicycle with a basket-load of twigs, and a white van advertising a printing firm in Rugby.

Within eight minutes, the two officers had returned.

'Don't even ask,' Marsh muttered as Ivan got out. 'And I suppose Dick Turpin came riding by, eh?'

'Nothing at all.'

Then Ivan had an idea. 'What about trying Small Copse Farm to see if my car's been dumped in there?'

'No way,' replied Marsh not even bothering to look in that direction. 'For a start it's all locked up: just a shell now, as you can see. Ever since the fire–'

'Fire? When?'

'Oh, a long while back – before I'd come here.' He cast a quick glance at his colleague. 'Terrible business, apparently. There was a brother and sister living there at the time. They'd taken over the cob-breeding after both their parents died. Probably due to one of the stable lads lighting up. Mind, it wouldn't have taken much after all, as the weather had been boiling hot for weeks.'

'That's what the inquest said,' Whitrow added, staring at the derelict building's ragged chimneys. 'Mind you, I've never been happy with that verdict. It's never felt right somehow–'

'Well, I'm sure Mr Browning hasn't got all

afternoon to spend listening to our theories on past events.' Marsh was jingling the car keys in one hand, obviously keen to be away to more pressing matters.

'But her own brother was burnt to death, and all those poor animals which were trapped in their stalls,' the constable added with feeling. 'In the end, Miss Middleton took a small flat in Stoneshanger, and just hid herself away, let herself go. That's what depression does to some folk, and in her case I wasn't surprised at all.'

'But you'd think she'd want to sell the place, get shot of it,' said Ivan.

'Yes, you would, but people always have their own ideas. Anyhow, eventually she married a doctor who'd just moved into this area. Dr Rook.'

'I see. So where do they live now?'

'Church House, Cold Firton. Nice place too.'

Marsh slid into the driver's seat then clicked in his seat belt. He turned to the potter standing next to the car. 'OK, Mr Browning, we'll keep trying, one way and another. If we maintain a low profile, one of our friends is bound to get cocky, a bit careless.'

But he didn't convince anyone – least of all himself.

After they'd gone, Ivan peered at himself in the driving mirror. He looked rough – in fact, bloody rough. Besides, it was getting dark and by the time he'd visited Mrs Rook, as originally planned, it would be darker still. No, thanks; he decided that however interesting she might prove to be about the markings on his hand, she'd have to wait till the morning, so when he got back to Tripp's Cottage he immediately phoned Church House with the number Gill Bunnett had given him.

The doctor's wife sounded intrigued by his request to meet her. Thursday morning would be ideal, at her house, she told Ivan, with coffee ready and waiting.

It was only after he'd mentioned Tripp's Cottage that she'd hesitated, and her goodbye had then seemed strained. He pondered on this reaction as he wandered through his chilly kitchen and into the adjoining outbuilding whose floor space almost matched that of the cottage. It was warm inside, with the red-hot glow from the kiln's open bung hole burning at him like a mad eye in the gloom before he switched on the strip light.

He turned up the pyrometer dial to the full glost temperature, and inserted both bungs into their snug spaces. Although it was cheaper to fire during the night, they were nothing less than his babies inside the kiln, and he liked to check on them periodically through their whole magical process.

As he listened to the elements reaching an even more intense heat, he set four dried planters on top of the kiln, at the same time resolving to try and see more of that intriguing girl in the Lamb and Flag.

Which made him think of Tania again. Tania Louise Bell – always immaculate, never a hair out of place, with her shoulder pads and chock-a-block diary. It was a miracle the two of them had even lasted together for five minutes. Ivan shook all his slip bottles and set them down in colour order on his workbench. But then the lonely don't often choose very well – he realized that now. It had originally been fear of the everlasting empty bed, the lack of laughter and shared music that had spurred him on to ask her out two years ago while she was still teaching at the City Technology College.

There'd also been her mother. Separated from Mr Bell back in the 1980s, she'd since categorized all men as feckless predators, and warned her only daughter against becoming in any way dependent, least of all on an artist and dreamer. Never mind that he'd landed a good job at a prestigious educational establishment in London – that never came into her calculations.

He'd only met this Mrs Bell twice, and resolved not to subject himself a third time to her inquisitions, let alone put himself up for prospective son-in-law. But Vicky Walker's death had decided that issue. Tania left him soon afterwards to take a post outside education, organizing conferences at some big hotel outside Leicester. Now, he mused, even a stay in a Midlands suburb with a brasserie meal and a study bedroom with Jacuzzi would never be an option for him.

That was still Tania's territory – and this was his. A rural one-and-a-half up, one-and-a-half-down, with an ice-box bathroom, but at least a big open fire in the lounge. Bought and paid for, like his then-brand-new VW, with the proceeds from the sale of his modern studio flat, leaving an emergency float in the bank to fall back on.

The cottage had been empty for five years before he'd moved in, but not everyone fancies living so close to nature, or so he'd reasoned at the time. Some people find a mass of trees oppressive, and wildlife unpredictable. Better the town street, or the village green than this little outpost of Nether Wapford.

From an old gate in his back garden fence, Ivan could walk straight into Wapford Forest – into sudden darkness even on the sunniest day. This conspiracy of oaks, as he called it, had regrown over centuries, keeping its secrets close to itself. And secrets there were, too. From the mysterious disappearance of his elderly neighbour, Mr Carp, the previous Christmas, to the recent discovery of adult human bones by an anthill at the far end of the plantation.

But it was nevertheless a place Ivan often felt impelled to visit, not just to collect browse-wood for his fire, but with his camera or sketch pad, to record bark textures, the interlocking limbs of branches beneath that invisible sky. It was best when the leaves lay underfoot, huge and fox-coloured. Best when the silence let him speak with his soul ... a soul, he knew now, which had been too long subsumed by timetabling, staffing – the greatest daily effort for the greatest ungrateful number. Yet, ultimately, even that hadn't been enough for those who'd wanted him conveniently out of the way...

He checked the pantry. There was one tin of sausages and beans left, plus a few slices of thin white bread. By eight o'clock, with the kiln now on 900 degrees, Ivan had settled down by the glowing fire with his most treasured book, signed by Noel Parr: *John Clare: His Life and Poetry*.

By ten o'clock, after a succession of lustful thoughts about that girl called Jo, in part inspired by Clare's longing for his own absent love, he was fast asleep. And, in the firing chamber, the opaque glaze had run its miraculous course, turning each red-brown dish and lid into a milky, ghostly white.

Marcus Webb stormed away from the drove, hatless, his coat dragging along the trail, the corgis following him. Siân felt sick, and realized she was wetting herself again, becoming quite sodden underneath. All the while her frightened eyes stayed on the unpredictable herd as Webb finally loped out of sight.

She saw her brother, Tomos, return, still swearing. He yelled for the dogs but none of them appeared. Only his wife, her fur collar turned up to her ears, a crab-apple blotch on each cheek. Careful to keep her distance from the turmoil by the gate.

'What's *she* doing here?' A neatly gloved hand pointed to Siân. 'That thing.'

'*I'm not that thing.*' The girl's anger brought just the slightest sound that no one heard. *'I'm Siân Richards. And one day, you piece of ice, you'll mind what you say to me.'*

Tomos was sweating even though the air was cold. His wife frowned as he came over.

'Have you lost your hearing, husband?'

'I heard you well enough.'

'So?'

'She's coming with us. Father wants her to see someone about her leg, and her voice. He's been going on about it for months.'

'Who?' Impatience sharpened the little painted mouth. Tomos glanced at Siân who was struggling to stand again.

'George Owen from Aberteilo. He's at St Bartholemew's Hospital now, so they say.'

His wife's mouth dropped open, revealing two rows of tiny teeth. 'Pah, I'd do more for a dog.'

Siân heard this and tried not to cry. Elen had always been jealous of Siân's freedom, that the mountains and rivers had once been hers for the enjoying. That Elen's own father liked Siân's studiousness, and she was Geraint Richards's favourite child.

'Why don't you take me instead?' Elen whined. 'We could follow in a coach and four, and when we get to London you can buy me a whole new summer wardrobe. You know, muslin, and the latest silk from France...'

Tomos passed his hat from one hand to the other, then, because he saw her father approaching in the distance, gave her the briefest kiss.

'I'm porthmon, remember. The chief drover. I go with the herd, not separately like some halfwit. I'll send word each week, mind. Now,' he looked over his shoulder. 'Let's go.'

Suddenly, Derryn Morris of the bakehouse appeared from nowhere, his thick hair springing from his white head like furze, his slanting pink eyes darting restlessly till he caught sight of Siân. He'd always liked little girls, especially ones like

60

her who couldn't fend for themselves. Just a harmless pastime, the albino would tell himself, and his generosity extended to adding extra dough to the loaf for any who called at the bakehouse.

Elen Richards didn't disguise her distaste at her husband's companions, and when the clergyman had finished his diatribe against the ungodly who no longer came to his church, father and daughter linked arms and walked back to the Glebe House.

'I see old Webb's got hisself a new nose,' Morris joked.

'Ay.' Tomos watched his wife disappearing. 'He earned it, fair do's.'

'As you're short of one man, I thought I'd go in his place. Me blood's a-boiling, that's for sure.'

The porthmon looked him up and down, the floury cuffs, the worn boots. 'What about your ovens?' he enquired.

Morris snorted. 'Me Mam can kick young Rhys out of bed for a change. Time he did a hand's turn.'

'If it's money you're after, forget it.'

'O' course money's always useful. I'd be a fool to say it weren't. But,' he smiled slyly at Siân, 'I could take care o' her.'

Tomos frowned. He'd heard of the goings-on in the Tafarn's back room. While he himself had been upstairs protesting at Lord Trelewis's encroachments and the resulting hardships for the smallholders, the likes of Morris had their breeches round their knees with girls barely grown to women.

61

'I dunno 'bout that.'

'Then you could fix your whole mind on getting this lot to England,' the other wheedled.

'I could. That's true enough.' He slapped his palm into the other's, and while Moses Evans from Horeb chapel joined them, singing 'Come, mine own Redeemer, come', Tomos fetched blinkers, mounted the cob and cantered round the herd to bring in the straying grazers.

'Ben!' he hollered. 'Dogs!' As the animals finally obliged, and after Morris helped Siân up onto the mare, letting his hand brush her knee as he checked the girth, the party set off, following the track from Pont Llwyd Farm round the vicar's house and down towards the Teifi.

A mist curdled over the river, blocking out the view beyond and the eastern edge of Lampeter's dwellings. It turned the day even colder and Siân shivered again under the coat. Although her knees hurt on the worn saddle and her feet tilted in the stirrups, her instinctive balance had never left her. Years of jumping on and off the wild ponies of Bryn Bechan now made the difference between being a mere nuisance and a burden – the difference between life and death.

'How's the Lodger a-doin' then?' Derryn Morris was alongside her, stroking the rough tweed of her arm. He knew the nickname her mother called her since she stopped being able to help around the house – she'd never be allowed to forget it. Siân could smell his sweat, feel the unwelcome weight of his white hand, and urged Collen on with a cluck from her throat. 'No need for that, my missy. Uncle Derryn's here to keep an eye on you.' His grip tightened, but Siân bent her head over and bit his hand till little pits of crimson showed through. 'Yer damned vixen!' He hit the chestnut's flank, making the mare rear then lurch into a headlong gallop towards the herd.

Siân shut her eyes, then prayed to God, pulling back on the slippery reins; but then her mount sensed her old home, the fern and the high-blown hills over Bwlch-y-Gwyn, and swung wide around the herd until the cattle lowing and Tomos's shouts faded away. The ground became spongy, soft as cushions, slowing the pony down.

Then, just as quickly, Collen stopped her gallop, her ribs heaving, and began to pick at the grass. Siân thanked God twenty times over, and, when her own panic had subsided, she watched the pony's two ears flick back and forth while crows, black as Elen's and her father's hair, settled along the old wall, waiting for early lambs. She clapped her hands at them, knowing only a gun would see them off, then realized with a tremor of dread that she was just as vulnerable, to them.

She nudged the pony on, the silence giving her space to think. Should she try to hide some-where? To live in the wild like Twm Sion Catti at Ysradffin, feeding off berries, stealing where she could? Or should she turn the mare round and head back to the drove, to the baker's ever-ready fingers and the hope of a cure in London?

Siân slipped her feet out of the stirrups and stretched her legs. The left one resembled a chicken bone on the vicar's Sunday table and didn't match the right in any way. In fact it looked as though it belonged to someone else. She hated it, hated it. After a cure she'd be able to show off her ankles like other girls, keep herself clean again; but, more importantly, she'd be able to hear her own voice again, even to sing like Gwen Prytherch at the Tafarn. Lucky Gwen, *she'd* not had a frightened steer open her skull, nor a Mam who'd grown hard as the stones up on Nantgarw... Still, hadn't Siân always buried her nail clippings under the ash tree near their cottage, after her Da had claimed doing so would help her grow into a 'top singer'? What more, apart from Huw Davies, could she ever want?

Siân returned her feet to the stirrups and urged her pony away from the grass it was grazing. Surprised by her rider's sudden resolve, Collen abandoned the sweet feast and turned herself round.

'*Goodbye, Bwlch-y-Gwyn, goodbye,*' Siân whispered, trying not to cry.

She heard Tomos still bellowing over the cattle; worse, she could see the baker waiting for her. But now nothing would deter her, and by the time the drove finally moved out of the village, her chin was stuck out resolutely and, despite her grief at leaving home, her eyes shone bright with purpose.

Three

The next morning, Ivan parted his bedroom curtains on to a veil of freezing fog. During the night a thick stealthy frost had covered his back lawn, and rendered the forest trees as one with the sky beyond them. The room was bitterly cold, and he could have grown a beard by the time the Dimplex radiator would have any effect, so, when normally he'd have stripped to wash, today the T-shirt went straight on under a new red sweatshirt.

He checked the top of his right hand again. That warm blemish was still there, more defined than ever, like a roseate miniature lifebelt on his skin. He thought of his impending visit to Church House, wondering what Valerie Rook would make of it and if somehow their two separate experiences were in any way connected.

Normally, he'd have phoned home to ask for advice, but both his parents had enough to concern them at present, with their own frail and elderly parents teetering on the edge of oblivion.

Downstairs he saw his mother's latest note from Downwellan propped up on the old mantelpiece, together with invitations to various local arts and crafts events, and bills from Potterycrafts for deliveries of clay and plaster. Maeve Browning was over-tired these days, not her usual lively Irish self at all, but had promised that when she and his father could find a spare moment, they'd come over to England and visit him. So how could he burden them with his problems meanwhile? Besides, he was old enough to have kids of his own, although that morning he felt those thirty-two years had doubled.

The Saxo had helpfully frosted up, so its door lock resisted the flimsy key. Ivan swore loudly, his breath billowing in the cold like a camp fire. It didn't improve his humour to deduce from by her moving curtains that Mrs Jonas next door was watching him. He'd run out of de-icer so first had to spit on then scrape each window pane with a wooden pottery tool, and finally wave his new cigarette lighter round the lock.

Eventually he managed to insert the key and open the driver's door. Inside, he was cocooned in a separate world of ice and vapour, until the dashboard vents blasted enough warm air onto the misted windscreen.

Suddenly, that same air grew even colder, matching the atmosphere outside again. Ivan's nose began to sting, and the hands fastening his seat belt grew stiff as those of a corpse. And in that chill, which seemed to pin him there to his seat like a butterfly specimen, came a repetition of that warm sucking sensation on his hand – almost a desperate attention-seeking – but from whom? And why?

Ivan watched helplessly as the original mark darkened then formed into smaller shapes – which were surely the indentations of teeth. Vicky Walker's teeth had shown below her lips, little blocks of ivory stained with blood, her tongue trapped silent between them.

Holy shit.

He started the car, reversed it badly, crashing the gear, then, still aware of the weird pressure on his hand, took the village road east towards his next appointment and, hopefully, some rational explanation for these so far inexplicable occurrences.

Two cars stood in the adjoining car port: a clapped-out white Lada and a newly cleaned red Saab. Ivan wondered briefly which was whose.

One press on the front-door bell was enough. It was as if Valerie Rook was already waiting for him, and even her smile was one of flattering expectancy. A small woman with a pleasant face and a light brown bob infiltrated by grey near her temples. Her clothes, Ivan thought, looked as if they'd been cobbled together from a charity shop. A thick green cardigan was zipped right up to her throat, and tights with their wool rubbed into little balls along her shins, matched her skirt. Her suede fur-lined boots, too, seemed well used, highlighted by shiny patches above the toes.

Hardly your typical doctor's wife, Ivan thought, wondering what sort of skinflint would let her go round dressed like that. Then he remembered Whitrow's comment about her depression. Maybe she still wasn't quite over it.

'It's good to see you, Mr Browning.' She glanced over towards the village street before admitting him into the bare hallway. 'Do come through. It's Michael's morning off and he's tidying the shed, though God alone knows he's done it often enough before.' Ivan followed her down the passageway, noting how she kept glancing back over her shoulder. Obviously uneasy about something, he thought, keeping his right hand concealed in his pocket.

'Can't you persuade him to get working on Small Copse Farm then?' he suggested, without thinking.

Valerie Rook stopped then spun round to face him. 'How did you know about that?'

'One of my students must have mentioned it,' he lied, now wishing the floor would swallow him up. 'Look, I'm really sorry, I didn't mean to upset you.'

'It doesn't matter. Nothing matters much...' Her voice tailed away as she moved on again. 'Anyhow, you're bound to hear all sorts of things, especially in a place like this. One of the penalties of village life, isn't it?'

Ivan merely grunted, working out how to make amends for his mistake.

Church House smelt damp despite the Rooks' occupation, and its pervading chilliness was only marginally challenged by electric storage heaters that were set on low. He also noticed how whenever she passed near one, Valerie Rook let her palm linger over the top vent to catch some of its minimal heat.

'I'm afraid it is a bit cold in here' – she pushed open the kitchen door – 'but Michael insists that cooler air's better for the lungs. And lungs are his speciality. Come in, do. This is the one place he says we can keep warm.' She went over to the electric kettle. 'Would you prefer tea or coffee?

And, by the way, now we've met, do call me Valerie.'

'Coffee'd be great, thanks. And my name's Ivan.' He looked around for any signs of children or pets but detected none. Like the other rooms off the hall he'd sneaked a look into, the kitchen was strictly functional, devoid of any obvious feminine touches, and, so far, there'd been no hint either of the old family farm or of the horses bred there. It was as if the woman's past life had been utterly swept away.

'Sorry if I sounded a bit critical of the village out there,' she began, 'but people here have hardly gone out of their way to make us feel welcome here, even though I've been living in the area most of my life.'

Ivan watched her switch off the kettle and pour boiling water into two National Trust mugs. 'Same for me,' he admitted. 'And as for my nearest neighbour, I reckon MI5 must have her on their payroll.'

'Oh, why's that?' Her hazel eyes took on a startled look.

'She's always peering out from behind her curtains as if she's keeping me under surveillance... I hope I make things interesting for her.'

'I'm sure you do,' laughed Valerie, then she grew more serious. 'So how's life been here otherwise?' she asked.

Ivan thought for a moment before replying. There'd never been many people he felt he could really trust since that minibus ordeal, but there was something about this woman he was warming to. It might do him good to tell someone else what he'd been through personally, even if she just listened to him without comment, so, for ten minutes, during which both their coffees cooled undisturbed, he relayed the events of that fateful night and its aftermath, barely pausing for breath.

The pain he felt, the subsequent treacheries discovered, all flowed out of him uninterrupted, as she stood taking in all the tragedy. Finally she came over and laid a hand on his shoulder. It was just what he needed: a simple act like that which Tania, for all her show, all her words, had never been able to manage. He looked up and noticed the woman's eyes also holding back tears.

'It's taken a lot of courage to go through what you've experienced, Ivan,' she began. 'And to have to give up a good job, a life in London you obviously enjoyed... I just hope you find some new friends here soon and the peace of mind to get on with your work.'

'I will,' he gulped. 'I'll be fine, thanks.' He watched as she poured milk taken from the fridge into a brown slipware jug. 'Just one thing, though – why your hesitation earlier when I mentioned I lived at Tripp's Cottage?'

A little milk slopped onto the floor. She snatched at a cloth from the draining board to wipe it up.

'No, no, that was when you spoke about that thing on your hand. I could feel *my* own skin prickling all over again...' She then carried the coffee mugs over, none too steadily. 'It comes and goes without any warning. Michael thinks it may be some allergy, but I'm not so sure. Mother used to say not everything has a rational explanation, and this makes me wonder if her psychic streak hasn't passed to me, because I've had other odd sensations too.'

'So when did this first happen to you?' he asked. He could have done with a biscuit but none seemed forthcoming. Better still, a fag or two, but this doctor's wife now had other, less worldly matters on her mind.

'It was late August, as I remember, over three years ago. We'd just moved in here and the weather was unbearably hot. Too hot to do anything much really, but Michael wanted to get everything shipshape before his first surgery in September.' She sipped her coffee and shivered. 'I told him at the time that it wasn't very realistic, unpacking things and ordering supplies, but there was no budging him, so by the end of that first week I was totally exhausted. I remember going upstairs to lie down, but you know how sometimes you can be too tired to sleep? Well, that was me, so I just lay there with the window open, listening to the birds singing in the yews...'

'And then?' Ivan leaned forwards, still keeping his right hand covered until it was time to show her.

'I felt as though something like a puppy was not so much licking as sucking at my arm, here. Sometimes the mark comes up quite red, at other times you can hardly see it, but still feel the heat.'

He studied the skin of her arm closely. The blemish on it was identical to the one on his own hand that he now showed her. A gasp escaped from her lips as her fingertips hovered over it.

Then her eyes met his. 'If you showed this to anyone else, as I did, mistakenly, they'd just assume you were into some sort of mutilation.'

'But you showed yours to Gill Bunnett?'

'How did you know?' Her neat eyebrows rose.

'She attends my class. We were just chatting the other night.'

'Oh.' A moment's hesitation. 'Your class certainly seems to be a hotbed of gossip.'

'Don't worry. She seemed very sympathetic.'

Valerie looked relieved.

'So what do you think is causing this?' Ivan asked. 'I mean, has anyone else round here had the same experience?'

'Well, the locals aren't going to come confiding in *me*, are they?' she said with an air of resignation. 'After all, I married a doctor, a professional man, didn't I? In their eyes I did well for myself. Too well after what had happened. Got myself a good meal ticket.' She leaned forwards. 'There's a lot of petty jealousy here, you know, tucked away behind the neat hedges, the pretty stonework. They seem to resent me owning a second home.'

'You mean Small Copse?'

'Yes.'

Ivan by now was aware of his stomach grumbling under the belt of his jeans, whether it was from nerves or the lack of a proper breakfast he couldn't tell.

'But no way has my husband, Michael, ever wanted anything to do with that place. *This* house is what he coveted from the moment he first set eyes on it.' Her forefinger tapped on the table. 'But after the old rectory was demolished at the other end of the village, the bishop and the church committee had someone from Stoke Wilton all lined up to move in here. A Reverend Richard Coombes. Quite a wow with the ladies apparently, even though he was in his early sixties. He was acting as a replacement for old Reverend Hutton here while he was in the hospice.'

'And?'

'Well, Michael being Michael, he got hold of some whizz-kid solicitor in London and had his searches and paperwork done two weeks ahead of the church authorities. That caused some resentment, but then there was the accident.'

'What kind of accident?'

'It was all very weird and tragic.' Valerie finished her coffee, frowning. 'The following May, Richard Coombes was knocked off his bicycle while riding along the Westhope Road. There were no witnesses to the incident and he was just left to die there in the road – would you believe that in a Christian country? But the locals knew he was carrying the takings from the St Dunstan's Fair in his saddlebag, which of course disappeared along with the bike itself.'

'I thought footpads and highwaymen went out with the arrival of the combustion engine,' Ivan observed wrily, at the same time disquieted by this accumulation of strange and seemingly unrelated incidents. 'Did the police never find out who did it?'

Valerie gave Ivan a look of such utter reproof that even though his mug was empty, he picked it up and pretended to drain it, such was his embarrassment.

'And you've been living here for over four months?' she said almost accusingly, each cheek now suffused by a deep red blush.

'Too long already, obviously.' Ivan stood up, scraping back his chair on the quarry-tiled floor. 'Someone tried to waste *me* on Tuesday evening. My five-month-old car got nicked as well, just down the road there – right by the Oakleys place, if you please. Cops couldn't find anything, though.'

Valerie shook her head. 'I'm afraid you could be waiting round here for police action a pretty long time.'

Then, as if this latest news was more than she could cope with, she glanced out of the kitchen window to where her husband was now trundling a loaded wheelbarrow away from the garden shed. Her eyes seemed suddenly faraway, her expression curiously detached. 'If only I could talk to him sometimes about things, that would help, but he's so focused on his practice mission. His premise is that although most people are born in pretty good order, Dr Michael Rook's remedies will make them far healthier. So,' she shrugged, 'there we go.'

An uncomfortable silence followed, in which Ivan rinsed out his mug and wiped it dry. He then wandered over to the window to observe the medical man who was now tussling with a heap of wire netting.

'Those Oakleys seem a pretty obnoxious lot,' he said suddenly.

74

She got up to join him, and together they stared out at the wheelbarrow still busy heading backwards and forwards.

'All of them regular churchgoers, if you please. It's Michael who sees them there, not me. I don't go to church any more. They're always ranged in the Oakley pew in their Sunday best – and I *mean* best.' She shot him a little glance. 'You know, Austin Reed, Burberry, none of your old Primark for them, oh no. And I reckon they contribute more than anyone else to the collection. Only last week Michael said they funded the vicar for a whole new set of hymn books.'

Ivan remembered his encounter at the old girl's cottage, then the taxi driver who'd soon lost his bonhomie. 'So who's *they* exactly?' he asked, as there'd been nobody listed in the phone book under Oakley. 'Do they have Christian names?'

'There's John and Harold...' For a moment she hesitated. 'He's married to Monica, then there's Stephen, though not sure in which order. Those three brothers look pretty much the same to me.'

So it seems, Ivan thought, wondering what she was holding back, and why.

'You must have had *something* to do with them once, though,' he ventured. 'They were your neighbours at Small Copse, surely?'

Her mouth tightened as she still watched her husband outside.

'They kept themselves totally to themselves.' She fiddled with the coffee jar lid and then produced a clean mug and teaspoon.

'But they go back quite a long way here, don't they?' Ivan persevered.

'Yes, they moved up from the East End in 1911, and rumour has it that the first Oakley married Alice Dawson and buried old William Wiseman alive in his slurry pit just to get hold of his farm, but somehow I don't think *that's* ever appeared in the parish magazine.' She bit her lip as if she'd already said too much, while her visitor felt a shiver trickle down through his spine. If this was just a taster, he thought, what might the whole story reveal?

'So not a very illustrious pedigree then?'

'Hardly.'

Ivan saw the doctor lean the wheelbarrow against the shed and remove his gardening gloves, as if he'd finished that particular task.

'We'd love to see more of you sometime,' she said, changing the subject in advance of her husband's imminent appearance. 'Though not in Michael's surgery, of course.'

'I'm not registered with anyone yet. I'm a total coward. Only got to smell a waiting room...' And it wouldn't be this man's, necessarily, Ivan had already decided.

She didn't reply as, with sounds of a door shutting, the doctor himself appeared and her unlipsticked mouth forced a smile for him.

'Michael, this is Ivan Browning. He's been trying to persuade me to join his pottery class up at the village hall next term.'

But obviously no handshake was forthcoming.

'Mmm.' The doctor frowned instead. 'Well I hope you're well versed in the Health and Safety regulations up there. Pottery-making is particularly fraught with hazards.'

76

'I am quite aware of that.' Ivan sat down again, suppressing his annoyance, aware of the other man's eyes now on his fingers.

'And a serious smoker, I can tell,' the doctor went on. 'You and I maybe need to have a serious chat about that.'

'Michael, please,' his wife protested.

'So, where exactly are you staying round here?' he asked as if the visitor was an itinerant.

'Nether Wapford, by the edge of the forest. Is that a problem for me, too?'

'No, no, my goodness.' The doctor then rubbed his hands obsessively around a block of soap under the kitchen tap. 'What was it Northamptonshire's greatest poet once said?'

Ivan then listened to Clare's 'Enclosure' being trotted out as if this man recited it every day of his life.

Like mighty giants of their limbs bereft,
The skybound wastes in mangled garb are left,
Fence meeting fence in owner's little bounds
Of field and meadow, large as garden-grounds.

'Of course, the whole system represented merely a cynical sop to the villagers,' the doctor added.

'What do you mean?'

Rook was drying his hands on a towel hanging behind the door.

'On the one hand giving them each a tiny token garden with the right to fire-bote and common of pasture, yet imposing rules of couchant and levant that determined who could put their cattle and pigs where, and when. No wonder disease was rife, with all those petty restrictions–'

'I really don't think our visitor wants to know all of that just now,' interrupted the man's wife, switching on the kettle again. 'But maybe he could come over for supper one evening and we'll talk more.' She eyed Ivan's ringless hand. 'Are you married, or is there a girlfriend you'd like to bring along?'

'I'm single – still looking. Thanks all the same.' He'd been thrown by this question fired with such directness, and first of all thought of Tania – her red-painted mouth, her sharp shoulders. Then he shook his head, realizing finally that she'd disappeared from his life.

Suddenly Jo from the pub came into his mental view. Jo with the lovely smile, the shiny hair.

He began to feel slightly uncomfortable. 'I'd better be going,' he said. 'I've got a kiln to unload and another to stack – it all takes time. If either of you is passing you're welcome to have a look round. Tripp's Cottage, it is.'

'That would be nice, thank you,' Valerie said, her neck reddening.

'Now then, Tripp's Cottage.' Dr Rook turned to his wife who was hovering by the kitchen door. 'Darling, do you recall when I first began researching the history of this area, all sorts of interesting little snippets came to light?'

The 'Darling' made Ivan wince inwardly.

'All I remember now is you sitting up in bed with at least ten books spread out on the eiderdown. It was like trying to sleep in a reference library,' she retorted.

Mention of the marital bedroom clearly

embarrassed her husband, and his mug wavered slightly as he carried it to the table. 'It's just that I like to get a good feel for an area.' He gave his wife a second stern glance. 'What's gone before, medically, socially, you know – to get it all in perspective.'

'So what about my cottage?'

'I have to be a bit careful here, Mr Browning, but I'm sure it came up in the context of some nasty incident... Long time ago, mind.'

Again, Ivan felt that familiar tremor invade his body. But the man had probably read up so much he was confused – probably thinking of somewhere else entirely.

'There are lots of little dwellings like mine dotted around,' he countered. 'I bet every one of them's got some story or other.'

'Ah, but this was different somehow.' Rook placed his upper lip over the mug rim and drew up his drink as might a horse. 'Quite different. Oh, in heaven's name why can't I think of it?'

'Don't bother now. It's OK. Let me know when you remember.' And, seeing Mrs Rook still sentry-like at the door, Ivan mentioned the starting date for the next term, then couldn't resist adding, 'You can make your own individual mugs if you come along. His and hers.'

Dr Rook, completely missing the irony, looked up at his wife, his lips glistening. 'I'm afraid the answer's no to that one, Valerie. Lace-making yes, that activity's much less risky to one's health.'

Her lower lip trembled, but her eyes never once strayed from her visitor's face.

Having at last said goodbye, Ivan found himself

outside in the still frosty front garden, thinking about this strangely matched pair. And as he drove down their cindery drive, between the graveyard and the thatched cottages, a murder of crows ripped into the air from a nearby tree, like storm-blown remnants of some huge bonfire, then disappeared.

'What do you make of all that then?' Elen Richards asked her father, the Reverend Meurig Jones, whilst watching the chaos from the parlour window; her ivory fan cooling her cheeks.

'It's what God makes of it that matters. However, more's the pity your husband made no Will before setting off. That would have shown a properly considerate side to his nature.'

But the young wife was transfixed instead by the scene unfolding outside, letting her father's words of piety and wisdom dissolve to nothing the moment they left his lips.

'He couldn't have picked up worse company to go with if he'd dug for it in the midden,' she observed.

The vicar of St Andrew and St Peter looked down at his daughter, his forehead wrinkling over his spectacles. 'I'd have a care how you speak, Elen. It seems to me that life at Pont Llwyd Farm has done little but coarsen your tongue.'

She tightened her once-pretty lips, her eyebrows arching in disdain as Siân rode by. Their eyes met and, for a moment, the drover's wife felt bile turn her stomach.

'And what about *her*?'

'I have nothing but pity for that poor creature.

We must remember God moves in mysterious ways,' his voice continued like the drone of hooves, his breath thin against the pane as if the mist had leaked in. 'And God only knows why Tomos can't wait for summer, when the tracks will be hard again and the sun warm on their backs.'

'Tomos has no choice. His father insists on it.'

'A pity your husband has even to be told. It's been three long years since her accident.'

'Well, I think she's a bad omen.' The young woman had ignored him again, pulling her shawl tighter around her slight frame. 'And I'm not the only one thinking that.'

He noticed how like her mother she'd grown, in both mind and body – the wife he'd buried just two years ago. Now like an alder that sucks the waters up into its greedy roots, she'd drawn on his isolation, his doubts, only to harden against him, he considered privately, noting the impatience of her sharp-boned hands fretting with her gloves.

'She could be the making of him,' he said at last.

'*What?* Are you serious?' Elen craned her neck to see the last of the Castlemartins go by. Then, still turned away from him, she took a deep breath. 'It may not be my place to say so, Father, but I think the solitary life has touched your mind. That girl needs to be sent to clean coal, where some "cropper" would soon knock her into shape.'

The vicar gathered up his pen and the sermon he'd been worrying over, and without replying left his daughter alone. When he reached the sanctuary of his study it was if his whole body, suddenly weary, expired into the one comfortable chair. It was once a beautiful specimen from the tanners in Dinas Powys but now forty years of fine stitching had been softened into loops by the damp, and there were two coarse patches at the end of each armrest, rubbed by his father's palms and his own during hours of contemplation.

He stared blankly at his translation spread on the desk before him. Some things he could control, the lie of the nib, the slant of the fingers, but others – the Reverend Meurig Jones shook his head – were beyond human intervention.

Elen slammed the outer door so hard his inkstand shook and, in the helpless silence that ensued, he set his hands to pray that his most willing pupil's journey be a safe one, and that she'd soon be returned whole to Plas Newydd.

Reaching Esgairwen, Tomos Richards borrowed two more ponies from Hector Lloyd, so the baker and the hymn singer could keep up more easily. A whole bay with a sly eye and a grey whose yellow tail had almost gone with the sweet itch were led out from the field and Siân saw how Morris struggled to mount. With no saddle, the animal took advantage, circling round and round, and when he thought no one was looking Morris landed a solid kick on its rear. He glanced back at her quickly, his face a knot of anger, and not for the first time she felt a tremor of fear pass through her body.

It would be the easiest thing just to turn away now, to go back home to Plas Newydd and be 'the Lodger' all over again. But why should such a creature as Morris condemn her to that fate for the rest of her life? He had the use of *his* limbs after all, and his speech too – God knew his speech, foul as bog water. So was he more worthy than herself? Siân followed behind the herd, with Moses Evans now bawling out 'Guide me, oh thou great Jehovah' in such a high falsetto she thought her eardrums would burst. At the end of the first verse, the baker threatened to take his head off his shoulders if he persisted.

Past Esgairwen the way veered north-east, rising more steeply, but wider, so the drove could pass six deep without risk of wandering.

'Llandewi Brefi,' Tomos shouted from the front. 'And no bloody tolls.'

'Any stopping?' Morris asked. 'My throat's like Mr Evans's brain 'ere, all shrivelled up.'

'Not till Abermadog. And don't ask me again.' The porthmon looked back at Siân, who was resting her weight on Collen's neck. She seemed to be asleep, but it was just her way of enduring the discomfort. She found it easier to daydream with her head on that coarse pillow of mane. She thought of Huw, of her father living in a crowded rented room in Dowlais and of all the things she'd do when that Dr Owen in London had made her better.

'Yer only porthmon 'cos yer've got a hearth,' the albino shouted. His resentment had been brewing since Esgairwen, seeing this younger man with the better-saddled horse, the wife with money, and a big fat purse at the end of it all. 'Ye forgets how it's I what puts bread in yer bellies.'

Moses Evans stopped singing for a while, cocking his little bird head to listen. 'Three's a crowd,' he muttered. 'And more so when one means to cause bother.'

Siân heard it all and realized that the pain of staying on the mare's back might be the least of her troubles. For a brief ungrateful moment she wished her well-meaning father had never mentioned his surgeon friend in London.

Tomos stood up in his stirrups and pushed his hat off his eyes. Even from that distance, his sister could see he was provoked. That his angry black eyes seemed to fill his face.

'You're lucky to have the extra work, man, God's leavings as you are.'

The baker's heels flayed the bay pony's ribs until he'd galloped alongside. This sudden surge caused four steers to buck and barge to the front until Ben snapped them back into place.

'Yer not such a porthmon ye can speak to me so.' Morris reined in alongside the cob. 'Yer've grown too far from where ye started out, Plas Newydd.' He sniggered then spat out a foul yellow spittle. 'That rat hole.'

Tomos kept his mouth sealed shut, his eyes focused on the steepening track. He knew if he riled this man any more the whole herd could be lost. This was wild unfenced country, and his investment, once loose, would never be traced. He urged the cob on, without speaking, and after a mile or so the baker drew back, letting his reins slacken, rolling his tongue around inside his mouth.

The sky took on the leaden dark of a winter

dusk. Here and there, pinpricks of candlelight showed from the dwellings scattered over the hills. Even rain might have warmed things up – or a breeze. But no, the stillness deepened, and by the time the noisy drove had reached Abermadog's first dismal holding, frost had stiffened their clothes.

Siân gritted her teeth and managed to drop from the pony. Her legs ached, burdened by her father's coat, but never would she cry or whimper in front of three grown men. *Never.*

The Ox and Bough was already full of farmers arrived for the Killing Ewe sale next day, but when Tomos Richards declared he was the porthmon from Nant y Fedw, and pressed a bag of coins into the publican's hands for the animals' keep, Cantor Rees soon found him a room. With a slap of his hat on his thigh, the drover then pushed his way into the crowded bar. Morris followed him, then Evans.

'*What about me?*' Siân pointed to herself, remembering with a pang Huw's halfpenny gone into the hedge, but the publican let the door swing shut behind him.

In the emptiness outside she could hear the bleating ewes, and followed their din round the back to where the yard had been corralled into sections demarcated with whitewashed placards: Llangybi, Bryn Mawr and Henfaes. The white skull-like faces turned to watch, but as she crawled under the lowest hurdle, the sheep jostled away to the far end, their cries even more plaintive, their lanolin smell choking.

Siân tugged her coat over her head and pulled

down the sleeves to cover her hands. Then, with the sheep settling again and the cold freezing the stars to stillness in the sky, she finally began to sob.

'*Noswaith da, Lletywrwr,* good evening, Lodger.'
'*No, Mr Morris, sir. Leave me alone. Go away!*'
'But, missy, we found a nice warm place for you instead.'
We? She strained her eyes in the poor light, but couldn't see anyone else.
'*I'm not going from here. You can't make me.*' Siân huddled lower against the rails, away from his grasp.
'Oh can't I? We'll see about that.'
The girl listened in the blackness for Moses Evans, for anyone, then realized in terror that she was on her own. With the baker.
The ewes had started up again, their fate just hours away. She thought if he'd left her alone a minute longer, she might have let them all loose into the night.
'I won't harm ye. And ye canna stay out in this till the mornin'.' His voice had changed, softer, more persuasive, but she remembered his hand on her thigh earlier. Remembered that look, those wet lips. 'Up ye come.'
Siân screamed, but the hubbub from the tavern drowned everything. She was just like another sack of oats, easy on his back but still fighting.
'Ye'll thank me for this, so shut yer noise.' He strode down towards an outhouse next to the stables, kicked the door open and shut it behind him.

Saddles, bridles and makeshift rugs lay on every surface. The deep damp smell of sweat and dung filled her lungs as rats scuttled from the feed bags leaving a trail of grain across the floor. Siân tried to gauge the door's position. He was rasping then sneezing as loud as a thunderclap. The dust had affected him and, during one protracted sneezing fit, she slipped to the floor and crawled out of the door. Morris was behind her, still heaving his sore ribs, but she was quick as a weasel despite the coat.

The back door of the tavern was ajar and the reek of homemade candles and stale beer enfolded her as she tried to stand. Suddenly a hand reached down and helped her onto a still-warm stool. The room fell silent as all eyes fell on her and then on Derryn Morris's huge frame which filled the door.

Four

Despite it being midday, there was no inkling of any winter sun, and frost still lay in sheltered pockets of grass, still whitened the stumps of old fencing and broken stiles along the verge.

Ivan glanced at the road where his Golf had been, and the pang of its loss hit him harder then than at any other time. He'd grown attached to the smart black car and to his books and the modelling tools acquired even before his teaching years. One in particular he had loved – fashioned from box wood and worn smooth from use since he'd first started art college. The more he thought about this special item, the more resentful he grew. Once he'd caught a kid at Linton Grove using it to clean a pottery wheel. After he had exploded, that kid never dared touch it again.

He saw the Wiseman's Farm's single smokeless chimney rear up into the sky and in that split second, he decided to make a call, to introduce himself properly and apologize for disturbing old Ma Oakley with his problems.

Ivan pulled up in the gap beside the new five-barred gate, from whose posts at either side extended electric fencing with a public warning not to touch. He then got out and locked the Citroën. The gate, surprisingly, was unpadlocked, and the heavy bolt slid sweetly to one side.

Welcome, he thought, *but not quite...*

With some apprehension he faced the farmhouse. Its dark ironstone walls seemed forbidding, its four roof gables blank, yet nevertheless all-seeing in that eerie silence. Yes, he knew he was being watched, but he too was surreptitiously taking everything in, looking out for any trace of his car in that surreal cleanliness. Then for some reason he glanced down and noticed an uneven trail of lighter marks across the stone slabs. He checked again, rubbing the toe of his boot into the nearest stain to shift it. But whatever it was had eroded the stones' surface and remained fixed. He remembered DC Marsh's remark about housewives.

Suddenly he heard a commotion from behind the house and, before he could react, two enormous lion-coloured dogs powered towards him, their jaws hanging open to show gums like wet pink silk.

He dived to the ground and lay holding his breath while they began to circle him, growling and pulling at his boot laces.

For a moment he silently recited a prayer, something half forgotten from his schooldays. But before he reached the end of it, he heard a woman's voice calling.

'Lodz! Krakow! Come here!'

Lodz? Krakow? Polish ghettos? This is really bloody weird.

The mastiffs skulked away and Ivan looked up to recognize those same immaculate green wellingtons he'd seen last Tuesday night. The rest was familiar too. A well-cut camel-hair coat and a strong-boned face above a colourful designer scarf. Her scent added to the air of money, as did her carefully cultivated voice when she introduced herself as Monica Oakley.

'I am sorry, Mr Browning. They are so naughty sometimes. No wonder we have to go in and collect our mail from town.'

She helped him up to his feet, like a woman used to dealing with things of such a practical nature, and it was only close up that he noticed her face was oddly pale, as if showing signs of strain. 'They've not messed up your boots have they?' Her appraising eye took in every detail of her visitor, without giving anything away of herself.

'No, they're fine.' He bent down to re-tie the laces.

'I'm sorry, too, about the way Harold spoke to you at his mother's home the other night. He's just rather worried about her insisting on hanging on there on her own these days. But she won't listen to reason. I'm afraid she's a very stubborn old lady.'

'That's OK. And I hope you don't think I'm intruding now. It's just that I wanted to–' But he didn't get a chance to finish.

'No, no, not at all,' she interrupted, still keeping a hand on his arm, guiding him subtly back to the gate. 'In fact, I'd offer you some hospitality, Mr Browning, but I've got to get lunch ready now for the old dear. She's refusing Meals on Wheels at the moment what with this BSE crisis and rumours of foot-and-mouth just down the road. It's all very trying, I have to say.'

She finally let go of him to open the gate. 'I've heard excellent things about your pottery class in the village. Mind you–' as she leaned closer, her perfume became even stronger – 'it does some of those people good to have their hands busy. It's just a pity you don't teach singing.'

'Why's that?' he asked, puzzled, noticing another lighter patch right under the gate as she closed it again behind him.

'That would keep their tongues occupied as well. At least while they've still got them.'

She then whistled for the two giant dogs, which loped along submissively on either side of her until the trio were out of sight behind the house. Her distinctive scent still hung in the air – clearly part of the charm offensive, he thought. Yet here was someone totally in control, calling all the shots; a clever, humiliating bitch.

As Ivan drove back to his cottage and the unpredictable outcome of the latest glost firing, his mind was submerged in a stew of impressions from the morning's strange encounters – unsettling thoughts that he couldn't erase. Hadn't the police noticed those lighter marks on the Wiseman's Farm drive? Why hadn't Monica Oakley grilled him further as to why he had turned up? After all, he'd been technically a trespasser. And, closer to home, what had Michael Rook been implying about his cottage? And, more crucially, what else did his wife, Valerie, know?

Ivan's hand fell on the cold wood of his own gate with its stiff latch, its singing hinges. He wondered now who else's hands had also pushed it open to access the brick-laid path. Who else in past years had been glad to return to the cottage's homeliness? But today that had all changed: the unknown past now threatened. Those invisible hands, those distant dreams of a welcoming fire and a bowl of broth were not now the sentimental meanderings of a sensitive soul, but an oppressive intrusion into the present.

He quietly cursed Dr Rook for his unnerving lapse of knowledge, and was on the point of inserting the front-door key when his ears picked up an odd noise. It was neither the blackbirds in the hawthorn hedges nor cattle herds on some faraway farm. This was different, more like the brush of leaves on a breeze, more human somehow. In fact, like whispering. Like that of the tragic thirteen-year-old whose life had ended in a gutter one wet November.

Once inside the warm studio, Ivan slammed the door shut as if to keep that insidious sound at bay, but it persisted, quite clearly now, as he walked over to the kiln. With the pyrometer registering 0, he removed the front bung to glimpse how his work had fared, yet was careful to avoid any accidental crazing of the glaze. A stream of heat met his face as he began to unscrew the kiln door.

Within, the glaze glinted in soft opalescence over the curves of the ware, and Ivan breathed a huge sigh of relief. Each casserole dish seemed in its place, nothing had tilted off its stilts or exploded. It seemed a miracle every time.

Suddenly, however, amid the potter's grateful

contemplation the whispering grew more distinct.

'*Help me... Help me...*'

He spun round, aware now that the temperature in the workshop had plummeted, that his skin felt cold and clammy, and once more, to his horror, that same soft sucking had begun again on his hand.

'This is totally crazy!' He stood unsure of what to do next. Ring Valerie Rook? Go and see Mrs Jonas next door? He felt dizzy and faint, while a real hunger – or was it fear? – welled up in his stomach. Then, as quickly as it had started, so the whispering died, as if exhaustion or feebleness had prevailed. His hand, too, was released and the kiln's heat once more restored the room to its former warmth.

With trembling fingers, Ivan cleared the top layer first and stacked the kiln shelves neatly against its legs. There was no need for gloves, no need for any later sanding down of bubbles or the like. These big-bellied vessels were perfect in every way and each one which he clasped to his body, before setting it on the workbench, seemed to calm him down further.

He scrutinized each piece inside and out, noting how the volatile cobalt had run like a river from the upper rims and diminished near the base. How the rich clay colour warmed through the opaque glaze on the roundest parts, and how well the pots sat, each with their own individual presence.

Then he re-packed the kiln with a new range of thrown soup bowls stacked right up to the top, one nestling inside the other. Next he began brushing batt wash onto the remaining spare shelves, for the latest glost batch. But as he worked the big old brush in the quick-drying liquid, he became convinced he wasn't alone in the room. Something or someone else was still there, determined to draw him away from an everyday reality which, until a year ago, he'd never had reason to question. Was he caught up in the residual energy of some departed soul? A former inhabitant of the cottage maybe, or even John Clare himself? For only last night, reading the man's gut-wrenching verses on loss and displacement, Ivan had felt a closer kinship with the poet than ever before. A kind of weird spiritual bonding, so that when, just before getting into bed, he'd stood looking out over the ancient Wapford Forest, imagining having to exchange it again for Islington or Finsbury or wherever, he'd felt hot tears sting his eyes.

Ivan sat at his workbench with the latest Potterycrafts catalogue, scouring its glossy pages for one or two more new dipping glazes, perhaps brighter colours for the spring shows. But his mind couldn't concentrate. Every word became *Help me*, every extraneous sound in the cottage the beginning of that piteous plea once more.

He'd felt that same presence, born – he'd realized later – of guilt, in his Barton Road flat. Night after night the victim's last words would steal his sleep and turn each day into a private hell, while over and over, in excruciating slow-motion replay, visions of her stepping off her kerb under his tyres drove out any other thoughts of coping, of even survival itself...

Still feeling hungry, in dire need of a fag, Ivan checked once more on the new biscuit firing. He could hear the elements labouring as the temperature climbed with both bungs out, the holes exuding a slightly noxious vapour as the last of the moisture was drawn from the clay.

Suddenly, as he was locking up outside, something tapped his shoulder. He started and promptly dropped the key into the mud. Then turned to see his neighbour, Mrs Jonas, with her cat on a lead. Quiet as the night, she was, never a sound, except when the grandchildren came round from Silverstone with her only son.

'Oi'm not 'appy 'bout that stink from yon things in there.' She pointed at his outhouse, and for the first time he noticed with a start that she had six fingers on her left hand. She then wiped her nose with her coat cuff, leaving a snail trail along its mangy fur. 'It's poisoning me air.'

Ivan stared at her in amazement. This was a new one. Usually it was how the magpies singled out his one rubbish bag and, as a result, a solitary tea bag or toothpaste tube might be left lying on the verge. Or a slipped tile after the gales. Or moss encroaching on his mortar. She was the Queen of Minutiae all right, and so far he'd found her observations rather quaint, epitomizing the old eccentric rustic bit, but this, about his very livelihood, was different.

'Mrs Jonas, I can assure you, it's only water being driven off. It's not Sellafield, you know. It's perfectly harmless. Look at me, do I *look* poisoned?'

She peered at him through her patched-up glasses and saw a serious face with dark brows still questioningly raised.

'Well, oi'm no doctor, so oi wouldn't 'ave a clue what's doin' with yer insides. Who knows?'

Ivan sighed. This particular bee in the bonnet was not going to buzz off quietly. Keep cool, he told himself. What can she do about it, after all?

'Tell you what I've been meaning to do for some time,' he cajoled in a voice once reserved for tricky fifth-formers, 'and that's to give you one of my garden pots. They're frostproof and you can fill it full of bulbs for the spring, pop it by your door, whatever.'

'Hmmph.' She looked up at the new aluminium flue protruding from the outhouse roof. 'When the Grimbles was 'ere all them years, Mr G did *useful* stuff...'

Ivan looked at her puffy little face, her almost hidden eyes. He'd never really seen her in close-up before, and wasn't sure he wanted to again.

'What do mean, useful?' he challenged.

'Oh, mending gates, building hives – used to keep bees out the back, ye know. An' 'e was a great one for re-wiring too. 'E did all mine for two bottles of home brew... It was elderberry oi used to make.' She was growing more animated as each memory unfolded, steering her right away from her original purpose.

'So presumably he did work on my place too?' her listener asked, relieved.

'Oh yes, busy from dawn till dusk was Jim, and his son, and when 'e showed me the bathroom what 'e'd put in, oi 'ad to 'ave exactly the same,

96

didn't oi?'

Ivan remembered the ton of junk that had lain around the property and cost him a couple of hundred quid to shift.

'Tell me, Mrs Jonas,' he planned his question to be as general as possible, 'did any of them mention having any problems with their hands – you know, funny marks, that sort of thing?'

Her expression was something to behold.

'Lord above, 'is 'ands was 'is tools an' they was perfect. As for 'er, oi can't say, but she never said owt to me about that. Why?'

'Nothing. Forget it.'

'Oi was never too sure about the wife, mind, but 'e was a lovely man.' For a moment she paused to remove her glasses and wipe her eyes. Ivan wondered if she might even have fancied Mr G.

'So what became of them?' His watch showed two o'clock. He needed to get to the bank, but also to discover what Dr Rook had been unable to deliver.

'It was all very odd when oi think back. Not like Mr Carp just wandering off the way he did. No, these folks 'ere seemed to lose the will, if ye knows what oi mean. Just seemed to go downhill – stayed more and more indoors, and then in bed. Oi know, 'cos oi used to see the top light on during the day, towards the end. Course their son had gone off to college by then.'

'The end?' Ivan felt as if one of his scale weights had settled on his heart.

'Just faded away. Both together – 30 November 1994 it was. We'd 'ad the most terrible rain all night ... like *Welsh* rain, Mr Carp said, and 'e should know. Used to go there sometimes on 'is holidays...'

Ivan was lost in thought for a moment, recalling the lack of any private individual's name on his Deeds.

'So who owned Tripp's Cottage before them, then?'

'Tripps o' course – one lot after another. Before me time, though.' She pulled her cat away from peeing against Ivan's tyres, whereupon a strange little growl came from its throat.

'Don't ye go doin' that to yer old mother, or oi'll let ye off this lead and then, pop, they'll shoot ye.'

'Who will?' Ivan looked perturbed. He'd not heard any guns at all since moving in, and the pre-sale search he'd also paid for confirmed that the nearest pheasant shoot was at least eight miles away.

'Oi's not telling, but certain folks come poaching at night. We still get muntjacs 'ere see, and when Mr Carp was, like, in his normal years, 'e 'ad twenty sheep or more in the forest. Mind, he lost a few every year. Oh yes, someone was getting free mutton all right. And when 'e made enquiries about the missing ones 'e started getting phone calls, death threats, you know. Not very noice at all for 'im, poor man.'

'But we'd hear any shooting, surely?' The 'we' was deliberately intended to unite him and his potentially tricky adversary against this unknown common enemy.

'Not with them silencer things. Anyhows, oi

don't want to end up like one of 'em poor muntjac deers, or the other buggers what wander around in there.'

Ivan unlocked his car, more depressed than ever. It was as if the cancer of mindless violence had spread into this particularly idyllic area's lymph glands, and there was no holding it back. The disease seemed terminal.

'Can I get you anything from town while I'm there? It'll be no trouble,' he asked, trying to sound normal.

'Oh all right then. That's kind. Oi'll 'ave a pack of four tea cakes and a large brown loaf if it's all the same to ye.'

He drove off, all too aware of ever more anxieties downloading into his mind, threatening his simple dream of being a country potter in an inspiring place, and as he put the car into third gear he could see Mrs Jonas edge nearer to his outhouse, still sniffing the air.

Ivan finished his shopping and went over to the Lamb and Flag where a row of suits from some local company stood by the bar, while a couple of lads in paint-spattered overalls mauled the fruit machine in the corner. Of the barmaid Jo there was no sign.

'What can I get you, sir?' a peroxide-haired woman asked him, talking over the supping heads between them.

'Lager and lime, please.' And as he quickly closed his wallet on Tania's photograph, he cleared his throat. 'Is Jo coming in today, d'you know?'

The woman gave him a knowing smile. 'She is normally here at this time, but she phoned in to say the baby's poorly.'

Baby? Ivan's face registered enough disappointment for the bar lady to linger once she'd passed over his drink. That was a new one.

'The way she describes him, he sounds a lovely little chap, her kid. Still, I don't know how she does it, working here, working there. S'pose she's got to, though. Bills don't pay themselves, do they? And I should know. I've just moved up here from Wembley. This was the only job I could find.'

Ivan returned to the same dark corner he'd inhabited yesterday – this time the electric fire was warming up, its fake logs beginning to glow. He felt as if another heavy stick had just struck him on the head, and yet he sensed there wasn't a father around by the way the woman had relayed the information. The poor girl was obviously rushing around to make ends meet, to save for her course in January and whatever else needed paying for.

As he smoked and drank in turn, he found himself wondering obsessively what Jo's baby looked like. Did he have his mother's smile, her big dark eyes? And the more Ivan wondered, the more he needed to find out. He drew on his cigarette until it was finished, then gulped down the rest of his drink and returned to the bar.

'You don't happen to know where Jo lives, do you?'

'Sorry, sir, but I can't go giving out our staff's addresses to strangers – be more than my job's worth.'

'OK, but if you see her, say Ivan called in and I hope the baby soon gets better.'

'Will do. Cheerio.'

It was dusk by the time he walked up Mrs Jonas's path and waited at the front door with her few provisions. A distinct smell of cat piss hung round the flower bed, and he was just about to leave the bakery bag on her step when the door itself opened.

She was looking dreadful, utterly bereft, and for a moment Ivan was tempted to put his arms round her.

'Oi'm so glad to be seein' ye,' she gulped.

'What on earth's the matter, Mrs Jonas? Tell me.'

'It's me little Marcie. She's gone.'

'Marcie?'

'Me cat – just after ye'd left,' she sobbed, 'oi'd opened this door to let her in but she must have slipped out again while oi wasn't looking. Oh, where is she? Where *is* she?'

Ivan scanned the neat front garden, and the darkening lane beyond. 'I bet she'll be back when it's grub time,' he said, but knowing deep down that the gloomy all-enveloping forest just feet away was no place for any tame home-loving creature.

'If yer in town tomorrow, would ye put this up somewhere for people to see?' She passed Ivan a tear-stained postcard with the cat's description and a phone number at the bottom.

He slipped it carefully into his pocket. 'I had my car disappear on Tuesday night. How's that for coincidence?' He hoped his loss might lessen hers, but no, and, as yet more tears crept down her cheeks, he promised to keep a look-out on his travels. He could still hear her crying as he let himself into Tripp's Cottage – crying that might, by some small stretch of the imagination, be the mewling of a cat far away in the depths of the wood.

By seven o'clock he'd put a meal in the cooker and lit the fire. He'd soon learnt how to save on logs by stifling the early blaze with house coal, and after twenty minutes it was this dense warmth which reached his body, sprawled out on the rug with a glass of cheap red wine at his elbow.

He found himself thinking of Jo and her baby again – where they might live and how he could get in touch, when all at once that soft, yet this time more insistent, lisping voice once again reached his ears.

'I can't stay here... I can't...'

Ivan sprang to his feet and charged over to inspect the four corners of the room, rattling a table lamp and knocking over a pile of books as he did so.

'Who *are* you?' he yelled at Van Gogh's *Postmistress*, then his wild gaze shifted to a photo of his parents on holiday in Cork and a charcoal study of his late aunt drawn when she was young. 'What the *fuck* do you want me to do?'

'I can't stay here... Help me... Help me...'

The sound diminished but as it did so his hand began to hurt – really hurt, and as he scrutinized it, tiny pinpricks of blood began to seep from under his skin, like before, conforming to that same strange ring shape.

He heard the oven timer ping the end of twenty minutes, but he couldn't just leave the cottage, abandon everything, not with the kiln reaching a crucial temperature. There was nowhere he could go: no escape.

He tried to rationalize the situation – something Tania was always so good at. In retrospect it seemed he'd always attracted clear-sighted women, ones untouched by dreams or nightmares, so much so that when he'd first mentioned John Clare to Tania, she'd thought it was the name of some local hairdresser. But this time the recollection of that didn't bring a smile. This time he needed someone different, a kindred spirit. He thought instinctively of Valerie Rook, and impulsively went over to the phone. But there was no reply from her number, and when the answerphone chipped in his words deserted him.

To his astonishment, the blood began to subside and the surrounding skin to gradually lose its redness. When he looked again a moment later, under the shadeless kitchen bulb, the area seemed unmarked – no trace of anything other than a smear of clay just beneath his wrist.

This was developing into some pretty crazy game. Now you see it, now you don't, but even though the bite marks had gone, he once more had the distinct impression he wasn't alone in the cottage.

It was as if that same invisible shadow was

another's breath, thickening his own air, and so unnerved was he by this sensation that when he came to retrieve his liver and bacon hot pot from the oven, it slipped from his hands to land upside down, and spread a brown mess over the kitchen floor.

That did it. He'd get a takeaway from the Balti House in Stoneshanger. Having cleared up and checked that the kiln was doing nothing untoward and would cut out at the right time, he locked up and walked over to the car.

He was just wondering if Mrs Jonas's cat had turned up, when he noticed lights in the forest. Too powerful for mere torch beams, he realized they were headlights strobing between the leafless trees. Ivan listened hard as he slid round to his outhouse wall. He could hear the muffled clunk of his kiln inside, his own breath short and tense, thinking of what Lily Jonas had said of the forest's nocturnal life.

Creeping round beside his picket fence, he crouched down near the corner post. Now he could definitely distinguish voices above the burr of some slow-moving vehicle. Suddenly a dull thud punctuated the night, then another. Ivan heard the creak of twigs become a longer smoother sound. It didn't take a genius to work out that whatever had just been shot was being dragged along the ground.

In that instant, the beams turned directly his way, and he was caught full face in their searching light.

Jesus. Shit.

With the reflex more of a trained soldier than a

104

potter, he threw himself in the winter-damp grass, so he could see out through the tufts – but not for long. First came panting, closer and closer, growing to a growl then a deep bloodthirsty bark. Ivan felt hot saliva dribble on his forehead, before giant paws clamped down on his shoulders. He recognized the same fishy dog breath he'd sniffed at Wiseman's Farm.

'C'm ere, Lodz, you fuckin' animal!' The man's voice was filled with such threat that the creature immediately left his victim and bounded back towards the trees where the vehicle's engine was now revving and ready to go. Ivan looked up to see the lights turn away into the deeper mysteries of the wood.

His clothes under the jacket were now wet through. He didn't dare move a muscle until whatever it was had vanished, then he stood up, disorientated for a moment. The night was too still, too oppressive without stars – the black clouds seemingly nudging the tops of the trees.

Ivan gripped the fence for support, trying to make sense of what he'd just seen. The Oakleys' Nissan, he was sure of that. But which of them driving it? And who or what had they shot? As he stumbled back into the cottage, he also thought about the neighbour's missing cat and hoped she'd had the sense to be elsewhere. But that foolish dog who'd given them away was probably now just a lump of dead meat, soon to be buried or bagged up to feed to the local foxhounds.

'Who yer with?' the stranger asked her at the Ox and Bough. 'Is it the lot from Nant y Fedw?'

Siân nodded, not for one second taking her eyes off the baker, while the man pointed at Tomos, who was trying to hide behind his tankard. 'How come ye let a young 'un like this be left out there?' he asked. 'What sort of porthmon are ye?'

'She's an evil little cuss with no business being on our drove,' the baker interrupted. 'But there was no telling her that. She wouldna' have any of it. She may look as crumpled as a widow's veil, but ye lissen to me, she's as cunning as the vermin in the straw.'

But Siân's face told another story, and while Cantor Rees showed the baker outside, then locked the door on him, the man who'd relinquished his stool rested a kindly arm across her shoulders.

'She needs a proper bed, in the warm. And in the morning, if there's been anything untoward happened, I'll go and fetch the constable meself.' At mention of the law, Tomos shifted uneasily, downing another sup of ale, aware of the collective disapproval becoming ever more audible whispers.

'I was going to see to it,' he mumbled, 'but she took herself off, didn't she?'

No one responded. There'd been enough young girls trailing the herds for no good reason, specially in the summer. Too young for such a thing, most would have admitted if asked. But this one was different, not just because she was crippled, and someone began clapping in approval as Cantor Rees came over to them, scratching his head.

'The only space left is by the stove,' he said to

her, gathering up an armful of smocks and leggings discarded by earlier patrons. The publican helped her into the kitchen and proceeded to make up a small uneven bed.

'There'ya my girl. Least it's dry.'

He closed the door behind him and Siân climbed gratefully onto the rags that smelt of so many other journeys, glancing up at the one dark window in fear of seeing the baker peering in. Then, reassured he was now well away from the place, she lay wondering whether Huw was thinking of her, and going over everything in her mind about a strategy for tomorrow should the outcast baker seek his revenge.

From the tap room, she heard some half-remembered ballad rise above the talk, the basses in their fervour taking over the tune, and as the cattle noises dropped in Halfpenny Field to become part of the night, she fell unconscious into a deep sleep.

When she woke, she found Rees's dog was lying half across her, his dried-blood breath full in her face. He growled as she moved away, then finally settled himself under the table.

Siân noticed some holes in her coat and knew rats had been in. She'd wet herself again and her skin and clothes underneath felt all sewn up together.

Suddenly the door swung open, the latch loud under an angry hand. Derryn Morris himself. He'd slept rough, that was obvious: his white hair was matted wet and looking a different colour on his head, his mouth ready for a curse. Siân felt her insides turn over and gripped the coat so hard her knuckles hurt, but the dog was advancing on the baker, snarling through his teeth. Then the man was gone again, leaving just the memory of the cold hatred in his eyes burning into hers.

'*Good dog.*' She patted him then crept past into the saloon, where the biggest woman she'd ever seen was sweeping the floor.

'*Where's he gone?*' Siân asked with her whole effort.

'Rats got yer tongue, then?' The woman stopped, out of breath. 'D'you mean Y Trafferth – Mr Trouble?' She picked a lump of damp sawdust off the broom head. 'If he's got half that dog's brain he'd be takin' hisself back to where he come from, and your Mr Richards ought to be more particular 'bout who he takes along with him.'

'Oh really, Mrs Fat-Ball?' Tomos, already halfway into the room, pulled his sister upright by the collar. 'And if I'd got a beast so lardy as yourself, I'd have to hire one of the new locomotives to carry it.'

Cantor's niece reddened, but had enough composure left to wag a plump finger. 'You couldna carry nothing over where you're heading.' She turned to Siân. 'You mind he doesn't take you near that bog.'

'What bog?' Tomos barked.

'What bog, my backside. The bog over Blaen-carreg, that's what. With all the rains it'll be more like the sea.'

'I'll ask you to keep your mouth where it

belongs,' he growled, then led Siân outside, still frowning, his head turned to the east.

The woman tutted, feeling sorry for such a frail little thing at the mercy of such rough men. She had half a mind to keep her back here and make her useful sewing sheets, keeping up the fire. Even giving her a proper wash over. But it wasn't her place to do that, she knew that. Besides, the child was bound to be someone's daughter, someone's kin.

Siân, meanwhile tugged on her brother's sleeve, even though she realized that was useless. His lips had all but disappeared they were so tightened, his eyebrows lowered like the black clouds heaping up over their heads.

'You're along with me only on account of your father. Don't you forget that, you little meddler. And what did he ever give me?' He jabbed at her arm. 'So just leave me be. I've talked to the ones I trust, and the way over Blaencarreg is passable. What's worse, tell me, a bit of easy marsh or paying tolls to fill the dead-weights' purses?'

The publican, who'd been stacking the night's rubbish in the yard, looked up. 'I've heard it's bad by there and all. If there's any trouble, ye'll be on yer own.'

Siân felt a stab of fear. Tomos's recklessness was more a madness, with this unknown terrain spread as far and dark as the dawn itself. She thought of Huw again and was in two minds to try and sneak off home, when one of the tavern's lads appeared with the cob and the chestnut held tight, one in each hand. Collen's ears were laid flat against her head, and Siân sensed they were both in a bad mood. Horses knew things. Never mind the men her brother trusted, what he should really be paying attention to was staring him in the face.

The black cob, Incio, was sweating. Froth spattered his neck like the Teifi's foam caught by the rocks near Nant-y-Fedw. His huge hoof struck the ground like a mourning bell.

'Be sober now, you.' Tomos tied him to the fence. 'It's not the time for tricks.'

He hollered for the gate to be opened and, as the herd made a move, he announced it was Evans who was to be 'driver' instead of Morris. The hymn singer slurred his thanks. To be a driver meant more pay and could add up to him being a porthmon, once he'd found a wife. But Morris muttered things Siân knew came from the devil's lips, and she was relieved to see him on the far side, more taken up with his current grievance than anything else.

The cattle breath rose like smoke, but the cold had calmed them, and they processed into the lane with Tomos and Siân at the head.

'Castlemartins won't like where they're going,' Cantor Rees observed to his niece from the window. 'They'll feel the water under their hooves, and that'll be that.' He stared after Moses Evans, slumped on his grey pony. The man had sung and drunk last night in equal measure, and now let his reins flap loose and his mouth hang open. 'Pity for them.' Rees closed the curtain and began counting out what Tomos Richards had paid him. Six shillings, in coins. The cost of four cheap coffins.

Siân was starving. Her stomach churned over and over and her head felt light as thistledown. She saw Tomos pull a piece of bread from his pocket and devour it in one go. Then another, and another, with no thought for her. Huw's potato would have been like manna from heaven, and as she surveyed the bleak hills leading down to Blaencarreg, she realized this remote brooding place was as far from any heaven as it was possible to be. Every old wall was a footpad's hideout, every tree a vagabond's vantage point.

Even the odd derelict mud dwelling was probably full of murderers, and when the Hereford coach had to stop to let the drove through, she saw nothing but evil behind its dark isinglass.

The noise grew worse, Tomos roaring instructions from deep in his belly as Morris kept the left flank from following a farm track up to the sky, and Moses Evans began yet another Williams Pantycelyn hymn for the hundredth time, oblivious to his pony's scouring in fear.

The lane became almost a holloway as it sloped down the hill, and the grass grew coarser, turning to reeds at the bottom. Nevertheless Tomos pointed straight ahead and kicked the cob towards a distant bridge which, unbeknown to him, was already half under water. But his progress was short-lived. The clay underfoot was sodden, without any firm hold. Incio whinnied and threw his head about, sinking to his knees as the herd ploughed on in panic past him, deeper and deeper down into the mud.

111

Siân looked around for the baker, her tormentor, but a group of cattle had broken away where he'd been, and there was no sign of him or the brown pony from Esgairwen.

She made a decision.

It wasn't desertion, it was survival. She turned Collen round, and in the ascent, away from the bog, the mare found enough tufted footholds until they were clear of the drove, well up the hill.

She realized that what she saw next would never leave her for the rest of her life, and there was nothing she could do except pray that Ben would have the sense not to go further. There was no sign either of the corgis who'd been up at the front snapping at the leaders' heels, and she feared the worst for them.

Meanwhile, Ben's black-and-fawn shape still wove amongst the runts at the rear and, for a brief terrible moment, he too disappeared, then scrambled up towards her, the bog dripping from his fur. Siân's breath stayed locked in her lungs as the scene below unfolded and one by one, after pitiful bellowing, part of the porthmon's livelihood sank without trace.

Five

Ivan woke on Friday morning with a serious hangover. After his edge-of-the-wood experience he'd finished the Spanish plonk and his cigarettes, then downed half a bottle of Bell's whisky – his father's intended Christmas present.

His throat could have taken anything after that bloody fright and, Christ, he'd have kept going with the drink all night if he hadn't crashed out senseless on the settee first.

He washed and dressed without too much thought as to what dry clothes he should wear, and, because his jacket was still sodden, he dug out an old denim job from college days and an even older pair of jeans. Having switched off the kiln and attempted breakfast, he went round to call on Mrs Jonas, aware of the fresh cold morning reaching his skin through the insubstantial cotton layers.

He tried her bell twice and, when there was still no answer, scribbled on a page of his Lifelong Learning diary his willingness to take a look for Marcie, tore it out and shoved it through her letter box. It included his phone number which, until now, he'd been reluctant to share. However, now was different. Very different.

On the way to town, Ivan found some old gum in the glove box and chewed it, keeping his window open for great gulps of clean air in case a local plod should be looking for ways to fill his notebook. By the time he reached the police station his breath was, thank God, more Ice White than anything else.

This time a middle-aged WPC was manning the desk. She was stocky, ginger-haired, and at least looking alert and interested, which encouraged him to relay in detail what had happened to him.

'We have to be realistic, Mr–?' she began when he'd finished.

'Browning. As in Robert.'

She ignored his feeble quip and kept her eyes squarely on his. 'That part of the forest, if I recall, is common land, public space, what you will. We try to do a recce there once every two months. Now I'm not saying that's an ideal situation, Mr Browning, but it does reflect the pressure we're under and–' her words were drowned by a fire engine in full flight outside – 'we do our best.'

'Look, I was set upon by one of the Oakleys' fucking great dogs.'

'I'm afraid that until East Wood becomes part of the estate of Lord Hickson, where his keepers have authority to protect the forest from trespass, we're powerless.'

'But you're the law?'

'On paper, yes. But incidents like that happen all the time round here – as they've done for years. We can't be in fifty places at once.'

'I recognized their Nissan, for God's sake, and the bloke was calling the dog Lodz.'

'Mr Browning, you must try and underst–'

'And I bet they've got my car in a thousand

bloody bits by now, flogging them off some-where.'

The WPC walked over to a large noticeboard and began pinning up several posters on car security and female self-defence.

'And what happened up at Radby End on Wednesday morning that was so important you couldn't come over to Cold Firton straightaway and help me? No one's said another word about that: nothing on the local news, nothing in the papers.'

She kept herself busy, ensuring that she wasn't positioned directly in front of him.

'You may not be aware, Mr Browning, that all our responses to calls are graded, and your request re a missing vehicle, I'm afraid, was a Grade 3 Deferred.'

'Deferred? That's ridiculous.'

The woman sighed. 'Grade 3 incidents do not require an immediate attendance, and include all those where deployment can be delayed for more than a few minutes, and those that can be allocated by way of appointment.'

'More than a few minutes? I waited twenty-four *hours*.'

'I'm sorry that wasn't made clear to you at the time but, as you can appreciate, that in itself illustrates our problem. Now, if you don't mind.'

'Well, my insurance company might not be appreciative that nothing appears to be happen-ing about the theft of my car; because that's what it is.'

'DC Marsh has already been in touch with them. They should be contacting you either tomorrow morning or Monday. And I'll pass on to them what you've just told me.'

Just then, the desk telephone rang and he was subsequently ignored. No more mileage in this, he thought, and pushed open the door leading into the forecourt where a drab little procession of solicitors and others was heading for the adjoining courthouse.

As he passed the Lamb and Flag, Ivan hesitated on its step and looked in through the leaded window prematurely laced by Christmas lights. His heart leapt in his chest. There she was. Chatting to a group of young women by the bar, the same happy-looking Jo in a silver-grey top. She looked fantastic.

He went in. 'Half a cider,' he said to her, feeling a blush creep up his neck. 'And whatever you'd like.'

'Thanks, but–'

'It's more than your job's worth. I know.' He grinned, aware of her companions dissecting him with their kohl-rimmed eyes. 'I came in to see if you were here yesterday,' he blurted out, then immediately regretted it.

'Really. Why?' Her tone was cool enough for him to take his change and retreat into his usual corner. The cider was too sweet. Inside his head was still a mess. It was all crap. Everything.

He slumped back against the old velour padding wondering what his cottage would fetch now, and where he could go next with the proceeds. He closed his eyes, suddenly exhausted.

Just then, a clean soapy smell reached his nostrils.

'Hi, it's only me.'

He woke with a start to see the bar now deserted and Jo sitting opposite him. 'Those were just some of my old mates,' she explained. 'I'm not bothered about them really, but they keep coming in to see me because that makes them feel better.'

'What do you mean, better?' Ivan left the rest of his drink untouched, aware only of her intense brown eyes and the strand of glossy hair which had drifted across her cheek.

'Because I'm a single mum, that's why. Got to work here, there and everywhere, then half of it goes on the cost of the nursery anyway.'

'Who needs enemies?' he said, a reckless idea forming in his mind. An idea which might just make him stay on at Tripp's Cottage.

'They're all so sort of old already, if you get my meaning. They've got their little bitchy offices, their PCs, think they've got it all taped...'

'Whereas you're going to be the Capability Brown of the twenty-first century?'

'Oh dream on, you. I don't know...' She suddenly looked defeated, turning a beer mat over and over.

'You've got to do that course, if it's pulling at you.' Ivan patted his own heart. 'This isn't a dress rehearsal, you know.' He leaned forwards, resting his elbows on the table. 'My lot in Ireland expected me to follow the old man into the haulage business. Can you imagine me driving some forty-tonner up and down the motorways all day?'

She smiled with a row of even white teeth.

'No, I can't.' Then she glanced back towards the bar where two farming types in muddy boots were studying the snacks menu. Ivan silently cursed them for arriving just when she seemed likely to begin talking. 'Best get moving, sorry.' Jo got up. 'The boss'll be on me like a ton of bricks otherwise. It's like sentry duty here. You've got to stick to your post ... as if I was in the bloody Boer War or something.'

There wasn't time now to find out where she lived, or to ask about the baby, and as Ivan left, exchanging a brief wave with her, he realized that neither had yet spoken each other's name. She was keeping her distance which was fair enough. After all, who was he? Some total stranger, probably too tall for her, too scruffy, definitely nothing like Westlife.

Ivan wandered out into the pub's rear car park, curious to see which vehicle might possibly be hers, so he could look out for it when he was driving around. He matched the muddied Range Rover, with its local dealer sticker with the rustics. There was also a motorbike and an old Cortina with DARREN and DAWN above its windscreen, then, last of all, a huge maroon Nissan Terrano which looked newly valeted – its heavy chrome sills immaculate – and on the front passenger seat was a box of pastel tissues. Like the other cars, there was nothing to suggest a baby, but, unlike its companions, the dealership was in Wapping.

He quickly checked for any evidence of recent welding or any paint re-touching, only to find the bodywork perfect as new. Disappointed, he made a note of the number. But something was puzzling him. There was something familiar about that particular off-roader's shape, its bulky profile, with the jutting body-coloured spare at the rear. But then, he reasoned, practically every second vehicle in that rural area was a 4x4 of some sort. No way could it have been the one he'd seen in Cold Firton. And no way could its owner be Jo.

On his way back to the town centre car park, with a disturbing possibility refusing to leave him entirely alone, Ivan halted by the double display windows of County Homes.

'You thinking of moving, then?' A woman's voice behind him made him whip round in surprise. It was Pam Barker – alias Mrs Swordfish – specialist in the art of asymmetry, with an unshakeable confidence in her awful work. She was clutching a bunch of dried flowers and the smell of fresh bread escaped from her carrier bag.

'Course not, Pam. Not now the class and everything else is going so well. No, I was just gobsmacked by the prices. They've gone crazy.'

She eyed him through her bifocals, her long pointed nose looking even more obtrusive in the daylight.

'You got a mortgage?' she asked.

Ivan's first reaction was, *none of your bloody business*, but as she still hovered, he had to think quickly.

'Lord, yes.' His solicitor had casually advised him about that line. People get jealous otherwise, he'd warned, they try and put you down, mention the tax man et cetera. So no one, apart from his immediate family and a young woman from the auctioneers, knew that Tripp's Cottage had been bought outright from a London sale.

'Keeps you at it, I suppose,' she sniffed, already half-turned to watch the passing traffic. 'Trouble is, my Gerald can't even get himself a tiny terrace cottage in Cold Firton to be near his mum. I just haven't the room, not with my old duck still to see to. Still,' she sniffed again, 'you've got to live with yourself, haven't you?'

He let her homilies and platitudes wash over him while he tried to shape the one question he'd wanted to ask someone since he'd left the pub.

'Tell me, d'you ever frequent the Lamb over there?' As casually as he could.

'Oh yes, me and Frank go to the quiz night on Fridays, which is tonight, of course. And then some of us from work' – she pointed over the High Street at Barker and Sons Electrical Retailers – 'usually go in for a snack there on Tuesday lunchtimes. Trouble is, there's not much bar food, not till their other chef's back.'

'What's up with him, then?'

'Malcolm?' She squinted at nothing in particular. 'Malcolm Cotton. Funny you should ask, no one's heard a dicky bird from him for a week now. Rumour has it he's just taken himself off for a bit of a break, but I tell you, there won't be a job for him when he gets back. Oh no.'

'So do you know someone called Jo working in there? One of the barmaids?' He waited anxiously to see what reply her busy little mouth would bring forth.

'Not to speak to, not really. Seems a pleasant enough sort of lass though. She joined in the quiz last week, that's about it. Not just a pretty face, I can tell you. She got all her answers right, and they was hard.'

'You don't happen to know her surname, do you, Pam? She may be interested in another class I'm starting up in the new year. Thought I'd mention her to the office in case it gets oversubscribed.' He began to colour again, to feel his skin burn. Whatever else the shopkeeper's wife was, she wasn't stupid.

'Oh Lord, I do believe you're sweet on the girl,' the woman said in an odd way, not for one second letting him avoid her probing stare.

'No, I've hardly met her.' He checked his watch – there was a full kiln to unpack and a range of urns to glaze. 'I'd better be off now. See you next Tuesday evening.' But as he turned to go, a finger prodded his arm.

'I've been here a good while longer than you, Mr Browning, and I've learnt not to get caught up with things that don't concern me.'

'I don't get what you mean.' Ivan felt a slight chill touch his skin and was aware that the town hall clock was nudging one-thirty. Yet she seemed to be leading somewhere.

'All I'm saying is, some things, or rather, some *people* are best left alone.' She tapped the side of her significant nose.

'D'you mean Jo? Why?' He thought again of the Nissan in the pub car park, but nothing else was making sense.

'I'm not saying.' Her lips disappeared.

'Well, who's this boss who's so hard on her, then?'

'Her uncle, isn't it?'

Ivan frowned.

'But, like I've said,' she went on, 'we've no complaints with the place. Compared to the others in this town, it's a palace. Now then,' Pam Barker's voice grew even more conspiratorial, 'there was something else I meant to tell you – first of all, in fact. I did have a mind to phone you.'

'Phone me? What about?'

'In case – oh dear, I don't know how to say this. In case you turned up on Tuesday night your usual jolly self.'

'Go on.' It was only early afternoon, but already the grey even light was darkening, bringing a slight drizzle on the breeze.

'It's Gill Bunnett. You need to be aware that her brother's gone missing.'

'Missing?'

Ivan knew from this woman's eyes that she was used to delivering gossip in small tantalizing doses. A bit like an artificial sweetener dispenser, he thought, except there was nothing remotely sweet about any of this. In fact he began to feel ill, as if some toxic vapour had seeped into his system.

'So Mrs Allen told me at the Drama group last night. Apparently she's seen the police searching out along the Wap.'

'Hey, that's the river near me,' Ivan said without thinking, his brain suddenly numb. For it was that stretch of water idling through the little valley just south of the village, which was a favourite walk of his, and, apart from the forest itself, a source of inspiration in his work.

'No, no. Up by Radby End,' she countered.

'Radby End? Oh Jesus.'

'I beg your pardon?'

'No, nothing.' He was aware of her startled expression. 'But I'm sure everything'll be OK. He may just have gone fishing, whatever...' Bland stupid words coming out, when he'd guessed the plods had been sitting on something since Wednesday morning...

The woman shook her grey head.

'That's impossible. He's never been known to miss his dinner before. Anyway–' she re-positioned the dried flowers in the crook of her arm – 'I thought it only fair to give you advance warning.' She eyed him over the top of her glasses.

'Thanks.'

He then watched her scuttle over the road and through an alleyway leading between shops, sensing that the gathering chill echoed the feelings in his heart.

As he passed the police station again, praying he wouldn't meet anyone else with yet more grim revelations to chip away at his little rustic dream, he saw a fresh notice displayed on its thick oak door, informing the public that until midday tomorrow any enquiries would be dealt with by Northampton police.

There was just the one message on his answer-phone when Ivan got back home, and with his head full of Jo's open friendly face and the

Swordfish's unsettling news about the girl's uncle and Tom Coles, Ivan pressed Play. To his surprise, it was Valerie Rook.

'Ivan, I'm feeling very guilty indeed,' the message began. 'There *are* things you need to know, and I should have said, but with Michael around it was impossible. Look, why don't you come over while he's at church on Sunday morning, say eleven-thirty? He keeps trying to get me to go too, but no way. Really, you'd think he'd give up after all this time.'

Ivan hovered over the phone. Her suggestion was compelling. Or he could ignore the whole thing altogether. An appealing prospect, but against his curious nature.

Go with the flow, he told himself, putting the kettle on the LPG cooker. God knew he'd got enough to do till then: cleaning all his tools, mixing up new glazes, playing midwife to the sixty soup bowls so carefully stacked and soon to be ready for decoration. That would be sure to get him back to base if nothing else.

The studio was as warm as a womb – the most welcoming sight in the world as he set his tea mug down, and, holding his breath, began unscrewing the kiln door. Suddenly the sound he'd dreaded since his Linton Grove days, with its often erratic kilns...

Clink clink clink

As he opened the door inch by inch, a mound of fired terracotta morsels of what had once been soup bowls slid to the front edge of the kiln and cascaded down at his feet. He forgot to breathe, staring in, surveying the rest of the wreckage.

There were no survivors, in fact barely any recognizable bits at all. Just one or two fragments showing the River Wap. His mind raced on. An air pocket, perhaps? A foreign body? No way. Not with repeatedly wedged then wheelthrown balls of clay. It was impossible. Since setting up on his own, he'd never even had *one* blow-up before, never mind this.

He went out into the afternoon drizzle, tears stinging his eyes. He kept walking round, past his own fence where the Oakleys' dog had found him, and into the black throat of the forest. Nothing could touch him now. Two weeks' work was just a heap of shit.

Ivan thought almost lovingly of his old man's lorries, named after rock stars – Jimi, Bob and Bruce. The idea of long-haul driving became ever more attractive with each step he took – a life of perpetual motion, not investing in anything much, just thinking of the next stop, and every meeting with fellow travellers just like ships passing.

When he was a teenager, in school holidays, he'd done a few runs up and down to Newry; sitting in king-of-the-road style, able to see into back gardens and fields hidden from the ordinary motorist. Then the slap-up breakfast in some greasy-spoon café, with the day's papers and the latest chart toppers on the radio.

Suddenly, as he walked, he felt something against his boot. Ivan bent down, could smell the same sweetish, rich smell as that hare. Something he'd never forget.

It was a cat. He felt its pointed ears, its thin red

collar. Marcie was as dead as the leaves which had almost hidden her. Ivan could feel the sticky blood around the neck wound – a gaping hole made by an air-rifle cartridge.

Oh God, help us. What now?

It was as if night had fallen two hours early. No moon, no stars, nor any inkling of the heavens beyond. The sky over Wapford Forest was the colour of old pewter and the drizzle that had begun that afternoon kept up its subtle baptism of Ivan's head, turning his hair a darker brown, dampening his denim jacket.

He'd have to tell Mrs Jonas, of course, but nothing would make him pick up that poor creature and deliver it personally. Instead, he heaped up the leaves over the corpse and left a stick protruding from the ground nearby.

As Ivan wandered deeper into the private domain of trees, along the track sometimes used by horses but rarely by weekend walkers, he felt all his thirty-two years slipping away like dead skin, his own memories receding to fuse with those of another harsher time. With the unknowns who'd lived and perished in this quiet backwater – whose souls seemed to reach out and touch him, like the bare winter branches of browse-wood themselves.

Yet he welcomed the shadows, the weak tears of rain which merged with his own, and as he reached the thinner band of oak and hazel where the common land curved downwards towards the River Wap, he knew deep in his Celtic bones he would always be the outsider from the city here, but nevertheless one who was breathing the same air of danger and mystery as those drovers, tanners and girdlers whose own bones had long since lain still in their unmarked, unvisited graves.

More rain, hard as the rods Geraint Richards was casting daily down in the Dowlais furnaces, and the wind forced the surface water along Martyr's Lane into shin-high waves.

At the Hen and Casket in Llancrwys, Tomos sat with his head in his hands while Siân gestured for food and drink from old Mrs Rice the publican, who'd already sent a runner for the constable.

'How many gone?' Moses Evans ventured, still shaken.

'Twenty-four. And the corgis too.'

Evans whistled through his teeth, and when at last Siân's brother looked up, it was as if an old man now faced her. His eyes were almost invisible.

'*I'm sorry*,' Siân mouthed. *'But I did try to tell you.'*

Tomos turned away. Like Evans, his clothes were caked with a uniform of mud which was beginning to crack round the folds.

'I'd say you was all lucky to be alive.' Mrs Rice set down three cups of cider, with a plate of black pudding that Siân devoured too quickly, biting her lip in the process. 'Unlike some.' The old woman's scorn was undisguised. 'And look at that poor girl there. You should never have gone near the river Carreg.'

'Did it for old Caradoc last September,' Tomos countered.

'That was September.' She brought over a rag and began wiping Siân's hands and face in such a way the girl knew she must have been a mother herself. 'And if you'd have followed this one's advice, you wouldna be sitting here now.'

She clicked her knotty fingers, whereupon Ben limped over and lay by Siân's chair. 'Nor this grand hound.'

Siân patted his damp head, a mixture of feelings churning in her head: relief that she wouldn't have to see Morris again, yet a deep guilt that she'd looked after herself instead of helping her brother. She tried to catch his gaze again, but knew the deadness there would stay for ever.

The hymn singer, however, was different. Siân had never seen a grown man cry and Moses Evans made no effort to hide his tears. They clouded his drink to mud while a farmer and his son in the far corner turned to stare and then brought their stools over.

'Ye won't be the first nor the last, while there's tolls,' the older man said. 'Those with a living to make aren't going to pay them. I tell you, there's trouble coming. Last week the booth at Bryn Iestyn was wrecked, and they don't know if Dai Watkins'll mend.'

Siân saw her brother shiver and haul his greatcoat up over his head, while the farmer's son went over to the grate and kicked the logs into life.

'I don't blame 'em neither. First, we can't run to keeping on any labour; second, we have to pay to use our *own* bloody roads.' He was flushed and angry, finishing his ale in one go. Siân noticed how his hands were thick and calloused, belonging more to an old man too.

Tomos sneezed and Moses Evans was wiping his nose on his sleeve, wishing he was back in his own bed, when a sharp knock made everyone start. The old woman who'd been slicing up a piece of bacon stood with her knife aloft.

'John James, Justice of the Peace.' A short pink gentleman introduced himself, leaving an oblong of night behind him. 'The constable's out at Esgair till the morning, but we got six of Mrs Hendy's lads down to Blaencarreg. They found your man.'

'Found our man?' Tomos repeated in shock, tilting on his stool so much Siân thought he might fall.

'And as close to dead as makes no difference,' James added. 'He's down with Dr Price until we can get word to his family.'

Siân's heart thudded in her chest. She could see it now. Nothing but trouble, with the baker's mother, Ma Morris at the head of it all. Tomos now feigned concern.

'As God's my witness, I thought he'd got himself clear. I'd swear I saw him coming up the slope, then' – he rubbed his hand across his eyes – 'he was gone. Bloody nowhere, wasn't it, Siân, bach?'

She nodded, ashamed of his lie, and of herself wishing Morris truly dead.

'You the porthmon?' James asked.

'Yes.'

'Licence?' The stranger then waited, while the

other fumbled in his clothes. The document was yellowed and folded into worn creases. James carefully unravelled it and set a monocle in his left eye. 'You've not had this long, sir.'

'No.'

'Is this your first run?'

'Second. I came through with a hundred. September fourth last year. Same route exactly.'

'Mmm.' The stout man looked across at Siân. 'Were you with him then?'

'No,' she whispered. 'But he was.' Her eyes fell on Moses Evans. He was thinking fast, she could tell.

'We'd not a second's problem,' Evans rose quickly to her brother's defence. 'We got to Gloucester smooth as Welsh butter.'

The JP handed back the licence, giving nothing away. Siân knew this man, grown comfortable on others' miseries, was too clever for that.

'You'll have to stay here until the next of kin are satisfied it was an accident,' he suddenly announced.

'What!' Tomos looked stricken, his fists large as rocks, and for the first time his sister saw such a terrible desperation that she felt fear all over again. 'Sir, I bought the herd last October, in part with my wife's money. And with twenty-four now gone I'm bloody doomed. I need to get this lot to Berkhamstead for fattening before their first sale, if we're not to starve.'

'Is your wife not understanding?' James probed. 'Would she be more satisfied if you rather than your companion had lain dead in the bog?'

Tomos lowered his head without replying, and

130

Siân realized now that all might not be sunshine and flowers back at Pont Llwyd Farm.

'He'll need new dogs *and* he'll have to repay Mr Lloyd for the pony as well,' Moses Evans piped up. 'They won't come cheap, neither.'

Mr James went over to the old woman, stuck his mouth against her ear, then returned. 'Mrs Rice says you can have two rooms for the duration, and there'll be just a half charge for the rest of the herd.' With that, he gave Siân a curious glance and vanished into the night. The silence in his wake was the same as before thunder.

'Imagining's the worst,' the innkeeper tried to ease the tension. ''Tis a pity we're not more like the beasts. Which reminds me, the grey may have to go.' She picked out the candle stubs from their holders on the table, and lit new ones. 'He's barely on three legs.'

Tomos groaned and banged the sides of his head with both hands. Siân swore she could hear some kind of prayer leave his lips, something she'd never witnessed before – not even when she'd lain trampled nearly to death. She too then said a silent Our Father for the animal. Incio had survived on account of his strength, but his nostrils had blown out blood the moment they'd reached the inn.

'Now, I'm going to give this young girl here a bathing over, and some clean clothes. We can't have her encouraging vermin. And you two,' she pointed at them, 'if you've got a whit of sense you'll shake that muck off yourselves and get some sleep.' With that, she took Siân's arm and led her through to a freezing room off the

131

kitchen, where a tin bath lay already half full of filthy water. She studied it for a moment, then made up her mind. 'It'll do: better than nothing.' She unpeeled Geraint Richards's coat and threw it into the corner. Then the rest of Siân's garments.

Siân cried out as the cold air met her skin. She tried to hide her growing body, but Mrs Rice was strong and lifted her into the tub. The girl's shrieks were mute, the splashing ignored, and gradually, with the application of a foul-smelling soap, Siân grew so stiff and blue that the woman took fright and quickly removed her own apron to wrap it round her.

'Wait, don't move.'

Siân couldn't, and the wait seemed an eternity. Her breath came out as little more than a sigh, and the effort of refilling her lungs was almost too much. The woman returned and hurled some clothes into the room. Men's things: a nightshirt and breeches that had once belonged to her husband.

'I want my coat. It's my Da's.'

'No, ye don't. It smells of the rinderpest as sure as I'm come from Adam's rib. I'll be throwing it away.'

Siân struggled free of her and, damp and half-naked, reached the saloon. No Tomos, no Moses Evans, no coat either. She remembered her father's single hair hidden in its pocket – her one precious relic – and hunted in all the bench boxes that lined the wall.

'Where is it? Where is it?'

But Mrs Rice had followed and now slapped

her back into the washroom.

'Under my roof you'll do as you're told.'

The nightshirt scratched like twigs, the breeches were baggy. Siân felt more uncomfortable than ever, and just as cold. She closed her eyes as the woman fastened the shirt buttons tight against her throat. Some mother this, the girl thought, and she found herself wondering whether if she'd perished too, Mair Richards would have even pressed a handkerchief to her eyes.

Overhead, she heard Tomos and his driver arguing. The louder the voices, the louder the old boards protested, and she could make out Moses Evans refusing to make a break for it with the herd. The old woman banged on the ceiling with a broom handle, then turned to stare at Siân.

'There's something about that younger one,' she said. 'He's got the same look on him as you. Is he a brother?'

Siân shook her wet curls almost too quickly. He was no brother – never had been.

'You're lying, girl. Still it's no affair o' mine.' She parked Siân by the dying fire for a quarter of an hour, then, with the candle lit, took her down a flight of stone steps to a tiny room.

The candlelight brought strange creatures crowding the walls. The damp smell grew stronger. It was like going down to Tartarus, and Siân held back. 'In here.' Mrs Rice heaved her body against a poorly fitting door and, once inside, left the candle holder on a ledge. When she'd gone, the flame expired, leaving an awesome darkness, a complete black void.

133

As a child, such things had never disturbed Siân. The night had been a friend bringing sleep, and she'd always felt safe in the knowledge that her father was below, watching the embers grow dim, planning ahead of the weather. For in those days the ewes and the sows still put food on the table.

But this was a different dark, threatening a tomorrow of uncertainties, making London seem like somewhere beyond the earth itself.

Six

Ivan ran back the way he'd come, with branches brushing his face and oak bark cracking underfoot. He felt strangely lightheaded, as if that brief journey to the edge of the forest had drawn him into a time recorded by ink on paper, whose stories nevertheless were beginning to entwine him, as if he too was part of those interlocking arboreal limbs. Both hunter and hunted...

After he'd delivered the grim news of his find to Mrs Jonas, and himself phoned her son to come over from Silverstone to bury her cat away from foxes, Ivan was pouring himself another whisky from the half-empty bottle when the phone rang.

He missed the glass and swore as a precious puddle spread over the table.

Valerie Rook sounded rather more agitated than usual.

'Ivan, you ought to know what's happened before it gets in all the papers,' she babbled breathlessly. 'It's that poor Mr Coles, they found him this lunchtime. He had his throat cut and was dumped in the river up by Radby End. The fruit and veg delivery man's just told me. I knew something like this would happen. I just knew.'

Ivan stayed silent, watching the whisky drip to the floor, remembering the kindly man who'd given up his time to help him, Ivan, out, and even bravely ventured into Wiseman's Farm on his behalf.

'Are you there, Mr Browning? Are you all right?' Fear, oddly, made her more formal – she was the doctor's wife again, instinctively keeping that little bit of distance.

'Yes, I'm here.' His insides, however, were numbed with dread.

'Look, I'll see you on Sunday as we agreed,' she said suddenly. 'I'd better go.'

His thanks dropped like a stone into a silent pond.

Having replaced the receiver Ivan glanced up at the massive oak beam which ran the entire width of the cottage. He wondered what strange kinds of meat might have once hung from its rusted hooks. A quaint feature he'd remarked on to the auctioneer, when paying his first visit. But, now, was it dried *human* blood he could see staining that old iron?

All at once his sight grew blurred, and in a gathering chill he held his gaze upon the largest hook, looking needle-sharp, curled up like a runt's tail. The vapour from his open mouth seemed now to coalesce into a single shape ... that of a pale salted carcass which turned imperceptibly in its own deathly momentum.

Ivan stared up at the apparition with half-blind eyes, trying to discern whether it was a largish pig or half a cow, but the more he looked, the more the form overhead took on the more definite shape of a human being with its neck snapped sideways. Suddenly he felt that mouth again on his hand, heard that same voice breathless with terror.

'Take me back ... take me back ... take me back...'

For the first time in his life Ivan felt as if his heart might be on the point of exploding. As if he, too, would soon be among that company of the undead.

A loud rap at the door behind him.

'Holy shit.' He nearly jumped out of his skin, and when he yanked the door open Mrs Jonas's son thought he was looking at a lunatic.

'Sorry to disturb you, Mr Browning.' The man backed away in alarm. 'Just wanted to say thanks from the old girl for finding puss here.'

Ivan let out a gasp of horror. The man was carrying a shovel, and barely on it hung the cat, its tortoiseshell fur streaked with blood, its eyes white as albumen.

'We're going to give her a proper burial, if you get my meaning, so if you hear any strange singing or whatever, coming from the back, that's us. My ma likes "The Lord's my Shepherd".'

It wouldn't have mattered if they'd brought the whole of *Cirque du Soleil* into Nether Wapford, Ivan knew that this latest outrage was one of the last nails in his own coffin. Maybe he wouldn't even wait until Sunday morning to see Valerie Rook. Maybe he should just put the bloody place up for sale first thing in the morning, and sod the next craft fair. His bowls were all broken, after all. Sod everything, especially that devious but tantalizing girl in the Lamb and Flag who happened to be the foxiest thing he'd ever seen on two legs.

'I'll bet you odds-on it's them Oakleys,' the

other man said suddenly. 'They're a fucking plague on the place – always have been. Them and the Dawsons.'

'I'm not arguing with that.' Ivan tried not to look at the cat dropping old blood onto his doorstep.

'And that plague has no bloody boundaries, has it?' The visitor cocked his head, thick black eyebrows raised. 'They bin poaching for years, selling off deer to London restaurants at five hundred quid a shout, an' when they gets bored, they have a go at anything else what moves.' He looked down at his slipping burden and adjusted the angle of the shovel. 'Trouble is, it could be the likes of us next time if we complain.'

Ivan thought again of Tom Coles but, as this man was still a stranger, thought it prudent not to mention anything. He was nothing if not a quick learner in this place.

'Anyhow, they're all bad fucking apples, and folks are too scared to stand up to them. I remind my old ma to lie low these days. She's seen a few things out there, but won't tell a soul.'

'Very wise.' The cat's smell was reaching Ivan's nose with a vengeance till nausea snaked through his body. He changed tack. 'What about Pikes Garage? Do you know anything about the setup there?'

The man snorted. 'Only that they're the bloody monkeys.'

'Monkeys?'

'Ain't you heard about organ grinders? Oakleys and Dawsons, get it?'

'I see.'

'Right, best be going now. Nice to have met you. My ma feels happier with someone next door rather than your place standing empty all the time. They couldn't give it away, as I recall, after those Grimbles died here. Went to two auctions before yours, so you were third time lucky.'

Ivan managed a weak smile, despite the stink of death growing stronger. One of the animal's paws suddenly slipped from the spade as if still alive.

'Come on, Marcie. You'll not be getting any sweeter this way. Nor is that poor bloody Coles chap with his throat slit open, poor bloody sod. Reckon they got his dog too, but no sign of it yet.' The man wandered away, still muttering to himself as Ivan closed the door. He leaned on it for a while, to steady his nerves, then he looked at the phone. How could he offer his condolences to Gill Bunnett now? She must be blaming him for her loss. Everyone would be.

His new-found life in Nether Wapford was collapsing like a house of cards, and he, The Fool, was trapped inside, powerless.

Siân waited quite a while, then pulled at the cellar-room door with all her strength, biting her lip anxiously as it screeched against the tiles. Her left leg dragged on the stairs as she went up, like her very own ball and chain. She listened: a cat somewhere tickling for mice; a loud snore, probably Tomos. There was no sign of the old woman, nor of any candles still lit.

She found another staircase, this time covered with old bits of carpet set down so badly the nails dug into her knees. At the top of it were doors to the left and right. She pressed her ear to both in turn, for any clue as to her brother's room. That same loud snoring from one, mutterings from the other. She chose the right-hand one and held her breath. What if she was wrong? What if she should wake Mrs Rice?

In the gloom she could see both beds were taken, and let out a sigh of relief. She went over to the first. In it lay Tomos, still smelling of the bog, his mouth wide open as if calling in the herd. His sister bent over him, wrinkling her nose.

'*Tomos?*'

He shot up in panic as if she were a ghost. 'What you doin' here? Nothing but damned trouble you are.'

'*Ssh! We've got to go – now.*' She repeated the same to Moses Evans, who was curled on top of his mattress like a baby, his breeches' buttons undone.

'For the love of God!' He quickly rolled from the bed to the floor, straightened himself up then let out the mightiest burst of wind she'd ever heard from either man or beast. 'Begging your pardon, what did you say?'

Tomos was fully awake now. He stood up and parted the thin curtains. The rain had dwindled to a drizzle and, far away over the Cambrian Hills, the first bleached sky of dawn appeared.

'*Morris is sure to come after us. He'll say you led him to the bog on purpose,*' Siân whispered. Each lisped word cost an effort, though she made barely any sound.

140

'She's right.' Evans smoothed down his hair with his hands. 'We can go up by Bryn Castell with not a soul to see us. If we wait here too long, and Morris dies, it could be bloody Cardiff Jail for us. Excuse me, God, for swearing.'

The two men held their filthy boots as they padded in stockinged feet down to the saloon. The door to the yard was locked.

'*This way.*' Siân led them to the washroom nearby where a small outer door opened to the push of Tomos's toe.

Most of the remaining bullocks were lying down, exhausted. One or two seemed in poor shape, staring at the small party of human beings with dull glazed eyes. For a moment Tomos was undecided, then summoned Ben to get them moving. The dog's tongue hung out like an old rag, but at that low whistle, he sprang to life and began nudging the herd up towards the farthest gate.

'What about our horses?' Moses Evans asked, as if the drover was contemplating walking.

'You fetch them last minute. They'll be heard on the cobbles but you get up on one and lead the other. Then you can catch me up.'

Moses Evans looked none too keen. The cob could be wilful and unpredictable, and he liked them small and amenable. Siân gave him an encouraging smile, then kept close behind her brother, struggling to keep up. Once or twice she slipped in the mud, but he ignored her as usual.

'Where's your coat, you sloven?' he growled as he unknotted the ropes on the gate. 'I can't be

141

seeing to you if you get the cramps, now, can I? You left it inside there, didn't you, *twpsin?*'

No tears, Siân Richards, not now. That coat was only an old thing. A thing, *remember?*

She watched as their one dog coaxed the Castlemartins into place, and wondered about those other steers still lying under water and the two little corgis which Tomos had reared as heelers. Could they have been still breathing? Would their short legs have been active enough to get them out? It was too horrible to think about. Drowning must be the worst thing. Worse than starving. Worse than freezing, too. But burning? She wasn't so sure about that.

'Bastards,' Tomos hissed as a couple of bullocks, impatient for the gate to be opened, bucked and galloped along the fence. Any loud noise might bring someone from the inn, but at least the night was still on his side. 'Now,' he whispered, and the hymn singer crept towards the stables.

Tomos climbed the fence and undid the gate from the other side. He could feel the intensity of the steers' eyes, could smell their proximity. He sprang back into the field and told Ben to track the leaders.

Moses Evans caught up with them, bringing the horses. Just the two, Incio and Collen, almost knocking him over as they sensed the cattle's surge.

'No saddles?' Tomos asked, frowning.

'No, couldn't see them nowhere.'

'Damnation. So where's the grey?' The porthmon's eyes roamed over the scene.

142

'Gone, like Ma Rice said.'

Tomos stared at Siân, and for one terrible moment she knew it crossed his mind to leave her.

'*No, no, please. You promised our Da...*'

'Why the hell not?' He stared up at the mass of black meat moving on without him. 'What's in it for me, sister, trailing you along?'

'Now, Mr Richards, sir. I know it's not my place, with you being porthmon an' all,' Evans passed the cob over, keeping hold of the mare, 'but you should take *her* instead of me. She's your kin, and God sees everything.' He then took off his jacket and heaped it on Siân's shoulders.

'*Thank you, sir.*' Siân smiled. The garment was warm and smelt of carbolic.

Tomos stood speechless, yet a trickle of doubt still crossed his face as Moses Evans pressed his hat on his head.

'Past Hereford, when you're baiting the horses, you'll pick up someone else all right, and more dogs to be sure,' he said, then began to walk away, but Tomos prodded his back, his fist full of coins.

'Not a word, if you want to keep breathing after I get back.'

'I don't need a bribe, man. What d'you take me for?'

'A goddamned traitor, that's what. Like all the rest who live over the Aust.'

Siân had never seen a man so stung, and in that silent second, hatred for her brother welled up enough in her chest to make it close to bursting. As Moses Evans disappeared, Tomos snatched at

Collen's reins and hoisted Siân onto the animal's damp back.

There was nothing for it but to grip hard, for the mare's winter belly sloped perilously away, and even before she'd moved off, Siân's ankles ached.

'Follow me, and no fancy notions, mind.' Tomos kicked the cob into a gallop up the hill, sending huge divots into Siân's face. A brief glance back showed Moses had vanished with the night, and only the Hen and Casket's silhouette huddled black against the sky. Then the mare lunged forwards, taking Siân to the top of the hill where pale dawn strands encroached on the darkness. It was then, against that vast infinity, that the full realization of her predicament sunk in. Now it was just her and Tomos and, whatever her fear, her crippling doubts, if she was going to survive, she'd have to trust her own instincts more than ever before.

'You wear that pony off her feet, and then what?' her brother complained.

Suddenly she felt a weight on her neck, then her skin being pinched as if she were a shot rabbit being snatched up from the field. 'This was *your* idea, remember that.' He squeezed tighter and, when she tried to scream, slapped his hand across her mouth. 'If we lose any more to your whims and fancies, sister, I'll see you pay, one way or another.'

Siân caught the madness in his eyes. *It's your wife you're talking about. Your mean and greedy wife.*

'And if Morris's brother catches up with us I'll see he gets you to play with first.'

144

He let go of her and kicked the cob on towards the head of the drove. Meanwhile the thought of Rhys Morris, the drunken waster who'd once thrashed her beloved Huw behind the bakehouse, filled her with an even greater terror and she urged the mare ahead while Tomos's continued hollering filled the night. Siân imagined he could be heard as far away as Hereford, bringing every constable and justice of the peace like moths round a lamp.

'Get to the left and keep them straight,' he yelled. 'Move!'

And Collen, as if understanding, wove a clever track through the herd and kept close to the first of the group, who were beginning to tire. Siân felt their horns brush her leg, their silage breath hot and foul filling her own lungs. Her knees made cup holes in the pony's sides as she galloped under new daylight towards that strange unfolding country down towards the Valley of the Irfon.

At the foot of Mount Eppynt, with much of the ground still mud, Tomos gave Siân a sixpence and sent her to pick up bread and a piece of bacon from the Ox Inn at Maesmynis.

When she appeared at the door, barely able to stand, the stares of the men inside turned to laughter.

'Whose is this pretty little bastard, then?'

'Oi, Blethyn, don't look at me like that,' said one of them, his old coat a size too small. 'My John Thomas has gone littler than a tadpole, and that's the truth.' He knocked his pipe on the table, then refilled it with a wad of tobacco, pressing it down with a huge thumb. He then smiled again at Siân who was trying to whisper her message to a girl, not much older than herself, setting out fresh candles.

'Yer'll 'ave to speak louder an 'at in this partic'lar farmyard.' The girl moved away to the wall where the sconces were clotted with dried grease. ''Sides, I'm busy.'

'She wants bread and whatever else you've got.' The man recognized Siân's frustration. 'And it looks like she's in a hurry.'

'I don't hurry meself for no one, least of all yeself, Will Hopkins.' She gave him a knowing glance, and Siân realized the girl didn't just work the ale pumps. Tomos was now even further away and she could hear Collen whinnying after him. Her sixpence burnt in her palm as she went out and stood by the mare, holding back tears, aware of the strangers in the inn watching her through the window. She couldn't mount, couldn't catch up now. No London, no nothing.

Maybe that's what he wanted all along. I'm such a stupid fool. When will God stop making me believe everybody. When?

146

Seven

Ivan had spent most of a miserable Saturday in bed, thinking of Tom Coles, listening to *CD Review* on Radio 3 and reading a new book of John Clare's early life in Helpston. The wind outside had been pounding the roof and south-facing front wall, bringing a rain so fierce, it threatened to push the windows in.

Now, with the distant Sunday bells riding over the breeze, he had washed and shaved and was on his way into his outbuilding to wedge up some more clay, when he saw the Stoneshanger *Herald* lying on the mat. He picked it up, puzzled. He never bothered to have papers delivered, nor did he usually bother with any local rags. If he wanted to find out about the next craft fair or whatever, he'd browse through *CREATE*, the county's free bulletin. No, someone had wanted him to see this. But who?

Its startling banner headline proclaimed: LOCAL MECHANIC MURDERED. The rest of the front page was full of the account of Tom Coles's brutal killing. How on Wednesday morning he had been found with his hands and feet tied with galvanized wire, how he'd first been almost decapitated then pushed into the River Wap to drift on the swollen current down to Radby End.

There were photos of the victim, of his wife and

147

two young daughters playing with a Border collie in their garden at Westhope. At the bottom of the page, under notice of the inquest and a private family funeral, was a short eulogy from the vicar of St Thomas's, Cold Firton, deeply concerned at such a violent killing amid the peaceful purlieus of his parish.

Ivan noticed his hands were shaking as they held the paper, so he sat down at the table to search again through every detail, every syllable, for a clue as to why this man had to die. Yes, he was a known crusader against rural crime, often sounding off on the local radio station and in the newspapers about how isolated communities were no safer now than in the past days of footpads. He'd also harassed the local police on their absence from the village streets and once, when a commemorative cherry tree had been vandalized in Sykeston, he'd undertaken a house-to-house enquiry himself.

Not the best way to make friends, Ivan thought, but surely not enough to warrant such a terrible end – unless someone out there was shitting a seriously large brick.

He looked over to the phone and, on impulse, found Bunnett R G, 6 Middle View Rise, in the directory and dialled the number. He let it ring, realizing no one would answer – that there wouldn't even be an answerphone to leave condolences.

He set the receiver down, his thoughts still reeling.

What about the local CID? Why had it taken them so long to make their investigation into this

148

murder known to the public? Who were they protecting? He then thought of Pike's Garage and the strange surly lad there. Who had he been phoning as Ivan was leaving? Phoning someone else to warn them off?

Ivan picked up the car keys, pushed both arms into his now dry leather jacket, and left the cottage. As he slotted the house key into the Yale lock, he thought he heard Mrs Jonas calling, but she was nowhere to be seen. And the harder he listened so the light lispy voice grew more distinct.

'Take me with you ... take me with you...'

Again Ivan felt that same warmth focus on his hand, but this time the gentle biting grew sharper, hurting, really hurting him.

'Soon ... take me soon...'

He screamed, then brought the sore hand to his lips to soothe the pain, but it was as if ooze from the teeth bites were filling his mouth – warm, gargly blood – so he couldn't cry out, couldn't even breathe.

He ran round to the side of the cottage and heaved up into the rough grass. Supper, breakfast, whatever was left inside came out in a spew of deep vermilion. He moaned as the residue dribbled from his chin, and hung like what he'd seen hanging off that shovel: those liverish innards, that putrid smell. He'd soon be dead too, dumped in some river with a hole in his head, he knew that now with a greater certainty than anything else in his life.

There was no one around; just his growing

paranoid panic and the forest trees dense and black as never before – their silent secrets and shallow graves sheltered by eternal darkness.

Ivan lurched back into the cottage and plunged his head under the kitchen tap, letting the icy water rinse out his mouth until his spit tasted normal again and the heat on his hand was no longer unbearable.

Whoever it was trying to make contact with him was as desperate as himself. But why? For what purpose?

'Take me with you ... take me with you.'

The voice urged once more and, as if to protect himself from its bleak insistence he pressed his head between his two hands, aware it was urgent that he go and see Valerie Rook, whether he was fit enough to drive or not.

'Hold on, miss.' It was Hopkins, pipe set between his weathered lips. He cupped both hands under Siân's boot, and noted her thin twisted leg. 'Up she goes.'

'Thank you, sir.'

'No saddle then?'

'I don't like them.'

'On your own, are you?'

'No. Er ... yes.' She felt dizzy with hunger, but was also aware from the way his nose wrinkled, that he could smell her pee. The other's eyes narrowed.

'I'll walk with you till you get where it is you're going, young lady. You're in no fit state to be doing much of this traipsing around.'

'I'm all right. Please...' Siân turned Collen to

150

face the track which skirted the hamlet. *Come on, let's get out of here ... he's wanting to know too much.*

Hopkins stared after her then broke into a run, his face growing redder with each step until he reached her and grabbed the rein.

'I got this for you.' Two lumps of rye bread wedged with a fish meat she didn't recognize. His lunch, obviously. 'Trout it is.'

Trout?

'You enjoy it now.' He pushed the offering into her pocket, wondering why it was a man's jacket on her back, and why she kept peering ahead as if her life depended on it. He'd noticed a drove of Castlemartins go by with just one porthmon riding bareback. And as she trotted away he put two and two together. 'You're with those runts just gone, aren't you?' he shouted. 'Better warn your man there's footpads waiting.'

A new fear made her hunger vanish as the track, hemmed in by forestry, curved away towards Builth. She was soon deep amongst a congregation of black pines giving off their wounded smell, and the wood owls' eerie chorus. There were tree-fellers in the distance and Siân imagined Huw was with them, calling out her name. But, no. God wasn't going to give her that much. Not today, probably not ever.

She heaved a sigh of relief when the patch of forestry ended and the dull sky reappeared; and within a few minutes, she could hear Tomos's shouts above the fractious herd. Siân spotted his hat and stick above the ambling mass of cattle moving uphill. He was letting the cob pick its own way, but she couldn't reach him without circling wide to avoid startling any of the stragglers into a bolt. It would only take one...

'Well, what did you get?' he barked.

'They only had ale, and that black brew.'

His eyes rested on her pockets but he didn't dare dismount to check. 'Liar.'

'I swear, honest to God. There was nothing but drink to be had.'

'Where's my sixpence then?' The branch he was holding scratched her cheek as she handed it over. His greedy fingers closed over the coin. 'I knew you'd be good for nothing, Lodger.' That word came like a rumble of thunder, then Tomos kicked his cob on. 'Stay at the back, d'you hear? If there's any trouble, whistle.'

Whistle? She'd never whistled in her life and worried about it so much she forgot to mention Hopkins's warning.

'Let's hear it then.' He waved the stick to keep the leaders back. 'Go on.'

Siân pursed her lips and took a deep breath. She slowly let the air out, picking up notes and making a tune. 'Ehedydd Bach – Little Lark.' Something her mother'd sung in happier days. Then Siân stopped, wide-eyed at her own prowess, and drew in her breath again.

'What d'you call that din, you *twpsin?* I want something *plain* I can hear.'

The hound, already confused, had left his position, ears cocked, and when she started up again, twice as loud, he yelped.

Tomos reined in and rested his stick on the withers, so one hand was free. She saw the blow coming and ducked as he toppled from his saddle. For a moment, he lay groaning on the ground with Ben creating such a ruckus the herd grew restive and began to quicken their pace.

'Jesus help me, you miserable baggage.' He got to his feet, snatched at Incio's mane and hauled himself aloft. Siân's trembling was nothing to his. His coat possessed a rage all its own, his eyes black as woodpecker nests. He wheeled round to see the leaders of the herd already in a trot, heads down and gaining speed.

'Keep 'em in!' he roared to the dog. 'Keep 'em in!' But their clamour rose above the quiet hill as they careered towards freedom, out of control.

'*Haiptrw ho!*'

Collen's instinct was to run with them, but Siân hauled her back till her own arms felt they'd leave their sockets. Those hooves, that smell, the devil in their eyes kept her away and, staring up at the weak sun, she tried to gauge south-east, to imagine where London was, that city she'd only seen in the vicar's old books.

Suddenly a voice she recognized, then a vision of Hopkins tearing past. He was too long in the leg for his pony, but she'd never seen anyone do such a gallop. Soon he'd overtaken her brother in pursuit of the herd and disappeared beyond the new plantation whose saplings lay strewn like wickerwork in the aftermath of the charge.

Siân held her breath as her mare picked her way over the debris. She wondered at the cost of the damage, for those trees would probably have been worth a small fortune, and not for the first time she considered turning round and heading away. But there was Hopkins again, with some bullocks hemmed into a corner, scouring black dung, their sides heaving.

'See those hooves?' He'd dismounted and crept as close to the group as he dared. 'They'll not go another mile without cues.'

'I'm not the bloody Dolaucothi goldmines, man.' Tomos joined him, suspicion all over his face. 'The beasts have all had new, and that's that.'

The farmworker shrugged. 'If they was mine–'

'Well, they're not. Now leave us be.'

Siân winced at his ingratitude, and felt the food still in her pocket. Without the stranger's speed her brother would have nothing left, with the steers roaming all over Powys.

At times like this, she missed her voice more than anything. She wanted to shout herself hoarse about how Tomos's pride and stupidity could only end in tragedy, and how she herself was too young to die.

'Where you headed then?' Hopkins wiped down his hog-maned dun with a wad of grass.

'None of your damned business.' Tomos shot Siân a warning glance so that she gave nothing away, and she prayed Hopkins wouldn't mention they'd already met. The lunch was beginning to stink in her pocket.

'It is my business when you're on Lord Trelewis's land.'

'That bloody English Tory.' But Tomos looked unsettled by the news all the same. 'What's he to you, anyway?'

'He pays my wages, that's what.' Hopkins picked up a sapling snapped in half. 'It'll cost

154

some to replant all this, you know.'

Tomos could see where this was leading.

'So?'

'So, I suggest we do a little business.'

'What d'you mean?' Tomos scowled.

'My brother's the smith down in Cardwardine.'

Siân saw Hopkins tot up the figures in his mind.

'You've got fifty-two beasts, each needing four pairs of tips.' He whistled through his teeth and she surreptitiously tried to copy him. 'That's four hundred and sixteen. That'll keep him and the family in victuals for a good while' – his smile was a challenge – 'and it'll keep my mouth closed.'

Tomos lifted off his hat and used it to hide his other hand that slipped into his pocket. He'd brought his pistol, the one employed for keeping crows off the lambs and foxes from the hen coops. She watched in mounting terror as the stranger came closer, his smile gone, and watched, still numb, as the blast felled him. Hopkins clutched his chest and made such a noise she'd never forget as long as she lived.

She tumbled from her pony and tried to reach him, but Tomos blocked her way, and for good measure fired another bullet into the fallen man's head. The echo of the shot trailed into the sky, as Hopkins's eyes fixed on Siân, like a dead sheep's, darkened by his killer's silhouette, the leaves around him all staining red.

'Move, sister, or you'll be getting one too.' Tomos pointed the barrel at her, briefly, before taking the dead man's feet and dragging him over to the edge of a shallow ravine. Having kicked

155

leaves and humus into enough of a heap to cover him, he called Ben away.

She struggled to remount, her heart beating like the winter hailstones against Plas Newydd's one window, her mind paralysed with shock.

'Keep behind, and if we meet up with anyone, lower your head. Understand? I do the talking.' Tomos ordered the hound to gather together those cattle which had scattered in panic at the sounds of gunshot. He kept Hopkins's pony close by as the reassembled drove then followed round Llanbedr Hill and past a sign skewed in the hedge for Rhydyspence.

'Toll. Dammit,' he muttered and, to avoid it, turned the bullocks to the right to take the Wye at Clifford. They seemed listless. That latest stampede near the plantation had sapped what extra strength they had, but the crossing was easy, turning the river water a thick ochre as they swam.

Eight

The road out of Nether Wapford sloped down past the old foresters' cottages to the bridge over the Wap. Drizzle still spat at the windscreen as the car met one pile of drifted mud after another, and Ivan noticed with alarm that the brown river water was only a few inches below the tarmac. He slowed down to watch its choppy progress, bearing a rigging of bent branches and the odd plastic carton swiftly out of sight. There was also a heavy-looking yellow feed bag bumping in and out of the bank as it too passed along.

Dawson's Farm would be flooded again at this rate, he reckoned – it had already suffered three weeks ago, when its fields had seemed like one vast mirror alive with drifting clouds. He'd checked out this same river just before deciding on buying the cottage, and was reassured it had never been known to breach its banks below the forest.

Now he didn't care if the bloody waters rose up and took the whole place away. His mouth felt stale, his head as if it had just hit a wall, and when a BT van came hurtling round Sykes Farm Bend, he almost met it full on.

Something about that close shave made him change his mind from simply heading straight for Cold Firton. Instead, knowing the Lamb and Flag would be open at eleven, he followed the signpost for Stoneshanger, and a quarter of an hour later was queuing up by the pub's main bar with all the other regulars chasing their pre-Sunday lunch drinks.

The same blonde woman was busily taking orders, giving change, pulling pints, while in the distant storage area a thickset man was tearing out the fronts of crisp packet boxes. But of Jo herself there was no sign.

'Is she around?' he whispered to the woman after choosing a pint of Worthington E. She glanced back over her shoulder at the man with the boxes and shook her head.

'No, and I wouldn't go asking any more questions about her.' She gave the thumbs-down sign. 'It's a bit hairy here at the moment, as Harold Oakley's not best pleased with being short-staffed.'

'Harold Oakley?' Ivan gulped. 'Is he her uncle?'

'Yes. What's wrong with that?'

'Nothing.' But there was – plenty.

This gets worse. So, she is one of them. Shit shit shit.

With an unsteady hand Ivan took his pint and licked its frothy rim before moving away. As he did so, he noticed out of the corner of his eye the stocky man coming back into the main bar area, so he returned to the counter for some pork scratchings – though they were the last things he wanted.

'And some barbecue crisps,' he added, for the first time looking at Harold Oakley in close-up. In the dark outside number three Church Street he'd not had the pleasure of studying those hard pale eyes, the nose twisted in the middle, the thin grim mouth.

'You again.' The publican glowered. He might as well have said *have your drink then, and piss off.*

'Sorry?' Ivan forced a smile. He was mindful of the blonde woman's anxious glances their way as she served her next customer rather too quickly and dropped his change on the floor.

'My wife says you came a-calling at our house the other day,' Oakley began as he reached up to set new spirits bottles in place, upside down.

'My car got nicked outside your place, remember? You'd have done the same.'

'I *don't* think so.' The big man leaned forward; now there was no one else waiting to be served. 'I would err on the side of politeness myself, and write to the owner of the property first.' He showed perfect, expensively cared-for teeth, just like his niece. His voice had taken on a more menacing tone, each vowel and consonant sharp as a razor so that the barmaid who'd just finished serving a customer, slipped her mac over her shoulders and left without saying goodbye.

Suddenly, the door of the lounge bar opened and a slim figure in a chic, fitted coat with matching brown umbrella made her way to the side of the bar and lifted up the wooden flap. 'Hi. Sorry I'm late.' She retracted the umbrella then pecked the man's cheek.

Jo turned to stare at Ivan, her smile quickly replaced by the same intense expression as her uncle.

'Oh I see.' The publican had missed nothing. 'I sense we have a little *quelque chose* going on here.'

'Oh Dad, for God's sake.'

Dad? Ivan blinked. So even the barmaid and nosy Pam Barker had been fooled. What on bloody earth was going on?

She slipped her coat off her shoulders and adjusted her pink V-necked jumper. 'Do me a favour. He's just some creep who keeps coming in here asking for me – you know, is Jo in today? Is Jo around? All that shit.' She flounced off into the storeroom without looking back.

Just some creep? Ivan felt as if he'd been lashed.

'Right, mister, a little word in your shell-like.' The older man cheeks, already highly coloured by a web of broken capillaries, were now a startling red. 'I'm *warning* you – so watch it.'

Ivan nevertheless drew himself up, his fists clenching on the bar top.

'You're not going to intimidate me. I'll do what I bloody like, when I like – and whatever it takes to get my car back too. You think you can rule the fucking roost round here–' He stopped himself, remembering Tom Coles. Still blushing with humiliation, he gathered up his snacks and his fags, and strode out of the pub before the other man could react.

He felt better instantly – like going to Confession, he imagined, although he'd never done that. After sprinting back to his car, he drove off towards the dual carriageway and the turn-off leading to Cold Firton.

He stopped just before the driveway into Church House as fresh drizzle began to fall.

He was still tense after Jo's rebuff, and what she'd let slip about that cunt being her father, and having knocked twice he stood back and

160

waited, sniffing at the Sunday lunch being cooked. Although roast dinners normally reminded him of home, rather than making him feel warmly nostalgic, this one had quite the opposite effect. He was also aware of church bells tolling through the thick graveyard trees, and the muffled sounds of car doors slamming as the congregation arrived.

There was no sign of the Saab he'd seen on Thursday, but maybe that was in the garage and the doctor had gone on foot for his weekly dose of religion. Valerie opened the door. He noticed she still looked pale, her hair scraped back and secured with a plain elastic band – courtesy of the Royal Mail – giving her face an even greater fragility.

Ivan glanced back down the drive, in case the doctor might have changed his mind about church, as she led him into the first room to the left of the hallway. It had dark blue wallpaper, two mismatching armchairs, plus ziggurats of medical books, an old Amstrad perched on a pile of assorted bedding, and some old outdoor clothes obviously awaiting a home. Hardly shipshape, Ivan reflected as she pushed the two old chairs closer together.

'Coffee?' she asked, lumping up both cushions.

'No thanks, really.' He toyed with his watch strap still smeared with clay, saw the second hand had stopped and it was out of sync with the clock on the mantelpiece.

'Do sit down. It makes me nervous when people hover.'

'OK, but bad news makes me nervous too. I've

161

just had a mystery delivery of the *Herald*. Not bedtime reading either, I might add.'

'About Tom Coles?'

Ivan nodded.

'That's a warning to you, then.'

'My thoughts exactly.' He rested his chin on his clasped hands sensing a sudden new chill reach his bones. 'Right, Valerie, I'm waiting.'

'Where to begin, that's the problem.'

'At the beginning of course.'

A faint smile, another glance at the open door, then Valerie took a deep breath.

'Although Michael's general knowledge is awesome, I've always been far more interested in what happens just *beneath* the surface of everyday life. Especially in a small area like this.'

'Were you born here?'

'No. I was a toddler when my parents bought Small Copse from an elderly couple who'd suffered some sort of breakdown. They never said much about it to us, but with hindsight I've a pretty good idea why. Anyhow, the place was a bargain, as Gloucestershire was getting far too pricey for the Middleton Section D Stud to keep going. It was too good an opportunity for my parents to miss.'

'I bet the Oakleys next door were chuffed.'

'Nothing they could do. My father's solicitor, who was just starting out, was keen as mustard. He got the searches done in record time and beat the Oakleys to it. Just like Michael with Church House here.'

'That went down well, then?'

Valerie Rook sighed. 'Well, at first there didn't

162

seem to be a problem. It was just Ena Oakley with the three schoolboys then – she'd been widowed a while back. But gradually as the lads got older with more time on their hands, I suppose, one or two things did happen. However, it wasn't until–' Here she tried to blink away her tears then rubbed her jumper cuff across her eyes.

'Go on, please.'

'Until my parents died – within six months of each other, in the end – and then, a week after Mother's funeral–'

She covered her face with her hands and stayed silent for a moment.

'I mean she was barely cold in her grave, for God's sake. It was evil, pure evil. It was as if the Oakleys were just biding their time till they were both dead.'

'What happened? Tell me.'

'It was 28 June. I'll never forget *that* date as long as I live. It was too hot for the horses to be out grazing, so Dick – he was my older brother – and I brought them into the stables adjoining the farmhouse, to keep the flies off.' She took a deep breath. 'He went into the tack room with the halters just as the phone in the house began ringing. I could hear it through the open lounge window, so I dashed in to answer it, then I spotted Harold Oakley wandering into the barn–'

'Harold Oakley?' Ivan interrupted. 'Did he often just turn up like that?'

Valerie Rook stalled. She looked up, tears glazing her eyes.

'Yes. And it was all *my* fault, can't you see?'

163

'I don't get it. What was your fault?'

'I've never told anyone else, not even Michael. I daren't.'

'You can trust me? OK?'

Another deep breath. All the while staring straight ahead, out of the front window. 'I already knew about that family's reputation from my parents. I *knew* he was trouble, but in those days, well, he was good-looking, in fact, very good-looking – and still not married. I'd had a sort of crush on him since I'd come back early from university. I'd been so lonely in London, you see.'

Ivan tried to hide his disbelief.

'So I automatically assumed he was there looking for me. When I'd finished on the phone, I tried to catch him, but he was charging out of the stables in one hell of a hurry. But the weirdest thing was him staring straight through me like I didn't even exist. I hardly recognized him: he looked liked the devil himself.'

'And then?'

'He pushed me aside from him and disappeared round the side of the barn. I followed but he must have leapt over the fence, as there was no sign of him, nothing. Then I smelt burning coming from where the horses were. Oh Jesus, Jesus... I yelled for Dick, thinking there'd still be time for us to get them out – after all, the door was still open – but he didn't hear me and some of the bolts to their stalls were so stiff. I was panicking, screaming till the smoke got to me. My fingers seemed like lead, there was nothing I could do. The roof beams were in flames– And the horses, those beautiful creatures... I'll never forget their terror, their neighing as long as I live.'

'But why would Oakley do that, for fuck's sake? Excuse my language. What was he hoping to achieve?'

'To extend the Wiseman empire, of course. There's ninety acres with the place. He wasn't expecting anyone to survive in there, what with the house gone up in flames as well. I was lucky because I'd gone for the phone.' But she didn't sound it.

Ivan listened out for any sound of the doctor's return, aware of the minutes slipping by. He found it impossible to imagine this woman in front of him ever falling for such a thug, but then hadn't *he* himself shown the same lack of judgement before? Pressed the same self-destruct button? And what about now, fantasizing about some girl in a pub he barely knew, who'd called that murderer *Dad?*

'As for poor Dick,' Valerie went on, 'I thought he was still in the tack room, but he must have gone back into the stables to check on me, while I was phoning 999 from the house...' She began to cry in silent heaving bursts of grief, all still too fresh, too real to her. 'Like I said, it was all my fault. All my fault.'

'No, it wasn't. We're just human, that's the trouble. Anyhow, what happened after that?'

'Two days later when I went back to the farm to salvage anything still surviving in the barn, I found something there.'

'Go on.'

'A cigarette lighter.'

'You don't mean *his?*'

She nodded. 'In all the confusion, it must have dropped and been kicked under the stack of old mangers in the corner, and they protected it from the worst of the blaze. Mind you, the police had hardly bothered with a search. They assumed it was just an accident. But I noticed someone else had been hunting around pretty thoroughly. I could tell.'

'I bet they had,' Ivan said wrily. 'So why wasn't the place made secure afterwards to prevent that sort of thing?'

'I couldn't afford to. You see the insurance had lapsed three months before. That was always Dick's responsibility, but he'd not been well and I' – she blushed – 'I'd got *other* things on my mind, hadn't I?' She turned her shamefaced gaze to Ivan.

'So did you show this lighter to anyone?'

Her expression tensed. 'How could I? I was just too scared to say or do anything to incriminate Harold Oakley. I was alone, trying to start a new life. I knew what that lot were capable of, can't you see?'

'What about the inquest?'

'A whitewash. The coroner made out Dick or one of the lads from Turwell who'd been there earlier had been sloppy with a cigarette – after all they were both heavy smokers. But how could I contradict that verdict? How could I show anyone the lighter? I was so shocked and terrified.'

Ivan nodded as, without thinking, she sniffed and wiped her nose on her sleeve. 'After that, I began going to church every Sunday, hoping to find some forgiveness for my madness in falling for him in the first place – and for my cowardice, but that Reverend Hutton only made me feel worse. As if hell was waiting just for me with its doors open wide. And then, would you believe, *they* started attending services.' Valerie Rook turned the little gold crucifix round her neck over and over. 'That was like the end for me.'

She finally produced a tissue from her sleeve and blew her nose. It looked red and raw.

'Well, I reckon you've done your penance a hundred times over,' Ivan said, aware that twenty-five minutes had passed. 'Now it's time justice was done. So where *is* this Oakley souvenir?'

He followed as she got up and crossed the hall into the lounge opposite. She unlocked the bottom drawer of a small scuffed mahogany desk, extracted an old Jiffy bag and handed it over. He held his breath as the article it contained, still gold, still intact, slipped into his palm. *HAROLD FROM JOHN. 9 APRIL 1976.* The inscription, darkened from smoke, was still clear.

'Sweet Jesus, this is *real* proof.'

'It's all there is.'

Ivan carried it over to the window where, despite the weather outside, the extra daylight helped. *ASPREYS* was incised on the back, an expensive gift.

'Look, is that solicitor you mentioned still around?'

'Kingsley Gilbert? Yes, but what's the point?'

'The point is that this vital evidence shouldn't be hanging around here. It should be kept secure. For Christ's sake, Valerie, this is important.' He slotted it back into the Jiffy bag, then she returned it to its hiding place and pocketed the key.

'I will when I'm ready.'

'Ready? I don't believe this. You might be too bloody late. Anyhow, what does your husband think about all this?'

Valerie Rook stood next to him by the window and fixed him with a look of fierce intensity. Her voice now sounded controlled. Every word precise and clear.

'I already told you I couldn't talk to him. But he must *never* know anything about me and Harold Oakley. If things get raked up again–' a hopeless shrug lifted her shoulders – 'then God knows... It's pathetic, isn't it? Small Copse is all I've got that's actually mine. A burnt-out shell and a heap of old clothes and stuff in the cellars. Dick wasn't married, so what remained came to me. Me, with the grottiest car in Cold Firton, who hasn't even got her own bank account or credit card. Who has to grovel for every last penny. Whose name isn't even on the mortgage. Now do you understand?'

For a moment Ivan was speechless. Things were beginning to slot into place. Then a grimmer scenario re-entered his thoughts.

'With the Oakleys around, you're not safe – you know that.'

'I'm not frightened of those cowards. Let them try.' She did not sound convincing.

Ivan shivered as the leafless trees outside waved their bony branches against the darkening sky.

The drizzle had turned to rain, slapping the window glass, obscuring the view.

'So presumably they've left you well alone since your marriage?'

'Not exactly. There's been the odd phone call – when Michael's out, of course. No one answering and caller withholding their number, and so on. I *know* it's them. And whenever I see them out and about I get those death stares. But that's to be expected.'

'Just think, they're probably kneeling piously right now in the Oakley pew, saying their bloody prayers, the sickos.' Then, sensing that now might be the time to ask; 'By the way, does this charming Harold have a daughter, around twenty or so?' The image of her smile, that toss of her hair came all too vividly, too shamefully to mind. The hips, the firm slim thighs, and what lay beyond...

'Harold and Monica?' She frowned. 'No, not that I'm aware of. Why?'

'It's just that I saw them both behind the bar this morning at the Lamb and Flag. Apparently the girl's got a baby son, and she called Oakley "Dad".'

Valerie Rook shook her head, puzzled. 'I've never seen any children or grandchildren. Mind you, I'm not exactly sitting up in the front bedroom with a telescope all day.'

There wasn't going to be much mileage here, Ivan could tell. Valerie nudged open both sun-bleached curtains to the extreme edges of the paint-chipped window frame, then turned to face him again.

'Anyhow, about your cottage. That's what we really should have been talking about today.'

'It's no big deal.'

'If you're worrying about my husband turning up after the service, don't. He always hangs around chit-chatting with the vicar, and besides the service doesn't end till twelve-fifteen.'

'Look, my problems are nothing compared to what you've been through.'

'That's not how it first sounded to me.' She went over to a pile of nylon sheets and began folding them more tightly, causing a faintly musty smell to fill the room. 'And, to be honest, I'm not surprised. Dreadful things went on there, apparently, right from its very first occupants. A lot of it's common knowledge round here, but after studying some of the local history for a while, I realized how much there was still to learn, and how to research it.'

'I'm impressed.' Yet Ivan felt suddenly cold. 'Go on.'

'The really odd thing was that whenever I tried to ride past Tripp's Cottage to get onto the bridleway behind, my horse would dig his heels in and refuse to budge. I'd have to dismount and lead him round past Mr Carp's old place. Even the riding school's given up going past your way now. There's definitely a presence there, something quite powerful.'

'Look at this, then.' Ivan pulled up his jacket cuff to show her his still-reddened hand. 'I swear someone's trying to communicate with me. And,' he added, noting the change in her expression, 'there are other strange things, like my kiln going

170

wrong... I'm not making it up. God knows, I just want a normal life there.'

'So did they.'

'Who?'

'The Tripps.'

'And the Grimbles?' He recalled what Mrs Jonas had said.

'Yes, them too.'

The lamb roast was burning. He'd always found its slightly sweet young meat repellent and, together with what else this so-called day of rest was delivering, his stomach was in revolt.

She left the room quickly then returned, her face flushed from the oven. 'They were bad times here after the Napoleonic Wars, believe me.' She started on a pile of ancient macs and coats – crossing over their sleeves in effigy mode, then folding and refolding as though she was packing for an army of ghosts. 'The country was still in debt, still poor, with every day new machines taking over men's work. Even though the Luddites had started up in Nottinghamshire, and we had the "Captain Swing" riots over in Finedon' – a hand waved in the general direction of the north-east – 'that wasn't making any difference. There was no sanitation either, so, like Michael said, you still had a quarter of the population dying before their thirtieth birthday – dysentery, typhoid and–'

'Cholera?' Ivan interrupted.

'That was the worst.'

'So what *specifically* do you know about my place?' He perched on the worn arm of one of the chairs, watching as the woman continued to make order from the jumble's chaos.

'After the fire, when I was living on my own in Stoneshanger, I couldn't face joining in the usual local things – you know, evening classes, rambling whatever. Every day was a huge struggle for me, but gradually what had happened to my family became a challenge. I *had* to know the background to this evil that had wrecked my life; to put the tragedy into context, if you like. So, from various newspaper cuttings in Northampton library, plus what old Mrs Tripp had told my parents, I was able to piece a few things together.'

'Mrs Tripp?'

'Yes – Caroline. She was our cleaner at Small Copse till just before she died.'

'Go on, please.' Yet Ivan dreaded what might come next. His insides felt as if a rock had settled there.

'Well, she and Robert Tripp were the last ones to live at your cottage. In the end they practically gave the place away to the Grimbles who came from Farnham and who fortunately didn't know anything. The Tripps then rented somewhere in Pury Vale, but after their daughter Edith left they both suddenly passed on. It was obviously the shock of it all...'

'The shock of what, for God's sake?'

'Edith used to write to my parents from Liverpool, where she had found a new job. She claimed it wasn't just the weird happenings inside the cottage, but also the Oakleys and the Dawsons who'd caused her parents' deaths. The twentieth of November 1943 had been the last straw.'

'Why?' Ivan checked his watch and added ten

minutes. Time was running out and he felt like a swimmer who'd merely planned a short dip but was now adrift in an infinite ocean of other lives, other traumas, pulling him this way and that, until the precious shore had vanished.

'Apparently her brother Graham, who was fifteen at the time, was sweet on Peggy Dawson. His parents didn't know, of course, but Edith did, and often warned him that no good would come of it.'

'Go on.' Ivan saw the rain intensify, the window now just a blur of descending water.

'But he wouldn't listen, and one day, when he'd not come back as usual for his tea, Edith went looking in the forest where they used to meet, and found him lying there, shot dead.'

'Oh Jesus.'

'Apparently she was so distraught she had to have a hysterectomy when she was only eighteen.'

'They're devils.' Ivan got up to help her with the final mound of twill breeches, moth-eaten hacking jackets, and hats whose brown velvet had been rubbed bare on the crowns.

'Anyhow, Walter Dawson, this present Roy Dawson's father, who was two years older than Edith's brother, told the police that they'd been fooling about like kids do. Except Walter had a rifle. His statement claimed that Graham had grabbed it and the thing had gone off, not once but twice. Well,' she said, picking up one of the hats and spontaneously placing it on Ivan's head, 'if you believe that, you believe anything.'

'What happened next?' He removed it to read the grimy label inside: *F. W. Middleton.* Its cavity

173

still smelt faintly of horse and sweat.

'The inquest verdict was accidental death. Walter Dawson just got a warning about taking more care with guns.'

'That's fucking unbelievable. Sorry, I know it's Sunday.' Ivan returned the memento to the pile.

'Edith knew it was Dawson's parents who'd put him up to it. They didn't want any Tripp coming into the family. Anyway, cruel justice I know, but Peggy was sent away to some boarding school near Southampton and apparently tried to kill herself.'

The doctor's wife stopped her frantic sorting and looked over at Ivan.

For a few seconds he was back in his cottage's dark hallway, with the whisperings, the earthy dampness, its heavy, lowering beam blotting out the day. Then seeing all too clearly that weird pale form twisting imperceptibly, exuding a strange chill.

'Are you all right?' she asked.

'I was just wondering – has anyone else seen a corpse hanging from one of the cottage's meat hooks?'

Valerie's eyes widened in surprise, then grew less focused as if dwelling on another distant memory.

'No, but Mrs Tripp did tell my mother there'd been moaning sounds coming from the outbuilding, at all hours of the day and night. And then, of course, there was the dog.'

'Dog?' Ivan frowned.

'They never kept one, nor did their neighbour, but this invisible creature went yelping on and on, as if pleading for something. She'd say whatever it was would only end up getting shot because of the Dawsons.'

'The Dawsons again?'

'Oh yes, sons of the devil himself, as Mrs Tripp would often say. Family originally from London – Bermondsey, I think – just as the railways were starting. Then Luke Dawson bought himself the biggest farm in Nether Wapford, didn't he? Easy pickings for him and his sons there. Anything that moved – *and* some that didn't,' she added mysteriously. 'You must know the place?'

Ivan nodded. 'Were they poachers then?' he asked, thinking of the white homestead and outbuildings stranded in the flood water.

'And anything else you can think of. In 1830 the three of them were all tried at the Lent Assizes and hanged up in Northampton, pleading for mercy, if you please, after all that they did. I don't think this county's ever seen such a bad lot.'

Ivan chose his next words carefully, trying to lose that repulsive repetitive image of the swaying corpse. 'Worse than the Oakleys, then?'

'Six of one, half a dozen of the other.' She finished stacking the last old riding mac and stared him in the eye. 'Look, the Dawsons *married* into the Oakleys way back in 1911 and have been together like mistletoe on an apple tree ever since. Mind you, there are whispers of them having differences.'

'Really? I wonder why.'

'No idea, but let's hope their days are numbered.'

Ivan moved towards the hallway. His time was running out. Valerie Rook followed, then suddenly snapped her fingers.

'This may be something or nothing, but I'd been meaning to tell you anyway. There was a short piece in one of the old newspapers filed in Northampton library. The *Mercury*, I think.'

Ivan turned round to see her face looking more animated than usual. 'It was about some strange girl who just turned up out of the blue in Nether Wapford. Apparently, she was wearing filthy clothes and riding a thin little pony – but, in those days, I imagine there were plenty of people going about their business on their own like that. I mean even youngsters would set off to find work in the fields, without a second thought. Not like today when everyone just sits in their cars.'

'So is it possible she stayed at my cottage?' Ivan's breath came more quickly now.

'More than possible, for I do believe old Mrs Tripp said her husband's father mentioned a young stranger who'd stayed there for just a short while, with his grandparents. She kept trying to run away, and a real worry to them she was when they were only trying to be Good Samaritans... Matthew and Hannah Tripp, it was, I think.'

Take me back ... take me back...

'Thank you, Valerie.'

He turned the door handle, feeling light-headed, unsteady on his feet.

'Are you all right?' she asked again.

'I'm fine. But you be careful now.'

Then he was outside in the same dank drizzle as earlier on, and as he reached the narrow

176

pavement, before he could duck out of the way, a Nissan Terrano hurtled down Church Street from the Westhope end, veered towards the kerb and splattered him copiously with mud. Before it vanished, he recognized the number plate: the same one as he'd noticed in the pub car park.

He didn't want to bother the doctor's wife again, but he was alarmed that if that was the Oakleys' vehicle, whoever the woman driver had been, she'd seen him come out of Church House. So he tore a page from his already depleted invoice book, and pushed a scribbled note to that effect through the letter box. He kept thinking all the while of that mystery girl who'd lodged at Tripp's Cottage so long ago. If it was her, why had she been so desperate to leave?

Siân stared across at England, this unfamiliar country, with its receding hills grey-green against the sky. Land of the *Saesneg*, the Saxons, whose inhabitants all lived to a ripe old age on bellies full of the best Welsh lamb and beef. No *potas mais* or tiny mutton joint for them, or just fat rind to last the week.

She herself had not tasted meat since she was ten and their last pig died.

In the distance, Siân could hear another drove stopped at the toll, and the shouts of its porthmon warning nearby farmers and road users of their presence.

Not so Tomos, who checked no one was following them, then kept his drove half hidden by trees along the river bank. It was three o'clock,

177

judging by the last of the sun, but there was to be no halt for them until Breinton just south of Hereford. That place at least, Tomos had announced, while stopping to relieve himself, was another county away from Powys law, with the possibility of finding extra hands to go as far as Tewkesbury.

His sister let him ramble on, fearful of doing anything to set off another rage: no whistling to herself, no getting up too near, and, more importantly, secretly stuffing the food Hopkins had given her into her mouth.

The Wye flowed flat and calm despite the recent rains. In several places the water had broken the river's banks and reflected the cold sky amid fields of grazing sheep with their new lambs. She was desperate to sneak down to the tempting tide, to wash herself, to lose the cloying smell of urine, to travel without undergarments if necessary.

The herd was thirsty, too. Whenever a chance arose for any to slip between the trees down to the river, it was taken, and Ben was fully stretched keeping the drove together. Siân watched their pink tongues licking the water, their ribs standing out, the bony rumps. They'd now need more than the week's pasture at Berkhamstead that Tomos had planned. A month more like, except Siân herself couldn't wait that long.

At least half of the Castlemartins were now below a selling weight, all had a doleful expression in their eyes and feet already sore. Once, when her father's best ewe was found rolled over in a ditch, Siân had bottle-fed its lamb until it was weaned. The gentle eyes, the soft nose had made that little creature almost a person, like another member in the family. But not these. To her, Tomos's stock were just brutes without a brain to share between them. Just like her brother in some ways.

Folks had wondered, after the trampling of his sister, how Tomos Richards could look another Castlemartin in the eye, let alone have their keep, costing as much as it did. But Pont Llwyd and its fertile acres had already gone to his head.

Never mind the cross-breeds coming out of Pembrokeshire, or Mr Johnes's fancy 'experiments' as Tomos called them. 'I don't want those mongrels in my fields. It's my land... *My* damned business.' How he'd boasted thus in the Tafarn every night. Yet everyone knew those low-lying two hundred and eighty acres had been bought in part with his wife's money. And, in turn, where had *that* arrived from? His companions sneered behind his back, knowing full well the answer: the Established Church. Small wonder the pews at St Andrew and St Peter were emptying. It had been that church's congregations' rents and tithes which had enabled Tomos Richards to build up his herds of 'runts', and become an envied Porthmon.

Siân had seen the way Dai Twp and the rest of the Tafarn gang eyed her brother when the drink had turned him bleary and offguard. And the poison of it all had spread to her own home, Plas Newydd, whose tin roof and shored-up walls proved no protection. Words and looks, like the air itself had seeped in and set one family member against the other – notably her mam and da.

If Tomos had only stayed with them, with his youthful energy they could have built up the pigs, bought a good ram, and maybe even started a small Vale of Clwyd herd – cattle which carried four times more meat than the blacks ... if Tomos had stayed...

But Elen Jones, the vicar's daughter had wanted those prospects for herself. Besides, in those days, Tomos took care with his appearance and cut a fine figure with his dark good looks, his fit strong body. He had also wooed her with surprising persistence.

Siân blinked such thoughts away. He'd halted the drove, yet none of the herd attempted freedom, instead they dropped their heads, letting their long curved horns brush the grass as they ate. Some slumped to their knees and grazed lying down. All were clearly exhausted.

There was no sound as Tomos tethered the cob and the dun to an oak. Siân then saw the mark of a dark cross on the small pony's back like a donkey's, and shivered under Moses Evans's jacket. For her brother was coming towards her, his hat slung back on his shoulders, its black cord tight across his throat. His gaze held a strange purpose, but stranger still was the smile that twisted his mouth.

'Lift your skirt, sister. I've got a good notion.'

The surprise of it left her hem undefended, and before she could push him away, he'd torn away her home-made pantalettes and grabbed at her pudenda as if it was vermin. 'The salmon'll be catching wind of this a mile away. Leastways your smell's had a use.'

'*Don't!*'

'D'you want supper or not?'

I don't care. Just leave me alone.

She tried biting him, always her best weapon, but he wasn't close enough. Instead he pinched her ear till it stung.

'You make one sound, Lodger, and you'll be floating down the river like that pig in the Teifi.' With his ear-nicking knife he snipped off a piece of the fine hair down below, which, to her consternation, had sprouted overnight on her thirteenth birthday.

Siân sat paralysed and degraded until the mare Collen wandered over. She patted her warm neck and the gentle creature nuzzled against her arm.

He's the devil. The filthiest man ever. Now what's he doing? Twisting it round one of his fish hooks, making a fly.

Siân's blush still burnt her cheeks as she stared at his skill. He'd always gone fishing, knew currents and temperatures better than anyone: and some said he was far better suited to this lonely pursuit than that of farmer. But now, even after her humiliation, he wanted his sister to admire his prowess.

'Count to fifty, and I'll wager there'll be a bite by then.' He cast into the Wye and let the bait drift into an eddy, dark and deep below a mat of dead fern.

Siân counted, not trusting his fickle mood, still shamed by what he'd done to her. '...*un deg dau*

... un deg tri ... un deg pedwar...' She continued, feeling dizzy again. The thought of food, any food was too much – but salmon. A treat not repeated since his wedding day at the Glebe House. '*...dau ddeg un ... dau ddeg dau...'* She was already tasting that melting flaky meat in her mouth when, with a flourish, Tomos landed something on the bank. A cock salmon, one moment thrashing its tail, the next, after he'd flogged it with a stone, still and glistening like some huge jewel, its eyes sunk into death.

'Get me some more kindling, sister. Move.' He'd soon made a pyre of twigs, muffling the snapping of them with his coat, and squatted down to place the salmon on top. 'I've been thinking,' he announced, prodding the fish with a stick, 'we'd better be keeping away from Breinton now, in case our good friend Mr James makes good pace on the roads. Bullingham might be better.'

She'd forgotten about the little pink man in Llancrws, for there were enough other demons following and, as she stuffed her pockets full of twigs, she prayed Derryn Morris wouldn't rise again from the nearly-dead, so she'd never have to see him again. The light was fading, blurring the outlines of the plantation against the sky. Anyone could be hidden in there, resurrected or not, and she crept quickly back to Tomos's fire.

'Hurry up, *twpsin.* I don't want the herd to be too near this river in the dark–' he waved a shiny hand at the Wye – 'or there'll be more dead bones.' Soon the struggling fire grew into flames, and Siân watched the salmon's mouth stay agape

182

and oddly waxen, while its skin spat and burnt to a creased paper.

She waited for Tomos to divide it, but instead, having filled his mouth and thrown the dog the burnt tail, he produced a kerchief, wrapped up the rest and secreted it inside his coat.

'You see what a clever brother you have.' He licked his lips. 'Now, on our way, girl. And cut out that look on your face. You're lucky to have had a whiff of it.'

And as the drover called Ben to raise the sleeping herd, Siân began to cry. Her expression, with her eyes squeezed tight shut, could be mistaken for tiredness, but not the tears which swelled large and salty, leaving grimy tracks down her cheeks.

Nine

As Ivan drove past the Stoneshanger turning heading back into Nether Wapford, he recalled a favourite stuffed toy he'd been given as a kid. It was a grubby yellow duck, and once part of the side seam had split, he'd begun pulling out its insides, bit by bit, until the creature became just a flat hollow shape.

That was exactly what this last week had done to himself, and now the prospect of having to scratch in yet more symbols of the River Wap onto twenty green-ware urns, or fiddle with the next set of slip-cast clocks made him feel it was all so irrelevant – all a wasteful self-indulgence. What the fuck did it matter if a lid didn't quite fit, when a man he'd only just met briefly had known a stinging blade at his throat? What the fuck did it matter that a little cobalt blue had fluxed into a copper-oxide green, when that same man's blood had turned the rain-filled river red – and, in the not-so-distant past, whole families had been destroyed by greed and malice?

He saw Dawson's Farm again, low and white, and seemingly harmless amid its pasture, where already pools of water had settled. He wondered what exactly was going on there now, surprised, after what Valerie Rook had told him, that its name hadn't been changed. But things *don't* change in the countryside.

No, that was exactly the point. And if privacy can be bought to keep wagging tongues at bay, they didn't need to.

He took care driving round the second nasty bend, then, having crossed the rising river and taken the slope up into Nether Wapford, he began to dream of who that mysterious young stranger from long ago might have been. As he tried to visualize her possible place of origin, her story, he was passing Tripp's Cottage itself without realizing it, heading west towards Banbury. Westwards, as though being pulled by an unseen will towards dark-clouded hills somewhere far beyond.

Siân knew what her brother was doing. Starving her gradually to death so Mam and Da would think she'd been refusing food again, like she'd done on and off since the trampling, and wanted to die.

But he wasn't going to win. Whatever it took, even if it meant grubs and worms, she *would* survive. She rolled over to face the sky, intersected by the dark bare branches above. Last night, there'd been no moon or stars which to her, were signposts in the Great Beyond, and the sky was now grey as an old shroud, with snow clouds edging in from the west. Moses Evans's jacket felt no more than cotton in the chill, and without her pantalettes, another wetting marked the ground underneath her.

Tomos was turned away from her, lying on his elbow, and she could tell by the sounds he made that he was eating the rest of the fish, after occasionally shooing the dog away to stay with the herd.

Siân felt the saliva of hunger gather in her mouth and run onto her chin. The cramps in her stomach felt so bad, she reached for a nearby bough and began to chew on its bark. It was sour and fibrous, and the moment it was inside her, she had to go and lift her skirt.

Tomos turned round. 'Hey, where you a-goin'?' His cheeks were full of fish.

Siân wiped herself and surveyed the Wye. She could swim, even with clothes, and now she'd have to.

Ice seemed to fill her boots, then the water rose over her knees till her garments spread about her, letting the river up to her waist. She saw him coming quickly towards her, an arm raised, Ben close behind, growling.

'Come back here, you piece of plague.' He threshed the water into the sky and reached her with an iron grip, delivering a blow that made her fall back into his arms. 'I'll say where you go and where you don't.' He pulled her towards the bank, while warding off the hound who'd fixed on his arm.

I had to clean myself. He pushed her into a pile of leaves. *'Where could I show myself without being washed? I'm not some animal, though you'd like to make me one.'*

'I'll teach you a lesson for going off like that,' Tomos roared as the hound still barked. Too loud, too long, as he'd been bred to do. 'Hush, you! What's that?'

There was a noise – men's voices. The crush of

dead wood. Three figures emerged from the trees.

Tomos stopped. Forgetting Siân, he ran back to his bundle and the pistol, but he was too late.

'Hands to the sky,' shouted the tall bearded one as he pulled a rifle from his boot. 'You an' all.' His eyes met Siân's, the other two followed his gaze into the grove. She tried to stand, covered in wet leaves. The strangers stared back at her, deflected for a moment, then focused again on the cattle, still as stones amongst the grass.

'Nice runts you got there, sire.'

'Nice bit o' money, I'd say,' added the fat one whose neck was hung with rope coils.

'These an' all.' The rifle pointed now at the horses, tethered together. Siân waited for Tomos to protest, but nothing came. He was as scared as she. 'Not bad neither.' The Beard gestured to the small rat-faced man to untie them. 'We need hosses.'

'*Not Collen, please.*' Siân stumbled towards them, pleading with her eyes, shaking her head.

'What we got 'ere then?' the Barrel Belly asked Tomos, 'a halfmade?' He then ran a hand down the dun's legs. 'Nice, these too, just the ticket. What d'you say, Tobias?'

The rat-faced man pushed Siân away with one gloved hand. He reeked of tobacco and Siân saw the pistol poking from his pocket. 'Bit small, but she'll do.' His worm-hole eye turned on Tomos whose upraised arms were beginning to flag. ''Sides, the saddle's worth a bit.'

'So, do we take all three?'

'No, just 'er. Better not be greedy, eh? Three

new hosses round the place will get too many curious looks. But we could run to a couple more runts ... six'll do for now.'

Siân sighed in relief, until she saw her brother's demonic expression as the steers were roped together and led away behind the screen of firs.

'They's not bin shod. Ye won't get far wi' 'em anyways,' the fat one opined, looking Siân up and down. 'And all being well, we'll be around again tomorrow.' The tall man nudged the air with his rifle, indicating for Tomos to keep his arms up. Siân started to whistle for Ben to give chase, then stopped. If the dog was shot, they'd be stranded. As it was, he remained crouching by her brother's feet, waiting until the thieves had disappeared in a drift of dust, then charged over to the remaining herd.

Tomos pulled his hat right down without speaking, then hefted his sack onto his shoulders. He came over to his sister, who held Collen's reins tighter than ever.

'May the devil burn those bastards' souls. Only forty-six left.' She was glad she couldn't see his eyes. 'I saw that ape looking you up and down. I know what he was thinking, and I've been doing some thinking too.'

Siân shivered so violently her jaws clattered together. She wondered what was coming next. 'Thirty pounds' worth of Welsh meat gone, but,' he came closer and held her, 'you'd get me more than that, as sure as night follows day.' His smile lasted only a second.

His grip on her tightened, her expression becoming one of disbelief as he spelt out his plan. 'Certainly wouldn't ask less, specially for a virgin. Some like a nice tight little place to go.' He picked up her hem and sniffed. 'But no one'll bite with you looking like this. First thing is to scrub, then wear something more like a girl of means.'

Siân now knew what he'd got in mind. She let out a shriek and tried to mount the mare, but he got there first.

'I knew there'd always be a use for you. Someone's looking after me.' He raised his black eyes to heaven. 'Thank you, God.'

'You're my brother!'

Her arms flailed the air vigorously despite her hunger. Her teeth were bared to attack, but he held her so close, so still, that the turmoil of her heart became his.

'And I'm your keeper. What I say, you do, or you can forget London. We're stopping at Bullingham, away from the main road, and come Monday morning, after two good nights' work on the Saturday and Sabbath, I'll have enough money to replace the corgis and the stock that's gone.'

Siân closed her eyes and wished for eternal night. She pretended it was Huw holding her, like he'd done after last Sunday's service. But no, Tomos was hurting her because she was his sister, and it was easy.

At the Farrier inn, a former forge near Lower Bullingham, Tomos Richards had to pay over the odds for night pasture and a pair of Jack Russells, both of them white with pink eyes like Derryn

Morris. The field was less than a half acre but no matter, for the weary cattle stood rib by rib, making no move to graze.

'Them's in real poor shape,' remarked the publican's son, a thickset clod in a tight-fitting apron. 'And they've no tips neither,' he tutted. 'They'll not make Warton, if that's the way you're taking.'

Tomos ignored him while digging in his pocket for money.

'One pound, straight and fair.' Tomos pressed a note into the other's hand. 'I want this young lady done up fragrant as a rose, with clothes to match. Can you do that?'

John Griffiths realized what the drover was after. He looked Siân up and down as he stroked the note. 'You his bit of biddy, then?'

Siân kicked him on the shin with her sound leg, but before he could retaliate, the drover gripped him by the collar.

'You've got an hour, sire, before dusk, or my note goes back in here.' He slapped his pocket as the young man went off to whisper with his mother.

The main room was filling up. There'd been a funeral at nearby Paylton, and those who'd walked over from the graveyard now stood in groups reminiscing on the life of the departed, while the landlord and his wife poured ale and set out a platter of cold beef on the sideboard.

When she thought no one was looking, Siân helped herself to a slice. The sudden food in her starving belly brought hiccups and unwanted attention. The woman wiped her hands on her apron and came over.

'I see'd what you did, young madam, and I got just the cure for them hiccups.' She dragged her into the room next to the pantry, where she boxed Siân's ears. 'That'll larn ye not to steal. How d'you think we can keep going if the likes o' you keep thieving?'

Somewhere, a fiddler struck up a tune, as Mary Griffiths tore the hymn singer's jacket off Siân's back. She then fetched a tub, bigger than the one at the Hen and Casket, and while the water was boiled over the kitchen fire, she pinned Siân's hair like her own and cut her toenails down to the quicks. She made a pile of the clippings and put them in her apron pocket. 'For the pigs, these. You can't be clawing a man to death now, can you?' Then her eyes alighted on what Tomos had done. 'Looks like the mice 'ave bin at it. You've not got the mange down there 'ave you? I've me customers to think of.' The woman brushed and re-trimmed the offending place, and stood back to admire her handiwork. 'There, that'll keep someone happy, I'll be bound.'

Next, she scoured both the girl's knees till they glowed like red amber, and ran her hand over the damaged left leg. 'I've an idea.' Her small eyes widened. 'When you're all cleaned up, we'll make a bandage on it. To look like you had an accident or summat. Now, give me a hand.'

Siân helped her drag the kettle to the tub. Drops of scalding water fell like sparks on her bare feet but no one could hear her. There was no way out of here. No escape, and as the fiddle playing grew louder, and men's voices joined in,

191

she thought again of Huw and her father, because they were all she had left in this hateful world.

An hour later, as distant bells pealed ten o'clock, Siân Richards had been seated strategically near the serving table wearing a blue woollen dress a size too small, with her hair primped into ringlets adorned with a matching bow.

Mrs Griffiths, having drenched her with lavender oil, had then given her a sandwich 'to keep yer strength up', and a piece of embroidery to work on. Siân had already noticed Tomos's drunken smile of approval, and now John Griffiths's eyes were on her each time he passed.

Ten

It was the rain that woke Ivan up, battering the Saxo's windscreen in a constant heavy rhythm. His bleary eyes checked his watch – Monday, 19 November. Time: 7.23 a.m. Limbo grey, and more grey, all around. Panic racked him as he stared out of the window for anything recognizable. But there was nothing familiar. Where on earth was he? What the hell had he done?

He got out into the soaking wind, and let huge drops of it freshen his skin to clear away his recent dream. But the water drumming on the car roof was like the noise of hooves on hard ground, and the discernible waft of sewage from some nearby treatment plant became the smell of horses and cattle locked together, buffeting their way through his subconscious.

Ivan turned to see a vague motorway procession of car lights, the wash of water thrown up by speeding wheels, and high above, in the dense darkening sky, he could make out the vaguely familiar arches of some massive bridge.

Suddenly, a deep engine growl and the blast of a horn made him spin round again.

'You gonna be all bloody day then?' Someone's anger, muffled by the weather, reached his ears. Ivan stared at the forty-tonner coming off the slip road, looming up behind him – its black diesel fumes soon choking his nostrils. 'You can't just park where you bloody like, mate. I've gotta get through here. Hey, you listening? I gotta get through.'

The lorry's grumbling roar grew louder as Ivan staggered towards it.

'Where is this place? And what's *that* over there?' he asked the driver, pointing to the hazy shape in the sky.

'For Chrissake, man, it's the Severn Bridge.' The young man leaned further out of his cab. 'You feeling OK?'

'No, I don't think so. God knows how I got here.' He put both hands to his ears as if to protect them from what he'd heard. He felt so tired, so tired ... and began to waver. Then he heard the thud of a door shutting, and something was thrown over his shoulders: some old mac smelling of WD40.

'Look, let's get you somewhere into the dry. I'll just move the rig on a bit, and shift your motor. Got some coffee left you can have.'

'Thanks,' Ivan croaked.

The driver helped him up into the cab, and repositioned his truck alongside the edge of the parking area's kerb. After doing the same with the Citroën, he walked back over and passed the key to Ivan who was still in a daze.

'I'm Gerry. Gerry Daniels. Who are you?'

'Not sure.'

'Oh bloody great.' The man switched on Radio 2, letting Procol Harum eke into the cab.

'It's Ivan ... Browning.'

'So what you bin up to, then?' Pulling out a battered Thermos, he poured out some dubious

194

black liquid. Ivan cupped his shaking hands round the plastic mug and stared straight ahead at the deluge hitting the windscreen.

'Been over in Cardiganshire somewhere. Then after that, other places ... all different.'

In my head, that was. In a dream.

'So you bin busy getting around?' His companion handed him a dirty rag to dry his hair, but Ivan declined. He could not remember motorways and traffic – only carts and desolate tracks.

'Which pub you bin in? Smells to me like you've had a few.'

Ivan was too absorbed in his hazy recollection to be taken aback. He could see a small white hovel with its pub sign, and a chestnut pony tied up outside...

'The Tafarn y Pluen,' he recalled with surprising clarity. 'It's a small place, a bit dark, but the singing, my God, it was incredible – *Clychau'r Bugail oedd yn henw, Gan yr hen fugeiliad gynt.*'

'You know Welsh then?' the driver asked, with a look of ridicule.

'No, never heard it before. Shit, what's going on?'

'You must have pulled in here sometime yesterday, and had a fucking good dose of shut-eye since. That's what.' Daniels tried to tune the radio so he could hear UB40 more clearly.

'I dunno.' Ivan took another gulp of the hot sweet coffee. 'Can't explain it really.' And now, as he tried recalling those marshy fields, those suede-smooth hills, the images slipped from colour to monochrome, the sounds of shouting and that strange high whistling diminishing to nothing the harder he grappled to keep it all clear in his mind.

'Bad dream, eh?' The burly younger man relieved Ivan of his mug, chucked the dregs out of the window and resealed his Thermos. 'Me missus gets those,' he chuckled.

Ivan managed a preoccupied smile. The odd thing was that apart from that pub, there had been so few people. It was just as if he had been visiting a bare land with just sound effects, everything kind of disembodied.

'Reckon you need a stiff brandy whatever, then take it easy. Where you from?'

Ivan hesitated, for in his mind he was now entering some small hamlet alive with white hawthorn blossom, the smell of burning hoof bone at the nearby forge... But no, no, that wasn't his home – nor was the old inn. They were just places he'd passed through, as might an unquiet spirit on its way to ... where?

'Let me think.' He saw again the pebbledashed semi in Downwellan, and then a tiny red-brick cottage with a dark screen of trees behind – interspersed with a barking dog, a crackling pyre in a woodland clearing, a desolate cry shredding the air, driving all the birds to cover. 'Nether Wapford, that's it. In Northamptonshire.'

'Hell, I go through there quite a lot,' Daniels volunteered brightly. 'Some nice spots there once you're away from all the overspill shite.'

'Sure, if you can turn a blind eye to what's really going on: poaching, car theft, you name it.'

196

The driver shot him a funny look and switched off the radio.

The atmosphere in the cab cooled. The man was suddenly in a hurry.

'Right, mate, I reckon you need to be off. And I gotta get going or the good folk of Stroud'll be having nothing on their toast tomorrow morning.'

Ivan craned round to peer through the tiny window in the back of the cab. 'What have you got in there?'

'Bloody marmalade, isn't it? Golden Heart, fine cut. OK, see you, mate.'

Daniels waited till his new acquaintance was back in his car, then unclipped his mobile, punched in some numbers and, as the red Saxo set off to join the M4 traffic heading east, his employer answered.

The gruff voice at the other end was almost drowned by the racket of a solitary dog howling – still grieving for its dead partner. But Gerry Daniels wasn't into distressed animals. Just the smack and the crack, and the black box-file full of notes, which would soon be passing into his hands amid the secret oily recesses of Pike's Garage at the end of a long run.

Services 15 miles – thank Christ for that. The words on the sign were just about readable through the downpour. Ivan saw his tank was low as he crept along in the inside lane, still completely at a loss as to why he was even here on the edge of England. And very frightened by the intensity of his recent experience.

Suddenly a truck cab reared up behind, then overtook, throwing up spray like an ocean storm. However, Ivan recognized its plain green sides, and for some reason, despite Daniels's apparent concern for his welfare a while earlier, something made his heart pound a little harder. That was a Northampton number plate, and as the rig disappeared in yet more blinding spray, Ivan logged the sequence of letters and numbers in his already cluttered brain.

Upon entering the hideously bright and busy service station Ivan went into the gents and, braving the giggling gaze of a couple of schoolboys, rubbed at his teeth with a finger, then ducked his head under the tap and positioned it under the blow dryer for three blasts of warm air.

Next, past the games and fruit machines, novelty rides and the crowded boutique, into the cafeteria. He'd already recce'd the lorry park for that same green truck, so no point in checking out all the tables to see if Daniels was there. But nevertheless as he stood in the slow-moving queue to pay for his breakfast, he kept a tired eye out. And, as he sat alone with his coffee and cold toast, it seemed that everyone who passed by was walking either too slowly or too quickly, and that any casual glance his way was laden with menace.

While he sat cocooned in one of the vinyl-padded dining bays, watching the ebb and flow of present-day travellers, his once-clear visions of that distant land were fading to shadowy flecks drifting across his consciousness – and when he attempted to recall those strange vowelless words he'd earlier spoken so fluently, and with such feeling, nothing came.

His snack finished, Ivan made for the exit, but stopped by one of the smeared glass panels to watch the torrent of rain from a gunmetal sky making lakes of water alongside each parking bay. He turned to face westwards, where, out of sight now, the Severn was already licking at its banks, where tractors were out gathering in the herds to the drier island dwellings, and all those impressions of another age continued slipping away.

But not his curiosity. Why bloody Wales of all places? Although he'd crossed the Irish Sea many times between Rosslare and Fishguard he'd no relatives in Wales, no familial connection with the country at all. In fact, he didn't even particularly *like* the Welsh – at least not those students he'd encountered at college in Belfast. Short arms and long pockets, to be precise, and ranting on about Plaid Cymru and the scourge of the *Saesnegs'* second homes. No, there must have been some other reason why he'd been drawn there, as a fleeting voyeur on some part of its strange bleak history. And for his peace of mind, he would have to find out why. But not just yet.

Only 11 a.m. and dark as dusk outside. Yet, despite the distractions of the world and his rowdy wife coming and going through the swing doors, and the incessant intrusion of mobile phones, Ivan composed a mental list of things to do when he got back home. In control again now, or was he? As he battled his way across the sodden car park, stung by the merciless downpour, he wasn't so sure.

Where Huw had the Celts' red hair, this one resembled a stone. Someone, most likely his mother, had shaved him close to the skull. Whatever, he had less charms than one of the bullocks, and she hoped he'd soon tire of her staring down at her handiwork.

The funeral party eventually dispersed into the night, still speculating on how long the grave must have taken to dig, given the hard soil. New voices took their place, and they settled down for some serious drinking in the far corner. Suddenly, Siân's needle stopped, as she listened.

'Have you heard, there's rumour of a corpse being found on Trelewis's land,' one said.

'Gwyn Price say he know who it be.'

'Who?'

'Hopkins, from Maesmynis.'

'I never.'

The fiddler's rendition of 'Roamin'' petered out and Siân saw Tomos turn towards the fire, now a fierce blaze up the chimney.

'And there's been footpads all along the Wye by Clifford Park.' One of the group set down his tankard. 'You wouldna' catch *me* on my own down there.'

'Mebbe 'e weren't on 'is own.'

'Well, anyhows, old Mudson thought he saw Hopkins's dun up for sale at Ploughfield this afternoon.'

'Today?'

''S right.'

'They didn't waste much time then.'

Silence, except for the fiddler's belch, and an

introductory cough from one of the men.

'Hey, drover?' He clicked his huge fingers at Tomos. 'Did you see owt as you came along?' His tone was suspicious, his ears keen. Constables weren't always to be recognized, Siân thought. She whistled and her brother whipped round.

'*We did*,' she whispered. '*There were three of them with a dun pony, just like you said.*' Her cheeks flushed, hot as the fire.

'Speak up, lass.'

'*I can't.*'

For Tomos had got up and stood close by, his hand clamped on her shoulder, heavy as a beam.

'She spins lies like a spider spins its web.' He tried jocularity but it ill-suited him. 'That's her trouble, but–' he let go, fearing more mischief from her – 'she's a clever little bitch in other ways, know what I mean?' He stroked her arm as might a lover. Siân winced and bent lower over the sampler.

One day, Tomos Richards, the devil will come and take you far far away into the darkness, where you'll never be heard of again.

'Well, then, let's be trying her.' John Griffiths untied his apron and put his hand under her chin. 'And let's see those pretty eyes all lit up, eh?' The two men winked at each other, while the others took their leave, still unsure about the dark dour Welshman, but unwilling to be witness to what might follow.

John Griffiths was rough. His cock as big as one of 'Ma' Morris's parsnips. Siân screamed and tried to close her legs, but the stranger was

201

already part of her, pumping into her secret places, bringing a blood she'd never seen before, and when he was done, he rolled away from her, buttoning up his breeches.

Tomos held out his hand. 'That'll be three shillings.' And by midnight the pound had been repaid; while, on the stroke of one, Siân Richards's first period had begun.

'Sunday is our day of rest, the one by God Almighty blest...' Mary Griffiths sang as she wiped up the ale slops and the vomit pooled under the tables. 'No more labour, no more toil, no more heavenly works to spoil.' It was a hymn she'd made up herself, and one she hoped the new Methodist preacher at the chapel would use in his services.

She ignored the girl, for although she was mute, there was a troubling look to her which spoilt the landlady's piety. And when her son appeared, with a swagger she'd not seen since her husband's rutting days, Mary Griffiths knew the peace of the Sabbath wouldn't be hers for long.

'It's cost us,' was all she could say, 'didn't you think of that? It's all back in the Porthmon's pocket now.'

'How could I resist after ye'd done 'er up so nice? What's a red-blooded man s'posed to do, Mather?'

'Think twice, I'd say. Now tonight, see she goes with Bragg and Pyeman. Mebbe old Roberts, too. That way we'll get it all back, and more.'

Bragg? Pyeman? Roberts? Siân's mouth fell open. She was sore, she was bleeding in a way she'd never seen before. She had to survive. When he'd gone outside, she started to follow.

'Where ye off to, girl?'

'*Ben*,' she mouthed.

'Who's he?'

'*Bytheuad. Dog.*'

Siân felt the cold air sting her cheeks. The frost had deepened in the night, and her boots slipped on the cobbles, and frozen water spread out from the drain. She saw a light in the adjoining barn, where Griffiths junior had gone to feed the boar. The smell was nauseating, both sweet and foul. She kept her hand on her nose and the woollen dress tight to stop the rags from slipping out of place, as she located the Hereford road. Having checked that the son wasn't following her, she kept close to the barn wall's shadow, until the verge curved away and down the hill to join the Dinedor Road.

By ten the sun was drifting through a clear blue sky. Her dress clung hot as a horse rug on her skin. Her smell different, and alarming.

Siân reached a field just as her left leg which had held up so far, began to buckle as if it didn't belong to her. Her insides felt as if a goblin had lodged there. She found a hollow spot, free of dung and thawed enough to rest in. Here, she pulled out the rags from between her legs and stared at what had come from her body. Then in a mixture of fear and shame, she pulled clump after clump of the rye grass and wiped herself clean, but with each dull ache, more of the same appeared. Was it some disease? An evil omen? Siân unravelled Moses Evans's jacket, which she'd rescued from that back room, and put it on again. It felt comforting, but never as warm as her father's coat would have been.

She finally curled herself up and, having said a prayer for Huw and her father, drifted into sleep.

'Who's you, then?'

Siân sat bolt upright to find another girl squatting next to her – someone so grimy she couldn't even guess her age, let alone distinguish many features.

'*Elen*.' Her lie was just a tiny sound, and her sister-in-law's name would do here.

'That ain't English, is it? You're one of them Taffies what come over and take our work, an'–' She peered closer. 'What's wrong with yer voice?'

There was so much Siân wanted to say, but couldn't. She gazed despairingly at her visitor. '*I can't speak*,' she whispered.

'And what's wrong with yer leg?' The girl stared at it till Siân stretched the wool over it, making a hole through which her knee stuck up more like an elbow.

'*Some bullocks ran over me*,' she mouthed and made a galloping movement with her hands. The urchin looked astonished, the whites of her eyes enormous.

'And you lived, after that?'

'*Only just*.' Siân decided to trust the girl, and rolled up her sleeve to show a purple cloven print above the left elbow. '*Why are you so black? Is it soot?*' she asked in turn, spitting on her finger and leaning forwards to touch the stranger's face. But the girl used her sleeve to rub the worst of it into one grey smudge.

'I go up chimneys for Mr Hubbard, if you must know.'

'*Chimneys?*' Siân recalled the one at Plas Newydd with a sudden pang of homesickness. River stone rising through the old tin roof, and full of birds when the grate was cold in summer.

'My master stands below me with the candle flame, and up I go – cleaning, see.'

Siân's admiration grew with every syllable. The proof was on the girl's hands, and on her shins chafed like bark. Her eyes were perpetually half closed and every pore of her young skin filled with black dust.

'*How much do they pay you?*' Siân's whisper was weakening with every word.

'Two for two pence. But I don't see none of it, oh no.'

The Welsh girl gasped. For the first time in three years she'd met someone worse off than herself.

'*And do you work Sundays?*'

'Course.' The girl pulled a piece of grass through her teeth. 'I just finished over in Lever Street.'

'*So what's your name?*' Siân asked by signs, wishing she'd still got Huw's coin to give her.

'Pansy. Pansy Palmer. Fourteen, and three days, of 5 Rowbottom Lane.'

She got up and brushed burrs off her legs. 'I gotta go or I get a whipping from me Big Man, but I tell you summat,' she bent down to whisper, 'there's police out looking for a Taffy and a cripple.'

Siân whitened. Here was the end of her dream of London staring her in the face.

Eleven

Still feeling dizzy, Ivan filled up the Saxo's tank, and dodged oily puddles on his way to pay the cashier. He also bought a packet of mint humbugs and a new phone card, then, having checked that the green truck still wasn't anywhere to be seen, unlocked his car and prepared to leave.

As he joined the line of vehicles also waiting to join the motorway, the engine idled in first, but when all was clear, and it was his turn to feed into the inside lane, heading east, the Citroën inexplicably held back, dangerously slow, to provoke a series of flashing lights and the collective rage of several horns.

Shit shit shit, bloody move, will you? he swore under his breath. He kept his boot hard on the throttle and toyed with the gears for the best torque.

He was now sandwiched between two giant transporters, his wipers unable to clear the front vehicle's spray, when suddenly he felt a distinct tug on his left arm, causing the steering wheel to move and take the car onto the hard shoulder.

'Jesus *Christ!*' Ivan wrestled with this determined hidden force, all the while trying to rejoin the flow of traffic. But the truck so close up behind gave him another angry flash and careered on past, followed by another, and another, until he was forced to stop altogether and switch on his hazard lights.

'*You've got to take me back ... take me back ... take me back...*'

That dreadful whispering again filled his ears, his head, then all at once it was coupled with the muffled barking of a dog – like the one he'd heard earlier on his involuntary travels.

Finally he closed his eyes, just like he always did whenever reciting Clare's haunting poem 'I am' to himself.

Into the nothingness of scorn and noise–
Even the dearest, that I love the best
Are strange – nay, rather stranger than the rest.

Another lurch of his small car as a juggernaut went close by, a siren of abuse trailing in its wake, yet Ivan still kept his eyes shut and imagined he saw the image not of anyone he recognized, but that of a girl, a pale oval face with huge dark eyes – eyes filled with such longing that he couldn't bear it any longer.

He blinked as this vision blurred into infinity and the external thrum from the M4 continued. 'Look, I've got two more pottery classes to do,' he found himself telling whoever it was importuning him. 'Just two, that's all, then I'm free – then I'll take you back.'

'*Promise me ... promise me...*' the voice insisted, until he weakened further.

'OK, I promise.'

He was shaking badly, waiting for that same tug on his arm, that other will strong enough to pull him off the motorway. But no, this time the Saxo obeyed sweetly, and it found the middle lane with enough throttle to keep it there.

With some relief, Ivan unwrapped a humbug with his teeth, as he finally turned off the motorway just past Swindon. When he switched on the radio, some Welsh hymn sung by a male-voice choir ebbed its melancholy into the car – but try as he might, he couldn't make out a single word of it.

There were no other incidents on his journey home, apart from a too-early darkness which seemed to have been flung across the sky in one fell swoop. The rain was easing, and by the time Ivan reached Nether Wapford it was an imperceptible drizzle, leaving behind a heavy dampness which almost solidified in his lungs.

When he'd unlocked the front door, to his surprise there was an envelope lying on the mat. On the front was handwritten *Ivan Browning. Urgent.*

He ripped it open and read the enclosed message with growing alarm.

Please call as soon as you can. I am very frightened. You must help me, Valerie.

Shit, what to do? He needed to get those urns in the kiln, do the worksheets for Tuesday evening, and organize price lists for a Christmas sale in Burcote. Apart from anything else, he was starving. Yet Valerie Rook's needs were clearly greater than his.

Ivan tried phoning her first, but her number was engaged, and a nub of fear began settling in his stomach as he wondered who it could be on her line.

The evening was still dark and moist, and, on the badly drained roads, pools of rainwater lay treacherously deep near the verges. As he passed Wiseman's Farm, Ivan noticed something different about the place. The gate was wide open and beyond, almost blocking out the unlit farmhouse, stood a couple of large green trucks whose sidelights cast a hazy glow in the gloom.

He wondered about the identical green one he'd encountered that morning – what it had really carried and where it had been.

Upon reaching Cold Firton, he saw that same Nissan parked outside the thatched cottages, and signs of activity in particular around number three. All the house's windows were lit behind carelessly drawn curtains, and as he drove by he could see three figures silhouetted in the open doorway. He slowed down and, as he stared, felt his heartbeat surge. One of them was definitely Jo from the pub, wearing skin-tight jeans and high heels, stunning and unattainable.

Shit.

He suddenly turned, without indicating, into Church House's drive, and made sure the Saxo was well hidden from the road. No way was he going to make his visit so obvious again, by leaving it by the kerb of the main road. And if Michael Rook himself was around, Ivan had an excuse for calling. However, the only car visible was Valerie's, and the Saab was missing.

She answered the door even before his second knock, looking suddenly ten years older. It was as if she'd just seen a ghost.

'Thank you for coming,' she whispered. 'I'm sorry to bother you but I've had a foul letter. More like a death threat, really.'

'Where's your husband?'

'In London till late on Thursday.'

'That's handy,' Ivan muttered. 'So who was on your phone just now?'

'He was, just checking I'm OK.'

Once the front door was shut, with the security chain in position, she ushered him into the cold front lounge full of dark auction-house furniture. When she switched on the light, he glanced first at the desk whose crucial bottom drawer seemed undisturbed, and then at a manila envelope lying on an occasional table.

'What's going on?' he asked.

'Please read it,' she said, her voice high and brittle. 'It came this morning. It's exactly what old Mr and Mrs Tripp used to get.'

Ivan studied the printed label, the Banbury postmark, and the first-class stamp neatly aligned with the envelope's corner. Then he extracted the folded sheet inside, mindful to keep his fingerprints to a minimum. His weary eyes widened as he read:

A WARNING, SO WATCH IT, MRS R.

He replaced the letter in the envelope, and looked Valerie in the eye.

'I told you the Oakleys saw me leaving here,' he said. 'I'm trouble as far as they're concerned, ever since my car went missing.'

'Look, it's me they're after, not you.'

But he wasn't entirely convinced. 'Haven't you told your husband or the police?' he urged.

'I can't do that.'

Ivan sighed. 'Look, there is such a thing as DNA testing now. You know, spit under the stamps, on the flap and so on.'

She shook her head in defiance.

'Then *I* will,' he said.

Suddenly she gripped his arm and he noticed her nails were bitten to the quick. 'OK, I'll do it anonymously,' he persisted.

'*No*. I just wanted *you* to see it. Anyhow, that's not all. Follow me.'

She reached the partially glazed back door and opened it. 'Hold your nose, mind. It's not very nice.' She pointed to the nearby drain.

Light from the kitchen window enabled him to see that it was covered by a pile of dog turds – a brown reeking heap carefully stacked.

'This is *totally sick*,' Ivan muttered and glanced round, wondering if it was some Oakley who'd nipped over the churchyard wall. Then he realized that anybody could have sneaked round just as easily from the front.

'You stay indoors. I'll just have a look round.'

He peered into the rhododendron bushes which separated Church House from the nearest of the three terraced cottages. No way could anyone have got through that dense foliage. Next he checked out Valerie's Lada, then caught his breath as he went closer. In the faint glow from the hall he could see that all four tyres were down – each with a gaping slit in their rubber.

Just then, he heard a distant siren drawing nearer from beyond the church. He ran down the drive and crouched by the wet hedge, expecting whatever it was to pass. Instead, an ambulance with its intermittent blue light strobing the street halted next to the Nissan. Seconds later a stretcher was carried over to the end cottage's door.

Other lights came on in the adjoining cottages and suddenly Ivan was aware of Valerie standing behind him, the smell of damp clothes noticeable.

'Here's hoping that's one less then,' she said flatly. 'And good riddance too.'

They both watched as the now loaded stretcher was shunted back into the ambulance, and Jo and a man who might have been her father climbed in after it.

'Who's that young woman?' Valerie peered into the gloom.

He tried to keep his voice bland, despite not being able to take his eyes off her.

'Jo Oakley, his daughter. The one I was asking about.'

'Oh right. I wouldn't be surprised if they've popped Ma Oakley off,' his companion went on. 'She wasn't exactly hard up, and that cottage is worth a good bit now.'

The siren picked up again and then the vehicle reversed into the Church House drive and sped off in a mist of spray.

Ivan led Valerie towards her car, a sudden tiredness in his step. No way could he tell her of his recent strange journey to Wales, or his encounter with Gerry Daniels. Her own plate of shit was already piled high enough.

'Look, I'll help clear that mess up if you've got a shovel or something, but there's also this, I'm afraid.' He pointed to the wheels.

Valerie let out a gasp, inspected the damage then pulled herself together and went to fetch her camera. As she took several photos with the flash, Ivan set to and cleared the drain with an old shovel, chucking the revolting mess over into the field behind. He left the implement propped up against the house wall for the rain to clean it.

'Remember, my husband mustn't know about any of this.' Valerie used the last shot, wound the film back and removed it.

'OK, but you ought to have a gate put up at the end of your drive,' he suggested. 'At least you could keep it locked.'

'Nothing'll keep *them* out,' she said. 'I can tell you that from past experience. Anyhow, now I have this,' and she patted the finished roll of film.

Ivan imagined he heard a car driving over the cinders towards them, but it was bare branches scraping the churchyard wall.

'Look, I must be going. Ring me if you have any more problems, right?'

'I will. And thank you again.'

He left Valerie hovering by her front door – a vulnerable yet defiant figure in the half-light. As Ivan drove away, he suddenly had the most overpowering feeling of helplessness – fearing that should the nutter who'd sent her that foul note go one step further, it was possible he might never see her again.

'Mr Hubbard said there was a man's body found over by Clifford just after a drove went through. He was half eaten by summat, God knows what.' Then Pansy noticed Siân's sudden deathly pallor. 'Hey, what's the matter? What's it to you, all of that?' The sweep girl stared at her as if she was already halfway into Siân's brain.

'Nothing. I was just thinking of that poor man.'

'That's not all.' Pansy wiped her nose, leaving a pale smear across her mouth. 'There's robbers out by the river. Mrs Dickens at the Post and Horses said Constable Burrows's got her son looking out as well as the Carter brothers from Pottery Lane.'

As Siân got up, the grass stung her hand.

'Where you from then?' Pansy demanded. 'If you're going same way as me, I'll come along with you.'

'No, no. I'm–'

'Hey, wassat?' The girl saw blood where Siân had been sitting, and before she could cover it up, Pansy had pulled up her dress. 'You bin hurt or summat?' She frowned.

'No.' Siân pushed the girl's hands away, tripping on her own hem. Then Pansy eyed her knowingly.

'You can be having a baby if that stuff don't come regular. Did you know that?'

Siân laid a hand on her own stomach, which felt bloated.

'So you're still all right. See what I mean?'

The Welsh girl nodded.

'You ever had a man inside you? Like this?'

Pansy wiggled a finger – more like a worm than John Griffiths's thing, Siân thought.

'*No.*'

Pansy looked disappointed. And if she'd had the time, would have furnished her new acquaintance with details of Mr Hubbard's predilections and those of the wheelwright over at Parson's Green. How the one liked girls of a certain young age, and the other would take his own grandmother if he could.

'Well, grab me hand, you. I'm goin' to see if we can get you a proper dress. Whoever gave you that must want you looking like an old woman. 'Sides, it's full of mess.'

Siân tried to say that she didn't want to look any prettier – at least not for what Tomos had got in mind – but Pansy was leading the way back into town, and down Argyll Street, a narrow lane of shops and brick houses squashed up together near the river. Siân could see the top of the city's cathedral and she smelt the fumes coming off a tannery works farther along.

Number 26 declared *C. Hubbard, Sweep and Handyman*, by means of a large green board on the wall adjoining the gate.

'Handy with his hands an' all,' the girl muttered as she pushed open the side gate. Then she hollered. 'Mrs H? Got someone for yer.'

The sweep's mother appeared immediately, a threaded needle clasped between her lips, her shawl covered by trails of coloured cottons. Two shrivelled eyes took in every detail of the Welsh girl. Finally she slid the needle out of her mouth and secured it below her collar.

'Any friend of Pansy's is welcome here. What's your name then, young lady?'

'It's no good you talking to her normally, Mrs H, 'cos she can't speak. She was in an accident, see,' the girl explained. 'And she needs new clothes.'

'I'm all right, really. I don't need anything at all.' Siân was blushing with nerves and a fear of her identity being discovered. *'I just want to be on my way.'*

The old woman was staring at her so hard that Siân averted her eyes towards a small brick outbuilding with the word PRIVY daubed in uneven whitewashed letters on its side, from which the unmistakable smell of ordure was escaping.

'If ye'd a mite more patience, Pansy, ye'd lissen hard and watch your friend's mouth. She *is* talking.'

Pansy bent closer and Siân grabbed her arm.

'I've got to go. Now.'

'Why? Mrs H'll set you up nice and proper in no time.'

'You don't understand,' Siân whispered.

'Well, tell us then.' Mrs Hubbard was now intrigued, and, seemingly being of a kindly if naive disposition, moved nearer and rested an arm round Siân's shoulders. 'Tell us so we can try.'

'It's my brother and that Mrs Griffiths up at the Farrier. They're going to make me do more bad things – tonight.'

Pansy and Mrs H exchanged a brief glance.

'I'd rather be dead.'

'What do you mean, more bad things?' The

216

seamstress frowned and Siân knew that the time had come to tell what she was up against. She wanted to make a new friend with Pansy now that her former friend, Eirwen had gone. Pansy wasn't sweet simple Eirwen, but she surely had enough of a good heart to be trusted. Yes, it was time to share things, and with plentiful gesticulations and both listeners lip-reading hard, Siân's story was eventually told.

'Dear God, child, it's a wonder I don't call the constable right this minute.' Mrs Hubbard was already by the gate before she'd finished. 'That brother of yours is not fit to be travelling with you. He should be locked up with the strays that come in off Dinedor meadows.'

'No, no. I must get to London. It's my only chance.'

Pansy who'd stayed silent throughout the girl's account, suddenly spoke. 'I'll tell you what, Siân. I've got one more chimney to do then I'll be straight back here. After that I'll become like your shadow, and you'll not be seeing your brother again on your own.' With that, she was off.

Siân hesitated, as a few wisps of cloud finally left the low sun clear.

'Come on in now, child,' Mrs Hubbard cajoled, 'and I'll get some tea going for you.' She helped the girl inside and, having seated her at the table, put the black kettle on the stove then stoked the coal underneath until a glow appeared.

'She's a good girl is Pansy. One of the best.' The dressmaker fetched a plain white cup from the shelf. 'O' course it's a shame she has to go up the chimneys, but I can't say nothing to my son,

Christmas – it's how he keeps a roof over our heads.' She then set a piece of buttered bread in front of Siân, who devoured it in one go.

Mrs Hubbard stared in surprise at her starving guest, then opened an old wooden cupboard from which she produced a cooked chicken, turned it over so the missing section wouldn't show, and placed a slice of the cold meat between two crusts of bread.

'Christmas won't notice a morsel like that gone missing.' She passed it over to Siân, watching as that too disappeared before she could scarcely blink. 'Now, you can tell me to mind me own business, but before he gets back I'm going to pack you up some victuals and stitch you up a skirt.'

'*Thank you, Mrs Hubbard. You're very kind, but I don't want to get you into bother.*'

'It's no bother, and if you was my daughter I'd see you went out looking nice, with a full belly to boot.'

Suddenly a sharp knock at the door made them both jump.

'Who be that, I wonder? Oh dearie dear.'

The second knock was louder, more insistent.

Instinctively, Siân hid under the table, glad its cloth reached down so far.

'Now who's troubling an old woman on the day of rest?' Mrs Hubbard grumbled, opening the door. 'Yes? What is it?'

Siân sensed whoever was there was making her anxious.

'Police, ma'am. Constable Burrows.'

'I don't want no police here. It's Sunday.

218

Besides, I haven't done nothing wrong.'

'I'm not saying you have, ma'am, and I'm sure the Lord will forgive us working on His day, but due to the special nature of the crime we're trying to solve, we have no choice. Now, I'd like a look round, if it's all the same to you.'

Twelve

The trucks previously at Wiseman's Farm had now gone and the gate was closed. Like its derelict neighbour, there were no lights to be seen anywhere, and Ivan drove the rest of his journey home as fast as weather conditions allowed, guilty at leaving Valerie and thinking of her obvious isolation within a strained marriage.

Suddenly he was no longer alone.

Badly adjusted double headlights were beaming in on him from behind, filling his wing mirrors with a blinding glare. The vehicle tailgated so close to him that if he braked as a warning, whoever it was would collide with the back of him. So instead he hogged the middle of the narrow road, concentrating on not letting the screwball get by.

All at once, while approaching Trappers' Lane on the left, Ivan saw a familiar green truck pull out to block his way. The number plate had been removed.

Gerry Daniels?

He slammed on the brakes and locked himself in. *Don't react. Don't speak. Don't look anyone in the eye. This won't take long – they can't block the way for fucking ever... Someone else's bound to come along.*

A man got out of the vehicle behind him and strode over to the Citroën. He was a thickset figure with an anorak hood keeping his face in shadow.

'You!' Then a loud knock on the window. 'You're into big trouble now with your meddling.' The stranger's weight rocked the Saxo back and forth. 'And we're running out of patience. But next time, *mon ami*–' big gloved fists pummelled the glass – 'next time, you and that nosy bitch won't be so lucky.'

Ivan now recognized the voice.

As a parting shot the bully wrenched the wing mirror askew, then kicked the tyre and shouted a command to the truck driver.

The man finally disappeared from view as the truck screeched back into the side lane it had emerged from. Then, as quickly as they'd come, both vehicles vanished, leaving Ivan marooned in a hell's darkness, beneath trees whose dislocated limbs scratched the car roof. He crashed into first gear then picked up speed ... 50 ... 60 ... 70...

He didn't care about speeding any more: anything to leave that goddamned road behind...

As he reached Nether Wapford, his lights picked up a flood warning sign. The river was well over the level of the bridge, like slurry under his wheels, and for a few seconds the car lost its momentum, until hitting the incline and pulling through and clear.

'*You promised me, please... You promised...*'

That same pale young face again seemed to form on his windscreen, yet was translucent enough for him to still see, through its moving lips, the first dwellings of his village.

Suddenly his engine surged as if this were a 20-valve Merc, not the cheapest hatch on the market. The Saxo seemed out of control, drawn by some huge invisible force right past his cottage, and along the flooded ruts of Syke's Way.

Ivan screamed in panic, screamed again, and wrenched the steering wheel round to take him off the road itself and up the bridle path to Sykeston. Only when a grassy ridge wedged the chassis underneath did he actually come to a stop.

'Christ Jesus, are you trying to kill me?' he yelled at his mystery tormentor, not sure if the engine was still ticking over. 'I'll be no good to you dead. Have you thought of *that*?'

What was he *saying*? Who was he talking to? What the *fuck* was he into? He had no doubt he was being manipulated. But where would it bloody end? Where?

His fags had fallen to the floor and he groped about to find them. Then he climbed out and locked the car, and stood to get his bearings. Outside was only a silent blackness. He'd once walked up this track in the summer just after he'd moved in here, and very pretty it had been too: one of the forest's outermost ridings, wide and green, with a wheat field the other side and the Norman tower of St Mary's church straight ahead.

Now, however, with the night rain picking up and a wind rising from the east, it wasn't somewhere to linger. He got back in the Saxo and crawled along in second gear until he reached the Queen Eleanor, a tiny public house on the edge of the village green. With relief, Ivan parked outside, glad of the early Christmas lights winking around the porch and the warm glow shining from the single leaded window.

The one main room was dominated by a huge open fire whose logs spat and crackled as they burnt. An aged dog lay on the hearthrug and, nearby, a young couple, probably not local, were removing their coats before studying the menu.

'Long time no see.' Bryn Mitchell wiped a glass tankard dry with an expert flourish and held it up to the light. 'How you doing, mister potter man?' He then put the glass down and focused on the new arrival's haggard expression. 'Or shouldn't I ask?'

'Some bastard was trying to drive me off Syke's Way, that's all. Seems to be a common feature of this area.' Ivan couldn't face relaying what had actually happened, just needed something calming to pour down his throat. He studied the evening's food offerings scrawled on a blackboard next to the bar, but nothing tempted him, even though his stomach felt like a hollow pit.

'Tell me about it,' Mitchell concurred flatly. 'They think the Silverstone racetrack covers the entire bloody county. So, what can I get you?'

'Half a bitter and–' remembering his lack of funds – 'a ham roll, thanks.'

He settled himself on one of the bar stools, feeling the fire's warmth caress his back. It had been a long, horrendous day. For a moment he closed his eyes, listening to the sudden crackles of the fire, the hidden songs as the oak logs surrendered to its flames.

'There we go, cheers.'

The drink placed in front of him glowed like amber. He'd tried to make a transparent glaze that colour once, but hadn't cracked the formula. He'd used either too much silicon carbide or not enough, the same with lead sequisilicate – all of it a delicate balancing act, with the kiln fire as saboteur.

Now the drink began to relax him, the couple's chatter in the corner drowned the noise behind the grate. And when the publican had taken their order through to the kitchen, he poured himself a half too and sat alongside.

'You heard about the chef at the Lamb and Flag?' he asked.

Ivan started. 'Only that he'd not been in to work.'

'Poor sod. He lived here in the village, you know. Just up in Park Street, number eight.'

Without fully knowing why, Ivan made a mental note of that address. 'What's happened to him?'

'Not sure if it was deliberate or what,' the man took a sip, 'but, anyway, they found him up in Wapford Forest. He'd hanged himself.'

'Oh Jesus.' Ivan stared at the froth in his own glass. Saw again that pale swaying shape in his cottage – the *deadness* of it...

'Apparently he left a note saying he'd had enough. It's the girlfriend and kiddie I feel sorry for.'

The young woman from the corner coughed to attract Mitchell's attention and, once he'd pointed out the door to the ladies' room, resumed his tale. 'Only eighteen she is, and the baby's not two months old.'

'That's dreadful.' Ivan nodded hello to Ann Mitchell, the landlord's wife as she delivered his roll then retreated. 'Do they know *why* he did it? I mean, what had he had enough *of?*'

'You tell me. Except there's always been some trouble or other since Harold Oakley took that place over.'

'When was that then?' Ivan asked as casually as he could. Never again would he give away too much. You never knew about people.

'May '98, and what a big palaver that was. Had an opening night with you-name-it, and Harold Oakley paid for it all – fireworks, the lot. And he's not stopped since, trying to tempt my business away by dreaming up this and that to get the punters in. Even gets his own niece to parade herself there. But don't you trust a word she says, either. Fibber's her middle name, just like the rest of them.'

'If that's Jo, she's his daughter, surely?' Ivan said bleakly.

Mitchell's surprise lasted barely a second, then he shrugged. 'There you go. What did I say? Can't believe anything they tell you. Anyhow, she's still a real looker.'

Ivan turned cold inside. 'What do you mean by her parading herself?'

'Exactly what I said.'

He couldn't shift Mitchell's disturbing comment from his head, and was still frowning as the landlord's wife brought in two plates of rump steak for the waiting couple. The dog finally woke

225

up and placed himself, alert, by their table.

'You sure you wouldn't like the same?' The woman looked his way. 'It's what the drovers always used to order at the end of a day.'

'Drovers?'

'Ah. So you *are* with us after all.' She mocked him gently. 'Yes, this was a regular stopping place. We've still got the Halfpenny Field next door that they used to rent out to house cattle. Mind you, the old forge belongs to the vet and his wife now.'

'Where did these drovers come from, then?'

'Wales mostly. Then on to London after their cattle had fattened up a bit. Or, if there were any fatstock sales happening in March, they'd sell them at those, rather than wait for the store sales in May.'

'Store sales?' Ivan had never heard the expression before.

'Stock that needs to grow a bit, young ones, but nice tender meat. Mind you, the Welsh breeds, especially the blacks with their long horns, were all called runts – small but dangerous.' She smiled at him again and rubbed one of the items off the blackboard with her cuff. 'Some drovers did settle in the county though. Found the living easier than back home.' She gave her husband a playful nudge. 'I mean Bryn's hardly your typical East Midlands name, is it?'

Ivan bit into his roll, trying to make connections, trying to recall what he'd experienced the night before by the Severn Bridge – and that strange language which had somehow flowed deep into his psyche... But no way would he tell these good people any of that, or an army of men in white coats might be round at the drop of a hat.

'The previous landlord had some old drawings which he told me he donated to the Local History Society in Grey Snorton. If you're at all interested, you could go and take a look,' she added.

'Like Wild West country it was at one time here,' Mitchell added. 'And wild's the bloody word again, if you ask me.'

Ivan drained his glass and pulled one of his business cards from his wallet, and asked if they'd display it somewhere.

'Delighted to. Some seasonal shoppers might come your way once they're full up with beer and feeling generous.'

Having thanked them, Ivan stepped out into the rain and pulled up his collar. As he unlocked the Saxo, he thought again of the Lamb and Flag's chef and what might have driven the new father to such an end. He also thought about Jo – how her whole life seemed now to be one big lie. But why? And if she was the tart that Bryn Mitchell had implied, why hadn't Ivan picked up on that and run a mile? Maybe she just had to do as she was told by her father. And Monica Oakley was hardly the sort of mother a daughter could confide in, surely?

Then Ivan had an idea. It wouldn't take him long, but he had to find more proof of that dodgy family's *modus operandi*. He located a Saxo Information Pack in the glove box, and tore off a blank piece from one of its pages. In the light from the one street lamp he wrote:

I would like to help you.

Then, having added his phone number at the end, he walked back up beyond the pub, past the village green, and into a short muddy lane lined with council houses.

Number eight looked totally unoccupied, but nevertheless he continued up its gateless path and pushed the folded slip of paper through the letter box. He then hurried back to the car before anyone could waylay him, the wind now slanting the rain diagonally across the nearby fields. His pulse was jumping with nerves. If that note got into the wrong hands, he'd be really for it. But, if what he suspected was true, that Cotton too, just like Valerie, had been the victim of threats, and God knows what else, how could he just stand by?

Mr Carp's house was still disconcertingly empty after his disappearance, and all the climbing greenery he'd so lovingly pruned back, now rambled over brickwork and windows alike, making the whole place look surreally like a piece of topiary. Lily Jonas, however, could be seen silhouetted in her nightdress against the light shining between her parted curtains. At least, since the cat business, she'd not been round to do any more complaining, but Ivan didn't doubt that, before long, things would get back to square one.

Ivan groped his way up the path, then suddenly

he stopped. A light-coloured feedstuffs bag lay popped up against his front door. A flicker of recognition dawned for, even in the poor light, he could see that it was yellow with green lettering: exactly the same one that he'd seen bumping along down the River Wap.

Alton's Molasses, it read, and he prodded the bag with his boot. Molasses were clearly the last thing it contained. When he eased apart the string ties at the top, he nearly fell back off the step as his stomach heaved. He'd seen an eye and a black nose inside, smelt the stale blood, and that was enough. He charged round to his elderly neighbour, banging on her door.

'Who left that dead dog on my doorstep?' he choked after she appeared in an old dressing gown pocked by fag burns. She went back in to fetch a torch, her lumpy behind sticking out as she bent down by the understairs cupboard.

'Oi can guess, can't ye? These are dark days all right.' She switched on the beam and followed him through the gusting rain back to his cottage. When he'd plucked up courage to open the bag a little further, the torchlight showed clearly a young, collarless Border collie, its legs tied together with twine. She let out a gasp of horror.

'Tha's Tom Coles's dog. Oh for Jesus's sake. Now why's tha' been left for ye, oi wonder? 'Ave ye been putting yer nose where it's not wanted?'

'Christ knows, but maybe because I've been asking a few pertinent questions.'

'Well, don't ye forget what 'appened to Mr Carp. And don't say oi didn't warn ye.'

The moment he'd unlocked his door, she was

in first and already nosing around. Ivan stepped after her into the tiny hallway and picked up the unsolicited newspaper from the small table. He located the dog's photo, a perfect match, then he dialled the police to report his grisly find. 'Answerphone,' he called to her, hoping she wasn't reading his post. 'I've been told to try Northampton.'

'Go on, then.' She turned to him, her eyes puffy, her breath still smelling of her last fag. 'Make 'em earn their money.'

When Ivan finally got through to HQ at Woolerton, the duty sergeant simply suggested that some passing motorist had just dumped the sack at random like they sometimes do in a divorce or break-up.

'I'm not a halfwit, d'you mind?' Ivan retorted. 'I've checked the dog with the photo in the paper. It's Fly all right. Tom Coles's pet. *And* I've got a witness that it was dumped on my doorstep.'

'I can tell you, sir, that every weekend the various canine rescue services inform us of at least five dogs disposed of in local rivers, et cetera. With farmers going under, it'll probably get worse. I can give you the RSPCA's number, if you like.'

'Bit late for that, isn't it?' said Ivan sourly. Then he glanced at Mrs Jonas who seemed to be egging him on. 'Supposing there's vital evidence here? Obviously whoever killed Tom Coles did this too, out of sheer bloody spite. So there could be vital clues on the dog itself, as well as on the feed bag. Why don't you come over immediately?'

'Sorry, sir, but I've made my point. Got to leave it there, I'm afraid. Another call's just come in.'

Ivan replaced the receiver and kicked the skirting board.

'It's like fartin' in the wind with them lot,' his neighbour observed. 'Tell ye what, though,' she made a move for the door, 'give me two secs to make myself decent and we'll bury him next to Marcie.' She hesitated as if that name had caught her unawares. 'That way, if they do decide to pull their fingers out and dig him up, least he'll be somewhere handy.'

At 11.20 p.m., wearing an old mac over her nightdress and with tears leaking from her eyes, Mrs Jonas, with a phlegmy tremble to her voice, sang 'The Lord's my Shepherd' once more, as Ivan lowered the feed bag into the ground. Ivan brooded not just on the poor dog – that was bad enough – but also on what this butchery represented.

The evil around him was now palpable. It seemed to be in every crow call, every stinging drop of persistent rain, and, as he spread the last of the sodden earth evenly with his spade and then relaid the turf, Ivan knew he probably couldn't hold himself together much longer. Something was bound to give, soon.

Siân held her breath, smelling the street on the constable's feet. His voice rumbled from a huge frame above her as she kept herself tucked up tight and silent, even though her leg was cramping.

231

'We're looking for two Taffies – one's a roughneck drover, the other's a girl who's not quite right, if you get my meaning.' He tapped his head.

'Why ask me?' Mrs Hubbard demanded, turning pink.

'She was seen coming by the end of your street together with a little red-head, so we believe.'

The dressmaker tutted, and Siân could tell she was annoyed. 'It's that Miss Pokerface from Albany gossiping again. She'll lie in her grave still a-snooping.'

'I'm not repeating who it was told us, ma'am, but we can't ignore what folks tell us. Jails'd be empty otherwise...'

Siân's heart thudded as the toe of his boot nearly touched her.

'All I'm saying is this girl would know where the drover man might be. So, I ask again, did she call here?'

'No, sir, I've not seen no one since my Christmas left the house this morning with his breakfast in his hand.'

Burrows sniffed Siân's teacup. 'What's this then?'

'It's mine.' The old woman was indignant. 'I always have a cup of tea at three o'clock.'

'Mm.' Siân heard him move away.

The constable pushed his way through the curtains, into the workshop beyond the kitchen.

'I've a mind to talk with your little red-head. Where's she now?' his voice carried back.

Siân bit her lip, praying Pansy wouldn't suddenly reappear and that Mrs Hubbard would

232

think of something quickly. An instant later her second prayer was answered.

'We don't have no red-head here. My son never trusts them – calls them tinkers' leavings, that's what.'

'You know, it's a funny world, Mrs Hubbard–' the man was moving things about, checking in her old wardrobe – 'but there's folks complain of us as dead-weights, and I won't mention that Mr Cobbett's name in polite company, yet they won't help us get to the bottom of things–'

She interrupted. 'I've always been one to help the law, and so does Christmas, too. Now then,' she fetched another cup from the shelf, 'would a cup of tea be needed? It's hard work out there, traipsing the street.'

Siân prayed that he'd decline, and he did, bidding the sweep's mother a terse goodbye as he crossed the kitchen again and went out, closing the door behind him. She let out a long sigh of relief and crawled out, her weak leg stiff and sore.

'I almost forgot you was there,' Mrs Hubbard helped her up onto a chair and drew the bolt of the door across, 'so quiet was you.'

'*I'm used to it.*' Siân smiled, and it was the sweetest prettiest smile the dressmaker had ever seen. '*And I know when to look like a statue, too.*' Then she remembered Tomos's mad eyes and how angry he would be, and a shiver of fear spasmed through her.

In the uneasy aftermath of the constable's visit, the dressmaker went into her workroom and set to stitching together a pair of pantaloons in such fine wool it felt like silk.

233

Siân sat with the garment close up against her cheek, reminded of her pony's soft coat, wondering if she was being taken care of. Also of Huw and his cold days in the forest. Tomos and those callous Griffiths would be missing her now, and making a fuss, but for the moment at least she was safe.

While Mrs Hubbard worked on a skirt, she plied Siân with questions about her home village. It mattered not that she heard no replies from her young companion, for she always had her imagination to supply them.

Never in all her sixty-six years had she seen such a poor creature – so thin, so ill-treated, and she kept busy at checking the hem was even, and the fit of the waistband perfect, sure in her mind that none of this effort would be wasted. By four o'clock, the new skirt was finished. She helped Siân to her feet, then held it up against her so its smart red and grey stripes were fully visible.

Siân felt like a queen, particularly when a matching grey blouse was altered to fit her.

'I'll be having a sewing machine soon, my Christmas says. He can get one from Hobdays, only wanting a bit of repair. Then I'll really be busy.' After dressing the girl, she brushed out Siân's ringlets until her dark hair was full of its natural soft curls. Then, to Siân's surprise, she nicked a stitch in Mary Griffiths's blue woollen dress and unravelled it into one large crinkly ball.

'And that's the end of *that* abomination,' she said, giving the girl's face a final wipe over. 'There.' She stood back to admire the transformation, then frowned.

'Now we can't have you still carting that old man's jacket around, can we? 'Sides, it's nowhere near warm enough.'

Siân watched as Moses Evans's kind donation was hung behind the kitchen door, and a shawl almost the size of a bedspread was lifted out of a wooden chest by the far wall. 'This is more the thing for a young woman.' Mrs Hubbard pinned it together at the front with a brooch in the shape of a fish. Not valuable, obviously, yet pretty enough. However, Siân tried to give it back.

'*Tomos will only take it,*' she whispered. '*Give it to Pansy instead.*'

But the woman suddenly seemed preoccupied. She looked first at the clock and then at the door, before sliding back the bolt and peering out into the afternoon.

'Pansy's late,' she tutted. 'Now I thought *you* was hungry, but she's worse. She'd never miss her tea. Specially on a Sunday.'

Under her new clothes Siân felt another shiver of anxiety.

'Her bit of the work never takes more than a half hour, for any house,' the woman continued. 'I'm just going to stand by the gate and see if she's coming.'

'*Mrs Hubbard.*' Siân touched the woman's arm to make her pause. '*Does Pansy live here – with you and Mr Christmas?*'

'Course she does. Where else has she got to go?'

'*So where's her Mam and Da, then?*'

'Mam and Da?' She let out a laugh which Siân thought the oddest she'd ever heard. 'My Christmas is her Da.' She kept her eyes fixed on the street. 'Her mam passed on in childbed, didn't she?'

Unwelcome thoughts threaded their way into Siân's head. What if Pansy did not come back despite her promise? Why had she made up that address in Rowbottom Lane and why had she called herself Palmer? And what was that sly remark about Mr Hubbard supposed to mean?

'I'd best be going, Mrs Hubbard,' she blurted. *'And thank you.'*

Siân tried to edge past her, but the woman suddenly got tight hold of the shawl behind her neck.

Thirteen

The wind woke Ivan, tearing at the jungle of bare wisteria entwined round the drainpipe and rattling the panes of the bedroom window.

It was 10.30 a.m., and Ivan's first thought was of his pottery class that evening: an unappealing prospect after what had seemed his lifetime in hell since the last one. He pulled the duvet back over his head, but nagging thoughts of the worksheets and preparations for the coiling demonstration prevailed. Within ten minutes he was washed, dressed and making his way downstairs.

Two letters lay at angles to each other on the mat, one with a handwritten envelope, the other franked by Reedman Insurance Services. He opened the latter first, to learn that a cheque covering the loss of his mobile and other possessions was being processed.

The thought of some imminent money cheered him up considerably, but as he opened the second letter, his empty stomach began to churn.

CHURCH HOUSE
COLD FIRTON

Tuesday 9a.m.

Dear Mr Browning,
I'm sorry to have to write to you in this vein, but

237

suffice it to say that I feel it unwise for us to have any further private contact, unless of course, your presence is part of any Art and Craft event in the village. I can't go into details here, but I trust you understand my somewhat delicate situation.

Good luck with your pottery classes, and my husband too sends his regards.

> *Yours sincerely,*
> *Valerie Rook*

What on earth had brought this on, Ivan wondered. He'd even planned to ask her to go with him to the County Record Office and check on what the Small Copse housekeeper, Caroline Tripp, had once revealed. *Damn.* He could feel the draught whipping in under the front door and suddenly, like the old days in Barton Road, felt more alone than ever.

He picked up the phone, then put it down, not really wanting to hear her rejection spelt out again. But the moment he replaced the receiver, it rang, making him jump.

'Ivan Browning speaking.' He heard coins dropping, then a breathy voice and what sounded like a baby whimpering in the background.

'You said you could help... I'm afraid my money's running out... It's Jeanette Yates, Malcolm Cotton's partner–' Her voice became a sob.

'Give me your phone-box number,' Ivan urged. 'I'll call you straight back.'

After he'd scribbled it down, he hung up and dialled. She answered straightaway.

'Where exactly are you?' he asked.

'In Sykeston, by the green. Look, I don't normally go phoning strangers, and you could even be one of *their* lot–'

'Who's they?'

'The Oakleys, of course.'

'For pity's sake, I run a pottery in Nether Wapford and I'm a Lifelong Learning tutor.' Here he paused. 'I'm really sorry about what's happened to you. Bryn Mitchell at the Queen Eleanor told me.'

'Have the police called on you yet?' She was trying to sound strong, in control. 'They said they were going to question everyone in Nether Wapford.'

'I was away till yesterday afternoon, but not a whisper so far.'

'Fuck them – and the Oakleys. Malc worked hard for them.'

Her anger was beginning to show. 'And to cap it all, that little slapper of theirs tried to take him off me. Making out like he was the only man on this planet.'

'You mean Jo Oakley?' He felt a shameful stab of jealousy, picturing her again – her perfect breasts, her smooth and lightly tanned skin. 'The one with the kid?'

'You must be joking: her spoil her figure for a kid? Anyway, I reckon there was a reason why she tried getting into his trousers. She was finding things out for them, wasn't she? Like she'd been ordered to, or *paid* to.'

'What things?'

Ivan was reluctant to hear any worse news

about the girl who'd had such an instant effect on him, and felt more depressed by the second.

'Well, my Malc was pissed off big time with them going after the deer and making loads of dough, while he had to bloody fight them for every measly little pay rise. In the end, he went to the cops, but they were bloody useless as usual – specially that Marsh wanker. Last September that was, and he reckoned he'd got the names of at least four London restaurants taking the stuff.'

'So how would the Oakleys ever know he did that?'

'Someone in the force must have told them. But the worst thing is, they're trying to make it look like he topped himself–' She broke off and Ivan could hear her choking back her sobs.

'Hey, just try and keep talking. See if we can piece some bits together?'

'The last time I saw him he was taping some Macy Gray for me off the radio. That was yesterday morning, just before I popped into town on the bus with Nicola to get some more nappies.'

'But I thought there was a suicide note, saying, like, he couldn't go on?'

'*He* never wrote no note! That was the bastard Oakleys trying to stitch things up. They put it in his pocket afterwards, I bet you anything.'

'But he'd not been in to work, had he?' Ivan urged gently.

'He was scared, wasn't he? Like you'd be, scared of what that bastard would threaten next. You wait till the bloody inquest. I'll be shouting it from the bloody rooftops that they snuffed him.'

Her language startled him. If she wasn't careful, he thought...

'Where's Malcolm now?' The question stuck in his throat.

'Northampton General. They thought they could revive him, I suppose. You see, when they cut him down, he wasn't quite – oh, Jesus, help me–'

'Jeanette, listen to me. Is there anyone you could go and stay with, out of the area?' He was aware of the baby beginning to fret.

'No, not really. My parents and brother emigrated to Canada, and I never got on with Malc's lot at all. They hated my guts, said I'd got pregnant deliberately. They live down near Eastleigh.'

Ivan tried the voice of reason. 'But, surely, in this situation they'd help you out?'

'No, never. Not them. I had to phone them yesterday, but they're refusing to see me or even Nicola.'

'Nice people.' Ivan saw the picture getting grimmer and grimmer. 'Thing is, you've got to get away, for the baby's sake as well. These Oakleys are getting desperate.'

'Well, I'm going to get kicked out of the house anyhow.' She took a deep breath. 'We'd got two months behind with the rent, and Malc's job barely paid enough to run his car. That's vanished too: silver Fiesta, nine hundred quids' worth. Mind you, I never drove it. Failed my test twice.'

Ivan saw all too clearly what had happened. The young chef had obviously been waylaid somewhere and his car disposed of. He now didn't

241

know what to say that wouldn't add to her existing worries, but just then Jeanette interrupted his thoughts.

'I suppose we could always go and stay with my mate in Banbury for a while. We did the same Nursery Nurse course at college together. Mind, I only did one year, 'cos by then I'd met Malc and got pregnant.' Her voice began to falter, then, without warning, she replaced the receiver, leaving Ivan's intended reassurance about his plan to expose the truth about the Oakleys, unspoken.

To take his mind off Jeanette's disturbing revelations for half an hour or so, Ivan went into his workshop, and opened up the kiln. He'd already cleaned out the firing chamber, so that not even the tiniest souvenir of that apocalypse remained, and now as the wind hammered the roof and powered down the flue, the firing chamber's pristine cavity gaped ready for his next body of work.

He checked that all of the urns' feet were free of glaze and set each of them on stilts on the freshly batt-washed shelves. Five shelves with four urns apiece: another full load – seven hundred pounds' worth, the most costly batch so far. As usual, for this type of glost firing, he set the pyrometer to 500 degrees and kept both bung holes open.

Then he sat down and wrote out the two worksheets on how to roll and assemble clay coils, the possible shapes and surface treatments – to blend or not to blend – and finally advice on colouring and decoration.

He checked his watch. There'd be time to nip into Stoneshanger to get these photocopied for each of his students, then buy some packed sandwiches and fill up the Saxo's tank. That was if someone else didn't have another agenda for him.

Having finished his errands Ivan crossed over to the Lamb and Flag just to glance in and see if Jo was there. Despite all he had heard about the girl, he could not get her out of his mind. However, to his surprise the premises were locked up, curtains closed, and a small notice had been pinned to the main door.

CLOSED UNTIL FRIDAY 23 NOVEMBER DUE TO FAMILY BEREAVEMENT. WE APOLOGIZE TO OUR CUSTOMERS FOR ANY INCONVENIENCE CAUSED, AND HOPE THIS MEETS WITH YOUR PATIENT UNDERSTANDING AT THIS SAD TIME. SIGNED *H.D. Oakley*

Ivan stared not just at the identical font to the threatening note sent to Valerie, but at the notice's oozing sentimentality.

So, did this relate to Ma Oakley? Had the old witch not made it back to her cottage after all? He surreptitiously pulled the note from its staples and slipped it in his jacket pocket, careful not to introduce too many of his own fingerprints, all the while wondering when and where the funeral might be and what Jo was currently doing with herself.

Midday now, and a sneaky winter sun the colour of mother-of-pearl glanced out between solid grey clouds. Although it was nowhere near spring, Ivan felt a certain sap rising through his whole body, a kind of courage, recklessness even – and Valerie Rooks's letter became a challenge.

The thunder trees that lined this all-too-familiar road were in turmoil – their top-heavy crowns railing against the wind, and scores of birds, he couldn't identify which, hung there buffeted to stasis, unable to fly. Branches littered the verges or lay fractured in the road, and several times he had to manoeuvre round them.

Wiseman's Farm was as discreetly quiet as a crematorium on Christmas Day, but at nearby Small Copse something was definitely going on. Ivan slowed down to see a green truck emerge from behind the farmhouse's blackened end wall, and suddenly pick up speed along the lengthy overgrown drive leading towards the gate. Every nerve of his hungry body was on edge – his sandwiches bouncing on the seat as he stepped on the gas – and just before he turned the bend into Cold Firton he noticed with relief that the road behind him was clear.

He swerved into Church House's drive. But where was her car, any car? And where the hell was anybody? He hurried round to the back, then he stopped dead – his heart pumping. The weathered back door was wide open, yet there was no sign of any tampering with the lock. Nor was there any key.

Oh no, Jesus, no... Not her too, please God. And where's her fucking husband?

244

'Valerie?' he called.

No reply.

Then he heard a powerful engine coming closer along the road and that same truck backing up the drive as if to block it off. He charged back and entered the house, leapt upstairs and into a spare bedroom, where he wrapped himself in the bedspread and squeezed under the bed.

Footsteps were tramping around downstairs now. He wished to God he'd left his incriminating car somewhere else.

'You stupid schmuck, Browning. Where have you got to?'

Daniels's voice sounded quite different from the time when Ivan had shared his cab. What the hell was he doing *here?*

Suddenly the crash of doors and drawers being slammed, and what sounded like an ornament shattering. 'We'll get you, mate, wherever you fucking hide.'

The intruder was on the stairs now, bashing some heavy instrument or other, bashing it on the banisters.

Ivan heard the medicine cabinet spill its contents on the bathroom floor, the shower curtain being ripped aside, then more less identifiable depredations. The guy was on a dangerous high, a space cadet all right, and this was bare-faced intimidation. With a jolt, Ivan realized what Daniels might be looking for.

'Come out, you nosy cunt face!' the same voice bellowed. 'I know you're here somewhere.'

Daniels was in the same room now, and Ivan could see his filthy boots less than a foot away from the valanced coverlet as again more drawers were hauled open and overturned. He pulled the bedspread over his face and prayed. There was enough other junk lying under the bed, for anyone searching to assume he was just another roll of bed linen.

Sudden whistling from below: three sharp blasts like he'd heard in the wood that other night. A signal, obviously, for Daniels turned instantly on his heel and careered back down the stairs.

'Any sign of our troublemaker?' bellowed someone sounding like Harold Oakley.

'Reckon he's legged it over the fields.'

'Take a look over that way, and meet me back at George's in half an hour.'

George's? George Pike? If so, how come Daniels was involved with that garage? And where had Tom Coles fitted in – or hadn't he?

The slamming of the back door brought an end to these thoughts, followed by the loud grating of a key in its lock. Gradually Ivan rolled clear of the bed and stood up.

How the hell had the thugs got in? And whose key were they using now? In the ensuing silence, the more he imagined, the worse it got. Not least that the crucial cigarette lighter might have been stolen. He kicked himself for not having checked the bureau in the lounge. That should have come first on his agenda.

Suddenly he heard a different engine start up and roar off up the hill towards Westhope, but when he got to the landing window to investigate, that same bloody truck was still parked outside.

He began patrolling from window to window, then snatched his breath. There was a figure he recognized outside, staring up at the house. It was Daniels. Then, as if satisfied no one was inside, he turned and sprinted down the drive to the safety of his truck. In two seconds he'd gone, leaving a pall of blue diesel hanging in the air.

Ivan strained to listen in case the silence that followed was a trap and someone else was still hiding inside the house. But having crept along the landing he soon realized that he was alone. Alone and probably bloody well locked in.

As he passed the hall phone he stopped to try it, but the line was dead. As dead as Valerie probably was. When he tried the desk drawer, his hand was shaking. It was unlocked, and he slid it open to reveal an ominously empty space.

His heart sank. The Jiffy bag had gone.

Ivan slumped at the kitchen table, remembering his last conversation with Valerie Rook. He noticed half a cup of cold tea and a Kit Kat wrapper in front of him. She must have been having a snack, been taken by surprise. He dared not think of the rest. Best to call 999 once he could get out of here.

Although the back door had been relocked from outside, the front door Yale lock opened easily, with a short turn of its brass handle. He slipped outside, noting the severed telephone wire by the front wall. His mind was in turmoil, sabotaging any logical appraisal of what to do next. He could go and call on Pam Barker in the new housing development nearby. Better still, he could phone the police from Radby End, the next village along from Westhope, then drive the longer way round back to Nether Wapford. That seemed the least risky option.

George Pike's garage looked as empty as the last time he'd called in. No sign of a green truck, or anything else either, and as he travelled the length of straight road where the Reverend Richard Coombes had been left to die, he prayed intently that somehow Valerie Rook had got away.

'Not so fast, missy.' Mrs Hubbard's eyes had suddenly hardened. 'You owe me for my favours.'

'What do you mean, owe me?' But Siân knew immediately she was in danger. Then she took her chance – she butted the woman off balance and scrambled out of the gate, up Argyll Street, not once looking back. She struggled past a group of Methodists on the street corner, too engrossed in their preacher's rantings to give her so much as a glance. Beyond and in front of a row of small houses at the top of the hill, she noticed a girl in shabby clothes kneeling by a doorstep and scrubbing it with all her might. Trickles of dirty water ran down into the road.

Siân tapped her shoulder and bent down to make herself heard. *'I'm looking for a Pansy Palmer. She's cleaning a chimney somewhere.'*

'The only Pansy I know'll be in Brick Street,' answered the girl without looking up.

Siân glanced around and noticed over the road a woman with a young child, both wrapped up as if they were in some snow storm, not a clear

248

bright February afternoon. She limped over to join them and took a deep breath.

'*Excuse me, but where's Brick Street?*'

'Brick Street?' The woman had caught the whisper, then looked her up and down. 'You don't want to go *there*, do you?'

Siân found this answer disconcerting, but persevered. 'Yes, I'm looking for my friend. She cleans chimneys.'

'Well, let me tell you it's not chimneys that get cleaned in that street.' The young mother pulled her child closer and set off down the hill, muttering, 'It's first turn right along from the Cathedral Arms.'

As Siân's suspicions grew, so her ungainly pace quickened. The shawl made her sweat even though the sun was now obscured by Hereford's Cathedral tower and dusk was beginning to dull the sky. But she kept on going, shutting her ears to the din of horses' hooves on the cobbles and the arguing of old men on the street corner.

The tavern was closed, its painted sign creaked above her head as she passed. Brick Street, however, was quite different and Siân took in the small parade of women on either side calling out and lifting their skirts, not to each other, but to any carriage and its occupants that passed along it. 'D'you want some company, sir?' or 'Sixpence a go, and cheap at the price.'

One of the women walked up to Siân. ''Ere. What you gawping at?'

'*I'm just looking for a Pansy Palmer, who works with Mr Hubbard the sweep.*' Siân, in surprise, realized the girl she was speaking to could not be more than thirteen, yet all done up with rouge and with glass baubles around her throat. The girl's cunning eyes roamed around, alert like some wild animal in the woods.

'D'you mean Pansy Hubbard? She ain't allowed to come 'ere no more on Sundays, 'cos he spent two nights in jail the last time.'

'*Who's he? What do you mean?*' Siân could feel her heart quickening. When the girl bent forwards to hear clearly, Siân nearly choked on her cheap scent.

'I mean her old man. After he's got her working up the stacks, he gets her cleaned up, then sees to it she opens her legs for whoever.'

Siân stifled a gasp of horror.

'But we don't like her round 'ere,' the girl sniffed. 'She'll do things no self-respecting orphans like us would ever try.'

'*Orphans?*'

'We work for ourselves see, not some lord and master.'

Siân couldn't listen to any more. Her one new friend had evaporated, just like Eirwen had done, and the air suddenly turned cold in the houses' shadow, while the prospect of an irate Tomos, and a night with those three men he'd spoken of filled her with dread. She wanted to tear off the clothes Mrs Hubbard had made for her, to have her dear Da's coat back, even Moses Evans's jacket – something familiar in this place full of strangers. But she had no money for anything else.

'Quick, hide.' The girl pulled Siân by the elbow into an alleyway between two dwellings, where a large black dog lay tethered. 'It's the constable!'

And sure enough, a heavy tread drew closer. As he passed the alley entrance, Burrows clearly didn't notice the two young girls squatting to pet the dog, their backs towards him.

'Whew.' The child prostitute stood up and brushed down her coat. 'He's a devil for coming down 'ere regular. Just turned Methodist, they say. Fire and bloody brimstone, him.' She gave Siân a knowing smile, as if she was a real woman of the world. 'As for your Pansy Hubbard, unless you catch her in-between beds and chimneys, forget it.'

'*So why was she down there?*' Siân pointed to the fields lying just below the city.

'Probably on her way to the Farrier for a wash – then whatever else they want her for, the crafty little bint.'

Siân winced. Why had Pansy ever bothered with her in the first place? Why go out of her way to show kindness, yet take her straight to Mrs Hubbard? She excused herself suddenly from her troubling companion and, instead of heading further up into the town, she cut through to Cromwell Street and retraced her steps along the Dinedor Road and up to the tavern.

It was almost dark and already a nip of frost was beginning to sharpen the air. When she arrived at the inn's front yard, she spotted Collen and Incio standing tethered to the barn wall half asleep. Nearby, the two Jack Russell terriers were frantically tearing at a pair of chicken heads.

Of her brother, or anyone else for that matter, there was no sign. Siân dragged her tired legs to the door only to find a note scrawled on a scrap of paper: CLOSED TILL FURTHER NOTICE. Panic seized her. Anyone could have stolen the unguarded horses. And what about the herd?

She struggled round the side of the tavern, and could just distinguish the Castlemartins grouped beyond the second gate, Ben lying close by. He pricked his ears when he saw her, but stayed at his post as she scoured the inn's upper windows. They were blank and dark, with no sign of life, so she returned to the door and brought the knocker down twice.

Collen looked up, then hung her head again, realizing no feed was imminent. Siân tried again, louder this time, bringing the Jack Russells fussing round her ankles.

Suddenly, a window opened above, and Mary Griffiths's head appeared.

'You'll wake the dead like that, my girl.' Her eyes peered down over pale sagging cheeks. 'Where's those fine clothes I fitted you up in?' she hissed. 'You sold 'em on, eh?'

Siân shook her head, desperate to hold the publican's attention before she disappeared indoors. Mary Griffiths hesitated. The lesser of two evils was to let the girl in, maybe. Otherwise her antics would surely bring that Constable Burrows calling again, and once today had been enough. 'Wait there and be silent, or there'll be one less of you setting off tomorrow.'

Siân stood listening to her progress down the wooden stairs, keeping a wary eye out for the woman's son. But the only other sound was the boar snuffling round its trough by the barn.

'Quick, in you come.' The woman bolted the door and sat Siân down on a bench in the stale dark silence. 'You stop there now and not a sound, or my boy will sort you out, understood?' Then she vanished.

Siân strained to listen for other sounds, till her patience was rewarded by the creaking of a bed in the room above, and people whispering. A man and a young girl, she was sure of it. Tomos and Pansy?

Fourteen

Radby End was an even smaller settlement than Nether Wapford, composed only of a triangular village green whose longest side abutted the main road. At the green's farthest end, along an unmade track edged by pretty ironstone cottages leading to the River Wap, Ivan could see the spire of All Saints church and its large white-shuttered rectory. The dark splayed branches of an ancient cedar tree moved in the gale against the sky.

This same wind drove unimpeded down the one street as Ivan struggled into the solitary telephone box, sensing curious but hidden eyes fixed upon him. His hand shook as he inserted his new phone card. He was about to betray a friend. But what choice had he, for fuck's sake? And while he waited for an answer from the police station in Stoneshanger, he expected to see his pursuers come swerving round the bend from Westhope at any minute.

Ivan's conversation with Detective Constable Marsh was quick and to the point. Not only had Valerie Rook received a death threat and was now missing, but also crucial evidence of arson twenty-five years earlier had been stolen from her house.

'Come on, Mr Browning. Disturbed patients frequently send doctors and their families strange material. It's a sad fact of life today, I'm afraid. And that Small Copse fire was unequivo-cally an accident, whatever may or may not have been considered evidence at the time or since. As for Mrs Rook, she's probably just gone out for the day. People do all sorts of daft things if they're preoccupied.'

'For Christ's sake, sir, the back door was open wide when I got there, and their house has been gone through. They must have got a key from somewhere, if they were able to lock it again. Doesn't that worry you at all?'

'Who's this "they" you're talking about?'

'Gerry Daniels and Harold Oakley. I saw one and heard the other.'

'OK, we'll go over and take a look, but in the meantime,' Marsh's tone grew more serious, 'there's one thing you yourself might consider...'

'What's that?'

'Try keeping out of trouble. Don't get yourself involved. Get my meaning?'

Ivan's stomach knotted. 'Oh yeah? Just like that?'

'I would recommend it.'

Ivan stared at the receiver as the DC rang off. As he left the booth he suddenly heard a noise. As he watched the road, he saw a motorbike approaching. Because the rider was wearing no helmet, Ivan could clearly recognize it was young Pop-Eyes from the garage. As the vehicle passed, an arm was raised, with the black-gloved hand thrusting a series of V signs.

By three o'clock, having taken a call from Jeanette Yates to say she was going down to the

Cottons in Hampshire after all, Ivan had turned the glaze kiln up to 1,100 degrees, after forcing down two ploughman's sandwiches. Around three-thirty he made another call to the police.

'Mrs Rook just phoned in a moment ago,' replied Constable Whitrow.

'Thank God for that. Is she OK?'

'Seems to be. She got home to find the break-in and phoned from McDonalds near Stoneshanger. She kept going on about us keeping her husband out of it. Now then sir, describe this Gerry Daniels.'

When Ivan had finished, to his amazement the constable suggested the man he had seen was in fact Anthony Pike, twenty-four-year-old elder son of the Westhope garage owner. In his chatty way he admitted they were another dodgy family, like the rest keeping just a short head in front of the law.

'Would DC Marsh have known about this alias?' Ivan quizzed him.

'Why should he?'

'And are these Pikes into key-cutting as well?'

An uncomfortable pause followed. 'They do have certain skills.'

At this, Ivan felt his late lunch begin to move towards his throat. 'So, for Church House read Open House, if there's a bloody key floating around.'

'I did suggest she change the locks ASAP, but, like I said, she was adamant her husband remains ignorant.'

Ivan sighed. 'Look, can't you pull those Pikes in, at least?'

'Nothing proper to go on, but let's just say we've got plans afoot, sir. I'm not at liberty to divulge anything at the moment.'

It was impossible to relax enough even to make a cup of coffee. His whole being jibbed at the prospect of revisiting Cold Firton to take his evening class. It was like standing next in line at some huge stinking slaughterhouse, the inevitability of the stun gun resting on his forehead.

Having checked on the kiln Ivan locked the outbuilding door and walked round the back towards the forest. Then he thought of those horses refusing to pass nearby, and decided on another route.

Instead of heading directly for the bridle track, he skirted around behind the neighbouring cottages.

In almost a year since Mr Carp's disappearance, nature had made a mockery of his once-neat picket fence. The lawn stood tall, and was now choked with weeds, a row of bare apple trees battled against the gale, and a loose tarpaulin on the old shed danced like a dervish on its roof.

Ivan walked on, head bowed into his jacket collar, hands deep in his jeans pockets, noting the tyre tracks criss-crossing in the rough grass where probably once carts full of oak bark had come and gone on their way between the forest and the tanneries in Northampton. Any 4x4 could easily come up to this western edge of the forest from the Sykeston Road and not be seen, and he wondered which way Malcolm Cotton had been brought there on his last journey.

Ivan sniffed the air and smelt that same smoke again – just the faintest scent of it dispersed by the wind from somewhere deeper among the trees. Daylight was ending as he entered that ancient domain of deer and fox, while overhead a flock of roosting woodpigeons tore through the tree tops, and from somewhere more distant a buzzard let out its mewing call. He trod over acorns long buried by the jays, through clumps of ink-cap fungi whose frayed caps dripped spore-black liquid, until he came to the electrified fence surrounding Lord Hickson's land.

TRESPASSERS WILL BE PROSECUTED

Ivan followed this barrier towards the Oxford-shire border, all the while the smoke was thickening, despite the sudden pummelling wind. The hazels rustled together, the oaks moaned in unison, as he instinctively clamped a hand protectively over his nose and mouth.

Just ahead in a small clearing, was revealed something truly unexpected: the charred skeleton of a car, still giving off heat. Ivan ventured closer, trying to guess the vehicle's make. A Clio? Fiesta? Too difficult to say. Whoever had set this up had done a thorough job: packing the interior with wood so it would seem like an unsuspicious bonfire.

He paced round the metallic remains, scrutinizing the wreck for any give-away signs. But like a true cremation, all had been rendered anonymous. For some reason Ivan kept walking on past, noting how some of the great trunks surrounding him bore a motif of oak leaves etched deep into the bark. Maybe to mark limits for the grazers of Nether Wapford? Or most likely someone exercising a knife.

Then he stopped in his tracks. A blue-and-white police cordon had been threaded round a circle of trees. As Ivan gazed upwards, his heart missed a beat. There, on one thick oak branch hung the most hideous sight he'd ever seen.

Tied at the tails, a bunch of headless grass snakes dangled and moved with the wind. He stared at them as if hypnotized, wondering who was warped enough to do such a thing. Was this some sick marker of where Malcolm Cotton had also hanged – beginning his journey into everlasting darkness?

Ivan began to run, his long legs raking over the ground already covered, his boots snapping branches, crushing the tracks of other recent visitors. And when he reached a point where the trees had been thinned, he stopped to lean against a rare and ancient elm whose lower limbs had been amputated.

Here he tried to compose himself, but his heart was throbbing in his throat.

Some time later, the Welsh girl woke up with a silent cry of alarm. Although the chilly room was still dark, she realized with a knot of fear that she wasn't alone. There was someone leaning over her, wearing a cape of sorts.

Pansy's hot little hand grabbed Siân's. 'I'm sorry for taking you to Mrs Hubbard's. I thought you'd be safer doing my business, but then I felt guilty, so I came here instead of you.'

Siân couldn't believe her ears.

'Write to me at the Cathedral Arms sometime.' Pansy released her hand. 'Don't forget.' And with that she ran to the door, unbolted it with a sharp clang of metal on metal, then was gone.

Siân tried to follow, but the dawn's heavy mist and the drumming of rain on the cobbled yard conspired to obscure her hoped-for friend for ever. Now other noises grew more distinct as the day lightened outside. The clank of buckets, of doors slamming, then men's voices arguing harshly. She recognized Tomos's over the rest.

Siân sat tight as the door to the stairs was pushed open, and the trio strode past her, hardly giving her a glance. She heard the cob whinny, then Tomos began ranting again.

'You couldn't wait for my sister, could you?'

Siân shivered at his heartless words. There was nothing to choose between him and Christmas Hubbard. And just by being there instead of her, Pansy had spared her.

The two local men pushed past Tomos, buttoning up their coats.

'God's truth, I wouldn't touch a cripple if it was the last fanny on this earth. I have some principles, sire, though you might not.'

When they'd gone, Siân waited in dread for Tomos to return. His hat was pulled well down over his eyes, and what little of his face showed was the colour of elderberries.

'So, I made damned well nothing last night, but Mother Griffiths got her cut, didn't she?' He found something in the bottom of an abandoned ale glass and drained it. 'Happy now, are you, canny little bitch?' He kicked at the bench under her. 'And there's more bad news reached me.' He pressed his mouth into her ear, his breath stinking like a cesspit. 'I've had word that Morris has reached Mount Eppynt...'

'*Morris? At Eppynt? Oh no.*' She could see the man now, his fists working, coming for her...

'So no more wandering off, d'you hear? If the likes of him gets you on your own, that'll be the end of you ... never mind me.' As they stepped outside, he whistled for the dogs to get busy, then stuck a hand in his coat pocket and brandished his pistol. 'But remember, I still got this, in case the baker and that layabout brother of his get troublesome.'

Siân turned away. How could she ever forget what that murderous weapon had already done? And, instead of suggesting he hide it somewhere in case he was searched, Siân checked her pony's bridle then mounted. As the dawn sky filled with black clouds from the west, great drops of rain began to fall. Soon Mrs Hubbard's new clothes were hanging off her like wet sails, heavy and cold. And, as the drove passed through Putley on Durlow Common, to the stares of locals going about their Monday business, her teeth chattered till she feared they'd fall out.

Every few yards, she'd turn to see if anyone was following them, but the Wye mist still hung low, providing a very useful cover for anybody up to no good. Another hazard was the new pair of terriers, who were too young, too noisy.

Occasionally Tomos would lean down from the cob to thrash them quiet.

'Morris could hear you critters a hundred miles off,' he muttered, landing yet another blow where it hurt most, so by the time another mile had passed, they realized Tomos Richards wasn't one to be ignored. By way of further punishment, at the next stop beyond Rye Street it was the other dog, Ben, who was given the bacon bone while they had nothing. Siân had never cared for their breed: in the trampling she'd suffered, it was the Jack Russells who'd kept going with the herd, and Flint who'd stayed with her, protected her.

However, a good day's progress, with twelve miles covered by mid-afternoon, and that same pale sun that yesterday had appeared only briefly, again edged out of the darkness. But Siân was soaked to the skin, and coughing so much that by the time the night stop came at the Green Parrot near Tewkesbury, she was first to the inn fire, where her new clothes steamed like the horses' breath as they began to dry.

Tomos had uttered barely a word to her all day, and his head, too, had often been turned for signs of his pursuer. Now, in the small public room of the ale house, he sat deliberately concealed behind the door, with both hands round his bowl of broth.

That night, he prowled about outside, listening to the owls in the nearby churchyard, then checking that the cob and the chestnut couldn't be easily untied, and ordering Ben to guard the field gate. When he finally came back into the taproom, the publican was already dowsing the fire while whistling some bawdy music hall song. 'Yer girl's in top room,' he said. 'Pity for her, in her condition.'

'It's I who needs pity.' Tomos picked a rind of ham off an uncleared plate. 'There's a felon after us.'

'Who be that, then?' the other man asked, his humming suddenly ending.

'He's from Cardiganshire: a baker by trade, with the name of Derryn Morris. Big and pink-eyed, too strong for most.'

'Another Taffy, then?' the publican stared Tomos in the eye. 'I don't want no trouble 'ere, mind. Only last October a man from Cardiff got killed in this very room over some girl or other. Excitable bloody lot, you are.'

'I felt it right to warn you, that's all, sire.' Tomos restrained himself from arguing. 'And we'll be away by first light, so I'll settle now.'

The publican wiped his big hands down his apron and produced an account book from his pocket, and a pencil as thick as his finger. But just as Tomos was handing over a note and some coins, he heard Ben start up outside, followed by the ominous thunder of hooves.

'*A curse on you all… You and your brother can rot in hell.*' Siân could never forget those frightening words uttered from Marcus Webb's bloodied lips.

Sensing imminent trouble, the publican of the Green Parrot had snatched the drover's payment, ordered both him and the girl to leave, then bolted the door behind them.

For the first time in her life she saw her

brother's face turn pale.

'Remember, sister,' he whispered, 'if there's any quizzing, we came by Brecon then over the Wye at Errwood not Clifford. Your neck depends on it.'

And just as he'd finished his warning, three riders emerged from the mist, their horses dark as shadows and blowing out white plumes of breath.

Fifteen

En route to his class, with the wind abated, Ivan rang the doorbell of Church House to check on Valerie, but the whole place was as quiet as the neighbouring graveyard, with no lights, no sound other than a distant night-jar flitting from tree to tree. The whole place exuded such an air of grim stillness he felt like a trespasser, and the longer he stayed waiting for any sign of her, the stronger his heartbeat pounded.

He made his way round to the side gate, as usual, unpadlocked. Just one flick of its latch was enough to take him through into the impenetrable darkness of garden beyond.

He ran his fingers along the old ironstone wall until they located the back door and closed over the knob, turning it back and forth. It was still locked. Good. Then something made him start.

A familiar smell. Not the damp evergreens which hung over the churchyard wall. No, this was quite different. Clean and soapy. *Jesus Christ!*

'Jo?' She must have rounded the corner deliberately quietly. 'Hell, is that you?' When his instincts said run, he reached out instead and touched a soft fleece. As she held out one hand, from the other something fell noiselessly to the ground. In the gloom it looked like an envelope. An all-too-familiar shape and colour. He bent down to retrieve it but she pushed him back with enough force for him to topple against the nearby water butt. She picked up the envelope and stuffed it out of sight inside the belt of her jeans.

'Just something for my old granny,' she replied, patting it in place. 'It's a get well card.'

But to him it looked too small for that, and surely the elderly woman had already died.

'Is she sick?' he quizzed carefully.

'She's just had a bad turn, that's all.'

'But why are you here? Or maybe I shouldn't ask.'

'No, you shouldn't, but I'll forgive you. Just this time.'

Now her beautiful face was up close. He suddenly felt weak.

'I needed to see Dr Rook. My Mum's ill too, now.'

Ivan thought back to his strange meeting with Monica Oakley, the drained face, her strange pallor. So maybe that was true, but sympathy did not come readily.

He nearly let slip that the doctor would be away until Thursday, but stopped himself in time. 'Where's your car parked?'

She sighed loudly. 'Questions, questions, Ivan. Don't you *ever* get tired of them?'

'Not when they're necessary.'

'And so's this.' She began trailing her fingers down his cheek, letting the tips of them circle round his ear and settle on the corner of his mouth. 'You were brilliant on Sunday standing up to Daddy like that. I like men who don't take shit.' Her fingertips now tracked his lips so lightly that they sent a current of desire through his whole body. 'Malcolm was the same.'

Ivan started. 'You mean the chef?'

'Yeah, he'd really let Dad have it. About the wages, the shifts being too long, and he never left off badgering him for a paid holiday. Poor sod, I think it got to him, all that moaning about stuff. Certainly couldn't have helped his depression.'

Ivan felt her hand moving down his throat, into the collar of his shirt. He held his breath. What Jeanette Yates had warned him of was slipping from his mind ... what anyone had said. For those fingertips had undone a button, then another, found a nipple and started to work on it.

'I fancied you when I first saw you. You know that, don't you?' she murmured.

Was this the same girl who'd rebuffed him only two days before – who'd made him feel smaller than a fucking leprechaun? But any doubts were replaced by an intense sexual arousal. Just like in the old days, too long ago. He extracted this same hand and placed it on his fly, half expecting her to withdraw it. But no, she knew what to do all right. Better than Tania, better than any of them. He felt sick with longing as she traced the growing bulge of him with her fingertips, then began to pull at the zip.

'Don't stop now,' he murmured, bringing his lips to hers. The kiss was long and slow. She let just the tip of her tongue tease his, and then, when he could bear it no longer, when his hand was already beginning its journey down the V of her jumper, between her breasts, she pulled away suddenly.

'Look, I've got to get back home now. I told

267

you, Mum's not well.'

Ivan gripped both her arms with a strength that surprised him. She struggled, kicked his shin, then ran from his grasp.

'And whose fucking mum are *you?*' he yelled after her. 'Who else d'you fuck about with, cock-teaser?' His reproach echoed into the night, to merge with the church bells' half-hourly toll.

In the ensuing silence, he was tempted to follow her and apologize. But it was already half-past seven, with the village hall waiting.

It wasn't until he reached his car that he recognized the same manila envelope wedged under one of his windscreen wipers. He snatched it up and checked inside. There was no enclosure but, under the car's feeble interior light, he could make out *Dr Rook* scrawled in pencil on the front. And inside, just under the flap: *I love you, Mr B... Jo.*

Still bewildered and elated in turn, he hefted his old reserve hold-all up the village hall's wooden steps. To say he wasn't looking forward to this, his penultimate session, would have been a gross understatement, and once he'd dragged all eight tables out from under the stage and attended to the temperamental overhead heaters, he stood by one of the windows to watch who'd turn up. His luminous watch showed exactly 7.45. This was a disaster. Normally Gill Bunnett would have been the first to show and get busy setting out crockery for their regular eight-fifteen tea break. Then Flora Deedes, the domineering ex-headmistress ... but not tonight, clearly.

He savoured Jo's message again, at first reading passion and lust into each flourish of every letter, as no graphologist ever could. Then, almost reverently, he slotted it back into his jacket pocket, allowing no doubts about the envelope's possible original contents to enter his mind.

The hall stayed empty until 7.50 when he heard car wheels grating on the hardcore outside. Then footsteps coming up the steps.

'Valerie! What are you doing here? I've been worried sick.' She seemed even whiter than usual. Her bottom lip trembling.

'So have I. Take a look at this.'

She dug in her vinyl bag and pulled out another manila envelope. This one was bulkier as if it contained more than just paper. It was also bloodstained around the flap. 'I was so scared this morning when I opened it, I just grabbed that damned lighter and got straight out of the house.'

'Thank God. Where is it now, by the way?'

'In here.' She patted the bag. 'Mr Gilbert, my solicitor, will be getting it first thing tomorrow. He said he wants the police to examine it properly next Monday once he's back from London.'

'When did you speak to him?'

'Yesterday. Why? I was taking your advice.'

Ivan frowned. Something was niggling him. 'And your backdoor key?'

She patted her coat pocket.

He scrutinized the envelope's contents: an oblong label, bearing that already familiar print, which said YOU ARE NEXT MRS R, and a clinical thermometer half smeared in blood.

'Jesus Christ. This is getting nasty.' He slipped them both back in the envelope. 'Once I've seen you home, I'm taking this straight to the cops.'

'No, I'll do that.' She snatched the envelope out of his grasp. 'I can't keep this a secret from them any more. I've had enough now. Michael will just have to get used to the idea that his perfect wife could see her own brother murdered and do nothing at all about it. I wasn't born on the day we married despite what his mother would like to believe.' She held Ivan's gaze with her tearful eyes. 'So there we are.'

Ivan cupped his hand under her elbow and guided her towards the door.

'Where did you go off to? I was thinking the worst.'

'After I'd posted that silly note to you, I just panicked and drove around in a kind of daze. Up and down the M1. Nottingham to Luton, I think. Some nice chap from Easifit came and changed my tyres just after you'd left.'

Ivan checked that all the village hall lights and heaters were turned off, then escorted her out to the steps. The wind had dropped, and a creepy stillness held them both to its heart, while high above, the moon slid between skeins of clouds and cast its intermittent light on Valerie's fearful face. No way could he mention Jo's presence outside her house. He had to keep secrets too.

Finally he said, 'I was actually there at your place when the heavy mob showed up. It was Harold Oakley, I'm sure of it, and Anthony Pike. Just after I'd seen his truck come out of Small Copse.'

She nearly lost her footing on the slippery step and gripped his arm.

'Oh Jesus, help us.' She turned to him. 'They could have killed you.'

'Never mind *me*.' He helped her down into the darkened car park. 'I was OK.'

'How on earth did they manage to break in?'

'Well, that lot aren't short of the wherewithal, are they?'

Her teeth began to chatter. The woman was obviously frozen. Time to get her back into her car and safely home. He could leave his here for a while.

When they arrived back at the still-dark house, Ivan found hammer and nails in the scullery and secured the back door with a wooden plank. He then suggested she could come back home with him and he'd kip on the settee.

'Thank you, Ivan, but I'll be fine now, don't worry.' She pecked him on the cheek with her cold lips and he watched her retreat back inside the front door. How would she be safe? Safe from the fallout that any of her revelations would surely bring? He didn't know. How could he know? But one thing was for sure: the fine scleroprotein threads of some unseen web of evil were tightening their grip, and, instead of just himself, there struggled inside it other frightened creatures. All with knowledge. All therefore targets.

Incio and Collen, who'd just come into season, meanwhile danced on their short ropes in the Green Parrot's yard until Tomos led them out of the way.

'You, Taffy,' one of the young men in black shouted after him. 'There's an honourable man, Will Hopkins, dead the way you just come, and we've got Reward notices signed by Alun George, solicitor and treasurer, County of Brecknock.' He pulled out a wad of papers and waved them at the Welshman. 'You got anything to say?'

When one fluttered to the ground Siân could read it from where she stood, and those black printed words filled her with terror.

MORDIWELL ASSOCIATION
200 GUINEAS
REWARD
WHEREAS

Some person or persons did on the afternoon of Tuesday 21 February or the following morning of Wednesday 22 February, brutally murder one Mr Will Hopkins, tenant of Gellionnen Farm, on the estate of Lord Trelewis, in Cwm Forest, Maesmynis in the County of Brecknock.

It is also recorded that much damage was done to Lord Trelewis's plantation, and moneys for replanting are sought from the perpetrator of this vandalism.

**signed Alun George
SOLICITOR & TREASURER**

'Who are you?' Tomos strode towards them, then stood defiantly, legs apart, frowning at the message. But Siân knew he could make no sense of it, being always too busy making money to have ever picked up a book. 'And what gives you the right to frighten the wits of my poor ill daughter here?'

Daughter? Siân tried to keep embarrassment off her face.

'Mordiwell Private Prosecution Association, Thomas Jedburgh Dickens to you, and them behind's Nathaniel and Francis Carter. And,' the man they called Rock Face went on, 'in case you're in doubt as to my credentials, my father's still a "Runner" in London—'

'But this is Herefordshire, not Brecknockshire,' Tomos argued.

Rock Face snorted. 'We assist our friends over the border whenever we can. Justice doesn't stop with fences, and this notice will be placed in every inn in every village, every town until Oxfordshire.'

For a moment, Tomos seemed nonplussed, then quickly decided that flattery might be a useful tool.

'Well, there's three very fine entires you got, sirs. Some good blood, I'd say.' He moved to stroke the leader's mount on the neck. 'We only got runts back home – just like our cattle.'

'So which way did you come from your homeland of runts, then?' sneered the taller of the Carters, clearly unimpressed. 'And don't you go giving us some tall story neither. We heard from the Ox Inn that your daughter here was after victuals there.' He clicked his horse on till it stood close enough to Siân to make her flinch.

'So, little hog-tied, you must have caught a glimpse of the poor deceased gentleman while you was there?'

'*We never went near Maesmynis,*' she lisped, barely making a sound. '*We came round by Brecon, that I swear. The Usk was full to overflowing so we kept south of it by Llanfrynach.*' She was straining at every syllable to save her life. '*We lost two of our steers as it was.*'

'So how d'you know the Ox Inn is at Maesmynis, then?' Francis Carter demanded, pulling his horse's head in tight.

'*My uncle goes there with his sheep three times a year on his way to Hay.*'

Tomos hid his surprise at her accomplished storytelling, while the three strangers glanced at each other from beneath their wide-brimmed hats. High above, the moon was losing presence to a lightening sky that promised a rare clear day.

'What happened to your saddles then, girl? Them at the Ox said the biddy rode bare.'

'*I've never ridden bare in my life. 'Tis a risk to my maidenhead,*' she retorted.

At this the men, even Tomos, sniggered at the surprise of it, until Siân continued to embellish her lie. '*But at Preston on Wye, by Blakemere, we met two footpads. They debated how they could get at least three pounds each for them, then snatched them away and ran off.*'

Nathaniel Carter, who'd been leaning forwards to catch her whispers, smiled with ugly black teeth.

'Well, we don't need to get proof just at this point, do we, us being married men and all. But lissen here, porthmon' – he faced Tomos, wagging a long bony finger – 'if we learn you've seen us off with falsehoods, you mark my words, as sure as the sun will follow that moon up there, we'll have you, and *her*.' He eyed Siân. 'Now, where you heading?'

Tomos was aware of the herd beginning to stir restlessly, to bump and barge around the gate. Every extra burst of temperament meant loss of condition for them, making it a longer and more costly time for the beasts to fatten later on.

'Winchcombe, south by Stow then–'

Suddenly he was interrupted by a chorus of guffaws from the three horsemen, and the terriers, hearing it, came running.

'I'll bet you five shillings they don't get no farther than the end of this road here.'

'Why's that then?' Tomos stood his ground.

'Them'll be walking on their bloody knees, that's why. Them should have had tips on a long way back.'

'It'll be grass all the way to Temple Guiting, then I'll get them done for Berkhamstead – if that's all right with you.'

'They your own, then?' Rock Face cast his stern features over to the field. 'You're not drovin' for someone else?'

'I don't handle money for anyone, never have, never will. They're mine, and they'll be paying for my daughter's treatment in London.'

That finally seemed to satisfy the trio, who began turning their massive mounts back to face the road.

'The reason I asked,' Rock Face half turned in

his saddle, 'is that if you was takin' *my* stock to the fairs, I wouldn't let you pass from my sight for one second.'

With that, they cantered away, the racket of their hooves lingering for a while in the still dawn air. Siân, still trembling, relayed to her brother the details of their grim poster with its huge reward of two hundred guineas put up by Lord Trelewis – until he told her to close her mouth.

Her lies earlier hadn't come easily. At home, it was considered a sin – the worst fault of all, claimed her Da. And as the sound of their interrogators finally faded away, she knew, deep in her chilled bones, that this was just the beginning. That wherever she and Tomos went, someone would be waiting or following, and that fear grew rather than diminished in her as the drove made its way up towards Winchcombe.

If she was expecting any thanks from her brother for her performance, none came. But it was clearly *her* duty now to concoct whatever stories she could, to stave off the law. And, to while away the hours along the old drove ways between sparse Cotswold fields, her imagination took flight.

While late February's sun hung low above the gentle hills, with Collen picking her way behind the cattle, Siân not only completely reinvented the past days' journey but also saw a future where that same sun beaming now into her unshaded eyes had become one vast glow, a fire almost, consuming all the wrongs of the past – and sending its fragments scattering black into the sky.

When she blinked and looked again, a flock of crows was passing eastwards, she saw the faces of Huw, of her Da, both smiling, waiting ... but more disturbing and persistent, was a succession of many strangers including, at the end, a young man whose hair was cut oddly, not of her own time. From his lips issued words that the Reverend Meurig Jones had once taught her, reciting from one of his new books.

This scene how beauteous to the musing mind
That now swift slides from an enchanting view
The sun sweet setting yon far hills behind
In other worlds his Visits to renew.

They weren't from William Wordsworth's pen, she knew, but someone else whose name she couldn't quite place. Yet, just then, that lovely verse seemed the most apt, the most relevant for a future she was sure lay ahead.

Sixteen

Following a gloomy Wednesday worrying about Valerie and catching up with his ever-worsening account, Ivan felt this was personal Thanksgiving Day all right, for by 9.30 on Thursday morning, with white sun and black cloud in equal measure, he was £300 the richer, courtesy of Reedman Insurance Brokers. They'd enclosed a cheque for the replacement of missing goods, and again reassured him they were still awaiting news from Stoneshanger CID about locating his VW Golf.

He instantly thought of all the things this tidy sum could buy. Maybe some designer gear to impress the lovely but elusive Jo; then, ashamed of this infantile notion, he thought again. More coal for the fire, that was it, some decent grub from M&S – or – even those special lustre glazes he'd been promising himself for months. But these pipe dreams paled into insignificance after listening to an answerphone message from Pam Barker, apologizing for her absence on Tuesday evening following Tom Coles's very private funeral at St Thomas's. She explained she wouldn't be attending the final session either as her son was coming back to Cold Firton after all to be with her.

There was shortly afterwards a call from Valerie Rook.

'DC Marsh phoned yesterday to check if I was

278

OK,' she began. 'He assured me that Michael wouldn't know a thing, and that investigations would be stepped up but I must be vigilant.'

'How decent of him. Did you tell him about the thermometer with blood on it?'

Valerie hesitated. 'No. I've had a think about it all but I can't.'

Ivan sighed his frustration as she went on. 'I thought he was being surprisingly loose-mouthed but he did come out with something else which I thought you'd like to know.'

'Amaze me...'

'That the police are planning to strike at Ma Oakley's funeral today.'

'Funeral?' *That's not what Jo implied.* 'Where's it happening? What time?' he asked.

'St Thomas's; three o'clock. The gist of it is they'll take the opportunity to pull the whole tribe in for questioning.'

'What about the Dawsons, their business associates? Did he mention them?'

'No. But who knows, they might be there too – one big horrible parry.' Her sharp laugh had nothing to do with humour.

Meanwhile an uncomfortable thought was worming into Ivan's brain.

'Why would he want to spill such information to you of all people? I don't get it.'

'Neither do I, but I'm going along anyhow, just to see what happens. And thank you for Tuesday. I won't forget it.'

Preoccupied, Ivan went towards his workshop with an uneaten sandwich. Was the copper losing it? No, impossible, for God's sake. And why would Jo the attentive granddaughter lie about something like that? Nothing was making sense any more. He kicked the studio door open in frustration.

As he approached, he just *knew* something was wrong. For a start, there was that faint smoky smell again, strengthening the nearer he got. As he began to unscrew the heavy firebrick-lined door he felt strangely isolated – more alone than ever despite Valerie's recent call.

Ivan coughed. It was definitely woodsmoke, even though he'd never tackled a raku firing or even used wood ash as a mottling agent in any of his processes. This was crazy.

He opened the kiln door just another inch to be almost knocked backwards by a thick acrid fug billowing through the gap. This wasn't from any wood, but something else. Choking and spluttering he made his way to his work-bench and picked up his overall, flapping it at the ever-thickening fog. To no avail; if anything, the atmosphere was growing more opaque, like cornflour dispersed in water.

Suddenly, yelps, quiet at first, then becoming more distinct, the same as that one dog heard during his strange dream journey. But now its tone sounded frantically defensive, as if trying to dissuade someone or something from coming near. But what did *this* phantom noise mean? What the *hell* was going on?

Ivan clamped both hands round his ears and slammed the kiln door with his foot. A moment later, having left the workshop, he glanced through the hall window and noticed a police car drawing up outside Mrs Jonas's cottage. Two officers got out and made for her front door, one carried a spade, the other a white plastic sack. They both looked grim, and when Ivan ran up the stairs, two at a time to look out over her back garden, the disinterment had already begun, with the old woman standing by, a hand over her mouth.

The filthy yellow bag eventually emerged and was swiftly transferred into the plastic one. The soil was replaced. The whole operation had taken fourteen minutes. He'd counted. As he stayed a moment longer, Ivan spotted the same police car cruising round to the rear of Mr Carp's house and heading for the western edge of the forest – the same way he'd ventured on Tuesday.

Ivan again braved his studio, relieved to find the worst of the smoke gone. But something altogether different had now replaced it – a quite unappetizing smell like raw mince when it first hits the frying pan. He thought immediately of abattoirs, and his stomach heaved as he opened the kiln door again.

The stench increased, and all at once there was another sound, not the dog this time – no, this was more subtle, almost human, an unbroken chant of pain which seemed to emanate from the urns themselves. Ivan stared inside. The high firing temperature had rendered the original buff clay body of each urn as white as bone, their carefully applied coloured glazes spirited away.

He pushed the kiln door shut again and rewound its handle tight, but that still didn't stop the woeful litany from filtering out and echoing through the whole room. Its ethereally plaintive notes persisted until, gradually, more definite vowels and consonants emerged, and in an instant, with a sudden lurch of his heart, Ivan recognized the song he'd heard sung at that Welsh tavern ... and this was the third time it had reached his ears.

'Who *are* you? Why are you here, for God's sake?'

The voice then changed to another familiar plaint.

'You promised me ... you promised...'

'Look, I've just about had enough.' With that, he stormed out and made for his car. He felt totally pissed off. His class had folded, his studio work was fucked up. There was only one thing for it. London was beckoning again.

But as he drove past Dawson's Farm towards Stoneshanger, he knew with a gnawing certainty that whatever life he'd have from now on would never be normal, never be simple – not after everything that had happened here.

He slowed up behind an elderly man leading a Shetland pony along the road. As he glanced at this strange partnership, he noticed a sign half buried in the hedge: Welsh Way.

So Ann Mitchell, the landlord's wife, *hadn't* been telling fairy stories. Those people with their strange and difficult language *had* shared this place, walked along it, lived by it, died by it no doubt, and for some inexplicable reason, Ivan suddenly felt as if his blood had chilled.

'Tripp's Cottage you said?' The young woman behind the desk at County Homes estate agents glanced up from her form-filling at the tall young man in front of her. 'So when would it be convenient for Mr Cartwright to call in and take measurements and give you a valuation?'

'Any time really, except this afternoon or tomorrow morning,' Ivan replied, noting her childish writing with each 'i' topped by a giant bubble just like some of his schoolkids used to do.

'He'll give you a ring to confirm a time. OK?'

'Fine.' Ivan then ventured, 'Tell me, are prices still climbing here? I paid eighty-five grand for it at the end of last June.'

'Things aren't too bad. But until the train services improve we may even see a drop.'

The girl got up and managed, despite her extremely tight skirt, to walk over to a nearby filing cabinet. From this she plucked out a couple of A4 sheets showing properties for sale. 'From what you've said,' she went on, 'these are similar properties to yours – detached, on the small side, but with good locations, some original features and a bit of history thrown in.'

A bit of history thrown in. So that's all it is? OK, if you say so.

She passed the pages over. The price tags made him blink.

'You *could* be asking near a hundred thou for yours,' she said. 'Mind, it's up to Mr Cartwright to decide.'

Ivan handed them back, an orgy of mental arithmetic taking place in his mind. The nearby forest, the meat hooks, the black beam, and the

283

old quarry-tiled floor – all were destined to help him on his way.

'At least let's get it on the market before the new legislation comes in,' she suggested, sitting down again.

'Legislation?'

'Vendors will be obliged to get a full structural survey done in advance, so that buyers are aware of any problems before engaging solicitors and so on.' She finished filling in his details. 'And I see you've not been there long,' she observed.

'Family reasons,' Ivan said quickly, and his expression was serious enough for her to say she was sorry to hear that.

'Have you a mobile?' she asked. 'They are handy with buying and selling.'

'No. I had mine nicked.'

More words of sympathy as she handed him her boss's card, a string of letters after the estate agent's name.

'I'm sure your cottage will be sold even before we put it in the window. The place sounds idyllic, and word of mouth's the thing round here.'

Ivan didn't bother to agree with her. As he closed the door behind him, he became aware of a troubled sky, of the lowering clouds edged by a viciously bright sun.

He should have felt elated at this first decisive move to resurrect himself, but in fact he now felt quite the opposite. He was a turncoat, a betrayer. Maybe when it was time to shell out for the survey, he could still change his mind.

Now that the sky had turned really dark, Ivan

thought of Gethsemane – and of that graveyard in Cold Firton where, in four hours' time if DC Marsh was to be believed, dramatic events were sure to unfold. And where, if he could only get Jo on her own, maybe there'd be a chance to talk... Why couldn't he get that girl out of his mind?

As people in the High Street moved purposefully towards shelter, Ivan stepped into the bank and paid in his insurance cheque, having decided that the fifteen quid in his wallet was enough to see him through the weekend. Then he made his way past the closed-up Lamb and Flag, which had a replacement notice on its door, and the newsagent's headline billboard reading: LOCAL CHEF'S INQUEST POSTPONED.

He bought a copy of the local paper and proceeded to the public library so he could read it in peace and quiet.

Ivan passed through the automatic glass doors and paused for a moment in the small foyer crammed with posters announcing events from terrier racing to a macramé exhibition. But one notice in particular caught his attention, advertising a lecture on Proust by some learned academic from de Montfort University. As a taster, a section of translated text, titled 'The Past', was displayed inside a typically French decorative border.

It is a labour in vain to try to recapture it. All the efforts of our intellect are useless. The past is hidden somewhere outside its own domain in some material object (in the sensation which that material object will give us) which we never suspected. And it depends on chance whether or not we come upon it before we die.

285

The first and last statements exercised his thoughts. Never mind his own past, someone else's was clearly roaming outside its own domain – and was with him now. But why?

Ivan tore his gaze away, and approached a woman at the desk who was setting out some tatty ex-library volumes for a book sale. He coughed to attract her attention.

'Can I help you?'

'Do you have anything here on local gangs back in the nineteenth century?'

'How far back?' She didn't look up from her dingy display. 'There's a world of difference between Wellington's day and Queen Victoria's old age.'

OK, Mrs Smart Ass, don't bother yourself.

He went over instead to the reference section where another woman was mounting a display of batik on the walls. At the two tables under the window three old men were buried in newspapers.

He sat down and joined them, to read the account of Malcolm Cotton's discovery on Monday morning by two lads cycling in Nether Wapford Forest. As they could get no reply from the three adjacent cottages, they'd pedalled over the Wap footbridge and down to Dawson's Farm where a Mr Roy Dawson, aged fifty-three, computer consultant, had called the emergency services.

There was nothing at all about the chef's supposed suicide note, or those headless snakes, or the freshly burnt-out car. To cap it all, the police were quoted as saying they couldn't yet decide if Cotton's death had been suicide or murder, and for this reason the inquest was postponed for another week.

Ivan folded the paper and stuffed it in his pocket. Either way, the poor sod had been a victim. He got up to look around.

The shelf labelled 'Northamptonshire Life and Times' contained a self-published work on the Lamport steam railway, two thin volumes on the growth of the canal system, and a thickish brown book with worn corners: *Notorious Gangs in Northamptonshire* by Mervyn Stanton, published in 1907.

Ivan's heart began racing. He cursed inwardly at having to share a table, but there was no alternative. However, the old guy opposite him had gone to sleep. While Ivan thumbed through the pages which contained Stanton's own versions of trial accounts as well as bleak engravings of the accused, the sky outside growled with thunder and the heavens opened.

By midday, he'd become acquainted with Thomas the Baker who'd turned 'approver' to save his skin, with Bacaunt and his tribe, with John de Aston and the Culworth Gang whose villainous days ended on Northampton Racecourse in August 1787. Next, after the Hollowfield Four, came George Catherall, 'Captain Slash', who was hanged shoeless on the New Drop in 1826. Finally something which made Ivan snatch his breath. It was a heading at the foot of one page: 'Northampton Lent Assizes of 28 March 1830', followed by the names *Luke, Noah and Arthur DAWSON.* The following pages had been crudely torn out.

He checked again carefully – there was nothing more to be had on them, and the proof was three jagged page edges close to the stitching of the spine.

His scraping chair startled the old man from his slumbers.

Ivan headed over to the issue desk and showed the damage to a girl who, judging by her youth, was probably there on Work Experience. She was busy stacking returned books onto a wooden trolley. 'Have you seen this vandalism?' He slapped Stanton's work down in front of her.

'Oh Lord.' A heavily ringed finger trailed along the tear. 'I'd better show this to Mr Gifford.'

Mr Gifford, too, fingered the rough edges where the yellowed pages had once been. 'Why would anyone want to do a thing like that? I don't think we can find another copy of this either. It's out of print.' He checked the details on the fragile flyleaf. 'Wilton and May stopped publishing just before the last war. I'm terribly sorry.'

'Did anyone take over their business? I mean, another publisher maybe? It *is* important.'

The older man frowned. 'No. They went bankrupt. What was it you were interested in?' he asked, skimming the volume.

'The Dawsons, tried in March 1830 ... Luke, Noah and Arthur.'

'Ah,' said the librarian enigmatically. 'Well there's the County Record Office, of course. Or, if you want to save petrol, you could get in touch with my brother.'

'Your brother?'

'Yes, he's called Charlie Gifford, and he covered quite a few local criminals in his dissertation at the University College last summer. It was also about enclosures and the growth of non-conformism, something like that. He's a mature student, working for his MA now. I can give you his number, if you like, as he lives only round the corner from the Leisure Centre.' He scribbled a phone number on a scrap of paper and handed it to Ivan. Then, picking up the damaged book, he marked it with a big black cross. 'Mmm. Someone didn't want that section left too public.'

'And I'll give you one guess who that was,' Ivan muttered to himself, charging through the sleeting rain to a public phone box opposite.

A boyish voice responded on the student historian's answerphone. Ivan left his message, and then went in search of lunch. A ham and mustard bap with a liberal spread of melted cheese on the top. Something filling and calorific for the afternoon ahead, at St Thomas's church.

Shop lights and Christmas displays did battle with the eerie onset of darkness as the Saxo crawled down Cobbling Street towards the roundabout. One thing was vexing Ivan: not one local paper had mentioned Ma Oakley's death or her impending funeral. Why was such a high-profile local family shrouding this occurrence in puzzling secrecy?

As he negotiated unexpected lakes of standing water along Welsh Way, Ivan was already visualizing the forthcoming funeral. Amidst black-coated figures huddled together, he envisaged Jo, beautiful and mysterious under her veil, catching his eye and smiling. *Come and get me... Come and fuck me...*

He narrowly missed a tractor spewing up shit all over his windscreen as it pulled out into Welsh Way, just ahead of him, totally blocking the road.

Suddenly it stopped, with its engine grinding, as an athletic figure in combat fatigues leapt down from the cab and strolled towards him, huge black-gloved hands held outspread on either side as if each defined finger was a threat.

The man tapped on the Saxo's window none too gently and, with a start, Ivan realized he was wearing a balaclava with just the eyes visible, blue and intense.

Ivan clicked central locking before opening the window just half an inch. The stink of manure met his nose and he could hear a dog barking in the tractor cab.

'I thought I'd better warn you, sir,' began the farmer, whom Ivan judged was probably his own age. 'There's flooding farther up. The Wap's come over badly. My poor bloody folks are stranded again, would you believe?'

Ivan was too bemused to thank him for this information. Something wasn't quite right here.

'Where exactly?' he asked. Why the balaclava? Ivan tried to work things out. Why bother to stop and tell him? And there'd been no *official* notice of flooding on the roadside.

'Dawson's Farm.'

'Dawson's Farm?'

'Second time in a month, poor bastards. I'm

OK up in Cymric there.' He indicated roughly eastwards with one of those giant black hands. 'At least I've managed to keep my ewes good and dry ready for lambing.'

'Cymric?' Ivan thought aloud. 'That's a Welsh name, surely?'

'Ten out of ten to you, sir. This *is* Welsh Way, you know. There used to be a drovers' route down near Silverstone, heading to Barnet then on to London. Anyhow, like I said,' he studied the small hatchback, 'you won't get through farther up, and that's a fact.'

'How are the local mourners going to get to the funeral?' Ivan tested him.

'What funeral's that then?' The blue eyes narrowed behind the two almond-shaped cut-outs.

'At St Thomas's, Cold Firton. Old Ma Oakley's, or so I heard.'

For a moment the man seemed genuinely blank. Or maybe he was just a bloody good actor.

'Didn't even know she'd kicked the bucket,' he said. 'Oh well, that'll set the cat among the pigeons. Watch this space.'

So, maybe Jo wasn't lying after all.

Just then, another vehicle pulled up right behind them, its headlights kept on. Ivan felt a familiar rush of panic.

'Right,' said the farmer, his tone hardening. 'Play acting's fucking over, Mr Browning. Time for you to make an exit.'

Before Ivan could react, the man had wedged a shotgun through the Saxo's window gap to prevent it closing – the barrel pointing straight at his head.

'D'you want him, Tony? Or do *I* have the pleasure?' He turned to his mate, whom Ivan now guessed must be Anthony Pike. Church House all over again, Ivan thought, except this time there was a gun less than six inches away from him.

He took a deep breath and, before the new arrival could reply, revved up and powered away from his assailant, mounting high up the bank, past the tractor. He heard the shot hitting the tarmac, and prayed nothing else was coming his way as he sped along the ancient drove road back to the bridge, and his turning into Nether Wapford.

When he finally stopped by Tripp's Cottage he was shaking from head to foot. And just as he was thanking God, and unlocking the front door, the phone in the hallway began to ring.

With the track drying up, and without the hindrance of tolls, Tomos calculated that the drove had covered fifteen miles by the time they reached Swell Borton.

As the herd heaved its way through the hamlet, Tomos argued with himself whether or not to continue for a few miles more to the forge at Maugersford, but before he could decide, Siân had drawn unnoticed alongside him, leaned over and bit his arm through the rough cloth to attract attention. His coat smelt of dung close-up, and the slap he left on her cheek stung as if a hundred bees had attacked it.

'You do that damned trick again to your brother and you'll sleep outside,' he barked, kicking the cob onwards to keep the herd going. *'Tomos!'* she breathed, not giving up. *'It's been too quiet. We need to stop soon and hide ourselves.'*

'Hide?' He glared. 'Why such a fearful little fanny all of a sudden?'

'Have you forgotten how much reward sits on our heads?' she replied, then pointed. *'Those fields there are quite empty. We could take any one – and there, look, three Scots pines. That means they welcome drovers. Can't we try there?'*

Tomos cocked his dark-hatted head, his restless eyes taking in the eerie stillness. Even the herd seemed subdued, shambling from side to side, with Ben and the terriers not pressing for any further progress.

'You got a feeling then, have you, sister?' he said suddenly.

'I feel it here.' She pressed a hand over her heart. *'God's truth.'*

'Don't you give me that gibberish. I get enough of that from the churchman back home.'

'You've got to believe me,' Siân begged. Already in her mind's eye she could see Derryn and Rhys Morris powering towards them, pistols drawn, and black revenge written on their evil faces.

It seemed her brother took a lifetime to turn the drove down towards the nearby farm, which bore the name Whitewalls on a large wooden plaque by its open gate. But then Siân gasped, for a menacing black cross had been painted over it.

There was no other dwelling in sight, and in this hollow of almost solid stillness, even the dogs sensed something was very wrong.

'Stay there and keep a watch out. Whistle if we

get company,' Tomos ordered her, then, having secured the herd in the field closest to the farmhouse, slid off the cob and walked towards the door which – like the gate – was already wide open.

He went through into the kitchen, keeping his hand on his pistol, and immediately smelt what he knew to be stale blood. He peered down at the roughly laid floor and saw a dull red trail leading towards the pantry.

The whole place had been stripped bare save for one or two tin plates strewn on an old wormy dresser, and an upturned stool with broken legs.

Tomos held his breath as he passed through the single shaft of dying sunlight appearing through the kitchen's one window, and headed into the pantry. He shielded his nose as the stink grew stronger. Then he let out a moan of horror. This wasn't some butcher's clean cut but the work of deranged madness.

Black as a piece of wet leather, the old man's tongue lay severed on his lap. His eyes, as much as the hardened drover could bear to look, hung by threads down each cheek. Behind him lay his dog with its head kicked in.

Tomos ran outside to heave the contents of his stomach onto the grass, and the two Jack Russells came to fuss around the spillage.

As she waited outside, Siân watched in alarm as Tomos wiped his mouth on his sleeve. The terriers ran into the farmhouse and came out again, yelping.

'Your feeling was wrong, sister, damn you. We can't stay here.'

He called the three dogs and gathered his reins before mounting. 'The law will think we did this, so hurry yourself.'

'*Did what, brother?*'

'No time now. Let's move.'

Never before had she seen him so nervous. And as she held the field gate open for the bullocks to emerge, she heard the familiar cry of '*Haiptrw ho!*' from behind the nearby hills.

Another drove, she thought, praying Ben would get the steers away before she and Tomos met anyone else in that place. She listened hard in the gathering dusk. It wasn't cattle this time, but sheep, their intermittent chorus growing ever closer.

She was right, the whole hillside behind the farm suddenly seemed alive with them. Then came another sound – that of men singing loudly.

Fe dynwyd hwnw ymaeth yn nghyd a 'i bwys a 'i boen
Mi ganaf un dragywydd am rinwedd Gwaed yr Oen.

Lanolin from the Welsh Mountain ewes' heavy fleeces filled her nostrils as the flock bumped by, their skull-like faces full of fear.

Tomos knew there was no avoiding this new encounter, and stayed alongside the moving bullocks until – to his own and Siân's relief – the sheep were well past them. Suddenly one of the drovers, seated on a muddy pony, galloped up to join him. Both men shook hands, then Siân saw her brother point to Whitewalls Farm.

'Don't touch that place,' he was warning. 'I know the fields look nice and free, but the devil's got there first. Best to get yourself out of here.'

'But this was to be our post for tonight – with Seth Box the bachelor. There's nowhere else for miles.' The man who'd introduced himself as Morgan signalled to his companion to stop the sheep from proceeding any farther.

Tomos took his arm. 'Unless you want to swing, I'm telling you, keep that lot moving.'

The little man with the straggling moustache then glanced at Siân.

'Very well, you done me a favour. Now I do the same for you.' He paused, looking her up and down. 'They *said* you had a young girl with dark curls, but with no talking in her.'

'Who's *they?*' Tomos demanded, a flicker of fear crossing his face.

'Call themselves Derryn and Rhys Morris, Nant-y-Fedw, near the Teifi. They'd just come through Bishop's Way when I met them.'

Siân's heart stopped beating.

'So they're ahead of us, then?'

She began to shiver as the stranger moved his pony closer and almost couldn't hear his reply.

'I warn ye, they've each got a weapon. They're spreading it about that you as porthmon chose Blaencarreg deliberately, to kill the one called Derryn.'

Siân pulled her shawl tight around herself. She just wanted this bearer of worst possible tidings to let them get on their way.

'No fair judge would ever believe such a trumped-up lie.' Tomos turned his cob and kicked it on.

The stranger, shaking his head, looked after them as the Castlemartins trekked away towards Maugersford. He was grateful not to be in their shoes.

Seventeen

'Ivan Browning here.'

'Charlie Gifford, just returning your call.' He sounded nothing like the librarian, that was for sure.

'Thanks for ringing me back.'

'No worries. Actually my dear brother's just phoned me about you and Stanton's old book being trashed. Still, it doesn't surprise me: desperate people do desperate things.'

'It's this cottage of mine. I've only been here four months and I'm curious about its past, so when your brother told me you'd studied the area's history, I thought you might have some gen on it.'

Gifford gave a little laugh. 'To be accurate, I mainly focused on those Dawson characters my brother said you were interested in. Look, d'you mind phoning me back? I'm a bit strapped at the mo, and phone calls cost money.'

'Join the club.' Ivan then dialled the number.

'Yeah, how can I help you?' Gifford continued.

'I'd be interested to see your dissertation,' Ivan finally replied.

'Well, I'll tell you something. The Dawsons wouldn't.'

'The Dawsons?'

'Yeah, Roy and the lovely Doreen. The high-tech King and Queen of Nether Wapford, Great

Britain, Europe – the world, you name it.'

Ivan decided to be straight with this man whose easy-going manner seemed an antidote to his own tortured feelings. 'I've just met their son on Welsh Way,' he began, 'with his tractor, blocking the way – and a gun, if you please.'

'Ah, angry young Andrew? That sounds about right,' said Gifford.

'Had a mate as well, Anthony Pike I reckon, who came up behind me, trying to put the frighteners on me.'

'You sure?'

'Well, I didn't actually *see* the other guy, but Dawson junior called him Tony, and I'm sure I recognized his voice.'

Gifford was silent for a moment. 'Well, if it's any consolation, I'm waiting any day now for my own head to be removed from my body. Or worse.'

'*What?*' Ivan started.

'Hey, it wasn't uncommon in these parts.' Gifford was on a roll now. 'Or else, to save time, they just cut out your tongue.'

Ivan felt sick. How could Gifford talk so glibly about these things?

'We should meet up,' the other man then suggested. 'I'm never one hundred per cent about these rustic phone lines, and whose big red ears are flapping. What about tomorrow night, Poacher's Arms in Broad Street? Friday's always fun in there.'

'OK, fine.'

'Make it seven, and I'll bring my work along in a plain wrapper.' He added, 'So what do you look like?'

299

'Joseph Fiennes minus the stubble, I'm told.'

'Whoa ... that's a grabber. See you then. *Ciao*.'

Ivan frowned, listening in the silence for any interference on the line, but the tone seemed normal enough. The thought then crossed his mind that the irrepressible Mr Gifford might be gay.

Two o'clock and one hour to go. But should he risk going to the Cold Firton funeral or not?

It wasn't just raining: it was as if the sky were one vast tub of water tipping out on the unfortunates below, so the Citroën's wipers could barely cope, and more than once it skewered on the treacherously flooded roads.

Ivan had felt tempted to travel the long way round to Cold Firton, but the ditches below Halsey Wood on the Radby Road were notorious and best avoided in even far less extreme conditions. So, wearing his shades for added anonymity, and an old dark overcoat from college days, and bringing his large black umbrella, courtesy of British Rail Lost Property, he processed to the village in the unlikely company of a cement lorry, a camper van and a slatted truck full of murmuring sheep. They left dark green dribbles on the tarmac in front, which then, diluted by spray and rain, ended up on his windscreen. He'd had time to look at Wiseman's Farm, expecting to see some activity at least, but again the place was gated and empty as if even the dead had deserted it.

In a rash moment, having entered the High Street, Ivan decided to park out of sight in the

Friar's Walk executive development, hoping it wasn't the Swordfish's front garden which was the closest to his car. The wind slammed his door shut and his umbrella – once opened – instantly inverted itself into a useless rag held by bent struts.

Nevertheless, despite his too-dark glasses, Ivan made his way across the road and towards the church, where a fresh grave heaped with soggy flowers and flattened ink-run cards of sympathy lay near the vestry.

He stopped in his tracks to read the new gold words, THOMAS RAYMOND COLES, A GOOD CITIZEN, incised into the grey marble headstone. Here was the reality of life in Cold Firton...

'You, God, up there,' he turned his face to the black sky, 'you'd better get off your backside, and sooner rather than later.'

Solemn organ music filtered from the church, soon lost in the downpour. He could see lights through the heavily barred stained-glass windows, but there was no-one else walking in, nor even vehicles parked. There was, however, over by the yews near the far wall, a heap of ochre soil waiting above an open grave.

Ivan went into the porch to disentangle his umbrella, and shake off the worst of the water, when suddenly someone from the shadows touched his arm. It was Valerie Rook, nervous and pale in a black coat. He noticed a slight blushing on her cheeks, her hair shorter than usual and its edges uneven as if cut in a hurry.

'Why are you wearing those?' She pointed at

301

his face.

'My shades? Just in case. You never know. How are things your end, by the way? Any word from Michael yet?'

She glanced in the direction of the nave as if expecting to be interrupted, then shivered. 'He phoned before I left. He should be back by ten tonight. I'm still not up to having to explain things, to listen to him sounding off ... not yet, anyhow...'

'Can I help at all?'

'I don't think so. Thank you all the same.'

Ivan glanced at his watch. The thing was still obstinately ten minutes slow.

'They're cutting it a bit fine,' he said.

Valerie leaned closer, to whisper.

'I'm not sure if this is good news or bad news, but it's *very* weird. You see, the Oakleys may not be coming here after all...'

'You're kidding?' As all anticipation haemorrhaged away.

'An old school friend of mine who runs the florists's in town, phoned a minute ago. She said the flowers had just been collected by Stephen Oakley to be taken down to London.'

The crafty bastards.

'That's where they're originally from though, isn't it?'

'Yes, but for some reason they used an Aylesbury undertakers, which I thought was odd. Not cheap either.'

Ivan returned to the subject of Ma Oakley. 'So was there any post-mortem on the old girl? It all seems so bloody hush-hush.'

'Michael had been out to see her the week before. Breathing difficulties, he said, possibly a mild pneumonia, but she insisted against hospital treatment.'

'I'd like to know who exactly called him out.' Ivan was now suspicious. 'So no inquest either?'

'I don't think so. Apparently she died naturally in her sleep.' Valerie sniffed, then blew her nose. 'All I do know is the church has been made to look a *complete* idiot, and, the vicar was telling me earlier, the gravediggers have been paid up front already. I suppose they could always keep the thing open, but trouble is, like he said, people don't like to see a gaping hole. I certainly don't.'

'I'm sure there'll be someone soon to fill it, the way things are going round here,' Ivan said darkly, reliving his confrontation in Welsh Way. He checked his watch again. 'So why's the bloody organ still playing? It's gone three o'clock.'

'The vicar still thinks the Oakleys will have a change of heart. Probably want to bury her near where she spent her last years.'

'I can't see that lot doing a U-turn and heading back up the M1 somehow.'

'If you want my opinion I think they got the wind up. After all, they'd have been here *en famille* ready to be bagged.'

It certainly looked that way. Ivan watched the rain pour down past the porch door. So why had Jo tried to mislead him? And *who* had tipped the plods off? Or was there a mole in the cop shop? That didn't seem such an outrageous notion – the newspapers were always full of police corruption. Besides, hadn't Jeanette Yates implied the very same to him?

Valerie Rook pulled her coat closer, holding the lapels tight under her throat. 'I feel really uneasy about everything at the moment,' she said. 'Receiving those notes hasn't helped.' She nudged her companion towards the door. 'But we'll get to the bottom of it all soon, don't worry. Look, I'll ring you sometime.'

'Are you busy tomorrow morning? I wondered if you'd like to come with me to the Records Office.'

For the first time a proper smile lit up her face. 'I'd love to. What time?'

'Nine-thirty, outside the post office in Stoneshanger. Now, what about that cigarette lighter?'

'I took it over to my solicitor yesterday morning. It's in his safe now.'

'Thank God.'

Half a second later Ivan was outside the church and running back to his car. Instead of turning left, curiosity made him turn right and, on passing the late Ma Oakley's cottage, he saw a new silver Merc parked by the kerb and a plump man hammering in a County Homes For Sale sign.

Meanwhile the vicar had emerged from the gloomy nave of the church and was warmly shaking Valerie's hand in the porch.

Tuesday 28 February, and with no word announced of the gruesome discovery at Whitewalls Farm the day before, the shoeing of Tomos Richards's herd at Maugersford took up most of the day.

The smith, his thrower and a helper worked from dawn until dark, first trimming the hooves then fitting two cues – or tips – to each hoof, occasionally expressing disbelief that any responsible drover could have skimped on these essential items for so long.

Siân, fascinated, watched this ritual of men pitting their cunning against brute strength. Each bullock was roped first, then, while the thrower took the horns, his lad gripped a foreleg and bent it at the knee as the thrower finally twisted the horns to bring the creature down. Its legs were bound fore to back with this same rope secured to a forked iron stake lodged deep in the ground. Thus was the beast made ready for shoeing.

She guessed that the lad helping was about Huw's age. He possessed a mop of fair hair and muscles which had glowed with sweat even in the early sun. Whenever the shoeing team stopped for water and a hunk of bread, away from the choking smell of singed bone, the youth, Joel Liles, wandered over to the strangely dressed but pretty girl and offered her a piece of his loaf and butter. Siân ate as if she'd had nothing else since she came on this earth.

By the time the forty-six bullocks were shod with eight cues apiece, and Cassiopeia's constellation flickered high in the sky, she'd found out that Joel Liles was an orphan with an uncle in Cheapside, while he in turn got acquainted with her little corner of Wales – with her precious Da and the mother she could never please. But not one word about Huw, whose birthday was tomorrow, St David's Day. That was *too* painful. But, she told herself, should she find a daffodil, or better still a Lenten Lily on that next day's journey, she would kiss it and wear it close to her heart.

To the Welshman's relief there were no reward notices up in the Naked Sailor tavern next door to the forge, nor had the innkeeper seen anything of a trio from Herefordshire, or the Morris brothers.

While Siân was giving the dogs fresh bowls of water and washing her face in the freezing pump water, Tomos settled himself inside at a table near the fire with the shoer and his crew.

'That's two pound and threepence to come to me,' the smith said to Tomos over a glass of black ale, 'and one pound two shillings for me thrower here and the boy.'

Tomos looked pained. The total was close to the price of two bullocks, and reluctantly he handed over a collection of coins, all worn thin from use. Then, completely out of character, he left his money pouch open and tapped the farrier's arm.

'Now, sir, I'm willing to pay you extra for you to see off two felons from here should they come a-calling from the Stow side.' As the older man looked bemused, Tomos elaborated further. 'They're lying in wait and would kill us if they could – me and my poor daughter out there who's going to London with me for a cure.' Joel Liles seemed surprised at this unlikely relationship but said nothing as he pressed some tobacco into a sliver of paper.

'Why? What you done?' asked the smith downing the rest of his drink in one go, his body giving off the stink of dried sweat with every movement.

'Nothing, sir, I swear on the Trinity.' Tomos made sure the man could see a five-pound note bearing the name of the Aberystwyth and Tregaron Bank but passed him two shillings. 'And here's a warning,' his finger stabbed the table for emphasis, 'they'll make bother for you, given half a chance. Derryn and Rhys Morris they are called.'

The other three men eyed each other before the smith finally took the money and thrust it in his pocket. At which the drover sighed with relief, and paid for yet another pint of ale as Siân came in from the pump, her face now glowing.

The Naked Sailor was filling up, mostly with local farmers whose faces were pinched leathery from winter work. Their local dialect was difficult to follow, but while Tomos drew up a stool for his legs to rest on and closed his eyes, his sister edged closer to the one they called Obadiah who, in between sucks of his old pipe, seemed to have the most to say.

'Whitewalls, that's it. Ain't never seen nothin' like it in all this unblessed world. There he were, poor Seth Box, with his old tongue sawn out of his mouth, his 'ands gone too, but worse–' Everyone listened intently, their drinks untouched. 'As Jesus loves me, 'is eyes was 'angin' down his face like marbles from a bag. And there's nothing left of 'is home neither. It's like a plague of vermin have been in and eaten the lot.'

'How do you know of all this?' someone asked at length.

'There was this hedge-layer and his son called in my place like they'd seen a phantom or summat.' The farmer stopped to bang his pipe on the table and discharge a pile of foul black ash. Tomos woke up, rubbing his eyes, then listened as the story unfolded. 'As I were sayin', they told me and the wife they'd seen two roughnecks riding out of Whitewalls, all loaded up so they could hardly move. Must 'ave been after 'is money 'cos 'e'd just sold off all his stock at Roundwell. Anyways, from what these hedgers could tell, them others spoke in some foreign tongue. Had two bays, one light, one dark. 'Course, after they'd gone, I rode straight round to Fulford to get the constable. Terrible business. Oh Jesus, I seen some sights with slaughtering beasts, but nothing like this – to a *man*.'

After that, the talk was of the dead farmer's colourful life. How he'd imported six Merino rams from near Adelaide and let them run with his black-faced Norfolks. The wool had made him rich, but never bought him a wife or children.

'Did the hedgers say which way these two were heading?' asked Tomos, noticeably nervous.

'East, towards Churchill. That means they're in front of you.'

'And they'll be ready for us,' Siân whispered.

It was getting worse with every minute of every day. Her chances of ever reaching the London hospital were slipping away like the water pouring over the waterfall near Nant y Fedw. Her Da's notion had come from the heart, she knew that, but all the same, a heart ignorant of the full wickedness of the world. For, apart from Ma Morris's vicious tongue and his overseer at the Dowlais Works calling him a *mais ddu*, a black turnip, Geraint Richards was an innocent in the ways of hard men, and she, at fourteen, had seen more evil in the past ten days than either he or her mother put together.

They had never even known their own son. But she did – this 'piece of plague' – and now her future, which depended on him, held nothing but fear.

Eighteen

Despite the foul weather and the deepening darkness of this Thursday afternoon, Ivan drove straight to Office World, to the south of Northampton, and bought a new mobile phone. He still felt cheated by Jo's absence at St Thomas's church, puzzled by her obvious lie about Ma Oakley's death. While he waited in the checkout queue, he also puzzled over how she'd never been seen attending that church with the rest of the clan, and how, apart from her irregular presence at the Lamb and Flag, she almost seemed not to exist. Who really *was* Jo Oakley? And the more he tried to fathom it, the more fascinating, more cruelly out of his reach she grew...

When he got home, Ivan was drenched. He lit a fire and draped his old coat over the back of a chair in front of it until the flames drew out the wool's moisture into tiny dew-like bubbles. This was the coat he'd worn on his first date with Tania. The same in which he'd stood and watched his Aunt Bridget's coffin smothered by wet earth. But now the familiar garment hung like a bad omen in the small room, relinquishing all its past associations to the flickering heat, freeing itself up for what might come next...

He made a cup of tea, binned the tattered relic of his umbrella, and headed into his workshop without any creative purpose at all. He found his fingers closing round the kiln door handle, opening it wide now, dreading any lingering smell of that choking smoke. But, no, nothing of that remained, just five shelves of ossified urns unchanged since the last time he'd looked inside, still perched on their stilts exactly as he'd first placed them, but somehow defying him to interfere with them in any way.

Their creator ran a tentative finger over the familiar curves, the scratched patterns of the River Wap, and then studied his fingertip. It looked as if he'd stuck it into a pile of bone ash...

As a student, he'd originally subscribed to *Ceramic Review* and pored regularly over the Potters' Problems pages, eager to learn how to avoid unnecessary mistakes, for, as even the most seasoned practitioners would point out, there were always unseen forces at work.

What would the magazine's readers make of all this, he wondered. What would anybody make of this total absence of both copper and cobalt glazes? They'd no doubt suggest that the pyrometer had failed, leaving the temperature to soar to the limit of porcelain, or that the glaze and the clay body were incompatible – so the former had crawled literally off the face of his work. But to where?

Ivan looked between the upper and lower rows for any sign of blobbing or spreading glaze, but the shelves were immaculate, the base of each urn clean and sharp.

He knew that some time he'd have to unpack the bloody kiln, then get it shipshape again, maybe to sell. But for the moment, it was best to leave things as they were. Let the dust, or rather the ash, settle until the time was right. But in his heart Ivan knew that time would never come, not here in Tripp's Cottage...

The phone ringing back in the hall stopped his reverie, and for a moment, once he'd picked up the receiver, his voice disappeared. He coughed once, twice, finally managing a whisper.

'*Yes?*'

'Douglas Cartwright of County Homes here, Mr Browning. You called in on us earlier, I believe. When would be convenient for me to visit?' His tone suggested he was a busy man.

'Er... I'll be in tomorrow afternoon.'

'Sorry, can't hear you.'

Ivan repeated what he'd said. It was as if that same bone ash had lodged in his throat, on his tongue. He needed to drink, then to spit it all out.

'Say four, o'clock then. I've a couple of other places to see as well.'

'*Great.*' Again it came out as no more than a croak.

Ten seconds later, Ivan had his mouth directly under the kitchen tap. This was freaky. He'd always tried to keep clay and glaze dust under control with a damp cloth and, even as a school teacher and on-going Marlboro chainer, had rarely suffered a bad throat. But he *had* inhaled *that* smoke, so maybe some ash particles as well.

'Christ, give me a break,' he spluttered, having rinsed and spat in the sink for the umpteenth time. What was truly freaky, though, were the darker flecks he saw spinning towards the plughole. And, when he'd trapped a couple of them between his thumb and forefinger and rubbed them together, a single dark smudge materialized – looking exactly as if he'd touched one of his burnt oak logs.

Wood and bone ... bone and wood ... even elm becomes ash in the end.

It was the first of March, and Huw Davies's birthday, but not a Lenten Lily in sight, as the Nant y Fedw drove processed down through quiet holloways and up along the dry Gloucestershire heathland.

Siân happened to look down and see a small lake set at the bottom of a fallow field – silver as the new day's sky.

'Tomos?' She kicked her mare on to catch up with him, taking care not to startle the bullocks moving sweetly enough on their newly shod hooves. *'Down there!'* she hissed. *'Look!'*

Two saddled horses were grazing by the water's edge, but of their riders there was no sign. Her eyes began to swim. She was hungry, cold, and the tiny room she'd occupied at the Naked Sailor had been alive with mice.

'Could be them.' Her brother slowed down. 'Now then, sister, I've a plan.'

Siân knew all about his so-called plans. 'You're to stay up front. Here, take my stick. And when I set these boys off, you keep up with them. Understood?'

Siân began to quake with terror. He was going to bolt the drove deliberately, and she'd got no saddle, just her poor knees to cling on with. 'If folks see *you* at the front, there'll be pity. They'll think, poor little biddy, the runts have gone wild on her.'

'*What if we lose some?*' she asked, still hoping to put him off. '*What if they can't be found?*'

'And I say, what's one or two next to my own life if those bastards catch me?'

My *life?*... But she had no choice, his mind was made up. Siân knew better than to test him further.

'Be gone with you, now!' He slapped Collen so hard on the rump that she reared, and then galloped at full stretch in front of the mass of black bodies.

Siân clung on desperately, with the icy air stinging her face, hearing with dread the thundering hooves behind. Knowing death must surely be not so far away, she shut her eyes to meet it.

The Castlemartins' mad sprint filled that early spring morning, thrumming the soil like the sounds of an army. It drove birds from the coppices and sent terrified sheep fanning away to distant corners of their fields. Upon reaching Little Clapton, the herd cleared the hamlet, with women and children running back behind their front doors, and dogs howling from their various places of safety.

Then moving higher again, away from dwellings and the works of men, away from trees and hedges – reaching just bleak brown grass against the sky. Siân's terror kept her urging the little mare on, feeling the animal's hot sweat seep into her own skin. She could hear Tomos at the rear, yelling at the dogs, but all she could think of was those treacherous black-tipped horns just behind and ready to skewer her if she slowed up for one second.

'*Haiptrw ho!*' she tried to scream, spotting a small farm and scattered outbuildings at the bottom of the next hill. But no one could stop them, or even attempted to, and when the drove careered past, Obadiah Willett's pipe dropped from his mouth and into the dung as he recognized the dark Welshman pass by, his coat flapping, long legs dangling below his cob's belly.

With relief Siân sensed the herd was gradually slowing behind her, and she let Collen's pace drop to a canter. The mare's sides heaved pitifully, her normally alert head casting from side to side in exhaustion. Siân patted her, promising her a good feed and a warm bed when their next stop came. The pony had surely saved her life.

As the drove's charge dwindled to a walk, Tomos stole up beside her, retrieving his stick and ordering her back to her usual place at the rear. She could hear him counting heads, but not a word of thanks to her passed his lips.

'None's gone astray,' he muttered finally, fishing out a crust from his pocket and ramming it into his mouth. 'And now we've got a good head start, we can make the Evenlode by dusk. That's as near enough Oxfordshire as makes no difference.'

'*Oxfordshire?*' Siân protested, seeing weary

spittle dangling from Collen's mouth.

'I'm not asking your opinion, sister. I'm telling you that's what we're doing. Place called Ramsden Worthy, though why in God's name the *Saesnegs* must call a place such fancy nonsense. Anyhow, Bernie Bowen told me he knew a lodging there with good grass.'

They'll need more than good grass, thought Siân, eyeing the bullocks' sweat-drenched ribs, their sudden loss of condition. Besides, the dogs, especially the little ones, were panting as if their last breath would soon come.

'You won't have anything left to sell at this rate, brother,' she whispered. *'Then what'll pay Dr Owen?'*

Tomos whipped round and banged his stick soundly on her one good knee.

'Who says *I'm* paying him? His bill will be sent to your Da. This is all his notion, not mine, remember? I could have saved this lot for the store sales in May when they'd have gone for double the price. But, oh no, I've got *you* to pander to.'

Siân hung back, letting the mare's reins slacken and her own pain-racked limbs recover. Mrs Hubbard's clothes felt as heavy as if she carried another person on her back, but all this, she knew, was meant to test her resolve. In less than a week she'd be with a proper medical man, not like that Dr Trieni – old Dr Misery from Dynfant. Tomos and his cruelty would have to be borne meanwhile: she had no choice in the matter. And, as sure as stars always bloom in a clear night sky, her time would come...

316

Nineteen

Ivan found the last remaining parking space outside the post office, hoping that Valerie's geriatric Lada wouldn't let her down in getting there.

Yesterday's rain had eased during the night, and patches of blue showed between the clouds, yet still the roads were shining wet, the drains full.

He waited for her white jalopy to appear, and sure enough he saw it turn up a side street and disappear, but the figure who emerged five minutes later, crossing the road towards him, looked nothing like the woman he knew.

She wore a brown cloche hat to eyebrow level, and an extra-long winter coat with collar up, and shoes that Ivan guessed were more for walking outside of town than in it. She had her hair scraped back to just below the hat brim.

Ivan opened the Saxo's passenger door for her.

'I could take the bus, you know,' Valerie suggested. 'The number 45 will drop me right opposite the Record Office. We don't really want to be seen together. You never know who's keeping a look-out.'

Ivan reluctantly agreed and pulled away from the bus stop where she joined a small queue, her eyes turned away from the street.

Having overtaken a removals van, he relaxed enough to spot some tree surgeons high in an oak coppice to the left, and the raw ochre patches where branches had already been lopped. He was thinking how yet another shake of the kaleidoscope could show him more enticing fragments of rural life. Despite his bad throat, Ivan sensed his old curiosity returning, and soon, with any luck, and Valerie's help, he'd be able to slot together some important pieces of the jigsaw which so far had eluded him.

At Woolerton he parked the car and waited till he could detect her in the middle distance, having been deposited by her bus, now picking her way across busy traffic. Ivan climbed out and was inclined to go and meet her, but the traffic was too dense, surging towards a five-lane round-about. He had to stay and wait till a succession of lorries and juggernauts rolled by.

Suddenly he heard a woman's screams from beyond them. Once the vehicles had passed, he could see a black taxi cab screech away from the red lights, cut over the central reservation and head back down the dual carriageway towards Stoneshanger and the M1. Too fast for him to catch its number plate. But it was a Pronto cab, he just knew. So who, then, had been driving it?

Nothing stopped for her. Vehicles simply moved around the stricken woman, honking their impatience with the obstruction as if she were some drunken bag lady.

Feeling sick inside, Ivan charged over the dual carriageway, dodging two clapped-out Fiestas racing each other. Valerie clearly had been hit, and lay in the outside lane of an exit road.

His stomach took a dive. Vicky Walker had lain exactly like this and, even though all his First Aid training said leave well alone, he'd taken the girl in his arms, and had cradled her until she died under the sodium lights.

'Valerie? Are you OK? Please try and answer!' he whispered.

She looked up at him in silence. Her head had obviously struck the concrete edge of the kerb, and blood eked from her scalp onto the tarmac. Just then a cacophony of sirens, and, as if by a miracle, all the traffic stopped. A police Mondeo appeared from nowhere and screamed to a halt. Soon a team of paramedics from an arriving ambulance had checked the woman over and lifted her onto a stretcher, her handbag being gathered up by one of the crew.

He felt sick and dizzy – this had been no hit-and-run accident, and when the two traffic cops invited him into their car for a statement, he banged his head hard on the door frame and nearly passed out.

In the Mondeo smelling of half-eaten sandwiches, the two-way radio crackled incessantly as Ivan spoke, each husky word a further strain on his throat.

'So, no other possible witnesses?' they quizzed him, once they'd taken down his basic details.

'You're kidding? Nothing bloody stops for anything round here.' Ivan held his head in his hands, his voice scarcely rising to the occasion. 'This black Pronto cab did a mad U-turn on the grass just up from here,' he pointed, 'then it buggered off towards Stoneshanger. You ought to go looking for it quickly, not waste time with me...'

'Now then, sir,' the darker man suddenly changed the subject and stared at Ivan in his mirror. 'Do we know you.'

'What d'you mean?' Thinking of that minibus again – every shocking detail of the whole ghastly affair. His stomach turned over, expecting the worst.

'Once you said Nether Wapford it clicked, of course. Tripp's Cottage and the dog-in-a-bag business.'

'That's nothing to what else has been going on.'

The two officers, in their vivid yellow gear looked at each other. One of them turned back to him.

'All we can say is that everything's adding up. And we're not so bad at our sums, are we, Dave?'

'Nope.' The other man then blew his nose repeatedly.

'So, rest assured, just because this whole business isn't hitting the headlines doesn't mean there's nothing going on. I believe, sir, that our colleagues down in Stoneshanger CID have given you some sound advice already?'

'You lie low from now on, Mr Browning, or we can't promise you'll get to grow old,' his mate filled in. 'There are some vicious types around.'

Those chilling words made Ivan clamp his arms round his body, as if to warm himself.

'So, may I ask what the two of you are doing up this way?' asked the darker one called Dave.

'I needed some info about my cottage from the County Record Office. I just asked Mrs Rook to come along and help me, as a friend...'

The men exchanged meaningful glances, and Ivan realized what was going on in their minds. It was pathetic.

'Look, chum, leave the digging to the professionals. That's our job, and it could get nastier than it is already. We don't want to be turning up next time with body bags.'

After Ivan had signed his statement, he was given both officers' direct-line numbers at HQ plus one for the local hospital's A and E department. Once out of the stuffy car he felt big rain drops hit his head. As he waited for a gap in the traffic so that he could cross over towards his car, he glanced back and saw Valerie's blood begin to spread thinly on the Tarmac.

'Mr Browning? Your friend can see you now. She's doing nicely, so we've put her in one of the recovery wards.' The staff nurse turned and bustled down the corridor in front of him.

He entered a bright crowded ward to find Valerie sitting propped up in a bed wearing an institutional nightdress, with a lint bandage perched on the side of her head. Her lips moved in a weak smile of welcome.

Ivan bent over her. 'I'm so bloody sorry...'

'What for? I wanted to go along – and I'll do it again if I have to. They're *not* going to win, I'm telling you. I'll do whatever else it takes. This has just made me more determined.' Her mouth firmed up stubbornly. 'I recognized who it was that hit me, even though I've not seen him for a while, and he had some sort of cap on. I'll never forget that angry face as long as I live. He's just as bad as his brother.' She lowered her voice. 'It *was* John Oakley, and that's what I'm going to tell the police when they come to see me.' She leaned forward towards Ivan. 'I'm not scared any more. Just bloody angry. And the day I can move back into Small Copse, this won't have been in vain.'

Valerie took his hand. 'I'm sorry to give you all this bother, but please let Mr Gilbert know, won't you? He's in Monkton Regis, 57 High Street. I don't think I can manage to phone him at the moment.'

'Of course I will. Don't worry.' He suddenly bent to kiss her cool forehead. She smelt of spring flowers. 'And what about your husband? Does he know you're here?'

'Not yet. Anyhow I'll just tell him it was my fault. My own stupidity.'

'Shit, Valerie, he's bound to find out.'

She suddenly looked tired, her head lolled back against the pillow. 'Leave it to me. There'll be time enough.'

'You'll have to excuse us now.' The same nurse had arrived, and began to draw the faded curtain round the bed. 'Mrs Rook needs some more rest.'

'When do you think she'll be out?'

'Could be Sunday with a bit of luck – if she keeps doing well.'

Once outside in the main reception area he dialled one of the police officer's numbers.

'They're both still out on duty but can I take a message?' replied a young woman.

'Look, I'm worried about Mrs Valerie Rook here in Northampton General Hospital. Someone tried to harm her earlier and she's *still* at risk.

She should have protection of some sort at least. I'll come back here myself and stay in her ward all night if I have to.'

'I'll see this suggestion gets passed on, Mr Browning. Both officers should be back at any moment.'

He then got through to directory enquiries for the Monkton Regis number and, having left a message about Valerie on her solicitor's answerphone, drove away from the car park with a heavy heart. Under a sky more grey than blue, with darker clouds mustering over to the west, he set off to join the ring road for the A43 turning.

Ivan noticed that those same problem trees opposite Burcote were now completely bare of branches, save for their topmost crowns which were host to a gathering of crows. He'd always missed trees in his built-up, overcrowded part of London, but here they seemed different, menacing, reinforcing his unease. He remembered his father once told him that oak trees scream when sawn, and so absorbed was he in this distant memory that he just missed hitting a giant sawmills lorry pulling out of a parking area in front of him. Christ, he was cracking up, big time... And time was running out.

There was no further stopping until the first dwellings of Ramsden Worthy came into view. By this time, the exhausted bullocks were dithering along the earthen track as if blind, barging, swaying and letting out such plaintive noises that Siân expected some to drop dead at any moment.

This was another place of stillness, as if the

village's population all slumbered late in their beds – save for one emaciated hound which slunk from one barn to another. The cottage windows were all closed tight, and no smoke came from any chimney, but more alarming were the open drains lying half full of an ochre liquid: sweet and fetid.

Tomos sniffed, then again. He halted the drove then turned in his saddle.

'That's the place – over there.' He pointed to a steep-roofed abode with the faded words Fiddler's Rest on a sign alongside. Ben was whining – he knew something was wrong. 'This air's bad,' Tomos then shouted. 'And Ramsden Worthy's dead with it.'

Siân knew it too. Something terrible had happened and there wasn't a living soul here who could tell the tale. She urged Collen to the inn's open doorway, where an old pump stood nearby. Water was needed urgently, the animals were all desperate to drink. She dismounted and tried to crank the pump handle, but before anything came, Tomos leapt off the cob and pulled her away.

'D'you want to kill us all, sister? Stay with the horses.' He then worked the handle himself repeatedly until a foul yellow liquid appeared, as if putrefying corpses in the spring water below had brought plague to all those who drank.

While Tomos herded the cattle into an empty barn and ransacked the bins for feed, Siân tied the horses up and stumbled into the ghost of the inn. For what else is such a place without laughter and men's histories against a ready fire, she thought, eyeing the spent grate, the bareness of everything. She shivered and drew her clothes tight round herself, feeling a hunger so sharp and constant she was sure she was going to faint.

The kitchen and store had nothing, not even a crumb, and the salting hooks hung bare from the huge beams. She pulled open more empty drawers, more empty cupboards, but whoever had got there first had left nothing. Even the chairs and stools had obviously been carted off. But, where *was* everybody, Siân wondered, as she began to crawl up the stone steps to the floor above. The smell grew more pronounced and filled her lungs as she pushed open the door to one of the rooms and stood in shock. What she saw in that darkened room she was sure would possess her for as long as she lived.

The four beds lay in disorder – their rough blankets, dark and stiff with blood and faeces, reached untidily to the floor which resembled a slaughterhouse. She recoiled, one hand tight over her nose, then heard a dog come leaping up the steps. Suddenly Ben, who had no reason to be away from the herd, was beside her, pulling at her skirt, urging her to leave.

She followed him outside, with that smell still lodged inside her, to where Tomos was already mounted and yelling for Ben. He then pulled a rag up over his mouth protectively.

They had to leave in haste or else join those he had seen lying heaped up in the barn, their feet, like white marble, curved up to heaven.

Nightfall, and the gathering clouds brought a soft

rain as the exhausted party finally halted by the Copper Coin outside Wychfield. Just ten miles from the Gloucestershire/Oxfordshire border.

Siân lay slumped on Collen's neck, her knees aching, her neck aching, but barely caring any more. It was as if that village of the newly dead had shown her the future. Her future.

She'd breathed its foul air, intruded where those dying souls had lain in their own blood and ordure, and now it was simply a matter of time ... and a time not too far away either.

'A dog's missing, dammit.' Tomos tied up the weary cob, then bawled for the absent terrier to show itself. 'Damned critter, cost me a three-pence, that did.'

Its exhausted partner had simply gone to lie by the hedge, until Tomos kicked it back into life. Siân watched helpless, too tired to intervene, as the little scrap went and cowered next to Ben whose tongue hung limp from his jaws. She should never have agreed to this journey. She should have fought against it, gone off and hidden somewhere. Better to live like a gypsy, she thought, than endure this continuing cruelty, for such was her increasing mistrust and hatred of Tomos Richards, porthmon, and a man grown mad for money.

'And as for Ramsden Worthy, no one'll go near the place again till they bloody 'ave to.' The publican's mass of grey beard seemed to move with his red lips as he brought over two platters of fat bacon and potatoes for Siân and Tomos. 'Mind, those Wellers from Lee Bottom ain't so fussy. Those vultures will have the clothes off yer

326

back afore yer blood's cold.'

Despite the welcome food which barely touched the sides of her mouth, Siân shivered at his talk of these local looters and pilferers who'd moved in on death so quickly. Vultures, the man called them, and vultures were scavengers who would take the plague with them wherever they went. 'Still, Ramsden Worthy belongs to the devil now, God rest their souls,' he continued.

'There was more than twenty in the barn there, naked as the day they were born,' Tomos announced, pulling a piece of fat from between his teeth. Siân gasped and tried to speak, but her brother's answer was to pull the jug of ale towards him, gulping from it in one draught. Then he buttered a lump of bread and crammed the loaf bit by bit into his mouth, never thinking, like Siân, to save some for the two remaining dogs.

'The cholera's creeping in, that's for sure.' The innkeeper then clapped his hands and a tiny figure dressed in miniature adult's clothes appeared with a cloth and a broom twice his height, and proceeded to clear up the un-occupied part of the room. 'This one's mother left this world only a week ago. Swelled up like a turkey, didn't she, Alfie? Left him with nothing. But still, there's always the Freak Fair at Lee Wood. That'll pay for his keep here so far.'

Siân felt a tremor pass through her, and wanted to put her arms around the tiny boy's shoulders as if to hold him there in a place of relative safety for ever.

Twenty

Detective Constable Philip Marsh vacated his bed well in advance of his alarm, not merely to spend more time on his ablutions and re-ironing his new cream shirt, which still bore unwanted creases from its Next packaging, but because a certain excitement had kept his mind on alert throughout the night, revisiting the events which had led up to his decision – to mastermind the Oakleys' permanent exit from Wiseman's Farm.

Their knee-jerking recklessness had gone too far, and no longer could he guarantee to keep the shit they'd accumulated from hitting the fan. After all, he had himself to think about – an officer with two commendations to his name, and an imminent step-up to the post of Inspector with the Metropolitan Police on the cards. No, he thought, opening his bedroom curtains to see the flat wet fields, part of the river Nene's flood plain, enough was enough. It was time to exert his authority.

Normally on Fridays he could take things rather more easily and substitute his Stoneshanger office and Whitrow's increasing questions for the weekly briefing with the DS and his team up at Woolerton. That change of routine inevitably meant a decent roast lunch and, if nothing was pressing in the afternoon, nine holes at the Danesbrook Golf Club in the company of fellow Masons, with drinks at the bar to follow.

However, today was different, and he'd already phoned HQ with his apology and convincing reason for absence – a tricky family matter near Coventry which needed his urgent intervention but, as he set up the ironing board and expertly moved the hot iron over his shirt front, he realized this fictitious 'family' which had served him so well in the past, had reached its sell-by date.

As Marsh steered the iron between the shirt's six buttons he rehearsed his contingency plan for his co-paymasters over at Wiseman's Farm. *Frighteners* would be a better word, he thought, smiling to himself, as he eventually unplugged the iron and left it upright to cool. Enough to see the problematic quartet of Monica, Harold, John and Stephen safely ensconced on foreign soil by early tomorrow morning.

Of course the girl would be present there too. But it wasn't simply for this new millionairess that he was making this special effort with his appearance. As Commander of Operation Exit he must inspire confidence and not a little fear in the older generation, and be able to field the Oakleys' inevitable awkward questions as to why he couldn't protect them any longer from their own stupidity. But once they were made to realize it was in their best interests to flee, then the way would be clear for his even closer cooperation with Roy and Doreen Dawson. Where the potential for *real* money and prospects lay.

Philip Marsh carefully bore his shirt upstairs and, as he passed the landing window of his new detached Persimmon home near Gayton, noticed that the weather was worsening and would be unlikely to change during the day. In the bedroom mirror he spotted an earlier shaving cut beginning to bleed afresh. He cursed as its dark stain persisted through the successive scraps of pink toilet paper he pressed tight to the side of his neck.

It was 10.30 a.m. and he'd deliberately missed breakfast. He'd finally inspected his brown suit jacket for the two nine-millis tucked away inside, and had just reopened his briefcase to check that the Oakleys' new passports were in place, when the phone in his study suddenly rang.

The detective held his breath, letting the answerphone begin to record a man's breathless message, relieved it wasn't his Superintendent checking up on his whereabouts. Then he snatched up the receiver.

'Yes?'

'Problem, sir.'

It was John Oakley. Marsh frowned as he eyed the young postwoman through his study window, making her way up the path to his front door. After the drop of post on his mat, he watched her swinging her hips as she headed for next door, and a flutter of arousal below his belt momentarily distracted him from the taxi owner who was now breathing heavily down the line.

'What problem?' Marsh demanded.

'It was my idea, sir. Just to get that Rook bitch finally off the scene. I'd got it all planned down to the last frigging detail and then she still gets a pulse, doesn't she?'

330

'Please explain.' The Detective Constable made a supreme effort to keep his voice even so as not to arouse this cretin's suspicions. '*What* has she survived?'

'I tried to run her over, didn't I? Just now. Up by Woolerton, and I think that cunt Browning recognized my cab. Her solicitor's only got to hand in that fucking cigarette lighter you said he'd got, and it's the slammer for the lot of us. Someone had to do *something*, sir.'

'I can assure you, Johnny, all will be taken care of. Now, where are you calling from?'

'Cab office.'

Marsh saw the postwoman climbing up into her van. Neat butt, nice legs – he smiled to himself. But not as nice as Monica Oakley's.

'Leave now,' he barked. 'Join the others at home and wait for me there. That's an order.'

'What the fuck for? Sir?'

'Do as I say, Johnny. I'm running out of patience.'

'Yessir. Sorry, sir.'

Marsh replaced the receiver with a shaking hand. He lifted his mac down off the coat stand, picked up his briefcase and set the house alarm. He then strode over to the garage, where a small but powerful drill lay in a neat slimline case hidden under rags in the far corner. Once he'd electronically sealed the door shut, he secreted this equipment in the boot of the BMW. With the doors open once more he waved to the postwoman who was now rejoining her van on the opposite side of the road. Marsh sensed a storm about to break, and swiftly settled into the driver's seat, at the same time switching on his dipped headlights.

The rain whipping round the side of Wiseman's Farm immediately sealed the visitor's darkened hair to his head as he left the BMW parked behind the main barn, out of sight from the road, and strode towards the farmhouse's back door. Suddenly the one remaining mastiff appeared from nowhere out of the gloom, instantly recognizing him, wagging his wet tail.

'C'mon, Krakow,' encouraged Marsh, lowering his head against the storm. 'Lead the way, good fellow.'

The dog obliged then vanished into the rain as the man let himself in, hung his dripping mac on a hook on the back of the door then made for the lounge and the hum of voices.

He'd never got used to the sheer opulence of the place. The sheer vulgarity of it all, and however many times he'd walked the black shag-pile carpets and taken in the marble-topped this, the gilt-legged that, he still had to hide a gasp of amazement at some of the stuff which had been given house room.

Monica Oakley was a totally different bird from Doreen Dawson, he mused, passing underneath the ornate chandeliers with their curling coppery leaves. The Detective Constable resolved that once his sprawling pile near Grasse in Provence was ready to move into as a second home, he'd go for quite the opposite. Simple white and more white. Letting the sunshine in...

His dark blue eyes then strayed from the

marble copy of an Italian nineteenth-century crucifixion, which took up most of a wall, to a large box full of tinsel lying near the staircase. Christmas decorations obviously awaiting the tree.

He frowned, spoiling his even-featured face, then kicked the thing across the hall, causing a trail of blood-coloured baubles to spill onto the carpet. Surely these clowns couldn't be contemplating Christmas here the way things were going? With Pike's threats of blackmail upsetting the Dawsons, and that fucking potter still nosing around?

'Deck the halls with boughs of holly? I think not,' Marsh said frostily as he came through the lounge's double doors, whereupon the murmuring voices suddenly stopped.

The five Oakleys looked up and the publican unnecessarily checked his watch – for the Commander was never late – and now he stood over them as they sat stiffly uncomfortable in their mourning black by the cluster of glowing fake logs and the accoutrements of a real fire.

Marsh saw Stephen Oakley's newly shaved head and could tell by the Little Rich Girl's eyes that she'd just had a fix and had glossed too extravagantly round the outline of her lips. He also noticed her fingers trembling on her knees as she perched on the arm of the red leather settee next to her parents.

'Thank you for being so prompt, but I'll start by saying I'm not best pleased with your antics of late. In fact, I'm fucking angry, especially with our cabbie friend here, whose cretinous actions this morning have got HQ's breath burning my neck.' His accusing gaze ranged from one Oakley to the other, alighting briefly on Monica who looked different in a way he couldn't quite discern, then finally the daughter. 'I've already bollocked Tony Pike for breaking and entering Church House last Tuesday.' He eyed Harold Oakley. 'And you, sir, should have known better than to step over that Rook bitch's portals.'

'Look here,' the publican protested, 'I've waited twenty-five fucking years to get hold of that lighter of mine.' The publican fumed. 'How much longer was I supposed to wait, eh?'

'I told you, I'd sort it.' Marsh sustained his stare until the man subsided against the red leather, his face now almost the same colour. 'So, wise up, you lot. I've managed to keep the lid on everything up to now, but Whitrow's bending his ear to Browning – the bitch's knight in shining armour – and that's bad news for us. I've got a tap on him now, by the way. But there's more. Pike's making trouble as well. Thought you ought to know.'

Five pairs of eyes looked from one to the other.

'The Butler?' Jo Oakley was the first to speak.

'Yes. His threat this morning to shop the Dawsons is the kiss-off for them, and us, I'm afraid. Dawson's going to close operations.'

'That's the first we've fucking heard of it.' John Oakley looked grim.

'He bloody can't. We're partners. We paid into it all,' his elder brother spluttered, while Monica Oakley's face was now white with anger, her lips a hard tight line.

'Take the Butler's tongue out. Simple.'

'Mummy, *don't*.' The Little Rich Girl chided her but was ignored.

'Then we tell Dawson not to panic. Like most men, he just needs reassurance.'

'It's too late,' Marsh said.

'What's Pike's problem then?' Monica's bayonet stare fixed now on Marsh. He was aware of his shaving cut beginning to sting again.

'Andy Dawson's been blackmailing Pike big time. So this is Pike's tit-for-tat, but his promised blabbing about Oak Leaf Distribution.com and your other – how shall I say? – extra-curricular activities, could reach my governor quicker than you could take a squat. So, my friends, you've no choice but to shut up your respective shops ASAP and get the hell out of here by 7 p.m. tonight.'

'What about the fucking Dawsons?' Monica again. 'They off as well?'

'They'll be next. Guaranteed. And after that I, too, will have to consider a change of career.'

A stunned silence followed, in which Marsh was aware of a paler, quieter Monica Oakley now staring absently at his groin. 'However, back to the present.' He tried to stay focused on the job in hand. 'Travel light. One small case each, maximum,' he continued. 'Take the Silverlink to Milton Keynes then the Gatwick connection. There's a flight to Geneva at eleven-twenty tonight. That's the last place anyone would look for you. From there try pootling round Lac Leman and the mountains whatever – get a bit of a winter tan and the rest. By the way, Harold, to make you happy, I'll be sending your lighter on to you.'

Harold Oakley frowned, gratitude forgotten.

'What about our bank accounts, for fuck's sake?' he growled.

'They'll simply be transferred, no problem. I have a friend in a very high place. And I mean high. His agent here will ensure you'll have sufficient francs when you arrive. By the way, his counterpart's address in Geneva is inside your new passports – Monobank, Rue Voltaire, and this contact will deal with you directly.'

Harold Oakley frowned. 'Monobank?'

'Money transfer people. Specialists. Trust them.'

'What's wrong with a Bureau de Change?'

'Plenty.' Marsh glanced at his watch impatiently. 'Not secure. They're being checked out for money laundering. Besides the Monobank exchange rate is way over what you'd get with that outfit.'

'What's the handling fee?' Harold Oakley was still clearly unhappy.

'A snip at three per cent. I have done my homework.'

Jo Oakley seemed impressed, but not the cab driver.

'What about the frigging Euro when that comes out?' he barked. 'I ain't having none of that monkey money in my pocket.'

'That's the least of your problems. Now, keep your mobiles charged up to receive me twenty-four hours a day. It's a safe line, remember. Leave the Terrano at Milton Keynes station. That'll confuse everyone.'

'But my wife's not well,' Harold Oakley protested, suddenly looking pathetic. 'Does she have to?'

'She'll live.'

'And *her?*' He pointed to Jo, then cracked his finger bones one by one. 'She coming too?'

Marsh threw him a reproving glance. In his eyes, a father should show his daughter more respect. 'Not immediately, no. She and I have some loose ends to tie up here first, starting with Browning.'

'What about Pike?' persisted Stephen Oakley. 'I could see to him.'

Marsh shook his head. 'Let's not get greedy, eh?'

Harold Oakley watched his wife get up from the settee. She pulled her short black dress down over her shapely knees.

'Stay in that gear and look bereaved,' Marsh instructed her. 'You'll be less likely to be stopped by my colleagues if you're on your way to a funeral.'

'What about the other Pikes?' the shiny-haired girl asked.

'A bit on edge, understandably. But they know the score.' The Commander fished inside his brown suit jacket and produced four scaled-down maps of Geneva city centre with a list of tourist hotels on the back, and, when he'd also located the four passports he handed them round.

'You're the Weavers now, from Huddersfield. Nice and ordinary, but with some useful inheritance bread, looking to retire amongst the eidelweiss and cow bells – you know the sort of thing. By the way, as you all know, there's one more load of horse coming in from Harwich tomorrow. Two million quids' worth which the Dawsons are redirecting to the store in Welton. Then when Roy's settled up with us, and sorted out your contribution, I'll make a move on *them*. Now *that* I am looking forward to.'

Jo Oakley chuckled and provocatively parted her legs, but Marsh eyed his watch instead. 'We'll be sealing off this farm the minute you've gone. Sends out the right signals, don't you think?'

'How long for, for fuck's sake?' the cabbie asked, but it was a bad move. The Commander didn't even reply.

'No shotties for anyone either,' he continued. 'Take my word, if a lump of metal's found on you, forget it. Once you're over there you can get tooled up as easily as buying chocs. The Swiss do a nice line in semi-automatics, all boxed-up and gift-wrapped too.' He glanced over at the girl. 'But for the time being she keeps the beretta and I'll take the rifle.' The two nine millis tucked away inside his jacket were his business.

Stephen Oakley bristled. 'Look here, I've already had to lose one of my dogs, and now having one of the goon squad take my rifle off me is the last bloody straw.' He got up and charged towards Marsh who neatly side-stepped.

Oakley fell against an armchair, picked himself up and stood close to the man who now fully controlled their lives. 'I'm getting out of here,' he rasped, then, turning to the girl, 'and if you've

338

got any bloody sense, you'll do the same.'

Marsh socked his cheek with a crunch of bone and sent him sprawling. Then, having emptied Oakley's pockets of a wallet and a hunting knife, his kicking began and only stopped when the poacher, having yelled for mercy, finally lay still, his pulse shallow.

The detective pulled one of the neat automatics from his back trouser pocket and chucked it at Monica Oakley who only just caught it between her manicured hands.

'Lose him,' he shouted, then turned to her husband. 'Get some rope and an old rag. *Vite.*'

Harold Oakley obliged like a wildebeest on the loose, muttering about his wife being too ill for this sort of caper.

Marsh ignored him, and knelt down to tie Stephen Oakley's hands and feet. The girl then watched Monica Oakley cut away the surplus rope with her own special mother-of-pearl-handled knife, which she promptly wiped and returned to her handbag.

This effort seemed to drain her and she had difficulty getting to her feet, so it was Jo Oakley who helped drag her uncle through the hall and out into the adjoining garage where John and Harold Oakley hauled him up into the off-roader's boot and pulled its cover over, shielding him from view. Meanwhile the rain was beginning to seep under the door and into the garage.

'Pay cash for your diesel and don't attract any fucking attention,' the Commander ordered Monica Oakley, suddenly aware of her thinning yet problematical blonde hair. He pointed to the black chiffon scarf around her neck. 'Wear that over your head. You'll be a nice discreet driver that other road users won't notice. Try Kent somewhere as if you're heading for Dover. But for Christ's sake, get a move on. Is your mobile charged up?'

She nodded, then he slammed the boot door shut, waiting while Harold Oakley activated the electronic door to open on to the dark morning.

Once the 4x4 had gone, and the garage door had closed once more, Marsh poked John Oakley roughly in the stomach. 'Shift those fucking cabs up to Westhope, but leave one here with a new plate on it for me. Got it?'

Oakley grunted.

Marsh then strode towards the utility room only stalling briefly to shout back at the two remaining brothers, 'I'll ring you in an hour. Just to see how things are going.'

'What about the dog?' Jo Oakley asked as he reached for his damp mac.

'Kill the fucker.'

The rain had eased. Marsh swiftly disabled his car's immobilizer and opened his door as the girl glanced round to check no one else was in earshot.

'And Uncle Johnny's five grand in the cab office?'

'Every little helps. Sure. But Dawson first, eh?'

Marsh settled himself in the driver's seat and pulled the seat belt over his body. 'Oh, and by the way–' he checked his hair in the rear-view mirror while she cocked her head attentively – 'make sure the sly cunt's got enough cash on him.'

'I love you,' she said, but her words were lost to the rush of tyres on water as the Commander sped away.

'What do you mean, Freak Fair at Lee Wood, sir?' The dwarf child stopped his labours.

'Never you mind, young man. Get finished now before we get more customers coming in.' The publican realized he'd said too much already.

The boy obliged without further questions, then when he'd swept the place spotless and wiped over the tables, he perched himself on the bench next to Siân, dangling his little legs. While Tomos snored under a print of the Duke of Wellington, the two of them used scraps of paper to see who could draw the most alarming face with the two pencils Siân had made by snapping one in half.

Her efforts showed mostly part-animal part-human images – a horse with an eyeglass, a devil with a cravat. After that she began one which looked exactly like her brother – his wild black hair, his cruel mouth – and Alfie thought that was the most scary. Then, strangely, after they'd both compared their efforts she took the last scrap and drew some of the odd faces she'd visualized recently on the journey.

'Who are they?' Alfie frowned, leaning over.

'Just some people I saw the other day.'

'They all look ill.'

'No, that's just the way they are. They're going to be my friends...' She placed the piece of paper inside

her shawl.

'Oh.' Alfie wasn't used to girls and their funny ways. So he screwed up all his little sketches and threw them in the fire. 'Have *you* had a bad belly yet?' His two grey eyes flecked with brown were turned on her and she shook her head. 'Well, I have, and my mama. But she went to heaven and left me here.'

Siân put her arms round him and buried her face in his soft blond curls, trying not to speculate on what the publican had meant earlier about the fair.

'You'll grow to be a big strong man one day, I know you will. And your mam'll be looking down at you so proud.' She was glad to be able to hide the tears which now fell on to his head.

'What about you?' he asked. 'You've got a bad leg and you can't speak right.'

'I'm going to London to see a doctor.' Her whisper felt just like hollow, empty words. *'I want to be able to sing again.'*

'If I pray to Jesus hard enough, you will.'

Throughout the rest of the evening, the inn stayed quiet except for the drover's noisy dreaming and the occasional bursts of childish laughter from the new friends. When at length Alfie kissed her sweetly on the lips and said, *'Nos Da,'* the way she'd taught him, Siân took the food scraps out to the dogs. Once Tomos had stumbled up to bed, she found another piece of paper and sat by the fading fire, writing a note to Huw.

1 March 1830.

Dear Huw,

I do hope your poor finger is better by now. I would kiss it if I could. I searched for a Lenten Lily today for your birthday but as you can see I had no luck. I cannot tell you where we are for fear Morris learns of it. We met up with a man called Rhodri Morgan from Cynghordy who told us that the brothers seek revenge on us after our accident at Blaencarreg Bog. But worse, there is a big reward for our necks. Also the cholera is here, but do not worry. However, some days I wonder if I shall ever see you and my home again. Has Father been back? I miss you so much,

your Siân

Outside, as the gentle Cotswold rain grew to a fierce rapping against the roof, she imagined she could hear all the open drains overflowing, spreading foul soil around the village in a sea of new plague.

The publican of the Copper Coin at Wychfield refused Siân's plea to send her letter without any postage payment in advance.

'One shilling to you, missy,' he'd said. 'That's for up to two hundred miles and I can't ask nobody to take it for less.'

So Siân kept it secreted away from Tomos and, once the drove had finally arrived at the Swan & Bucket, she stole the two pence which fell unheard from his pocket while he dismounted.

That was something at least and who knows, she thought, there might be more to come. But that seemed as vain a hope as wishing for the sun, for the weather seemed even colder here, with a strong easterly wind blowing more rain over the Hertfordshire fields.

The cattle looked such a sorry lot, bunched together in their fattening field, that when a few locals did come by to view these new arrivals, they walked off again, shaking their heads, saying better those runts had stayed put in the land of goblins for the pennies they'd make.

Tomos called after them, 'I'll show you, you miserable *Saesneg* dogs. They're fine cattle. And when I leave this place I'll be a rich man.'

Siân who was hiding out of the rain wished she could believe that. Wished with all her weary heart she could believe it, and that London would be next.

Her bed in the attic room she'd shared with the servant girls had been far too small, too hard for any comfort, and when Siân woke early next morning to the sound of them laughing and tittering as they dressed, she felt as if she was paralysed.

'Hey, cripple, you getting up sometime?' the taller of the two called out, tying her lank hair back into a knot. 'Or are ye waiting there all day for Ned with his needle?'

When she turned to use the mirror, Siân tumbled out of the bed, and began raining blows on the servant girl's back. All her misery, all her fury filled her with a strength which finally

344

brought her tormentor to the floor.

'Mr Potter, sir, come quick! Evie's being murdered,' the other yelled down the stairs.

Siân didn't remember much of the next few minutes' confusion, except that both she and Tomos were forcibly pushed outside the inn and the bolts of the Swan & Bucket drawn fast behind them.

Twenty-One

It was one o'clock on Friday, with an ominous sky but less rain as Detective Constable Marsh walked away from Monkton Regis's main car park towards a pair of phone booths situated outside the post office. He'd made sure the gear he needed was tucked safely inside his mac and the black BMW faced the main road for a speedy exit, if need be. His ticket would last two hours, enough to cover all eventualities.

He dialled Gilbert's number three times, each time replacing the receiver just before the answerphone took over. He smiled to himself. Perfect. The solicitor's secretary was never there on Fridays, and the idiot was away in London until Sunday evening.

Marsh paced along the High Street, unnoticed by those out shopping or looking for lunch at one of the small town's many hostelries.

Suddenly his mobile rang, and quickly he pressed Talk. 'Yes?'

'HQ here.' He recognized Harold Oakley's voice. 'Just had some news from Westhope.'

'Not a good time now. Hurry up.'

'The Butler's cold.'

'Jesus, you fucking sure?'

'Definite.'

Marsh stopped in the doorway of an insurance company, suppressing another smile. Things were going well: one down, one to go. He thought of the restorations which were under way in Grasse. New roofs, new *fosse septique*, nothing but the best...

'This one's too close, and the shit'll stick to us,' Oakley went on. 'What the *fuck* do we do?'

'Get out of there the moment M's back. Anything from her yet?'

'She's just past Luton. Traffic's shite.'

'Damn. Don't make or answer any calls – even with mobiles. Understood? The lines may not be safe.'

Oakley grunted his puzzlement and ended the call, and the officer slotted the phone back into his jacket pocket. Hastening past assorted shops and offices, with every step his conviction grew that a little humility might have saved Tony Pike's skin. Eventually Marsh reached his destination.

KINGSLEY GILBERT
SOLICITOR FOR OATHS

Plus a whole load of the man's letters filling up the grubby brass plaque.

The front window, equally neglected, bore a vase of dusty plastic flowers. Marsh looked up and saw that the flat above still had a letting agent's board dangling from the wall. He breathed a sigh of relief and studied the window again, checking that no one was checking on *him*.

As Monkton Regis still remained largely a repository of the genteel and well-heeled, so that crime here was minimal, unlike in the surrounding region, there was as yet no CCTV surveillance in the High Street. Marsh once more was grateful.

The police officer repeatedly wiped the smooth soles of his shoes on the doormat, George Pike's carefully crafted Yale key at the ready. He had slipped gloves over his shapely fingers and with one turn of the key in the lock followed by a gentle shove from his shoulder, the front door opened on to stale air as in an auction room. He peered round, listening for any sound however minute. Just silence except for his breath in and out, and he moved swiftly into a small back kitchen where sachets of darjeeling tea and decaffeinated coffee lay on the one worktop next to a clean cup and saucer and a mini pack of digestives. The adjoining WC, complete with its dingy packs of Izal toilet paper stacked up on the cistern, was also empty.

There were several messages waiting on the answerphone, but he left the machine untouched, knowing exactly what he was looking for. He carefully felt along the old wood panelling that covered one wall, until he suddenly detected a slightly raised edge under his fingers. Behind was the safe, cleverly disguised, as Gilbert had once foolishly boasted. Marsh held his breath and, keeping an eye on the street outside through the window, extracted his new diamond drill from its neat navy case and plugged it into a nearby socket. He'd done his homework from the maker's complex specifications and after fourteen minutes of accurate probing, the safe's lock slowly yielded.

The item itself took just ten seconds to locate, then the officer began checking the solicitor's untidy desk, opening the drawers one after the other, scanning cupboards full of files, finding nothing else relevant in Valerie Rook's dossier.

Just then Gilbert's phone rang several times until the answerphone crackled into life. Marsh stopped to hear the message.

'Ivan Browning here, Mr Gilbert. I'm a friend of your client Mrs Valerie Rook. I'm not really happy about leaving this message on your answerphone, but I'm afraid she was knocked down by a taxi cab at about nine-thirty this morning near Woolerton. She's anxious that you know it was a deliberate attempt, and she swears John Oakley was the driver. The police in Northampton have now got all the details, and I did urge them to contact you. One last thing, please don't contact her husband about this. Thanks.'

Cursing the caller, Marsh swiftly exited the office with his tool kit secreted away once more, confident there'd be no prints anywhere, just steel dust on the carpet that any skilful burglar might have left. Outside, he felt a surge of sweet relief at knowing that the only real hard evidence to be levelled at his fleeing paymasters was now deep in his trouser pocket, and potentially far more valuable than any police pension.

Marsh glanced up and down the High Street cautiously, then strode off towards his waiting car. He switched on Radio 3, to *Le Nozze di Figaro* from the Met, and sped away, relieved the girl had kept to the agreed tight schedule, and wondering if the co-director of Oak Leaf Distribution.com at Dawson's Farm might have seen fit to give them both a last-minute pay rise.

'Now see what you've done, you devil's daughter!' Tomos lashed out at his sister, who reeled, clinging to the gate, then collapsed with Ben crouching beside her.

'We'd an easy billet here, you bitch. Now we've lost our beds, and the herd have lost their grass.' He began to kick her, until a passer-by paused his hand-cart full of wood and called out to him.

'She's just a child, sir. Leave her alone at once or I'll send for the law.'

In the aftermath reigned a bruised silence of anger and resentment, while the local church bell pealed quarter past the hour, and yet again the drove had to be moved on.

When Tomos had begged the innkeeper to let them stay until at least first light, he was ignored. So now, still in darkness, the Castlemartins with just the sleepy terrier and a dispirited Ben, made their way along Wychfield's main street until the wilder darkness of unknown countryside opened before them.

By eight that morning, with the wind still up, Siân and Tomos had reached Woodview House in the Lee Bottom road, and were ensconced in Betsy Turrell's front parlour. She was a farmer's widow who made some income from letting her one spare room and also the three-acre field near the house, which led down to a stream.

The woman, hunched and frail on her birdy ankles, was soon busy with providing broth, bread and a slice of ham for the starving travellers. She even ventured outside to give the two dogs some scraps. When she returned, both plates and bowls were licked clean, and her customers seemed close to sleep.

Tomos roused himself to enquire if the cholera had come calling yet.

'Don't you even say that word, mister. I've heard such terrible things about folks farther west, with them scouring like lambs and all tied up with the cramps. But no, thank the good Lord and his mother we've not had the one case here.' She stacked the dishes and carried them into the adjoining kitchen. 'When you think of that fat old king,' she went on, 'it's a disgrace. While he sits around in Windsor Castle in comfort, his people meet their Maker lying in their own muck.'

Tomos, not wishing to waste precious time discussing the English monarchy, dipped in his pocket and drew out some coins.

'I'll pay you now for the week, then. God willing, the runts will be well up to selling weight by then.'

Mrs Turrell held out her skeletal hand for the silver. 'Have a care not to take any one-pound notes at the sale, as they're worthless,' she warned, then glanced at Siân. 'I expect *you'll* be staying for the Lee Wood Fair next day?' she asked, then began counting the money with moving, silent lips. 'It's the finest for miles around and cheap to get in,' she continued eventually. 'It makes St Bartholomew's look like a flea circus.'

Fair? Siân suddenly remembered that one of the publicans had mentioned it too, in a sinister sort of way. She thought instantly of produce and mechandise. The kind of fair that Nant-y-Fedw held every Monday in June, when the woollen goods, the fleeces for spinning, the honey and vegetables would all be set out on a piece of land by the Glebe House.

'Oh, that's quite the place to see the woman with three breasts, or the man who stands on hot coals while he downs a pint of ale.'

The Welsh girl stared open-mouthed as the widow continued. 'People can make their fortunes at Lee Wood, if they've something really queer to sell.'

Meanwhile, Tomos had pulled off his reeking boots and was picking dirt from between his toes.

Siân couldn't believe what she'd just heard – a woman with three breasts? And then a sudden anxiety overtook her as she thought of the midget Alfie – and that reference to herself.

'*It sounds horrible,*' she gasped.

'Depends on how my sale goes.' Her brother's dark eyes now bore the glint of secret purpose. '*I'll* be deciding, anyway, not you.'

What does he mean – depends on how the sale goes? A ripple of panic passed through her.

'*But what about London?*'

Tomos shot her such an evil glance, his mouth set like a dog's when about to snarl, that Mrs Turrell scuttled away to keep out of trouble.

The days before the Lee Wood sale were spent in a constant state of alert for either the Morris brothers on their bays, or the Carter thugs and Rock Face Dickens, to whom Siân knew her brother had foolishly revealed their first destination.

Her hopes of London were fading like those early mists above the Wye, but some tiny spark of her one dream still remained. And to that end, while Tomos mostly slept, she'd sit on guard, on a little tapestry stool by the parlour window and watch the road outside. If it was fine, she'd sometimes take Collen from the stable as far as the hamlet of Burnt Offing to the west, whose name by its strangeness wouldn't leave her mind. Or she'd ride over to Much Winding on the east, knowing that, with every step the pony took, this was the way to London, and to Dr George Owen's healing hands...

But by the Saturday, two days before the sale began, all the surrounding roads and tracks were too packed with other droves or with cottagers bringing in their produce to sell off the cart. The mare wasn't used to such numbers, and the last thing Siân needed was for her fearful antics to attract unwanted attention.

Twenty-Two

Ivan pulled up his jacket collar against the rain and headed towards the Lamb and Flag. There was scarcely anyone else around, just some guy in a Corporation mac poking at litter in the gutter. Ivan went round to the rear car park, and stopped dead. There, out of sight from the main road, in the corner nearest the kitchen wall, stood the maroon Nissan Terrano with its Wapping sticker.

He sneaked closer, aware of the total silence: not even a heating vent purring inside the pub as he walked past. He pressed his nose against the Terrano's passenger window, and saw that the vehicle was completely bare. Even the box of tissues had gone. He couldn't help reflecting that these Oakleys were so slick, so clever, they imagined nothing would touch them. Except that maybe today they had gone too far. Perhaps they'd picked the wrong target. For the doctor's wife seemed to have acquired iron in her veins, and his admiration for her was increasing by the minute.

He then checked the pub's side entrance where the replacement notice of bereavement was still in place. The early Christmas lights were all out, of course, but as he peered into the gloom beyond the leaded glass, his heart began to quicken. There was definitely someone behind the bar. Could that be Jo? Was it possible she was in there tidying up, sorting out the till? His mind raced on, because somehow it didn't matter to him what anyone said about her, or about the vile family she'd had the bad luck to be born into. She was the foxiest girl he'd ever come across, and hadn't she recently touched him up with her magic fingers? Hadn't she even written that she loved him?

His hand was poised to tap the window glass when, with a gasp, he realized it was Harold Oakley lifting up the bar flap and coming towards him.

Ivan ducked below the level of the door's glass panel, and, to the amusement of the litter-picker opposite, scurried along the pavement and into a nearby florist's, where a tall bespectacled man stood at the counter, watching his bouquet being assembled.

'So how many years is it, Mr Dawson?' the overalled shop girl asked him, adding a final touch of gypsophila to the spray, before pulling a length of decorative wrapper from a dispenser.

Ivan gulped on realizing that six inches away from him was the owner of Dawson's Farm, in the flesh. The man's face was grey and unhealthy looking.

'Twenty-four, and not one year too many.' His voice was smooth and pitched low and, like his son's, had no trace of the East End in it. Mr Respectability himself, with his immaculate mac and polished black shoes. When he pulled out a wad of notes from his wallet he told the girl to keep a fiver for herself.

She handed over the wrapped flowers with a huge smile. 'Ta very much, Mr Dawson.'

'Thank you.' He hastily returned his wallet to his suit pocket and turned to leave. Ivan noticed that his eyes looked hard, reptilian, the mouth mean and thin. He felt a shiver pass from top to toe as he realized he'd just been in the presence of someone quite ruthless, quite evil. In fact, he was so disturbed by this encounter that when the girl asked him what he wanted, he could merely point to a bunch of white rosebuds.

Outside again, he stopped a schoolgirl to ask if she knew where Pronto taxi cabs were based. His throat still felt sore, his voice below par.

The pupil, stuffing her chewing gum into her mouth, pointed up Cobbling Street towards the racecourse. 'Next to the butchers,' she said.

That's appropriate, thought Ivan. 'Cheers,' he said.

The wind kept pushing him along from behind, as he tried to shield his flowers from the worst of the weather. They'd cost him nearly eight quid, and he'd never bought flowers before in his life – not even for Tania or his mother. Now it seemed his life really wasn't his own any more.

As Ivan passed the butcher's window, which was full of purple offal and trays of tired mince, he almost missed the alley alongside. He checked that no-one else was around, before venturing along the weedy gravel strip which led to a Portakabin at the far end.

There was an air of desertion about the place and there were certainly no taxis evident. Even the neighbouring red-brick properties seemed empty and neglected.

As he drew closer, however, he noticed a faint glow shining between the tattered notices on the Portakabin's window, which displayed Pronto Cabs' rates for Northampton, London and elsewhere.

Pressing himself up against the glass, Ivan realized that someone was indeed inside. He heard the telephone ring and a girl's voice answering.

Jo? No, it couldn't be.

He plucked up courage to push at the door, but it was locked.

By now she'd seen him, so he made a decision. There was no way he was going to run off. He tapped on the glass door panel and showed her the flowers.

'For you,' he mouthed.

'Fuck off.'

'Jo, please. I must talk to you.'

He stayed put. He'd no choice, so he stood his ground, waiting.

After five long minutes, he could scarcely believe his eyes. She was making for the door with key in hand.

'You've got a cheek,' she hissed as she opened it just enough for him to squeeze through, then locked it again, shoving the key into her jeans pocket. The single, badly lit room smelt of fags, and there was only a small trace of her usual posh soap. But it looked busy, quite a lucrative little set-up, he thought, noting the switchboard console and the Silverstone racing calendar

357

replete with memos he could not decipher.

'These are for you,' he said sheepishly, handing over the roses. 'They should last quite a while.'

'Longer than you will if you don't lay off poking around people.' She gave the flowers a perfunctory sniff, deposited the bunch in the kitchen area then sat down again at the long desk and started up her calculator. Obviously a word of thanks was too much to expect, but that didn't matter though, nor her acid warning. He was still in thrall, unable to take his eyes off her slim firm figure, her perfectly fitting blouse, the short suede skirt, that ever glossy hair.

'Thanks for your note,' he ventured. 'The feeling's mutual.'

She lowered her head, avoiding his eyes, and he noticed a tiny speck of blood at the base of her parting.

'Is your shin OK then?' She looked up, half smiling. 'Sorry I kicked you.'

'It's fine.' Ivan edged closer, took a deep breath. 'Look, d'you want to go out for a meal tonight?'

'I can't, thanks.' She crossed her long legs under the desk. 'Got too much to do here. Perhaps another time.'

The chill of rejection touched his heart. But he knew he had to move things on, for everyone's sake – to find some truth amongst all the lies, and discover where exactly Jo stood with those dodgy relations of hers. But here, in her presence, his resolve faltered. The matter of Ma Oakley's funeral was too risky, might drive her away from him altogether. That could wait.

'So you work here as well, do you?' as casually

as he could. 'Isn't this your uncle John's outfit?'

She swung round in her swivel chair, her dark eyes fixing intently on his.

'Look, Mr Browning–'

'Oh come on, Jo. You called me Ivan before, remember? Even Mr B would do.'

A tightening of her lips. 'I've got all this VAT stuff to tot up before I can go.' She checked her expensive-looking watch and frowned. 'If these sums aren't done by–' Her voice faltered. 'If they're not done, then I get no pay for *anything.*' She faced her work again, this time seeming subdued in a way which alarmed him.

'Well, why don't you just say fuck off to the lot of them? Christ, Jo, you'd get a job anywhere. I don't understand.'

'You would if you hung around here long enough.' Her lips moved on to mouth the figures as her fingers tapped the keys, fingers which had so recently driven him wild. Whenever she reached a sub-total, a print-out emerged from the top of the calculator which she tore off and filed. Ivan watched transfixed. Even shovelling shit, she'd be a vision. But vision or not, there were still questions to ask. He cleared his throat.

'Were there any taxis of yours out North-ampton area this morning?' he asked.

'Not sure. Why? Let me check.' As she flicked through a grubby pad, Ivan craned to decipher the blurred soft-pencil scrawl, but it was impossible to pick out any details.

'Friday 23 November. Uncle Johnny to Middleton Tysoe at 9.40 a.m. Then Uncle Johnny to Stoneshanger Bowls Club at 10.30

a.m. Cabs taken for servicing the rest of the day. There you go.' She closed the pad. 'Satisfied?'

'Where's Middleton Tysoe?' Ivan was doing some instant mental geography and thinking that Friday afternoon was an odd time to be servicing taxis.

'Past Sykeston on the way to Banbury.'

He felt chilly, even though the one oil heater was belching out an acrid warmth. This was getting him nowhere. Either she was making things up or he and Valerie had been drastically mistaken.

'Does anyone else drive for Pronto on a Friday?' he ventured, pushing his luck.

'Don't be dumb. No, it's just him. Now, is the twenty bloody questions over?' A twist of her chair and Jo got up. 'Would you like a coffee? I'm having one, sod it.'

She went over to a grubby worktop where a stained kettle, next to his roses, sighed into life. After she'd spooned some Tesco instant into two stained mugs, she turned to face him. 'Look, why d'you keep bothering with me? I don't understand.'

Ivan suddenly found he couldn't look her properly in the eye, his real answer locked in his throat.

'Because I like you. You're different.'

She laughed but it didn't seem in mockery. It was more a sad reflective laugh, saved for just herself. 'But I've told you nothing but lies. I'm just not nice to know.'

The urge to take her in his arms was overpowering. He was longing for her so much, it

360

hurt. He wanted to tell her how she'd been on his mind since the day he'd first met her. That he couldn't imagine ever wanting anyone else as long as he lived. And he still had that note from her in his pocket: part of him now, for ever.

'You've got your reasons,' he offered instead. 'Who am I to judge you?'

'True.' She passed him a mug and went back to her seat. 'And if I told you *everything*, you'd probably understand why. But I can't – that's how it is.' As she began totting up again, Ivan became aware that the longer he stayed here the more risky it would be for both of them.

'Just one thing,' he said suddenly. It was worth a try. A whim. 'Have you ever heard of the poet John Clare?'

She swivelled round to face him again, this time her face was transformed by what seemed a genuine pleasure.

'Yeah. Course. He was the only thing that kept me going in that shit-awful Holmlea place.' She then bit her lip as if she'd said too much.

'What's Holmlea?'

'Oh, some stuck-up boarding school in Essex. Mind you, your local peasant poet wasn't what I was supposed to read, oh no. It was meant to be Carol Ann Duffy this, Sylvia Plath that... I got well pissed off with all those ranting women.'

Ivan recalled Tania's response to that same question – that John Clare might have been some hairdresser. This was amazing. 'So you know about Mary, then?' he asked her, trying not to show that he found the coffee undrinkable.

'Mary Joyce, the farmer's daughter? Course I

361

do. She never married, after they parted, did she? Died in 1838. God knows why they didn't just get on with it, then he mightn't have ended up where he did, poor fucker.'

'Exactly.' But Ivan's smile quickly faded. He put his mug down. There were noises outside: tyres on gravel, the purr of an engine. He checked the front window where, between gaps in the notices, he could make out a black vehicle drawing closer.

'You'd better disappear.' Jo jumped up and ran to the far end of the hut where she began frantically unbolting another door. Ivan took over, managed to wrench the rusty thing across and slip outside into the back yard, just as the main office door began to open.

'Give me a ring,' he whispered to her. 'I'm in the latest phone book, OK?' With that he crouched low amongst the wheelie bins, his heart lurching, as she secured the door behind him.

Even though rain was now cascading off the bin lids, Ivan could vaguely hear her and some man he assumed was Uncle Johnny arguing about where the flowers had come from, then a shouting match about the job he'd given her not being completed, ending in what sounded like a slap. The bastard was hitting her, not once but twice, then a third time. Ivan could tell she was crying, then silence fell as the main door slammed shut, vibrating the whole Portakabin as if it were made of cardboard.

He wanted to sort out the cruel fucker but that might only make things worse for Jo. He'd never felt so helpless, so bloody frustrated and, as he

362

finally negotiated his way between old oil drums and rusted machinery, he realized that something major was up.

Why was their pub still closed to the public, with Harold Oakley himself fiddling round the till in semi-darkness? Why was Jo doing emergency accounts for the taxi firm? Were the Oakleys thinking of bunking off? If so, why bother with servicing the cabs? Or were they just tying up loose ends? Of course he didn't know anything for sure, but as he squeezed through a narrow gap which took him into the butcher's domain next door, this premise wouldn't leave him.

And if they were all doing a flit, what about Jo? Yes, what about Jo, who'd actually loved reading John Clare? That seemed a miracle – like finding a diamond in a dung heap, he thought.

'Sorry, got a bit lost out there,' Ivan explained as casually as he could to the stout woman butcher who'd eyed him suspiciously from her storeroom. 'Bit of a maze round here.' He must sound a right weirdo. 'Do you mind if I go through your premises?'

She gathered up a stack of off-white wrapping paper and took it round into the smelly shop. 'So what were you up to, may I ask?'

'Trying to get a taxi sorted out for Monday with those people next door. Got to go to Gatwick. Job interview in Spain.'

Whether the woman believed him or not, she did not seem to resent his presence but busied herself writing up new price tags and sticking them into piles of tripe, pale fleshy innards which seemed almost alive when she disturbed them. Ivan repressed a desire to heave.

'No point you bothering there with that lot,' she announced to his surprise. 'My brother's just seen a load of their cabs on some transporter turning into that garage up at Westhope.'

'Pike's garage?'

'That's the place,' she confirmed. 'Now, d'you fancy something tasty for your supper tonight?'

Ivan hesitated, eyeing what was on offer. In the end he plumped for the least-harmless-looking option – home-made sausages.

As he left the shop he sneaked a glance down the adjoining alley at the Pronto Cabs Portakabin. Whatever vehicle had interrupted him and Jo earlier had now completely vanished.

By Sunday, 7 March, there was still no sign of their pursuers. The air in Lee Bottom grew thick with the stench of the passing beasts, and the shouts and curses of those keen to feel money in their hands after the lean winter months.

Church bells clanged out the hours as the procession of livestock grew. There were types of cattle Siân had never seen before – like the short-legged russets, black-and-white and speckled, or the Herefords with their curly brows.

Young men, old men, mounted or trudging, often drunk and unsteady, even though it was the Lord's Day; but some sober, with children, wielding great sticks. It was as if a secret world had been magicked from all those surrounding silent hills and fields. And it seemed to her as if those same fields produced bigger bone, more flesh than that raw wind-blown world she knew around the Teifi.

Tomos was also comparing these beasts with his own. Was there more meat on their loins? More condition in the coat and less rib showing than on his stock? And the answer was unfortunately, yes. He'd stood unobtrusively and scrutinized each passing animal through the window, until the main street grew quiet and dark, so that when Betsy Turrell appeared from the kitchen to place bacon and cabbage on the table for supper, he was angry and unreasonable.

'Your bloody grass hasn't brought a half inch on my stock,' he complained, wagging a brown knotty finger. 'So what have I paid good money for? I'll not get more than a pound apiece tomorrow.'

Siân didn't dare whisper to him that if he'd done more feeding up with hay and swedes when the herd had first arrived, and less sleeping all day, things would be different now. And how could *she* have interfered anyway? Would he have been grateful for her opinions? No. It would have meant another knock on the head or a kick somewhere else that hurt.

Mrs Turrell busied herself without answering at first. Her late husband had often warned that it was always best to ignore difficult folk. Like a fire, he'd say: easy to start, hard to put out. But her husband wasn't there now, and besides this rough fellow needed putting straight.

'You can't blame me, sir,' she argued. 'That grass out there's the finest in Hertfordshire. I've had no complaints before.'

365

Tomos kicked a chair to the floor, making Siân jump up in fright.

'You pay me some of my rent back, madam, or you might not *have* a field to let out any more.' He was red from the ale, red as the devil himself.

Siân tried desperately to intervene but Tomos pushed her away, even more inflamed by the old woman's stance: hands on hips, facing him in defiance.

'I'll have you know, my son's a constable here, and,' she pointed at Siân, 'I have a witness to your threat.'

The girl's heart quickened, and she watched her brother in despair.

'Now I'll give you ten minutes to get yourself and your herd off my property, or I'll be calling on him. He's only a short way up the street, and –' she gave the Welshman a knowing stare – 'you look the sort to be in bother already.'

Tomos didn't even stay to finish his tankard. By seven o'clock, with the daylight almost gone, they arrived at the sale field from the west, with Ben and the one terrier almost run to death to keep the Nant Y Fedw herd intact.

On the way, Siân prayed for the morning, then added another plea that the runts would fetch a good price, because in that uneasy heart of hers, she knew her life depended on it.

A hedgerow for a curtain, damp weeds for a bed, Siân had no sleep. As the cold darkness lightened and the moon took its long farewell over Wendover Woods, her bones ached. It seemed that each and every one of them had drawn in the earth's moisture, so that when Tomos prodded her with his stick to get moving, she could barely stand.

'Shift yourself, sister. We need to get them to our pen now.' He looked more red-faced than ever: the strain of keeping watch all night, and knowing his runts looked poor against the rest, made him dangerous. So, without protest, she helped guide the drove down through the designated field into the area marked WELSH, where six pens of equal size lay one next to the other.

Unlike the sales she'd seen back home, this one would be a formal affair, with officials constantly strutting about in black hats and cravats. The only carts permitted were those selling produce, and they were lined up on either side of the gate. They carried butter, milk and cheese from goats – strong, sour-smelling and certainly not tempting to her appetite. Horses and ponies were not permitted access, nor dogs once the cattle were penned ready to enter the small, fenced-off selling ring. So, when the sale began at nine o'clock prompt, she was left in charge of both Incio and Collen and the two dogs, up by the ale wagon.

After an hour of looking around, fearful of spotting Morris or the Carters and Rock Face Dickens on those massive black stallions, she fell asleep with the new sun's warmth on her face. As the morning progressed, so did the number of tottering louts who thought it a lark to leer at her or tease the cob into showing his teeth.

Woken by a stray dog, she prayed again. 'Dear

367

God, let him have two pounds apiece at least. Just two pounds, dear Father, please.'

By midday, with the sun now well up and showing every stain on Mrs Hubbard's bedraggled garments, a hungry Siân saw Tomos leaving the field with his head down, his hands plunged deep in his pockets.

Twenty-Three

Ivan had skipped any kind of lunch, even though he was famished. There were urgent things to do instead, like checking round for any dodgy fungal growth or beetles lurking in corners, then covering up any woodworm holes on the narrow wall beams.

By three o'clock, he had wiped out the bath and hidden his mangy facecloth, swept the kitchen floor and put out the rubbish.

Ivan was just on the point of opening wide the curtains to let in more daylight when the same silver Mercedes he'd spotted by Ma Oakley's house drew up outside, and a portly besuited man emerged. If this was Mr Cartwright, he was an hour early. Spotting a traitorous nest of cobwebs in the dark corner created by the main beam, Ivan deliberately made the man wait a few seconds before opening the front door.

'Douglas Cartwright, County Homes. Pleased to meet you.' His hand was pink and clammy like those sausages, his bottom lip full and permanently moist. 'Apologies for being premature, but it was the only way I could fit you in. You know how it is – Netherby Hall and Grafton Manor Farm – two of the largest properties in the area. All in a day's work.'

After a quick look round, he whipped out a steel tape measure and, none too accurately, Ivan thought, logged the dimensions of the ground-floor rooms.

'No proper gas supply, I see.' He sniffed round the cooker's two rings. 'Why not electric? Much cheaper and safer.'

With every stroke of the man's wretched pen on the pad, Ivan could see his own investment turning into a millstone round his neck for as long as he lived.

'No central heating either?'

'I prefer an open fire.' It was an effort to speak.

'Hmm.'

The back door had jammed in the damp. The sash window in the hall wouldn't budge, and when the estate agent's suited elbow accidentally nudged the wall alongside it, a layer of damp plaster fell to the floor.

The podgy man was busy scribbling. 'Let's look upstairs, eh?'

Ivan led the way, only barely registering the sound of some heavy vehicle stopping outside.

At least his bed was made, even if the sheets were somewhat greyish. Thank God, too, he'd evicted last summer's flies from the windowsill.

The visitor opened the wardrobe door on a heap of unwashed clothes. 'Mmm, could squeeze in another room at the end, with a bit of luck. Not listed is it, by any chance?'

'No.' Ivan now heard that same vehicle drawing away but thought nothing of it. Plenty of agricultural stuff took a short cut through to Sykeston this way.

They headed back downstairs. Cartwright turned to him. 'Mr Browning, now be honest with me, have you ever had any trouble from the natives round here? You *are* obliged to say when the purchaser's solicitor asks you.'

'Nothing at all. I've got a really quiet neighbour, Mrs Jonas.' Why had the slimy git brought this up? Did he know something about the cottage's past? Or had he some other agenda altogether?

'No burglar alarm, I see.' The estate agent made another negative jotting, then stretched up for one of his fingers to trace the curve of a meat hook jutting from the central beam. 'I'd have thought that essential out here.'

'I've never felt I needed one.' Ivan's mendacity was growing, but still Douglas Cartwright didn't seem to be convinced. He let his finger rest on the hook and frowned.

'As for these hooks. They don't look good. No, sends out the wrong signals entirely.' He then tore himself away from that particular bit of the past and looked towards the half-open door which led from the hall into the adjoining studio. 'OK, according to Angela's notes, this is a workshop,' he began. 'But I'd better warn you. Not everyone wants one and usually they're tacky cobbled-together eyesores.'

He let out a grunt of dismay as he stepped inside then paced round the four walls, tutting all the while and prodding the floor with the toe of his shoe. 'Big problem: we've got damp here as well.' He peered at Ivan over his rimless glasses. 'Probably just an earth floor underneath. Didn't you have it investigated before you handed over your money?'

371

'No I didn't, and anyhow it's kept warm by the kiln. I've never smelt any damp so far.'

'Oh dear.'

Time to rattle the bastard's cage, Ivan thought. 'I still reckon this'll fetch more than old Ma Oakley's cottage, what d'you think?'

But his mention of the deceased woman's name merely made the man's mouth close up, and he moved on more quickly as if to deter any further awkward questions.

Cartwright didn't even so much as glance at Ivan's finished pots set out along the shelves, nor did he show any interest in the kiln. No, Ivan could see this wheeler-dealer was only interested in how many bunk beds could be shoe-horned into each room, how many sleeping bodies could lie here with the forest in the background, whispering through the night.

But it seemed he was wrong.

'To be truthful, Mr Browning, this is pretty uninhabitable.'

Uninhabitable? Jesus Christ!

'If you want my honest opinion, it's like stepping back into the Dark Ages.'

'But that Angela lady in your office reckoned at least a hundred grand.'

'I'm afraid she gets rather carried away. She's only been in the job a month.' Just as he pulled the cap off his pen again, a terrible farmyard whiff began to penetrate from outside, only slight at first, then, as the seconds ticked by, becoming a choking, almost solid odour.

He ran outside, Cartwright following with a crumpled handkerchief pressed to his face.

'Where's your bloody cesspit?' he yelled.

'There isn't one. I'm on the mains.'

'So what's *this* then?' The other man picked up a stick and poked through some flattened weeds at a rusty manhole cover that Ivan had never noticed before. The hole it was meant to cover lay less than a foot away – and was now filled to the brim with rotting stinking slurry.

Both men stumbled round to the front of the cottage where they encountered Mrs Jonas already at her door, pinching her nose. To forestall any trouble, Ivan approached her with a false grin.

'Sorry about the pong, Mrs J. We're getting it sorted straightaway, no problem.' But she'd already spotted the suited estate agent, and slunk back indoors.

'This is a real no-no, Mr Browning. In fact, a serious health risk. You'll have to get this mess sorted before I even *consider* whether to take on the property or not.' He replaced the pen and pad in his pocket and made for his car.

Ivan tried not to inhale, but he was seething. That muck had been dumped there deliberately, yet there were no clear tyre marks. This was like the persecution of old Mr and Mrs Tripp all over again.

Cartwright fastened his seat belt, the window open barely an inch. 'Best you get rid of it quickly, Mr Browning. Just get Pillocks to auction the place. I believe that's how you acquired it originally.' He then did a rapid three-point turn and disappeared in a spray of mud.

Ivan cursed him, and whatever psycho had

gone to all that trouble just to warn him off. Finding it hard to shift Andrew Dawson's name from his mind, he found *Yellow Pages* and looked for Septic Tank Operators. Thank God, there turned out to be a firm in Daventry, not too far away, but they quoted him £75 plus mileage. The price he would receive for ten soup bowls.

He slumped down on his old settee, oppressed not only by the invasive odour but the bleakest sense of despair he'd ever known. Why not have someone come along right now and put a bloody great yellow cross on the front door? *Place of Plague?* It sounded good – absolutely right, in fact.

Two hours later, the rumble of an unfamiliar engine outside made Ivan leap towards the hall window. A giant brown tanker with the words Toprank Liquid Waste Disposal painted along its length, was drawing up behind the Saxo.

A man in blue overalls jumped out of the cab, then straightaway pulled a mask out of his pocket. Ivan forestalled his knocking on the door.

'It's round there,' he pointed along the side of the cottage. 'Someone's just dumped a load of muck on me while I was asleep,' he fabricated.

If anything the stink was worse than earlier, and he felt ready to keel over. The man frowned, scratching his head.

'Christ, man, this is fucking *cow* shit.' The man stared at it in disbelief.

Ivan thought about Andy Dawson again, but he'd only ever mentioned keeping sheep. He watched, with his hand over his nose, as the vacuum pipe was unravelled and dragged towards the manhole, as inch by inch, its contents were sucked away.

Afterwards, with the lid secured and weighted down by a number of old concrete slabs, Ivan offered the man a cup of tea and stood with him in the kitchen, waiting for the kettle to boil.

'So, apart from this little caper, what's life like in these parts?' asked the Toprank man as Ivan poured boiling water onto the tea bags.

'Sure you really want to know?'

'That bad, is it?'

'Let's just say I'm planning to get out, and leave it at that, eh?'

'Well, it beats me,' the other went on, staring out of the single window at the forest blurring with the now darkening sky. 'You got all this lovely scenery, all them wild animals and stuff, and yet–' He paused for the right words as Ivan opened a packet of digestive biscuits and passed it to him. 'It's always the *people* who foul it up, every time. I mean, take what I heard today on my way over here.' His crumbs settled on a V of pullover between his boilersuit lapels. 'It made my bloody hair stand on end.'

'Go on.' Ivan was feeling suddenly cold.

'It was up by a place called Westhope and–'

'Westhope?' That word now had as much of an evil ring to it as Cold Firton.

'Yeah, that's right. Quite a nice spot, really. I stopped to fill up at this one-hole garage, George Pike & Sons.'

'You struck lucky to get served, then,' Ivan said sourly. 'As you were saying...'

'Well, I was just picking up my receipt from Mr Pike, when some kid with weird eyes comes running in screaming that his brother's been found lying in some open grave at the bloody churchyard down the road.'

Ivan slammed his mug down, slopping tea on the draining board. That same black oblong pit had haunted him since the moment he'd first seen it.

'Was he dead?'

'Sounds like it. The kid was wailing on about how there was blood everywhere, and he couldn't get Tony to wake up.'

Ivan's brain was in a frenzy trying to work out who might have murdered the man, but the driver was still talking thirteen to the dozen.

'I was just left standing there while they ran off round the back somewhere, so I decided to move on. Anyhow, as I was leaving, this green truck thing appeared with just the man in it and drove off. God knows where the kid went. Like I was saying, you don't expect that sort of thing amongst the deer and the dicky birds, do you?'

Ivan didn't answer and began writing out a cheque for ninety quid, then they parted in silence. As the tanker moved away, he happened to look up and saw a huge tawny owl breast over the cottage and swoop towards the trees.

The owl of death?

Tomos's demeanour spelt bad news. God hadn't listened at all and that would be the last time Siân would beg Him for anything.

Tomos kicked a stone, which struck her good

leg, and Siân flinched, seeing his hands now menacingly free of his pockets.

'Ten shillings each,' he muttered, sending another stone flying. 'Damn the *Saesnegs*. Damn them. I've been humiliated more than any man deserves.'

Tomos slumped down on a discarded crate to count his meagre takings, while Siân stroked Collen's neck, wondering where the mare would be taking her next, while his bitterness poured out.

Then, to Siân's great confusion, her brother looked up with a hint of a smile creeping across his lips. A smile that had come too quickly, like the sun darting through storm clouds.

'London it is,' he announced, 'tomorrow.'

'*Tomorrow?*' She could scarcely believe it.

'Tomorrow. And now we need to find us some lodging.' He got up and stretched like a dark and ominous scarecrow against the sky. He whistled for the dogs, then gathered Incio's reins and mounted.

Brother and sister made their way to a newly made road signposted London 23 miles, with warning of a toll to pay at Morton Bridge. Tomos whistled softly to himself, occasionally humming some old drover's ditty picked up on his last trip to Hereford.

Siân hadn't seen a sweeter sight than that signpost in all her fourteen years, and to her, at that moment, twenty-three miles was nothing. Her treatment, her cure, lay just around the corner. She turned to look at her brother and, for the first time ever, whispered to him '*Thank you.*'

But that was too soon, for as they rounded the next bend leading into King's Langley, she noticed with a start another sign nailed to a nearby oak.

FREAKS TO VIEW AND FREAKS TO BUY!
THEY AWAIT YOU HERE AT
LEE WOOD FAIR.
Turn right at the Shearer's Arms crossroads, then travel two miles down Hawkswood Lane.

Siân felt a knot form in her stomach as they rode by, for Tomos's eye was on it, trying to read the lettering. Normally, she'd have helped him out, but not this time.

But that evening there seemed something wrong with her brother as they sat in the Shearer's Arms just outside King's Langley. He'd ordered the best steak with onions for them both, followed by apple tart like she'd not tasted since those occasional Sunday suppers at Glebe House before the Reverend had buried his wife.

Later that night, as Siân lay awake listening to the clock downstairs strike half-past eleven, she began to hear a faint neighing from the stable. But she was too absorbed in her own thoughts to think anything amiss. Why had Tomos appeared so cheerful on the way south to London, despite his disastrous sale? Why had he paid for such a good dinner and even let her eat her fill if there'd been so little to celebrate?

She watched him from her bed in the shared room as he tossed and turned over and over, and the longer she gazed, the more clearly she realized she knew the answers. And they lay less than two miles away at the Lee Wood Fair. He was planning to recoup his losses with *her*.

Siân reared up with a thudding heart as Tomos Richards resumed his snoring. She slipped out of bed, and crept along a creaking passage full of other sleepers' dreams until she came to the main saloon. Here she stopped and held her breath, for someone was already in there. It was a young woman sprinkling new sawdust on the floor.

'*I want to see to my pony,*' Siân explained. '*She's been off her feed.*'

The girl silently unbolted the outer door for her and returned to her duties as Siân made her way in the moonlight towards the stables. She patted Incio affectionately on the head, before letting Collen out, with Ben following. She could hear the remaining terrier whining as she slipped the bit into the mare's mouth, but for her there could be no stopping. It would be London on her own, if need be, and there wasn't a second to lose. Once she'd found the mounting block, she was soon aboard her little chestnut and ready to move off.

But suddenly a large hand gripped her rein and held Collen fast. It was a man whose hair was white as whey under the moon, his pink eyes fixed on her as hard as glass.

Derryn Morris the baker.

Twenty-Four

From:Roy.Dawson@Crowbar.com
Friday 23 November 2001 15.08
To:C.Gifford@Rightserve.org
Subject:Respect

Dear Friend,

Despite our continuing requests you have persisted in bringing your inaccurate and, moreover, slanderous work to fruition with no thought as to the consequences, either for this family, or, ultimately, for yourself.

I would suggest therefore, as a gesture of goodwill on your part, and for both our sakes, that you bring any hard copies of your dissertation together with all back-up disks to our door by midnight tonight. And there, I guarantee, the matter will end.

In anticipation of your understanding in this matter,

Yours faithfully,

R. L. Dawson

Send and auto delete after opening.

Roy Dawson leaned back in his office chair and stared out beyond his console of computer screens through the farmhouse's new dormer window. It had taken him over half a precious hour, since he'd returned from Cold Firton, to access Gifford's latest email address. The gay had been changing them as often as his underwear, just to keep himself one step ahead of them. Except that in matters technological, he, Roy Luke Dawson, was unbeatable. The Mouse Wizard one newspaper had called him just after Oak Leaf Distribution.com had been formed with a hefty wad of funding from Brussels, and a not so public contribution from Wiseman's Farm, buying into his expertise.

Now his irritation was growing and the day wasn't over yet, not by a long chalk. And when he reached for his coffee, he found even that was cold.

He turned to his filing cabinet and pulled out the latest letter from Kestleman and Amory, his solicitors in Bishopsgate. It seemed they were getting nowhere in their legal efforts to prevent Gifford's university from allowing the dissertation to be published.

He was apparently barking up an impossible tree, for they stated the mature student had introduced nothing that wasn't already in the public domain. As it was, Dawson had already run up costs of over £28,000, and did he really want to lose further serious money and face possibly years of litigation in so doing, only to adversely highlight the Dawson family still further?

He crushed the solicitor's letter into a ball and hurled it against the window, then removed his glasses and pinched the bridge of his nose.

'Roy?' His wife called from the floor below.

'Andy's on the phone.'

Immediately Dawson tensed up. If that inadequate couldn't be bothered to speak to his father directly on his office number, why should *he* bother with him?

'Roy?' Her heels were tap-tapping towards him up the wooden stairs.

He stayed facing the rain as she entered his study behind him, her perfume filling his private space with a dark sickly sweetness. She still clasped the handset in her red-taloned fingers.

'It's about Pike, for Christ's sake, Roy.'

'Which one? There are three of them, remember?'

'It's Anthony. Our Andy says he's been killed and his brother and father have vanished. Hiding somewhere probably. Andy was over near West-hope trying to get some slurry tank organized when he heard about it.'

Roy Dawson logged off the message to Gifford and clicked on Authorized Viewing Only.

She was still close enough to pry over his shoulder and see Stoneshanger Medical Centre come up on screen.

'We'll all be under suspicion, you realize that?'

'Everything's under control. I've seen this coming since October. Pike's been sailing too close to the wind for too long.'

Her smell was nauseating, her aggression equally unwelcome – as ever, just under the surface. While he quietly resolved matters, she would create a galaxy of unnecessary emotional chaos.

His father had been right, of course. Twenty-four years ago Doreen Miller, grocer's daughter from Banbury, had been a half-hearted choice of wife – in fact a distant second to the striking blonde he'd really wanted all along, but she'd turned out to be a high-class bitch calling all the shots before dumping him for another.

'Can't you say just one word to Andy?' Doreen Dawson pleaded, holding out the phone. 'He's worried he'll be fingered by the police for this murder, and he's going nuts about paying his mortgage. Just put his mind at rest, please.'

Dawson snarled dismissively, 'Apart from his arsehole, his whole bloody body's been at rest since I shelled out for Cymric.' He then slid his chair along towards a new Dell super-size monitor where, after a couple of seconds, a series of carefully scanned blackmail letters loomed large and pathetic. The end of a love affair. He gestured for her to take a look.

'Whose are those?' she whispered, at first not recognizing the writing, and aware her son might be listening. 'Oh my God.' Her red lips then brushed the phone. 'He'll be with you in a minute,' she reassured before pressing the handset against her thigh.

'As you can see, our Andrew's quite a prolific correspondent.' Roy Dawson scrolled down through his son's litany of increasing hate, jealousy and confusion of feelings for Tony Pike.

Doreen Dawson gasped, momentarily forgetting the phone she was holding.

'These I'm getting rid of,' he announced.

Click click. *Deletions confirmed.* Click OK.

'When faggots fall out, I'm afraid things can get

a little unpleasant. Now,' he turned to face her, her mouth distorted in shock. 'What you were saying? Andy?'

She passed him the phone and he cocked his head against it, then shrugged.

'Gone. Oh dearie, dear.'

'For God's sake, Roy, you know where this always leads. He'll be round here again, stalemate as usual. Nothing sorted.'

'But when he does call, we'll see him, like we always do. Like the decent parents we really are. Now, I have a lot to do, so if you don't mind...'

His chair spun round to face the sky once more, while she stood there motionless.

'Look, he'll have to start living in the real world like everyone else, and about time too.' His long white fingers brought the Medical Centre's home page into view, showing a clutch of friendly faces brimming with rude health.

'But that farm's his entire *world*. He's been really trying to make a go of it. OK, you gave him the deposit, but why not the mortgage repayments as well? You can afford it. He's your *son*, Roy, not some stranger.'

'I'm not going through all that again.' By now, he'd reached Personnel and a smile twitched one corner of his mouth.

'I think you *enjoy* seeing him struggle,' Doreen Dawson taunted. 'It gives you some kind of thrill. And now our business is closing down – maybe that's our punishment.'

'No, no, my dear, please. You've got it quite wrong. That's what our former partners in Cold Firton would *like* to think. No, we're merely relocating onwards and upwards. The sky's the limit, eternity's the limit ... while our friends up the road are having to cover all their grubby little tracks. Much good has that grand Oakley pew done them, or their hymn books.'

He waited until the nuisance woman had gone and he was alone. Now he could safely begin.

PATIENT FILES M–R. *Please click for authorized access.* Click. *Please provide code word.* PYTHON. Click. *Strictly confidential.*

'Ah.' There she was. Monica Elaine Oakley (née Shaw). Complete with recent photo, too. What a woman. He still hated her, of course, for humiliating him all those years ago. But how could he ever forget that insane passion she'd once stirred in him? That all-devouring lust? His memory lurched into rewind and he savoured again that best, brief part of his life as clearly as if it was all yesterday.

It had been late spring: warm enough to make love out of doors. In fact right under Donald Carp's nose while he was tagging his sheep and, hearing her moans, the shifty git had taken a peep. It wasn't just that; he'd known too much all along. So that last New Year's Day he'd made an excellent bonfire without too much smoke. Just another bit of forest clearance, another ash pile mingling with the rest.

He stared at the patient's medical details. 8 September: Negative smear test. 17 September: Biopsy on neck of cervix. 27 September: Wertheim's hysterectomy and chemotherapy to begin immediately...

His hand clenched the mouse. His lips tightened. A small rash of pink settled on each sharp cheekbone.

Scroll down...

He viewed the previous day's grim entry then sat back in his chair.

So, there *is* some justice, he thought, allowing that same mean smile to return. Then he thought of the girl, so like her mother in many ways. Her intelligence, the same need for flattery, but, most of all, that overriding need for money. And because her birthday was imminent, and she deserved something different, he'd create her very own website for the whole world to see. Adorned by oak leaves naturally, for he was never one to shirk on artistic touches. But the content ... ah, well, there'd be no holds barred with that either.

He checked his watch. A little dark blood was lodged between its strap and the face even after thorough cleaning. He'd have to wear another for his visit to Church House after Dr Rook had finished his supper, to help him set up the new PC to enable him to work more from home.

By 4.30 p.m. the website was finished, and he studied its graphic disclosures with a certain pride. Certainly his talents had never deserted him when he'd needed them most, and this was no exception. Then he made the new program secure and clicked close.

Roy Dawson stood up to unlock his wall safe and extract the sole set of keys to George Pike's hangar as well as a brand-new carving knife which now bore no trace of Anthony Pike's blood. Nevertheless, as he went downstairs and headed for the blazing woodburning stove in the kitchen, he repeatedly wiped the blade against his trouser leg, thinking how, with his eager assistant's help, the whole procedure had seemed much less complicated than carving a Sunday chicken.

Then, with his wife safely ensconced in the conservatory at the rear of the farmhouse, he left by the kitchen door and made his way across the Tarmac, to where an almost full septic tank awaited him. He prised open the lid and wrinkled his nose as Pike's keys made a slight sucking sound then vanished.

'Well well well, if it isn't our little Lodger.' Just to hear that voice again made Siân shudder. She tried kicking Morris away but the iron strength of his grip on her knee pressed her leg even tighter to Collen's side, his fingers working their way up her thigh. 'Mmm, not as soft as our Eirwen ... nor so ready for it,' he whispered. 'And now she's got a Morris bach in her belly ... out in May, it'll be.'

Eirwen? Eirwen Pugh? No, it can't be. Never in a million years...

Siân felt sick. So *that* was why her best friend had left Nant-Y-Fedw so suddenly. This man was evil, loathsome and, like herself, Eirwen had always been frightened of him. Or *had* she? That possibility was too painful to dwell upon now. Besides, Siân had herself to think about.

'And now, brothers,' Morris hissed towards the

stables, 'we know where the porthmon will be. So let's get on with it then.'

By now, almost paralysed by terror, Siân could just make out other voices from inside, the clack of hooves in the stalls.

Those Carters are here as well. Oh my God!

They'd known Tomos would be somewhere round Berkhamstead, and for a shilling any publican would confirm it. So that's why she'd heard whinnying earlier in the night. The dogs had probably received a slap or a kick; they both seemed subdued.

She had to act, to get away, now. She whistled, the loudest, sharpest sound she'd made since her trampling, and Ben leapt for the man's throat, toppling him backwards. Then she kicked the mare on with all the strength she'd ever possessed, and Collen lurched forwards, almost stumbling, then galloped away as she'd once done on the hills over Bwlch Y Gwyn, with Ben following them out into the road. The road to where, Siân didn't know, and just now, didn't care.

A shot whistled past them, then another. Her scream of fright was as chilling as the dark cold midnight as Collen took her away from the five intruders now pushing open the inn door, silencing the poor cleaning girl and entering Tomos's room.

As Siân rode on, eventually slowing to a walk, images of everyone she loved passed through her mind, while distant shots and the neighing of horses fractured the still night air. Huw, her Da,

Eirwen and even little Alfie … all once so real, but all fading now.

Except for the 'friends' she had yet to meet: the ones whose lives would surely one day entwine with hers.

The roughly made road became a track, taking them through ancient holloways, newly frosted, whitening more every minute like the glaze on her Mam's best Sunday cups as she strayed not westwards to home nor south to a dream of a cure, but north to a hostile place and other strangers' hearths.

The night folded itself around them, and Siân reined in Collen by the gateway to a ploughed field that seemed to spread as far as the world itself – its ridges, lit by the dying moon, stretching away to infinity.

She tied the chestnut to one of the posts and settled herself with Ben in a grassy ditch, which because of its depth was luckily untouched by the frost. Here she curled up next to him for warmth and slept fitfully until next morning, when a pony and trap occupied by two lads and a girl, about her age, trundled by; their giggling sounding strange after the previous night's horrors.

Siân sat bolt upright as they passed, keeping a tight hold on Ben for fear he'd chase after them. She tried to stand but her legs had gone numb.

'*London?*' she whispered. '*Is this the right way?*'

The trio stared at her, then exchanged glances and broke out into raucous laughter.

'London, you says?' The girl winked at her

companions. 'Just you keep on goin', little gypsy.' She pointed towards a distant church spire. 'Straight through to Pitstone Green – can't miss it. Then on from there.'

She slapped the brown gelding into a trot before Siân could offer thanks. However, she'd seen their evasive eyes and just sensed they weren't telling the truth. But what else could she do? There was no one else around, and the sky had grown grey all over, like an old blanket, with no hint of sun to guide her.

'*Ben, point your nose in the right direction for us, please.*' She stroked him, waiting until he'd finished pulling at the grass and sicked up a vile green ball at her feet. He turned and followed the same way the cart had gone.

As she clambered up the bank to mount Collen, she knew that her past had somehow been severed for good by that cold night's journey – and the unknown was all that awaited her.

Twenty-Five

As the day's low cloud evolved into an early dusk, so Ivan's voice worsened. Depressed by the loss of that ninety pounds, he was in too much of a bad mood to call Pronto Cabs to see if Jo was still there. He wasn't going to risk being made a fool of by her, even if her voice was all he really wanted to hear.

And then there was his meeting with Charlie Gifford – an unknown quantity. For two pins he'd have put him off, but that might be downright stupid. The man would have his dissertation with him, if nothing else.

Ivan had finished the last of his Strepsil tablets and was now on a whisky laced with the dregs of an ancient cough mixture. At least this concoction seemed to make his throat less tender, but his voice box stayed resolutely feeble, so that when he answered the phone, Valerie Rook momentarily wondered, from her hospital bed, if she'd contacted a heavy breather instead. She explained to him that she would be getting out of there on Sunday.

'Look, I'll drive you home. What time are they letting you out?'

'No, please. I've already booked a taxi. Woman driver only, as recommended by the nurse, so don't worry. There are some errands I need to do on the way home. Besides, Michael's got some conference to go to. Look, there's a shocking piece of news... It's too dreadful–' Her voice wavered. 'I mean, I know that Tony Pike was into all sorts of shady business, but he was still a human being. He's been *butchered*, Ivan, his head almost cut off. Oh, heavens, I think we've got a serial beheader on the loose.'

My God, Tom Coles all over again.

The Toprank man hadn't mentioned that detail. Ivan's chest tightened.

'Michael says the police have erected a kind of tent thing over the grave and there are dog-handlers scouring the land behind the graveyard.'

'Any hints as to who might have done it?'

'Nothing. But George Pike and his other son have disappeared.'

Ivan thought about the Oakleys probably also preparing to run. Maybe this was why. Maybe this murder was their last gesture. But somehow it didn't connect. From what he'd gathered, the Pikes had been their loyal servants, launderers of anything dodgy the Oakleys wished to dispose of, so why waste one of them?

'Look, Valerie, I've decided to put my cottage up for sale. I'm getting out of here while I've got some sanity left.'

She gasped, then there was a long pause. 'You can't. Not now.'

'It's not just the threats and the malicious vandalism. No, the whole scene here's getting weirder and weirder. It's really scary. I get burning smells, and some frantic dog barking, and now, to cap it all, my latest batch of urns has fired to a weird white powder.'

392

There was another pause as the patient gathered her thoughts.

'That's odd. I've started smelling burning too. The other evening I was just using the hair dryer, when I could hear a crackle-crackle sound coming from it, so I turned the thing off. There was absolutely nothing wrong with it, but when I checked my hair in the mirror, some of the ends were badly singed. It was really frightening.'

Ivan recalled her uneven haircut when they had met at the church. Suddenly he felt a prickle of heat on the back of his own neck, as if a hot poker tip had brushed against his skin.

'Look, Valerie, I need you to help me. I have this strong gut feeling that someone from the past is trying to reach us. Why, I don't know. When you're back home, I'd like you to find out who were the doctors at Cold Firton and Nether Wapford around the time when that Hannah and Matthew Tripp were alive, from say 1820 until 1860. That should do it. Check if there were any significant occurrences then.'

'I wouldn't know where to start. I'm only his *wife*, remember? My job is to keep the kettle permanently ready, not go raking up the past lives of the medical profession.'

'Well, ask your husband, then. Come on, Valerie, think of *something*...You see, according to Mrs Tripp, her husband's great-grandparents took in a young girl, a complete stranger with possibly a Welsh connection. Now that must have been quite a thing, someone arriving in a backwater like this, speaking in what must have seemed to them like a foreign tongue.' He added,

'On Monday I'm going to have a good snout round in the Central Library and the Record Office. Maybe second time lucky. I keep seeing an image of this young girl's face; she's very pale – stricken, I'd say, as if she'd been to hell and stayed there ... though thank God there's no frantic whispering any more nor those burning sensations. Look,' he ended, 'I've got to move on with my life. Maybe *you* as well.'

She sighed audibly, then fell silent with unhappiness. For a moment, Ivan could hear the rattle of trolleys, the hubbub of other voices.

'I'll do what I can but, knowing my husband, I'm not promising much.' Then to Ivan's great surprise, she added, 'I want to help solve your mystery. More important, it sounds like *she* wants us to solve it.'

The ward was getting even noisier.

'What do you make of this, then?' he almost shouted over the racket. 'The Oakleys' pub is still closed, though I saw Harold Oakley lurking in there today. It doesn't make sense for them to be losing all that custom. And it looks like their taxi business is folding up as well. D'you reckon they've all legged it to the Costa del Sol?'

'No, not them. There'll be another grieving family yet, you'll see. They seem to have a blood lust and they don't know how to stop.'

She lowered her voice, even though no one else could be listening. 'Something else I heard from my husband. There *is* a Jo Oakley. He had to write some report on her for the probation service, just after we'd moved here.'

Ivan's stomach tightened.

394

Probation service? What the hell's this about?

'What kind of report?'

'It was about her having to be weaned off hard drugs a few years back.'

'Go on.' But he didn't really want to hear it.

'Apparently, and this is confidential, she attacked the trainee nurse assigned to her. She found a knife somewhere.'

Ivan's frown deepened. He tried to forget the sudden violence of her kick to his shin at Church House. 'Where's this supposed to have happened then?' he demanded. 'Her posh boarding school?'

'Michael wouldn't say, but apparently she was only fifteen at the time. Look, Ivan, I know you like her, but you don't know what you might be getting into. And if anything happened to you–' Her voice tailed off, as if she'd said too much already.

'So is she still hooked?'

'I don't know. Michael clammed up then. I'm sorry if it's bad news.' Valerie sensed his dismay. 'I'm only trying to stop you getting hurt.'

But his thanks were muted and they both hung up in an air of unsettling gloom.

Armed with yet more throat medicaments from a late-night chemist, and unable to shift Valerie's surprise news about Jo from his mind, Ivan threaded his way through the crowded car park behind the Poacher's Arms and approached the saloon bar door.

The illuminated pub sign overhead showed a bucolic figure with a bloodied hare slung over

395

each shoulder, no detail spared. Ivan recalled the other carnage seen in his friendly neighbourhood forest, and felt a sudden yearning to spend the rest of his days amongst brick and concrete, on busy well-lit streets where at least your stray pervert is likely to be recorded in fuzzy-grey on some CCTV screen, not secreted away in a dissembling rural idyll.

Both bars were packed, probably because the nearest rival pub in Cobbling Street was still closed, and Friday night wasn't Friday night out here in the sticks without getting seriously pissed or getting hold of some downers for the weekend. Ivan gravitated towards the counter where a young barman was trying to serve the entire darts team in the quickest possible time. 'Excuse me,' his voice was only just audible, 'I'm looking for someone called Charles Gifford. Is he around, d'you know?'

The shaven-headed barman stopped and grinned at him. Thirty-something, going on twenty, Ivan thought, with a white T-shirt and black jeans both a size too small.

'That's me. Sorry, I should have warned you I work here part-time.' The barman proffered a damp hand then, all too aware of the surrounding thirsts closing in on him, he turned back to his customers. 'My shift will end any minute, soon as Rob shows up. Can you hang on till then?'

'Sure. I'll be over there.' Ivan pointed towards the door, where a two-seater table had just been vacated. He deposited his scarf there while he fetched a pint from the lounge bar next door.

He found his thoughts once more preoccupied by Jo, wondering where she was right now. If she was ever likely to give him a second thought. OK, she could be sharp with her tongue, but to deliberately *attack* someone with a knife? That was scary, but was it true? Even Bryn Mitchell and Jeanette Yates had it in for her. Each with their own agendas for doing her down. But one thing was for certain, she wasn't in this pub; and he felt an intense wave of yearning wash over him.

'Cheers.' A tipsy girl at the next table tilted her glass of vodka and lemon at him and Ivan then suddenly realized who she was: Angela from County Homes. 'I heard about your cottage from my boss,' she announced for all to hear. 'He reckons it's a bit of a dump and you ought to get shot of it, quick as you can.' She then went back to tittering with her friend, ignoring Ivan's look of scorn.

Gifford raised the bar flap and came over. He had poured himself a pint of lager too. His leather jacket was draped over his arm, and he carried a Safeway's bag containing something bulky. He then propped it up against the table leg.

'For your eyes only.' He patted it. 'Hey, I noticed you were chatting up the delightful Angela Cartwright.' He settled himself opposite.

Cartwright? 'Not that estate agent's daughter?'

'Stoneshanger's very own Mr Blobby.' Gifford stared at him. 'You look like you've seen a ghost, if you'll pardon me. Sounds as if you've lost your voice as well. Having fun out there?'

'If you call having a ton of cow shit dumped on your doorstep fun, then yeah, I've been there, done it,' Ivan croaked.

'That's an old trick round here. Tell me more.' Gifford eased his toned body back against the wall, his drink soon dispatched, as Ivan catalogued the threats and malicious incidents that had befallen him ever since that fateful Tuesday evening. By the time he'd finished, his companion was leaning forwards, chin propped on his hands.

'Hey, I'm having a real problem getting my head round all this, that you've become *such* a *bête noire* to all these creeps.'

'The irony is, it's *me* who's been wronged. I got my car stolen in the first place.'

'To them that's immaterial. But keeping control, keeping the collective nose clean, keeping the law at bay, well, that's another matter.'

'You mean the Oakleys?'

'The Dawsons *and* the Pikes, too, let's not forget.' Gifford continued, 'I've just heard about that junker Pike, and I'm telling you him getting topped was just waiting to happen.'

'Why's that?'

'I knew him from when he became a reserve on our cricket club team last summer. Trouble was, he literally got *too* cocky, get my meaning?' He gave Ivan a lopsided grin.

'Yeah, OK.' Ivan was wondering where all this was leading.

'I'm surprised our Tony didn't pounce when he got you in that truck of his on your own. He was the biggest tart north of Watford.'

398

'But a useful one, it seems?'

'Oh sure. A real busy bee with that truck, and well paid for it too. I mean we're talking a minimum of two grand a month. He used to brag about it, trying to impress me.' Gifford framed his beer mat with a well-tended hand and turned it round and round. 'D'you know, he had a Boxster tucked away in that poky hole of a garage at Westhope? But unless you knew where to look, you'd be wasting your bloody time. The pumps are just a front there, but underneath, boy, they've a huge fuck-off hangar of a storeroom. Quite a little goldmine for all concerned.'

'So what did Tom Coles do to upset them?'

'Blabbed a bit too much. End of story.' The edge of the beer mat hit the table like a guillotine. 'So you see our Tony was making one or two other folks jealous, but he liked that. Gave him a bit of a buzz.' He broke off, seeing Ivan's empty glass. 'Can I get you a refill?'

'My shout.' Ivan got up, and, as he returned, noticed that the veins inside each of Gifford's elbows were darkly raised.

'I don't think we need look very far to find who nearly cut his head off.' Gifford reached for his fresh glass.

'Go on.'

'Well, Pikey was ringing – pardon my French – Farmer Giles no less.'

Ivan's eyes widened as he thought of the possibilities.

'Yep, tasty pasty Andy Dawson, our very own little snorting snowbird.'

Ivan was puzzled by this remark, but

nevertheless let Gifford continue.

'Trouble was – is – that Andy's not doing very well in the duckets department. Clapped-out old equipment, practically *giving* his stock away left right and centre – so if whispers of foot-and-mouth come true, he'll soon be done for. He gets more from selling cow shit these days. So how did boyfriend Pikey make him feel?' Gifford smiled. 'You just think, if *you* were up to your thighs in that stuff every day of the week, while up cruises lover boy in the Porsche...'

However Ivan was thinking of their intimidation of him in Welsh Way, realizing now that he might find the answer.

'But why do that to *me*? It doesn't make sense. Has he got his own slurry tank?'

Gifford smiled. 'Dream on, mate, he's a primitive up there – spreads the muck by shovel off a cart. My theory is someone else paid him to make your life a little – how shall I say? – more richly flavoured. After all, he could do with the dough.'

'What for? Why me?'

Gifford's laugh was deeply unnerving. 'Someone clearly wants you out of your delectable cottage, then, having slipped the agent something to verbally demolish you, buys it up cheap at auction and, hey presto, makes a tidy pile.'

'Cartwright was responsible?' The disease was spreading. Ivan hadn't even thought of that one. He remembered the estate agent's performance with his handkerchief. It was all a set-up.

'I've heard rumours about his *modus operandi* on more than one occasion.' Gifford affected a mysterious tone. 'I'm surprised the Oakleys let him near their old granny's bothy.'

'He already knew I'd bought my place at auction last year, and that no one else wanted it. So why does he think it's worth anything now?'

'Because rural property prices are shooting through the roof, that's why. Anyhow, what was I saying? A mate of mine at the cricket club reckoned he could sniff some shaking down going on between our boys.'

'Shaking down?' Ivan was puzzled.

'Blackmail, right? That Handy Andy had been sending Pikey letters, emails and so on, threatening to shop him to the law unless Pikey coughed up. Now that sort of thing's not nice, is it? But he's desperate to keep that farm. It kept Pikey up to scratch, I suppose, and Andy probably forced him to waylay you in Welsh Way.'

'So why doesn't Dawson senior just help his son out if he's so loaded?' Ivan had almost forgotten about his beer.

'Why doesn't the devil possess a soul? You tell me.'

'Maybe they just don't approve,' Ivan suggested, vividly remembering what Valerie had told him. 'I heard from a local woman that back in the mid-forties Roy Dawson's father, Walter, shot some boy because a Dawson girl had got keen on him. And then the killer gets off with a bloody warning, if you please. They may also have a problem with gays,' he concluded.

'They've got a problem period.' Gifford said bleakly, toying with his glass. 'Have you ever been to the Snake House at London Zoo?' he suddenly

401

asked. 'You can stand there all bloody day waiting for signs of life, and then suddenly, hey presto, out pops a head, briefly, then back in it goes for another twelve hours. But, instead of the Snake House here, we have our very own Dawson's Farm.'

'So why do they still live there if they're so rich? I don't understand.'

'Would *you* give up a property worth nearly two million pounds? Oh they're clued up all right – and nasty, very nasty.'

'What about the local cops, they're clean, are they?' Ivan had lost all interest in his drink.

Gifford paused. 'Yeah, far as I know. Slow as hell, mind, but bent? I don't think so. They'll get there eventually, when the moon's turned to green cheese, maybe.'

'So, tell me more about these Dawsons.' Ivan wanted to pin him down for some hard facts. 'I mean, what do they actually *do* in the scheme of things these days?'

'Our charismatic Roy's a proper fixer. On the public front he's set up computer systems for both the Medical Centre and the local council – stuff like that. On the old QT, however, it's the internet that's his fucking world. His business, Oak Leaf Distribution.com, deals in freight, a.k.a. hard stuff, from mainly Bulgaria and the Netherlands, with timetabling and distribution to major cities in the UK all sorted without stepping out of the farm. He uses Oakley's truck drivers and pays them and Pikey to drive, with Pike's underground garage being used for storage and servicing.'

'All Ma Oakley's idea, so I heard.'

Gifford paused uncomfortably and went on.

'Anyhow, there's nothing sticking to Roy's little white fingers once he's bought the stuff online, oh no, clever bastard. And I'm sure Handy Andy's farm is tied up with it somehow.'

'And Dawson's wife?'

Gifford shrugged. 'Who knows? That witch probably keeps a pet crow in the bedroom.'

Ivan felt a sudden shot of excitement hit his heart as Gifford reached down then placed the package he'd brought with him in the middle of the table.

'Your dissertation?'

'Correct, but,' he looked round warily, 'not to be broadcast *anywhere*, or we'll find ourselves taking a dip in the Wap.'

He pulled back one side of the carrier bag to reveal a black spiral-bound typescript. On the front was a label:

THE RISE OF CRIME AND CRIMINAL GANGS AFTER THE ENCLOSURES A NORTHAMPTONSHIRE STUDY

by
CHARLES W. GIFFORD

Ivan extracted the substantial thesis and began flicking through its index, which listed Baptists, Calvinists, Methodists and Quakers. 'This is all about religion, like your brother said,' he complained with a frown.

'You have to read between the lines, mate.'

Gifford showed large strong teeth once more in a smile. 'That's just the backdrop, so to speak.'

Ivan selected odd pages to study, the sub-heading 'Body Snatching' being the first to catch his eye, and, as he glimpsed the name Luke Dawson, his curiosity was soon fully kindled.

Gifford's account was graphic and succinct, dating this lucrative activity as flourishing between the years 1827 and 1829, when freshly exhumed corpses were crammed into four-foot-square hampers and dispatched to St Bartholomew's Hospital by post-chaise.

'This is bloody revolting.' Ivan looked up to see his companion looking rather pleased with himself. Then he received the distinct impression they were being watched by some bloke in a dark coat over in the corner. He hesitated.

'Read on, good man. This is the never-ending story of simple country folk.' Gifford got up. 'Same again?'

'I'm driving, so better make it an orange juice, thanks.' When he looked again, the man had gone.

In the growing hubbub around him, Ivan tried to concentrate on how this grisly enterprise had been curtailed by greater vigilance around the local churchyards.

Luke Dawson and his two married sons, Noah and Arthur, then diversified into producing a range of cruel and illegal poachers' traps which they manufactured at the farm and sold all over the county. They themselves also poached anything that breathed, mostly for sale at Smithfield with no questions asked.

By the time Ivan had finished that particular section, Gifford was back.

'So they were all eventually hanged in 1830? What did those missing pages in Stanton's book reveal?' he asked.

'Not a lot, I imagine. I think our friend cobbled together his own woolly version of events, unsavoury enough to make your ordinary reader prick up his ears, with the odd olde illustration or whatever to give it atmosphere, but without enough detail to satisfy the professional researcher. According to the Swanimote records which I found–'

'Swanimote?'

'Yeah, the forest courts. There was one held in Sykeston as late as November 1829. Most of the others were abandoned at the end of the eighteenth century, but I reckon they kept this one going to deter the likes of the Dawsons. As you'll see, it makes interesting reading.' Gifford turned to a facsimile page detailing all the charges, fifteen in all, including physically threatening the forest warden and damage to his cottage, and bearing at the end a seal bearing a single oak leaf. Ivan stabbed his finger on the faded signature.

'But they were all three acquitted. That's crazy.'

'So what's new? They probably slipped the old judge a hefty wad, and here we go again.' Gifford glanced up to smile greetings at a young man in denims on his way out. 'I just had to know how they finally ended up. I mean, they were hardly likely to break the habits of a lifetime and bunk off to a monastery somewhere, do the sackcloth-

and-ashes thing, were they? Besides, they owned a big freehold farm, not tenanted like the others. So, I did some more rootling. Mind you, it was like pulling bloody teeth.'

'How d'you mean?'

'When I went to check the County Record Office last spring, all I could find were the parish records for Cold Firton. No mention of them having a Christian burial at any of the local churches–'

'Surprise, surprise,' Ivan interrupted.

'Yeah, but I still wanted to know exactly *why* the three finally ended up in jail, and what the charge of murder related *to*.'

'Murder?' Ivan visualized that forest again – its multitude of dark secrets maybe never to be fully told.

'Well, that's all Stanton's account gave us. With no *detail*, and that's what I was really after. To find out what they actually *did*. So I asked at the CRO to see any recognizance books or calendar of prisoners which would include that particular date, 28 March 1830, at Northampton Lent Assizes. And guess what?'

'Go on.'

'They claimed they'd gone off for re-binding, but I reckon the bloody Dawsons were leaning on them to keep the records secret from the likes of me or anyone else interested in investigating their murky past. Course they'd know I had a deadline for this dissertation, so I'd likely never be going back there.'

'But *you* were still curious,' Ivan suggested.

'I *was*, and I kept making enquiries. It's then I

started getting emails, scary stuff actually warning me off. Word about my *oeuvre* must have got out somehow, as does everything else round here. I even got one today. Dawson wants this on his doorstep by midnight. As if...'

Ivan stared at him.

'Did you mention this to the cops?' he asked.

'What, me? No, mate, I want to *live*, get my MA behind me and bugger off to Oz – maybe do my PhD out there. Don't know how my brother sticks this country.'

However, Ivan felt a creeping unease return. 'But you reckon the local cops are clean?'

'Dunno for sure about all of them. Just a whisper in the breeze.'

Ivan, still thoughtful, closed the thesis and returned it to the carrier bag.

'Do you know about Jo Oakley?' he asked suddenly.

Gifford shrugged. 'What about her?'

'Anything.'

'For starters, she's not really an Oakley. Never was, never will be. No, they adopted her when she was about ten or eleven.' He gave Ivan a knowing look. 'Whoever rides her is on a fucking loser, I'm telling you. And not just because she didn't get a cent of the old girl's money.'

Before pulling open the pub door Gifford glanced back with a smile, but too quickly to notice the full extent of the damage he'd just inflicted. Ivan wanted to follow him and ask more, but what was the point?

All the way back to Tripp's Cottage, he brooded

on the day's revelations, on how things were slowly beginning to connect, but heightening his unease, not reducing it.

As Welsh Way proceeded, narrow and dark away from the A43, Ivan shuddered to think of how he had just unburdened himself to someone he'd never met before.

Past Dawson's Farm white under the hanging moon, set out like a harmless string of child's bricks, back home to where the forest's unquiet spirits were biding their time.

With her ears still tuned to possible pursuers, Siân steered Collen through the bleak morning air towards Pitstone Green, which promised to be a sizeable hamlet where surely she would find assistance to get her on the right road to London.

However, the four dwellings set alongside one narrow track, were now little more than the black remains of a devastating fire. A Need-Fire, she wondered. Had this too been a place of plague or the rinderpest?

There wasn't a soul around, and her hunger was now so intense she tore new hawthorn leaves from the hedges and crammed them into her mouth. Collen, too, snatched at whatever she could, stumbling occasionally, and when she finally cast a shoe along the way, Siân realized she could never afford to get it replaced.

The landscape grew more hilly with every mile covered. The surrounding tree tops sealed off the sky, creating a silence she found unnerving. It was as if the Goddess Rhiannon had cast her spell and nothing was yet awake. But more unnerving still was coming across a sign proclaiming the county of Buckinghamshire.

This can't be the way, surely? Siân felt a rising panic, suspecting that all along she'd been heading north and not south.

Suddenly came the sound of boots behind her, the growl of another dog. She turned to see Ben standing in defiance, and envisaged some other huge beast soon tearing his throat out.

'Leave him be,' she whispered to her own dog. *'I don't want you hurt.'* But it was too late. The two animals circled each other then locked together until the thickset man used his stick to beat them apart. When Ben withdrew, blood from his slack jaw peppering the ground, Siân noticed with dismay that one of his ears was also torn.

'Six o' one, half dozen o't other, I'd say,' said the man in an accent she could hardly understand. 'C'mon you.' The stranger whacked his hound's scraggy haunches until the poor creature skulked along behind him. 'Pick someone yer own size.' Then he turned to Siân. 'I'll give ye a shillin' for yer Welsh Hound.' He pointed at Ben. 'He'd be a tidy worker for me. What say ye?'

Siân stared at the man now arrived alongside her, not fully understanding his dialect or his purpose. But when she saw both his pockets stuffed with a dead rabbit apiece, she shivered and kicked Collen onwards.

'I wouldn't sell him for twenty pounds,' she mouthed. *'I'll be needing him for London.'*

'London?' The poacher's mouth slid open to a black toothless smile. He took a long stride and clamped his hand over her leg, just as Derryn Morris used to do. 'That seat of sin lies *that* way, missy.' His ugly head gestured back the way she'd come. 'And no place for a fine one like yersen to be thinkin' of.' Siân saw how his fingernails were edged with blood.

If she turned Collen round now, this man could easily block the whole track with his bulk and strength, and his dog would most likely see Ben off for good. She'd no choice but to head forwards, and a few moments later was cantering away from his mocking laughter, which mercifully grew ever more faint.

Collen and Ben slowed to a walk as the track became merely two deep wheel ruts, a muddy gulley between the silent fields and silent woods as a soft yet persistent rain began to fall.

Another hamlet appeared, populated, Siân thought, more by souls of the dead than by anything living. Her hunger was now making her dizzy, and she clung to Collen's mane as they passed a painted sign for Bring Upton, then another, standing by an empty yard, saying, D. Weatherall – Cartwright in faded letters. She recognized the trap that had passed her earlier, now tilted on its end, with no trace of either its pony or the occupants' cruel laughter.

This strange land seemed full of ghosts: they hovered in the covering cloud, in the thickening rain, slowly stealing her dreams. For London and Dr George Owen were simply hollow sounds now in her head, fading with each of the mare's halting steps.

Twenty-Six

As soon as he woke on Saturday morning Ivan contacted the unfortunately named Pillock Auctioneers of Market Harborough and arranged for them to visit Tripp's Cottage, to assess a reserve price. They'd already got several other properties in the region listed for their December sale, and no, he wasn't yet too late to be included in their catalogue.

Oliver Pillock assured him that his company had no direct connection with Douglas Cartwright, a man he barely knew.

'I've got to be careful what I say here,' he explained. 'I've got my business to think of. That's not to say he's not tried it on in the past, mind. I have to say we once did get a call from this Cartwright gentleman, going on about subsidence.'

'Subsidence?' Ivan croaked, alarmed. That was a new one.

'Oh yes, but we know that game of old. If he wants any of the properties, he'll have to pay the going rate. The market's still strong – different to last summer.'

Ivan thanked the man and went out into the cold clear air to check that the prehistoric cesspit hadn't been tampered with again. He saw Mrs Jonas approaching, sporting as a new hair-do a mass of wiry grey curls.

411

'You missed the police last night.' She toyed with her extra finger.

'Police?'

'Ye weren't here. They called round to warn me to make extra sure all me doors and windows were locked both night and day, and not to open the door to anyone oi didn't know.'

The winter sunlight, bringing everything into a sharp relief that cast vicious black shadows on the frosty ground, did nothing to soften the menace underlying her words.

'Things are getting serious, then.' He watched the smoke from her chimney trail away towards the trees. 'Did they say *exactly* what's going on? I heard a rumour the Oakleys are scarpering.'

'No, nowt like that. But, as ye mention them lot, the milkman said when he called at their place this morning, the gate was all tied up with barbed wire like Bosnia or somewhere, and not a soul around.'

'Very odd, isn't it?' But all Ivan could think of was Jo.

'Oh, the police did say ye was to give them a call sometime. Oi was going to come over and tell ye.'

'OK, thanks.'

'DC Marsh here.'

'You asked me to phone.'

'Glad you did, sir. We want to advise you about your security – and there's something else.'

'Oh yeah?'

'One of my men spotted you in the pub last night with our friend Charles Gifford. I'd better warn you the man's a Class-A junkie and a pusher – not the best of company.'

So that was the bloke in the corner.

'Can't I go for a bloody drink whenever I want?'

'Mr Browning, Charles Gifford has also been a close associate of Wiseman's Farm. Need I say more?'

'My neighbour heard the place was all barricaded up this morning.'

'We did that.'

'Why?'

'Let's just say that when the fox returns he won't find his earth quite so accessible.' Marsh drew in his breath, keeping his voice even. 'We're getting warmer.' There was a pause, a tiny click on the line which Ivan missed. 'But be careful. Gifford *wants* trouble, and consorting with him in public could be a mistake on your part. Lucky it was not one of the Dawsons who saw you. Now, I must away.'

Suddenly, Ivan sensed a drop in temperature, and his ears picked up that dreaded whispering again as it filtered into his cramped hallway. It seemed more insistent now with each repetition of the familiar plea.

'Take me back... Take me back... You promised me...'

The words seemed to grow to a shout, circling round and round inside his ears. Then, before Ivan could escape into the living room, it soared into a scream – the most piercing wail he'd ever heard, as if all the misery in the world was caught in its raw primordial power.

413

It was a last cry that devoured the cottage, the sky outside, the forest beyond, swirling into the hollow oaks, those mighty pollards, which once would have become the prows of ships, the pews for church and cathedral, or browse-wood for the common people's hearths.

That despair now deafened him, now moved him inexorably as he flung open his front door, and propelled him back towards the waiting trees.

Siân woke with a start. Ben was growling while Collen had stopped in her tracks.

'Hey up, where d'you think you're goin'? This is my field.' A figure almost seven feet high stood blocking her path. One huge hand held her rein, the other a gun. He looked like a farmer, rough and raw with wild bushy eyebrows. Ben wisely kept out of his way.

Siân kept her eye on the weapon. *I want to go home. I've got to get back to Wales.*

'Do you now?' He bent down to run a hand up and down each of Collen's legs in turn, and tutted. 'These won't get you far; she's got two spavins and she's nearly lame. Needs proper shoeing and a rest. 'Sides, the rain's set in till morning.'

Although the man was repulsive, Siân knew he spoke the truth. The pony had barely managed to carry her the last few miles. Without her she would be lost, and the weather was looking grim.

'So why not stop over with me and the wife tonight? Jesus, girl, your hound looks like a piece of string.'

'*I've had no choice,*' she protested.

'My name's Isaiah Crook, of Crook's Farm over there. And if you've got any sense you'll come with me.'

She looked to Ben, as if a mere dog could advise her. But his nose was busy by a sack that Crook had dropped by his feet.

'Moles,' the farmer explained. 'Little bleeders. Velvet devils, my Maggie calls 'em. Come and meet my new wife. There'll be a slice of mutton and a cup of milk for you.'

Siân was too tired, too starved, to refuse. Besides, Ben was even letting the stranger pat his head, something none of Tomos's men had ever been able to manage.

The untilled field sloped down towards a cluster of buildings encircled by pines, and Siân thought with longing of the drovers' inns back home.

'We've had the rinderpest here twice over since Michaelmas.' Crook flung an arm wide to show the empty acres dotted by the scars of Need-Fires. 'Satan's curse to be sure,' he muttered, untying a gate through which a stony path led to the barns. 'Not one cow left for us – just the sheep and the milking goats.'

Siân could hear them bleating from inside the barns – a welcome sound after miles of silence.

A black half-breed dog ran towards them, but, curiously, after the man's whistle, bounded away again.

'Maggie!' the farmer suddenly hollered. 'We've got a little Welsh biddy to join us for dinner!'

Siân blinked at the woman emerging from the farmhouse doorway: a hunched-over figure, clearly a dwarf just like little Alfie, except she was completely bald and possessed just one good eye, the other was simply a fold of skin below the eyebrow. Siân's famished stomach began to stir the wrong way, but her faculties hadn't entirely left her. With a supreme effort she urged Collen back up the hill, and through the still-open gate, the little mare barely able to put one hoof in front of the other. This man had obviously bought his new wife from the Freak Show and at present that was more than Siân could bear.

Twenty-Seven

It was cold enough for Ivan's eyes to water. Not a whisper of wind entered that eerie cathedral of trees where the pillared oaks locked together overhead, still dank and wet under an invisible sky.

But there was nothing remotely holy about this place where the breath of souls who'd suffered and died in its sheltering darkness seemed to have condensed into black pools edged by rotting leaves and fallen branches. No, this was where the devil had once walked with other cloven beasts – the boar and the high-deer – and watched and waited for his time to come again.

Ivan rested against a giant coppiced trunk whose roots sprawled half-buried like the leathery limbs of a forgotten people. His heart was busy, urgent, and he could feel the rough bark through his sweatshirt, his flesh against wood – ash on ash to be shifted to nothingness by a puff of air.

That scream inside the cottage still haunted him, lingering like tinnitus in his ear as he passed from tree to tree and farther into the dark. And, despite a gripping terror at what the forest gloom might hold, he gave way to its pull, like an iron filing drawn towards a magnet, as if beyond his own control.

He saw a fallow deer dart behind a huge holly

417

bush, felt the sudden rush of wings between branches overhead, then watched a white feather spiralling downwards into his quaking hands. It was then he realized that he was not alone, and Ivan stopped to listen hard as a regular footstep on the forest floor came closer...

Sliding behind the nearest tree, and tucking in his elbows tightly, he held his breath, feeling torn by a dilemma. He was meant to go on, not stop here. That force which had brought him so far into the wood wasn't finished with him, so, with a pulse thudding in his neck, he stepped from his hiding place to obey it. He gasped. A slim, hooded figure in black was standing in the near distance. Male or female, he couldn't tell, but whoever it was stood motionless, staring at him as if checking him out. Then something long and dark like a rifle was slowly raised.

'Jo?' This was mad, crazy. 'Jo, is that you?' And, if so, what was she doing here? 'Hey, put that *down!* It's me, Ivan. Shit, put it down.' His voice, still hoarse, seemed useless, and in that instant he saw all his past life fast-forwarded through his mind – until the stick was jettisoned and the girl started moving.

She spread out her arms with a cry of pleasure as she ran towards him. She looked pale, dishevelled, as if she'd been sleeping rough. He gripped her tightly, felt her heart pounding through the duffel coat, several sizes too big. Her usual clean soap smell was now transformed to a damp earthiness.

'For God's sake, how long have you been out here?' he asked, stepping back to look at her and noticing her wide eyes, their irises merging with the pupils' dense brown, her colourless lips. He saw leaf fragments on her shoulders, then how her right cuff was smeared with something dark like blood, although there was no sign of a cut or wound.

'Since last night. I had to hide. There was nowhere else for me to go. I've never been allowed to make friends here – otherwise I might have shacked up with someone, and got beyond their control.' She planted a kiss on his cheek. 'I couldn't risk leading the firm to your door, now could I? You've had enough on your plate already.' She suddenly looked embarrassed, not meeting his eyes.

'The Oakleys?'

She nodded. 'Yeah. Bird Dog's got a gun and the bloody mastiff. Oh Ivan, I'm so bloody scared.'

He pulled her closer again. 'Who the hell's this Bird Dog, then?' he asked, checking around over her shoulder

'Stephen Oakley. He's the one who hunts.'

Ivan recalled those headlights in the darkness, the slavering dog. 'So why's he after you?'

'Because I'm dangerous to them. I know everything.' She pulled away from him and began to pull leaf debris out of her hair.

Ivan shivered. Now every tiny movement around them could spell death, every bird call might be a whistle from their stalker.

'So why's that blood on your cuff? Did you get hurt?'

'No,' she sniffed. 'It was already there when I

put it on. God knows who's been wearing this thing before.' Jo sneezed, not once but three times. Ivan thought she looked about to cry.

'You've had a tough time with them,' he said. 'I overheard John Oakley roughing you up in his cab office.'

'He's another prize shit,' she almost spat out the words.

'Look, we'd better get you somewhere warm,' Ivan suggested, 'and quickly. Come on, my cottage isn't far.'

Ignoring the ever-present pressure on him to move deeper into the darkness, he hurried back with her the way he'd come, sensing that although he was helping her, he was also letting someone down. That other pale, terrified face.

'So, where is your family?' he asked as daylight began to appear through the trees. 'Are they lying low somewhere?' He felt safe to probe.

'They've all gone bunking off to Norfolk. Sea View Hotel, Cromer, they said. Just to reassess things, before making their next move. So I did the good citizen bit and informed the plods of that.' She patted the bulge in her coat pocket. 'I had to, didn't I?' Her unusually huge eyes fixed on him. 'It's sickened me what those Oakleys have been doing. I mean, when I first came to live at Wiseman's Farm I thought it was bloody great: my own bedroom, TV and bathroom, the life of luxury. My God, in all my eleven years I'd never seen anything like it.'

'Why eleven? That's quite old for adoption.' Ivan gently prodded for what he hoped was finally the truth.

'I've never talked about it to anyone, I mean being adopted's like being disabled or something, isn't it?' Again those beautiful eyes fixed on his.

'Don't be daft. I'm just surprised those lot were *allowed* to adopt.' They had reached the back gate.

'Are you really? The Social Services are always boggled by money.'

They crouched down by the studio wall to check if it was all clear. With a frantic turn of the key, Ivan unlocked his front door.

'Quick, get inside.'

As she stood in the hallway, she looked more slight, more vulnerable than he'd ever seen her, her dark eyes immediately scanning around for windows through which they might be seen.

'I'm putting you in terrible danger.' She shivered. 'You don't deserve this.'

'Neither do you. Come on, I'll get the kettle on. I've got tea, coffee, cocoa...'

'Nothing. I'm fine.'

'Go on, something to eat?' Ivan persevered.

'Maybe later, thanks. I just need to make sure he's not hanging round here. Then, if you don't mind, I'd like to wash my hair, get all this shit out of it.'

'Course, feel free.' He bounded upstairs to check the water heater was switched on, then he came down and put on the kettle, listening out, like her, for any unusual sounds.

He made two mugs of coffee and put them on the kitchen table. That's when she began to talk.

'I've seen a lot of what the Oakleys have done, and what they're capable of. I even heard my so-called father talking about what they'd do to Tom Coles, how they were going to chop him up and give him to the dogs.'

'Oh, Christ, no. That was my doing.'

'No, it wasn't. They'd already had enough of him causing them trouble. Then there was that vicar bloke, earlier,' she went on.

'You mean Richard Coombes?'

'Yeah, that's the one.' She seemed vaguely surprised that he knew the name. 'They even got baby Pike to pick up the money from his saddlebags once they'd run him over. They allowed him a wad for being nifty.' She picked up her coffee and returned to the tiny window, still hunched in the old coat as if it were some sort of protection.

'The one with the weird eyes?'

'Ugh, he was foul – a real weirdo. Porno stuff everywhere. Always got his hand in his boiler suit, tossing himself off. At least his brother treated me decently. I mean, I know he was bent as a corkscrew, but basically he was OK. They had him all tied up too, didn't they? Used to call him the Butler. Can you do this? Can you do that? My God, he should have kept away from them – but who says no to some easy dough? I'm from Cowley originally,' she said simply. 'Wasn't exactly peacherino there, as you probably know.'

Ivan didn't answer. The picture was getting clearer. She'd been so grateful to her wealthy new parents that any urge of self-assertiveness had been carefully suppressed by her. 'Then they were trying to drive you out, by nicking your car and that other shit. That's because you'd dared to go to the police. You were an unknown quantity to them, the *bastards*.'

Ivan paused. That was the first time the disappearance of his car had been linked to the Oakleys by an Oakley. She really was adding the finishing touches.

Suddenly the telephone rang, and they froze. 'I'll just let it ring, see who's on the answerphone,' he whispered. But as soon as his recorded message began, the caller rang off.

'Try 1471,' she suggested. She watched him dial, then shake his head: no joy there.

'Someone's checking on us, I fucking know it.' Ivan had turned white.

'I'm sorry.' She pulled up the hood of her duffel coat as if about to leave. 'It's all my fault.'

'No it isn't, and you have to stay here.' He pinioned her arms. 'We're in this together and we'll sort it. If your bloody uncle wants to put the frighteners on us, let him try.' But as those brave words fell from his lips he realized that, for both of them, there was nowhere to turn.

If he informed the cops he'd got Jo Oakley with him, they'd be round like a pack of hounds and probably arrest her. Nor could Valerie Rook be approached for help and be put in danger. It was as if a dark shadow hovered over Tripp's Cottage.

He thought of the almost empty fridge. At some point he'd have to risk going into town, but he daren't leave her here on her own. The rest of the weekend loomed like a curse and on Monday morning, the auctioneer's niece would come calling.

The quandary deepened as he couldn't involve

anyone. Round here, the name Oakley was a kiss of death.

'Look,' he began, 'we could try finding you a B&B or a hotel. Have you got any cash or a credit card?'

'I know you're trying to help,' those wide eyes again, 'but I don't think I can trust *anyone* round here any more – only you, and I'll be fine stopping here for a bit, if you'll have me.'

'Of course. You know that.'

'I've got Stephen Oakley with a fucking great dog on my tail. He'll kill to order, and is probably in spitting distance at this very moment.'

She turned to face him, with a deeper frown. 'My so-called parents, aren't they nice people? They fucked *me* up big time, I can tell you, but not any more, oh no. I've got big plans now, and they're nothing to do with them.' Her whole face seemed to suddenly glow, as if she'd been privy to some kind of vision.

'So why didn't this Stephen just force you to go with them since you know so much? After all, you could shop the lot of them, as you just said.'

Jo gave him the oddest look, one that turned her into someone he almost didn't recognize.

'He's not that much of a dick-head,' was all she said, and Ivan felt a new tremor of unease. 'Even though he has shaved himself bald.'

Ivan felt a growing wariness in her presence. There was something too dogged about her wanting to hang on there at Tripp's Cottage. It wasn't as if she'd gone to wash her hair or accepted a Pot Noodle or whatever. Dammit, she would not even take her coat off. What was going on? Why suddenly did he feel he couldn't trust her? And who, or what, was she waiting for?

'You OK?' she asked suddenly.

'Yep, fine. I'm just worried that something really shite's going to happen.'

'Well, if it does, we've got each other.' She smiled again. 'Why don't you go and light that fire? I like *real* flames. They have fake logs at Wiseman's. I suppose they think smoke's too much of a give away, they're so bloody paranoid.'

Ivan hadn't thought of that one, though he'd several times noticed the farm's smokeless chimney on even the coldest days. He hesitated about drawing such attention to his own place.

Fibber's her middle name... He recalled Bryn Mitchell's remark about the young woman still hovering in his hallway, and a swell of doubt and mistrust rose up in his mind.

As Ivan finally knelt by the grate, criss-crossing the kindling wood, he didn't notice her check her watch and smile to herself.

He was just nudging a corner of the newspaper with a lighted match when the ringing of the phone suddenly pierced the silence, making him drop the match onto the rug. As he picked it up and threw it back onto the fire, Ivan was aware that, after a few rings, Jo had snatched up the receiver.

'Could you try later, OK? He's just setting fire to the cottage,' she said in a strange voice, and, just as Ivan reached her, replaced the receiver.

He was getting more tense. Something was going on here. Something he couldn't *quite* put his finger on.

425

'Who was it?' he demanded, rubbing his singed thumb on his jeans.

'Some guy called Charlie Gifford.' He noticed she was eyeing him closely.

'Never heard of him,' he lied badly.

An uncomfortable silence hung over the cottage as the fire struggled to life and slowly began to warm the living room. She pulled her hair free of its pony tail, to fall round her face.

He was wary now of letting her out of his sight – the girl he'd most desired in his whole life now suddenly symbolized his worst fears. It was unreal; he was going barmy, just like his favourite poet – seeing evil everywhere, with no let-up. Or was he?

'Jo?' he said suddenly.

'What?' Her attention was focused even more keenly on something outside.

'You know you felt you could trust me?'

'Yeah, so?'

'Well, how do I know I can trust *you*?'

She swung round, her eyes ablaze like he'd never seen them before, their whites huge and wild, like those horses he'd seen in Westerns as a kid. Her mouth had tightened – the lips no longer pretty, the smile just a memory. She looked mean, she looked deadly, and she stood between him and the open living-room door.

Ivan stared at her apprehensively, his insides lurching.

All at once there was the sound of breaking glass which seemed to come from the far side of the cottage.

Ivan pushed past her into the hall then on into

426

his workshop where, to his horror, he saw a rifle muzzle poking through the pane at the top of the outer door, and above it he could make out the crown of a deerstalker hat.

'Christ, who's that?' he gulped, for a split second turning to face her.

But Jo's only reply was to thrust her hand into one of the duffel coat's pockets and pull out a small hand gun, complete with a silencer. It was pointed straight at him as she advanced into his workshop and made for the window.

Ivan felt sick inside, but had to act. While she was off guard for a moment, glancing out, he took a deep breath. In an instant he'd charged back into the hall and dived out of the front door. A shot whistled past him to lodge in the verge. He crouched by the Saxo and frantically yanked open the door. Once locked inside, he floored the throttle. Another bullet grazed the car's paint-work.

'Christ Jesus, Christ Jesus...' Ivan could scarcely breathe, could scarcely see where he was going. Then he realized he was passing Dawson's Farm, going over the bridge, with the low afternoon sun in his eyes.

He was heading for Church House.

But what about the fire he had lit? It was unprotected. Just one spark could send the whole place up in smoke. But even that concern wasn't enough to turn him round.

He punched 999 on his mobile, giving them the address of Tripp's Cottage and his mobile number. He explained how he was escaping from two armed people in the vicinity. Then, with a bolt of alarm, he realized that Valerie was still in hospital.

'Oi! Where you goin'?' The farmer began to limp after them with the dwarf following. 'You'll not get far, I'm warning you, and if you do, it'll be the Workhouse.'

But as the Welsh girl finally drew clear, she suspected all Crook had wanted was to add her to his weird collection.

The farmer's shouts faded as Siân reached the top of the incline and turned the pony along a track leading towards flatter terrain, towards fields with budding hedges, the odd church spire, or at least some habitation. Then, having rested both her companions, she could press on with her plan.

As an early dusk purpled the sky, she resolved to stay mounted, but to let Collen graze her way along, taking her time. They soon passed a sign nailed to a fence bearing the word Northamptonshire and, farther on, she spotted the flickering lights of a town. Back home at the Tafarn, she'd heard how a couple of local drovers would regularly bring cattle to this same county for the leather trade. Merlin Williams and someone called Dic, from Gors Goch they were. Maybe, if they were around, she'd find a way back home with them. Maybe.

Late in the afternoon, Siân discovered an empty barn set well back in a field which looked as if it hadn't seen a plough in years. Its internal beams were hung with several old deerskins abandoned by some poacher, and the smell of rotting hay was choking. Nevertheless Ben was content to lie on it and so keep guard near the opening while Collen leaned against a wall with head bowed.

Siân curled up nearby, gripping her rumbling stomach. She drifted in and out of sleep, half dreaming that she'd be running away like this for ever, as huge black crows flew in and out, thieving hay for their nests.

At dawn, with no inkling of which day it was, Siân woke when the silence she'd grown used to was broken, for outside the barn the folk of Monkton Regis were clattering their way along the poorly surfaced road, bearing goods for sale at the town's weekly market. Siân rose to look.

Carts almost toppled under their loads of wood, farming tools, and the artefacts of other trades, woven baskets and home-cured sides of pig alongside winter produce of every description. To Siân it was incredible that all this commotion could arise from this seemingly bare and depopulated landscape.

The traders themselves were of small stature, with fair and ruddy colouring, whereas the Welsh back home were mostly dark. But it was their expressions which she found most alien, their mouths set grimly, their eyes unfriendly and fixed ahead, as if solely concerned with the prospect of making money.

Hunger overcame caution. She moved from the barn entrance as the smell of fresh loaves almost made her faint. With Ben at her heels she reached the verge and waved to a baker's cart. The man ignored her, urging his horse on faster but, as if by a miracle, one wheel caught on a large stone making the cart rock from side to side.

Two loaves tumbled from the rear, as the driver cursed Parliament for not attending to the dire state of the highways or the needs of decent people trying to earn a living.

She snatched up these treasures, before he could notice anything amiss. They were made from wheat and still warm – the sweetest things since Huw's last kiss. Siân pressed one against each cheek and scrambled back into the barn, aware of Ben's jaws dribbling with anticipation. He and Collen were given half a loaf apiece, then she stuffed the other into her own mouth.

As new clouds spread over the sun, and rain began to darken the stones outside, she noticed Mrs Hubbard's clothes were beginning to split in places, and soon she'd look more like a tinker than ever. Another good reason for getting on her way. If she was found here, they would definitely stick her in the Workhouse. So she waited until the last cart was out of sight, then used the last of her strength to mount the weary mare and direct her back to where the road had last forked.

This turn-off was almost overgrown with weeds, and led away from where the sun had been seen beyond the distant oaks. So, Siân judged, this route must be heading west, safely away from that town she had seen last night.

The rain now soaked her hair, gathered in the folds of her shawl, as the hills returned and black-faced sheep and their early lambs appeared. Cattle with unfamiliar markings stood watching her slow progress, all facing her way. As the track continued over a full stream, Ben and Collen stopped to drink, before entering a dense forest the like of which she'd never seen at home, or even on her journey with Tomos.

This was a place of giants: trees whose vast trunks were three times the girth of a man, and whose greening arms wrestled so tightly overhead that no rain penetrated below. She saw small speckled deer leap to hide, like quicksilver, and pigeons drifting between the new leaf buds. Sounds of a busy saw could be heard from somewhere farther in, men's voices shouting, echoing through the oak pillars.

Then, suddenly, a gunshot, sending a spray of birds up from the branches. She felt Collen tremble underneath her, saw Ben stop rigid, unsure what to do next. He then lowered his nose and began to follow a path through dense-sprouting bracken, away from the sawing and the sounds of death. He barked once for her to follow. She had to trust him now more than ever – what else could she do? There had to be *someone* around to point out the way west. Someone who might even know of some Welsh drover returning home. And the way her dog seemed full of fresh purpose made her hope that a new and welcome page would soon be turning.

Twenty-Eight

The Cold Firton road was creepily quiet. No traffic, no horse-riders, and the River Wap, despite all the recent rain, flowed smoothly under the bridge, in complete contrast to Ivan's mood. His mind kept blanking for he was back again in that dense hell of a forest, where his dream of love had ended.

He was also crashing the gears, veering from camber to camber, and when he saw the rolls of barbed wire heaped up round Wiseman's Farm gate, the Saxo nearly climbed up the verge exactly where his Golf had been waylaid.

He was feeling foolish, no question. He'd seen thirteen-year-olds, for God's sake, swooning around so in love they couldn't even hold a Biro. And he'd been no different. Just nearly twenty years older, that's all, but no bloody wiser. *Sad bastard.*

Peering into the rear-view mirror, Ivan smoothed down his hair with his left hand. He looked so bloody rough.

Then he spotted her. Valerie Rook. He stared again. Surely not? She wasn't due out of hospital till tomorrow. And he hardly recognized her, walking towards him now, a lipsticked smile forming on her face and her step quickening.

He saw smart new clothes on her neat little figure: cream chinos and a matching top. Beige court shoes on delicate feet. She looked years younger as she approached his wound-down window, but when she noticed his expression her face dropped.

'Ivan? What's wrong?'

'How come you're out of hospital? Are you OK?'

'Bit of a headache still, but nothing much else. But Ivan, you look terrible–'

'Can we talk?' he interrupted.

'Course. Michael's just left for that conference in Warwick.'

As she stepped into the car, he saw no trace of her injury, apart from a fine red line under her hair. Her light perfume filled the car, and lingered even after she got out to unlock her front door. He parked behind a large clump of rhododendrons, out of sight of the road.

She was aware of his eyes on her, her unsteady fingers, the key not connecting properly. She heard Ivan's footsteps, felt his breath on her neck as finally the door swung open. Her heart was leaping. She felt like a sinner, entertaining a younger man like this in her husband's absence.

She turned to smile at him. 'I'll put some coffee on, and there's lasagne I can heat up if you're peckish.'

'No thanks. I've just had Jo Oakley and that uncle of hers trying to kill me.'

'*What?*' Valerie paled.

'She took a couple of pots at me. I'm not kidding. After I met her out in the forest, and invited her in for her own safety.'

Valerie Rook gripped the banister, then let her

hand slip down to rest on its comforting ball-end. 'You can't be serious.'

'I bloody well am, and I'm probably not doing you any favours by coming here, but I've nowhere else to go. I had to get out ... and I forgot you were meant to be in hospital.'

Valerie brushed past him into the kitchen.

'I understand, but I *did* try to warn you.' She pulled two chairs from under the table and gestured for him to sit down.

Ivan tensely perched on his chair, turning his mobile round and round on the place mat.

He held out a hand. 'You did. So where's the rap on the knuckles?'

Valerie Rook placed her own hand on top of it. Surprisingly light, with pearly nails. It felt nice. Reassuring.

'Have you told the police?'

'First thing I did. They'll ring me back if there's any news. The place will probably burn down meanwhile, but I don't give a toss for the dump any more. This has bloody done it for me.' He leaned back and sighed.

'What about that voice which whispers to you? The one who's trying to tell you something?'

Ivan shrugged. 'I haven't got to the bottom of it, but there's *this* to deal with now.' He straightened himself. 'Look, I don't know what happened to the rehab treatment your husband mentioned, but I swear Jo Oakley's definitely on something. I noticed her irises were bloody huge, and the way she can suddenly change mood just like that.' He snapped his fingers so loudly, his companion flinched. 'There's no problem her getting hold of the stuff either. That's what those Oakleys arrange with their mates, the Dawsons.'

Valerie Rook got up to open a cupboard. She found a plate and set four Kitkats on it in a neat arrangement, as if this could in some small way compensate for the insane world outside her door.

She then ran water into the kettle. 'They're probably all of them snorting and injecting behind their posh front doors ... and she's no different.'

Ivan was frowning when silently she brought his mug over, then some sugar which he heaped into his coffee without thinking.

'You could always stay here with us till things calm down,' she went on. 'I'm sure Michael wouldn't mind.'

She looked at him expectantly – her eyes enhanced by a soft blue shadow, her hair the same colour as autumn leaves.

'I'd love to, but...'

'But what?' She came over and stood behind him, that subtle perfume reaching him again. He felt her light fingers touch his hair. 'What do you think I've got to live for here? If I was one of his bloody patients, I'd get more attention. It's as if I'm just another ghost around the place' – her voice was thinning – 'as if my life's already over.'

'Oh, come on.' Ivan got up. 'Surely you've talked about that together. I mean, how long have you been married?'

'Three years five months three weeks and two hours.'

'And still counting, eh?'

All at once, Ivan took her in his arms. Heard the kitchen clock mark out the next few minutes as she began to cry against his shoulders, her tears darkening his old leather jacket. Her whole being needing him as no living person had ever needed him before.

They left the kitchen and moved along the sun-slatted hallway to the stairs. His mind was lurching from one emotional image to the next – from Jo Oakley to this woman who was now leading the way. From the dark depths of that wood towards a pool of shining light.

The fresh coffee prepared afterwards was hot and very welcome. They stood close together by the kitchen window, without speaking, looking out to where, just the other day, Dr Michael Rook had been so obsessively tidying up. But there were, Ivan mused, clearly some aspects of his life that control freak couldn't organize.

He studied Valerie's hair, where it seemed as if the wind had taken control, and her face was changed by a glow he'd not seen there before. The lonely years of pretence and making-do erased by a single encounter, while the winter sunlight had cast her skin and the sheets almost in the same soft tone, caught her lips and her teeth as she'd climaxed, both bodies entwined like fallen branches.

She finally broke the silence. 'While you were in the shower, I phoned the police at Stoneshanger, to confirm your earlier call.'

'And?' Ivan was not terribly excited.

'I was passed to DC Marsh who said they were already checking. Apparently all the Oakleys and the other two Pikes have vanished into thin air. It'll be in the papers tomorrow.'

'Any mention of the Sea View Hotel in Cromer?'

'No, why?' Valerie looked puzzled.

'Jo Oakley reckons her lot were planning to go there – or so she informed the cops.'

'There's loyalty.' She nuzzled closer and pushed a strand of hair off his forehead. 'Look, can't you forget about that lot now? Let the police deal with it then. I couldn't bear it if–' She stopped, a slight blush appearing. 'Do you still want me to go with you to the CRO on Monday?'

His reply was to lift her hand and kiss it. He then stepped into the hall.

'Right. Places to go, people to see.' But he was still seeing an image of Jo Oakley with that gun, the crazed eyes. Why hadn't there been a dog with Uncle Stephen? And was it really Charlie Gifford who'd phoned like she'd said? Or was that some cosy prearranged call between uncle and niece? If not, why suddenly pick *that* guy's name out of her hat?

He felt confused again, his wits dulled when he most needed them. The fact that Gifford's name had come from Jo Oakley's lips was seriously setting off alarm bells.

Ivan extracted his mobile and tried Gifford's number.

No reply. No answerphone message either.

'Who are you calling?' Valerie asked, looking concerned. She was already by the front door.

'Just checking on someone I met last night. He wrote some bad stuff about the Dawsons, past and present, so he's probably in deep shit too.'

She frowned. 'Leave well alone, that's all I say to you.'

'OK.' Ivan kissed her again on the mouth, this time more fervently and she opened the door on to the bright daylight.

Valerie Rook watched him walk to the car sensing his shiver as he trailed a hand along the bullet scar on its paintwork. He reversed the Saxo round, ready to go, then wound down his window and shouted something she didn't quite catch. Was it 'I love you'? She couldn't tell. But once he'd gone, she squeezed her eyes shut, praying for his safety.

This rain feels soft like a veil, and is in for the day, I know. And if I close my eyes I can pretend it's Welsh rain coming from the sky over Bwlch-y-Gwyn. If I keep my eyes closed a little longer, I can see again all those strange faces which I've seen in my mind before. But they're people I've never met in my life. They still look unhappy, but why? If they're somehow going to be my friends then perhaps I'll find out... I wonder if Ben can see them, too, since he often barks for no good reason, as if to protect me.

We're now quite alone, coming through the outer edge of a wood where younger trees, all different sorts, line a wide pathway. And yet at the end there seems to be a tiny hamlet, just like Nant y Fedw except its cottages' walls are brick not mud, and with tiles on the roof, not reeds or tin. Each is surrounded by a patch of garden, whereas Plas Newydd dwellings led straight on to Wern Common. Only the last dwelling has smoke coming from its chimney – the other two seem empty.

Ben's good ear is cocked for the scent of foxes, but Collen's rolling badly and I fear, unless we stop soon, she'll give up altogether. This new lane brings mud up to her fetlocks so we keep to the higher grass bank. I can smell cooking – but something else, like at Ramsden Worthy. My heart suddenly sinks remembering that dreadful place. Holy Jesus, suppose the plague is here as well?

Tripp's Cottage is signposted and looks a neat and tended spot, with chickens and a cockerel pecking around a coop. Yet as we draw closer, the stench of human waste from the overflowing cesspit gets stronger. Ben is nosing the air. I pray for him to keep his jaws tight together, for fear what this bad air might carry.

A young woman is swilling a bucket of yellow water round a drain. A little boy comes out to stand by the gate, then runs towards us, not caring he's without a coat in this damp weather. He's full of questions which I can't answer loudly enough, and this seems to amuse him. He claps his hands, as a grown man appears.

'Mama! Papa! Come and see. She can't speak a word, and I think they're lost!' The parents both stare at me in puzzlement, then pity. We must make a strange sight.

At least, this must occur to the little lad, who begins to chant, 'Make a picture for me, Papa. Make a picture of them.'

'Later, son. Can't you see they're wet through and exhausted.'

'Do it now, Papa. They look so funny.' He is getting tearful.

Such tactics pay off, for his father resignedly pulls a piece of paper from his pocket and, with practised strokes, completes a quick sketch while his wife quietly continues her task.

'Now then, Eddie' – he hands him the drawing, which the child kisses with glee – 'now, go and tell your brother we have company.'

There are three rooms and a barn here, while at home we have just the one living space over the other, but instead of our own use of a stream of clear mountain water, Hannah Tripp must pull a bucket from the well. It's a deep hole which reeks of foulness.

She's pretty enough – like her home, but is tired in her eyes from keeping the twins busy so her husband can work on his drawings and the repairing of old furniture. Their clothes are worn and have been mended many times over, and though the household chattels are old, they're polished up to shine: a copper jug, the spoons, the stewpot above the fire. That's what I could smell in the lane outside as I arrived. She keeps remarking on my pallor and suggests rest. After which I can stay for a while and be a help to her with the twins in exchange for free board and lodging. But that isn't my plan at all, and I mustn't be persuaded, however kind she is.

I have been given one of her older dresses and an ancient shawl which came from her mother – it's not very warm, but at least dry. She's also promised to give my letter to a friend who frequently visits Stoneshanger, assuring me that is the best chance of it reaching its destination. I cannot whisper thank you enough times, however my heart hurts more than ever with my longing for home. I can't explain how this

440

dark place with its forest affects me, and Ben too, for he refuses to leave my side.

Although the Tripps are kindness itself, and Eddie especially is so sweet to me, I sense that something evil is in the air. I feel so strongly that disease and death are present that I spend each minute of night and day wondering how best I might leave them without giving offence.

Twenty-Nine

Tove walk was a crescent of neat semi-detached homes, mostly with pretty ground-floor bay windows and the tired brown front gardens of winter. Ivan parked some distance down from number fifty-eight, after turning to face the way he'd come, just in case. Also, if the man he wanted didn't want to see him, he didn't want to risk being seen first and his visit possibly ignored.

The house itself seemed unoccupied, no lights on, no car outside, no sound of TV or radio, as Ivan walked quietly up the path so as not to arouse any neighbourly interest. As he pressed the front-door bell he noticed the door was fractionally ajar. Having glanced cautiously round at the curving street, and guessing all was clear, he stepped over the 'Hello!' mat and into the hall.

'Charlie?' he called out. 'Are you there?'

The smell was bad, like old meat. This wasn't right at all. The place was too quiet, and, judging by the clumsily closed bureau drawers, with bits of papers jutting out untidily, someone had already been in there before him. He also noticed that the answerphone had been unplugged.

Ivan peered into the lounge, dominated by a large framed photo of a couple in their mid-thirties, whom he presumed were Gifford's parents, with two boys in shorts, both wielding

442

cricket bats.

The small kitchen led into an even tinier dining area, furnished in IKEA, whose wall was covered by a huge print of the Sydney Opera House. That dazzling white shell against a ridiculous blue sky seemed like one man's dream in a dangerous English winter... A prospect no more, Ivan knew deep in his gut as he climbed Gifford's stairs, careful not to touch the banisters.

The smell of decay intensified as he climbed, hanging thickly over the landing as he pushed open the bathroom door to find the mirrored bathroom cabinet had been disembowelled and an array of harmless medicaments strewn mostly in the bath. His heart was on overdrive now as he tried first what was obviously the spare bedroom. Here he found a surprisingly up-to-date and still switched-on computer amid the detritus of a junkie's life.

Empty syringe boxes from Spain, used needles tipped by dark blood abandoned in an old ice-cream carton – but of the drugs themselves, nothing, all carefully cleared out. Someone had been diligent. Someone who needed a fix badly?

However it was the Viglen screen, dominated by a yellow triangle, which attracted his attention: *Error Message! Server Unavailable.*

Recalling how the man had talked of his emails, Ivan swiftly pulled his jacket sleeve over his fingers and pressed the Rightserve symbol to check the inbox. But there was no shifting the Error! sign. Someone else had already seen to that.

Then he noticed the familiar Safeways bag

amongst other junk deserted on a sofa bed. He checked inside it, then slipped the thesis inside his jacket.

Ivan then made for the larger bedroom. Even before he'd turned the door handle, he realized this was going to be grim.

'Oh Jesus, God, oh Jesus...' he muttered, backing away.

One glimpse of that naked bloodied corpse was enough. His stomach churned like a cement mixer, needing to vomit, and he lurched into the bathroom. He flushed the WC twice, then, again using the end of his sleeve to cover his fingers, stumbled down the stairs and closed the front door behind him, the sweet-and-sour taste of death still in his mouth.

'Noah Dawson's child died in the night, and his brother's daughter's ailing bad,' Matthew Tripp informs us as we sit round the table, and I notice after this news that no one, including me, has the slightest appetite for what Hannah has put on our plates. The leftover rabbit reminds me too much of what I've seen already, and the boiled barley's like maggots. I can see the Tripps are frightened and more so when, later on this same afternoon, Eddie complains of stomach cramps and his hands have turned blue, which is nothing to do with the cold.

Two days of watching him suffer. Two days with nothing to ease his pain. Even Mrs Hamer, the doctor's wife, who calls and says her husband is too occupied with others to visit, fears Eddie may not last the night.

He must have his father's strength, for next day he's improved and wants to play at making a house of branches with his twin, Jack, by the forest. Matthew and I stay awhile, and, seeing them happily amused, we leave them to go and clear the chicken run.

Suddenly, we hear a shot. Next thing poor Jack's crying that Eddie's been killed by a man who came out of the forest. He thinks it was one of the Dawson brothers as he's often seen him around the village. But I ask why would someone do that deliberately? Unless it was some terrible accident...

Matthew Tripp insists on going straight over to Dawson's Farm with or without the constable from Cold Firton, but Hannah reminds him that although the three farmers there dress more like London people, they're violent men who could kill him as well and then where'd the last of his little family be?

Ben howls as the small body is laid on the table. So white and thin after the cholera. Eddie's lips are like carved marble, his fingers still clenched round a piece of wood.

It's past midnight, with the storm hitting every corner of the cottage. Suddenly, from my bed in the barn I see candlelight pass under the door, but think nothing of it.

This morning should never have come. I'm the first to light the fire and that's when I see him. Matthew Tripp. His dead eyes rest on me as I scream for Hannah with my whole being, yet only my soul can hear the sound. And whatever is said to her, she won't be consoled

Dr Hamer and his wife attend to everything: the cutting down from the meat hook, the taking of the body for burial, at great risk to their own health. Without Mrs Hamer especially, what would the villagers do? She's spoken with me several times and knows what I want most, but advises me against leaving the cottage, at least until the epidemic has passed.

'People here are frightened, Siân,' she said 'They aren't thinking reasonably. There's never been such a disease here before and you wouldn't be thanked for spreading it.'

Those words stay with me every second of every day, but can't change anything: I have to go. And while Hannah has gone to St Mary's church in Sykeston, tired from weeping, dragging Jack behind her, I leave her my precious two pence and fit Collen's bridle.

The forest is darker, more gloomy than before. I'm damp and cold. My stomach feels as if it belongs to someone else, but I'm not afraid. Not even when an old crone not long for this world steps out at me from behind a tree. She reads my lips, urges me to leave Nether Wapford if I have any sense. This stranger manages to give me new hope, for when I ask for Wales, she points the way west. She also speaks of someone called Idris Roberts, a drover from Cardigan expected at Dawson's Farm that very afternoon. It's less than half a mile away, and, despite the stories of Eddie's death, it's a place I must try.

As I turn Collen towards the river, there are more shots from within the forest, at least six, louder than ever. Then the cries follow. My mare can't take me fast enough from this terrible place.

Still more rain, as if heaven, or is it hell, has more to

spare. Sharper, harder, forming a mist over the river. The path alongside brings us to a small footbridge, beyond which I can just about see the flat acres of Dawson's Farm.

I can also make out ewes and lambs everywhere, but so far no sign of any cattle drove.

I kick Collen on, but here she stops and nothing will move her. Ben, too, holds back when normally he'd show more interest in the sheep.

My one chance to get home safe seems to be slipping away. I've no choice but to tie Collen to the bridge end, with enough rein for her to graze, then I stumble along with Ben to the farm gate.

Thirty

Ivan pulled over into a lay-by, still in shock. He noticed there was just one message on his mobile. It was from DC Marsh, sounding slightly less composed than usual.

'Mr Browning, this is just to say we arrived at your cottage at 14.22 hours and found the door open but no sighting of either of the two characters you mentioned. Constable Whitrow will be waiting there till you get back home. We made sure to put the fireguard in place.'

Two characters? Why couldn't he even accept they were Oakleys?

On the journey back, Ivan realized he had almost wanted the unguarded fire to do its worst, for those flames to spill over, to gorge on the old hearthrug, devour the whole fucking place and silence its troubled spirits for ever.

The rain returned as he drove up the sloping village street and he prayed that none of Gifford's neighbours had spotted him visiting Tove Walk. The expected police car stood outside his cottage, and, as he drew up, the middle-aged constable opened his front door.

'Just check first that nothing's been taken, sir.' Whitrow let Ivan head past him into the kitchen, where he furtively deposited the Safeways bag in the fridge.

'So the two Oakleys had already buggered off

448

from here, then?' Ivan knelt and poked the now-dead ashes in the grate.

'We can't accept for positive it was them. I know you said it was Jo Oakley but you didn't actually see *him*, did you?'

'No. But she said–'

'We've got to be very careful, that's all. Or knuckles will get rapped – mine especially.'

Ivan contained his anger by continuing to beat what was left of the fire with the poker, till clouds of ash landed on the rug around his knees.

'Mind you' – Whitrow watched him without any reaction – 'we found plenty of grass disturbed round one side.'

'What about a rifle cartridge or the ammo *she* used?'

'Sorry, nothing doing.'

'The bloody rifle went off – I heard it. And you can see where the car's been scraped. She took two pot shots at me.'

Whitrow sighed. 'Look, if you can think of anything this girl actually touched when she was here, just tell the forensics chap. He can check over your car as well.' He moved towards the front door. 'I'm sure you've seen the general procedures on the telly.'

Ivan searched around for the mug Jo had drunk from, but it had vanished. He then went and stared at the phone, noticed someone had replaced the receiver the wrong way.

'Have *you* used this?' he asked.

'No, sir, got my own.' Whitrow patted his mobile, fitting snugly against his belt.

'Something else for your forensics wallah to

look at then. They've obviously been busy.'

'Leave it to us,' said the constable rashly. 'Now then, for your own safety, just keep indoors, and call this number if you have any more problems. We'll have it all sorted ASAP.'

'But they're all on the run now, aren't they?' Ivan pressed.

'Who told you that?' Grey eyebrows lifted in surprise.

'Can't say for sure,' Ivan shrugged.

As he watched Whitrow reach the Sierra, he felt powerfully tempted to call him back and tell him about Gifford lying slaughtered in his own blood. But, no, he couldn't. The poor sod would be found soon enough. Ivan was racked by the guilt, his stomach felt like a big empty urn.

Big empty urn...

Something made Ivan go to the workshop – darker inside now as the shattered door pane had been covered by a nailed-on piece of board. He switched on the light and sniffed the air. It smelt perfectly normal. He then walked over to the big aluminium oven and, without pausing, un-screwed the locking handle and pulled.

Ivan blinked. Felt that familiar dizziness again. There was nothing there, but the moment he peered closer a sudden heat passed through him, leaving his spine a core of exquisite pain. With this sensation still lingering, he stared into the kiln again, and this time saw twenty small pyramidical mounds of ash.

White ash, bone ash...

He covered his head with his hands and sat on the one old chair by his workbench. For a moment it seemed that desperate sucking on his hand, the whispering, the reason for his mystery journey to the edge of England and that strange and terrible scream, all resided in that place of burning.

Ashes to ashes...

Ivan got up, approached his kiln once more, and blew each of the piles to nothing...

Rest in peace, whoever you are. Please God, rest in peace.

And he could begin the process by scrutinizing the dead man's thesis.

Ivan extracted the thing from the fridge and hurriedly laid a new fire whose gentle warmth he hoped would calm him down.

But the pages were chilling. Some he recognized from glancing at them the previous evening, but when he found a sub-heading that read, *'The Effects of Common Land Loss on the Village of Nether Wapford,'* his pulse began to quicken.

Those villagers who formerly enjoyed the benefits of pasture for commonable cattle were powerless to prevent its enclosure by Lord Hickson and his wardens. The loss of this right to common pasture in 1820 was a massive blow to these 'in-town' inhabitants who had previously been permitted to keep three cows and ten sheep on the forest's commons. They were now without a vital food source and other useful by-products. Even the cutting of underwood which, tied into faggots, provided a family's fuel for the winter months, had now become illegal.

Thus we find increased incidences of depression among the population, and an unwillingness to give their strength and skills for another's gain, which no amount of attendance at church or chapel could alter. The folk of Nether Wapford gradually succumbed, in greater part than any 'out-town' settlement, to drunkenness, poaching by whatever means, and the ravages of disease. But, far more sinister than this, there arose a lack of good neighbourliness and a hostility to incomers.'

Ivan nudged the coal and the one small log to drive the creeping gloom from the cottage, before he flicked over to the next page.

On 11 March 1830 the cholera arrived, affecting every single family ignorant of its symptoms: cramps, diarrhoea, unbearable pain. Those with privies situated away from their wells and dwellings, or those who left home for the duration, survived. However, these latter often unwittingly carried the disease further afield with them, and any stranger to the village was therefore viewed with deep suspicion.

Life in that rural backwater sounded too grim to be bearable. Not so different from now, Ivan mused, searching the Notes and Bibliography for Gifford's sources.

To his surprise he discovered the name Robin Grimble, Grey Snorton Local History Society. A surname like that was surely too much of a coincidence. Suddenly he succumbed to an attack of coughing. To soothe his throat, Ivan drank some of his father's Christmas whisky straight from the bottle, leaving only an inch left.

'*Shit!*' Instead of relief, it brought fire to his throat. He felt he was choking and quickly drank some more, finishing the bottle. The flames in the grate spat at the rain coming down the chimney –sounding vengeful, defensive, not cosy at all.

On impulse, he fetched his mobile and after dialling 192 got Grimble's phone number.

'Robin Grimble here,' a young man's voice, sounding a touch impatient, with a TV on in the background.

'Ivan Browning. I've lost my voice.'

'Can't you speak up a bit?'

Ivan was on the point of giving up, but was somehow impelled to continue the uphill struggle. Maybe it was the mental vision of a pale anguished face, those sadly moving lips whose words obviously fell on deaf ears all those years ago.

'Do you belong to the Grey Snorton Local History Society?' he managed to croak.

'I'm its president.'

'I really need to come and see you as soon as possible. I live at Tripp's Cottage.'

There was a pause during which Ivan could hear the TV being switched off. By then, the man's tone had completely changed.

'My God. You don't really? It used to be ours.'

'I'm afraid I do, and I've had some pretty weird experiences here. Please, I need anything you've got on Welsh drovers round here about 1830 – or about a young girl turning up on a pony out of the blue.'

Ivan could tell Grimble was deliberating with himself.

'I'll come to you,' the young man said suddenly. 'I've been meaning to take a look at the old family home since I moved down here from Carlisle. It's only fourteen miles away, but I've been putting it off, as one does. You know how it is.'

'Tomorrow?' Ivan wheezed painfully. 'Say eleven o'clock. Or will you be at church?'

Grimble laughed strangely. 'What? No thanks. I'll see you then. By the way, I've got a silver Peugeot 206.'

Ivan thanked him and returned to the thesis but, apart from what he'd already sussed with Gifford, there was nothing else that might solve the riddle of that frightened yet insistent presence at Tripp's Cottage.

He then realized with a shock that if this same work was found in his possession, he wouldn't have a leg to stand on. There was no other way: he'd have to destroy it.

He unravelled the black plastic spiral binding carefully, washed it free of prints, and placed it in his workbench drawer along with some others he had used to impress into clay. Next, he took batches of four pages at a time, and tore them into small pieces before assigning them to the flames. Sudden angry licks of fire rose blue-green with each fresh sacrifice.

When he had finished, the paper ash was almost indistinguishable from that of the oak and the coal. Even so, Ivan hustled the remains with the poker. By the time darkness had fallen he was fast asleep with the fireguard in place.

'What the *fuck?*'

He'd been rudely awakened by the telephone in the hall. For a moment he struggled to get his bearings – he'd been dreaming of somewhere else, far away ... that land of wild bare mountains and rivers spilling towards pastures dotted by herds of long-horned black cattle. He'd seen them swimming a ford, followed by men on rough ponies, brandishing sticks. Watched as they stumbled to dry land again, to shouts of *'Haiptrw ho!'* He'd smelt the acrid sweat of beasts in perpetual motion ... dead meat on its way.

He staggered to his feet, groped his way towards the intrusion. First of all he thought it must be Valerie

'I'll be back, don't you worry,' said the androgynous voice, muffled and mysterious. His stomach went into freefall.

'Who are you? For God's sake...'

'Remember what I said? I'll be back.'

Then just the empty burr of the dialling tone.

Holy shit.

He stared at the receiver, realizing that any of Jo Oakley's prints would now be overlaid by his.

Jo? It was her. He knew it. And he was getting the hell out of here.

The closer I get, so the smell of cattle grows, and that other smell that hung about Tripp's Cottage. Two men come out from one of the barns, both dressed in black. The younger man is taller than the other, but neither

looks like a farmer, and I wonder to myself how they keep themselves so clean. Even the yard is spotless, like a best parlour.

The younger man holds an evil-looking dog – not of a breed I recognize. Already Ben's snarling for a fight, but a black boot kicks at him between the bars of the gate, and for the first time I'm afraid, wishing I'd not left Collen behind. My stomach suddenly turns over, hurting as if full of stones... Is there still time to get away? But the shorter man suddenly pins my arm down on top of the gate.

'Who are you?' he asks. 'Some tinker, eh? Some damned no-good?'

'Siân Richards, from Nant y Fedw, Cardiganshire,' I reply, unable to even hear my own whisper. This one's impatient, while the other man looks more curious. I must strain my lungs to repeat the words. They both look me up and down, all the while, their eyes like pieces of ice.

'A mute it is.' His hand is still heavy on my arm, and Ben's trying to make him leave me be.

'I'm looking for Idris Roberts, the drover,' I say. 'Has he called here yet?'

'Idris Roberts left here at ten this morning.' The taller man points to over beyond the farm, and my heart sinks. 'See, there's the runts we bought – a hundred and twenty, and not a one gone sick.'

'Not like our poor innocent Constance and Gabriel.'

'No indeed.' His voice seems different, strange, and while I glance at the Castlemartins grazing in the distance, thinking that there's no need for me to stay here any longer, the gate is pushed open, knocking me off balance. Ben's tugging at my dress, as to keep me away from them – but too late. Four strong hands are

456

four hands too many for me.

Collen whinnies from the bridge she's tethered to. I can't bear to hear her.

'Fine little pony, that. Fatten it up for a nice bit of meat, eh?'

'Patience, Arthur.'

'Her, then. Why not?'

'I've a better notion for one who's brought the plague to us.'

Brought the plague? My God, what does he mean? I shake my head and deny it.

'We've just lost our children. Dead and buried deep.' The one called Arthur stares at me with such an evil look I feel my cramps getting worse. 'All what you done, devil's daughter.'

Devil's daughter? What are they saying?

'It's in her eyes.'

'Cover them up, then.'

'Bind her arms and legs while you're at it. She'll make no sound.'

'You're a droll one, Noah.'

Take me back ... take me back. I'm biting, kicking. Ben's barking again. But it's no use.

They lift me up and carry me for a while, then throw me into some cart. At least I assume it's a cart, as it rocks up and down. Then, all of a sudden, Ben's thrown on top of me, his rough tongue hot against my cheek. He's whining as the wheels shift underneath us then settle. Some barn door slams so hard it empties my head as a bolt is knocked in place. Oh God, help me ... help me...

I smell a different death inside here. I try to think of Huw, of Eddie, and all those dead I saw two days ago. I am all of those people – now and for ever.

Where's dear Collen? What they're doing with her I daren't wonder, but whisper to Ben that when the door is next opened, he's to escape and find his way back to Wales, like other drovers' dogs do.

Wales? For a moment the place is all lost to me, but as I think harder of it than I've ever thought anything before, I'm on the road home to the sounds of sheep and cattle and the shouts of men... But where's Mam? Where's Da? Where's the Reverend Jones who taught me so much? The smallholders' children who once played in the river?

And then, in my mind, I fly up to Maen Lefn, the standing stone above the common to find those unfinished letters, H D loves – but what's this? I can't believe it. I won't believe it. There are new letters where mine should have been. Instead of S R, my initials, there's G P. They can only mean Gwen Prytherch, the singer from the Tafarn y Pluen. I can see the letters so clearly ... so clearly.

Huw's fallen in love with her, and her singing, I know it now. But he was my dream for so long. Now I've nothing left ... nothing.

Thirty-One

Ivan didn't sleep well that night. Instead he listened to the thunderous rain sloughing off the roof, and cascading down his centuries-old walls. Gifford's bloodied corpse and yesterday's shocking encounter with Jo Oakley went round and round in his mind like one of those fairground rides.

Why had she phoned him later like that? Why scare the shit out of him? What was her bloody game?

He turned over in his lumpy bed, pulling up the duvet to cover his head. That phone call was a threat he couldn't drive from his consciousness and, when a grudging dawn touched the sky outside he slunk downstairs and left the receiver off the hook.

His throat felt no better

Feeling like shit, he pulled on his jeans and sweatshirt over his pyjamas and made a cup of tea.

He wondered idly what Valerie Rook was doing now. Then, glancing outside into the desolate murk, he thought of the cholera all those years ago – how torrential rain just like this must have flooded human waste out of the ground to seep around the cottages, spreading it far and wide to contaminate whoever trod on it with bare feet, touched it with their hands, or even children who put their faces near it in play. He found himself wondering if that same ghostly wayfarer from Wales had succumbed, and the longer he sat there, the more impatient he became to learn the facts.

Valerie was going digging among the County Records next morning, but there was no guarantee she'd find anything much. No, he had to find someone else connected by *blood* to that long-forgotten time. Stanton's missing pages and Gifford's researches were all very well, but he, Ivan Browning, had to get to the root of it all soon.

And that probably meant confronting a Dawson. But which one? Handy Andy was now probably a murderer, so more than likely lying low, while his parents – like the Oakleys – were the sort to magic a starving Rottweiler from somewhere.

No, he should leave it alone, just get out now – leave the bloody place while he still had a chance. But somehow he *couldn't*. That other presence had become as real to him as anyone else he'd met here. Those strange dreams of that different country were just as vivid in his mind as the dismal view in front of him now. If he were ever to live peacefully with himself in the future, he had no choice. And so it rested with what he perceived as the lesser of two evils.

Having made this decision, Ivan left a message on Valerie's answerphone, telling her he was going to Cymric Farm in Welsh Way, and that he was leaving now. He remembered he had to get back by eleven o'clock.

Ivan bought himself one of the few remaining copies of the Sunday Gazette from Nether Wapford's one-horse newsagent and stared in disbelief at its bold black headline.

LOCAL FAMILY EVADING ARREST

Ivan returned to the comfort of his car, his mind racing.

The front page and inside page carried several photographs: Harold Oakley as mine host at the Lamb and Flag bar, next to a shot of his wife, Monica, taken some years ago on an exotic holiday. John Oakley posing outside his Stoneshanger premises with his trademark cap pulled low over his brows, while Stephen Oakley had been snapped by the vestry door of St Thomas's church. The last looked very dapper in his Sunday best, and obviously he was the youngest of the brothers. But why no photo of Jo? Or any mention either? How come *she* managed to keep such a low profile?

The attendant piece requested the public to be on the look-out for a maroon Nissan Terrano with a London number plate and a Wapping supplier's sticker in its rear window.

Stoneshanger CID were obviously playing this one close to their chests, he thought. Drip-feeding the readership with a bare minimum? Then he started. At the end of the final column was a short paragraph noting a firearms incident at an anonymous address in the south of the county. He suddenly felt cheated and angry. What the *fuck* was going on?

He slapped the newspaper, folding it in half. No wonder there was so much growing mistrust of the media. A year ago, following Vicky Walker's death, he'd been crucified wholesale by them. This time around he'd been airbrushed out. And as for Charlie Gifford and Anthony Pike, or even the latter's missing family, there'd been absolutely no mention.

Ivan checked his watch. He was almost in two minds now about pursuing his next rendezvous. He then reasoned that he was at least suitably warmed up to handle any more piss-taking.

It was 10 a.m. Not too early for a farmer, he decided, starting the engine and setting the wipers going at full speed. But even then they could barely cope with the onslaught of rain as he pulled out into Syke's Way and eased down the hill.

There was just the one light on in Dawson's Farm, and a trickle of white smoke against the gunmetal sky. The River Wap was rising fast, and looked browner than ever. Again he thought of the cholera epidemic as he entered Welsh Way and slowed down by a narrow turning to the left. There was a shabby sign stuck in the hedge: CYMRIC FARM – Free-Range Eggs, Manure for Sale.

With his heart in his mouth, Ivan knew he could still turn back, but things had gone a bit too far now. If that ghostly scream hadn't almost torn his head apart, if he didn't think whoever it came from hadn't suffered enough, he wouldn't be here now – risking his neck to give them both peace.

'Not until you find me ... find me...'

Well, maybe here was where he could start.

The narrow Tarmac lane, encroached upon by untrimmed hedges, soon deteriorated to infill rubble and this in turn became a churned-up viscous mud – a yellowy clay which had spattered all the old junk strewn on the bald patch of grass in front of the run-down farmhouse. Ivan noticed a pattern of wide tyre tracks leading towards the line of outbuildings to his right. Some of those were stone-built, some knocked up out of rusted corrugated sheets, standing alongside an ancient-looking Dutch barn containing unprotected hay bales which had blackened in the damp.

Before Ivan came to a halt on the one clear space, two skinny collies careered out from one of the barns and leapt up at the car windows, leaving filthy paw prints, their mad barking enough to wake the dead in all the nearby villages.

'Gerrin, you two!' a voice hollered after the din. The moment a man in camouflage gear appeared, they slunk away in the rain.

Ivan recognized the farmer's physique but, without the balaclava this time, was surprised by his face: strong, good-looking, but without any of the ruddy weathering of a typical outdoor life.

Tasty pasty Andy – an apt description, thought Ivan, especially the crop of sandy-blond hair.

He left the Saxo unlocked, with the key still in

the ignition. It not being his property, this was a huge risk, but he knew it was the best option for a quick getaway if need be. He had stuffed the offending newspaper under the passenger seat.

Low cloud now hovered over the rain slanting in from the east. It muffled the collective bleat of ewes and lambs and, from somewhere, a distant cow. Ivan noticed huge slipping middens by the Dutch barn, their stench seemingly unaffected by the weather.

'Hi.' He walked directly towards the man, coughing to clear his dodgy throat, aware of his trainers sinking into foul slurry puddles. 'I'm Ivan Browning, remember me?' He held out his hand and, to his amazement, the guy took it, his grip hard and warm. 'And before you say anything,' Ivan took the initiative, 'I've not come here to get even with you for all that crap you probably dumped on me. I just need your help.'

'Help? Christ, I can't even help myself.'

'Actually, I think you can.' He was amazed the man hadn't denied his accusation or told him to shove off.

Instead the farmer's blue eyes focused on him with unnerving intensity. 'How? Please explain.'

Were these the same eyes that Tony Pike had stared into just before feeling the blade in his neck? Ivan swallowed, tempted to run.

'I'm being haunted by someone at Tripp's Cottage and I know it's a girl who came from Wales. Whatever happened is over and done with, I understand that, but unless I can discover more about what happened to her there, I'm going to go bloody mad.' He tapped his head and waited, while Andy Dawson kept up that unrelenting gaze, rain trickling from his hair onto his collar.

Finally the farmer cupped a hand under Ivan's arm. This surely wasn't the behaviour of a man afraid to show his face. Either he'd been spared from any investigation into Pike's murder, Ivan surmised, or else he was still that same bloody good actor.

They reached the front door, its paint flaking to leave bare damp wood. 'Is it too early for a beer?' Dawson asked, not bothering to remove his boots. 'Sounds like you could do with something for that throat.' He kicked the front door shut behind them and, to Ivan's alarm, locked it.

'A drink'd be great, thanks.' Better keep him sweet, Ivan told himself, as he looked round for another means of escape. His visitor took the lead along the dark hallway, laid with its original stone slabs and littered with an assortment of footwear and old outdoor clothes.

Ivan noticed a rifle propped up under a row of stained waterproofs on coat hooks, and in a rush of panic remembered that intruder at his cottage.

'Voilà.' Dawson indicated a door to the right, leading into a huge kitchen where one ancient wooden table bore a selection of empty beer cans. The six unmatched chairs surrounding it were in varying states of disrepair, while in a corner next to the one bare window stood a butler's sink, like his own, piled high with dirty plates and saucepans.

Ivan could hear the dogs still barking outside as his host unpinged two cans of Kronenburg 1664 and handed one over.

465

'Cheers.' He tipped back his throat to reveal iron-taut neck muscles. Ivan realized that if this man chose to put one on him, he'd be hammered like a fly under a rock. With a lurch of his stomach he recalled the man's handgun.

'Cheers.' His voice croaked pathetically.

'So, you've got a spook over there, eh?' Dawson chose the least fragile chair, and indicated for Ivan to take another. 'I had heard about that. Little birds, you know – the ones still alive, that is.'

'It seems that in the early nineteenth century, some young girl showed up from nowhere and stayed at the cottage with a couple called Hannah and Matthew Tripp,' Ivan began. 'Not for long mind, but long enough for something tragic to have happened. Apparently there's an account in a copy of the *Mercury* kept at the CRO.'

'Ah, the CRO – a rather large thorn in the side of my nearest and dearest.' Dawson gave a wicked grin. 'I keep telling them you can't keep public knowledge out of the public domain, but will they listen?' He rested on his elbows, clutching his can. 'Oh no, they'll throw good money at fucking parasite lawyers to make sure the Dawson records are never shown the light of day, and I mean we're talking thousands of bloody pounds... Christ, I could have had some new shearing gear, my own slurry tank – you name it.'

So, Gifford *had* been right, after all; there were obviously enough cows to warrant one.

Resentment fuelled the farmer's every syllable.

It was clearly a bitter young man who faced his visitor, but was he dangerous? Was he a killer? Ivan wasn't yet sure...

'For Christ's sake, I keep telling them it's over and done with,' he continued. 'The sins of the fathers can't be visited on the sons, or we'd never move off square one. But they just go deaf on me.'

'Look, I'm talking round about 1830, though I'm not exactly sure of the date yet.' Ivan was trying to pin him down to specifics. 'But I do know that a certain Luke, Noah and Arthur Dawson were tried on 28 March that year for murder, and hanged the following month.'

The farmer edged his chair closer and lowered his voice almost as if his parents were in that very same room with them.

'Course I'm ashamed of them, like I am of Walter my grandfather – who wouldn't be? What I do know is that, unusually, those three – father and sons weren't given the option of transportation. It was the New Drop in Angel Lane, full stop.'

'So what crime did they commit that your family is so frightened of becoming public knowledge?'

Dawson slugged heavily at his drink. A man of big appetites, Ivan thought, without the dosh to satisfy them.

'They burnt someone alive.'

Ivan let out a gasp of shock. And suddenly that same heat he'd experienced yesterday passed upwards through his body – a searing, melting sensation beginning at his feet.

'Oh Jesus Christ.' For a moment he closed his eyes.

'You musn't breathe a word of that to anyone,' Dawson warned, 'or I'm in deep deep shit, and I don't want to be saying ta-ta to my inheritance after everything else I've bloody well had to put up with. There's something else too. Apparently it was all done in secret.'

'Where?' But Ivan already knew.

'In Wapford Forest, about half a mile in from your place.'

'Who was the victim? Any idea?'

'Some young girl or other. Both Arthur and Noah had just lost kids to the cholera, and they reckoned she'd started it, bringing it in with her. A kid in the house she was staying in had died as well. Also there was something odd about her, apparently, some kind of strength.'

'You mean, like she was a kind of *witch?*' The word had a flavour all its own.

'I'm only guessing.'

'How do you know all this? From the Session's recognizance books?'

'You must be kidding! I heard it all from Mr Carp down the Queen Eleanor. Bit of an amateur historian, he was. We often had a pint together as I used to shear his sheep – the ones that weren't nicked, of course. When he'd had a few, he'd sound off about what he'd found out, even though I told him the wrong ears might be listening. Poor old fucker, but at least he seemed more clued up than most of the other clods round here. They never found him, though I have my theories.'

Ivan thought this might be the best time to make a move, before he was drawn into a deeper, more dangerous discussion about *them*.

'I have to go now. Someone's coming over at eleven.' He pushed his chair back. 'But thanks for all that, Mr Dawson. The jigsaw's beginning to piece together.'

'I wish mine was.' Dawson was suddenly pinning Ivan's arm down with a big heavy hand. 'Hey, d'you remember what Philip Larkin once said? They fuck you up, your Mum and Dad. Well, it's fucking true.' He withdrew the hand. 'And, d'you know, people round here say to me, hey Andy, what's with all these acres and good drainage, and you have to go round like a tart, doing this for a buck here, and that for a buck there?'

Ivan tried to stand, but Dawson clearly still had things he wanted to say.

'You know what's next then? Got foot-and-fucking-mouth in a farm over in Turwell, and that'll be winging its way straight here. Shall I show you my feed barn with no bloody feed? The hay down to six bales already and it's only November? Oh yeah, sure.' His tone was hardening, like his face, in that darkening room.

Ivan saw the rain hurl huge drops against the window.

'And what I have left to bloody live on wouldn't keep a fucking rat happy.'

Ivan knew he had to go. This was getting too personal. The pale face was colouring, the massive fists clenching at the injustice of his lot.

'They are fucking unreal, my pater and mater.

469

And they're so loaded. I mean *fucking loaded*, while I've got a mortgage I can't pay, and the bank about to foreclose in two weeks – unless I come up with sixty grand.'

For a second Ivan felt sorry for him. He then envisaged Tony Pike lying in that open grave, his blood mingling with the damp soil... Yet there was no trace here of the crack which Gifford had implied Dawson used to excess. No evidence of anything other than a struggle to survive hard times on the land.

'Look, I hope things work out all right.' Ivan hauled his jacket collar halfway up his head and made for the hall.

'Oh they will, they will. And you're coming with me to see how.'

His visitor spun round. 'What d'you mean?' A stab of fear shot up and down his body.

'I mean you'll accompany me to Dawson's Farm.'

Ivan froze. 'I can't, sorry. I've got someone coming to see me.' It sounded pathetic. He was also a bloody fool to have left his new mobile in the glove box.

'Ah.' Andy Dawson reached down into the pocket of his fatigues and produced his own mobile – a blade of straw wedged in its holder. 'Give them a call, say you've had a change of plan.' His voice sounded different, slower, in a way that was more frightening.

Ivan took Dawson's phone with a numb hand, then tried to remember Robin Grimble's number, but couldn't. 'He'll just turn up and go away, I suppose,' he said, handing the mobile back. 'No problem.'

'Good. Let's go.'

The farmer moved off in front, only pausing in the hall to pull down an old Barbour from the rack and sling it over his shoulders. He then picked up the rifle. 'You never know,' he said, seeing Ivan's face turn white. 'We might just meet a friendly neighbourhood pheasant.'

As he unlocked the front door, Ivan said a silent prayer for whatever else was about to follow.

At that moment, Dawson grabbed Ivan's sleeve tightly and, having secured the farmhouse door, escorted him through the driving rain towards that same filthy Land Rover with which he'd intimidated him just days ago.

But something was different, Ivan could sense that. Every aspect of Andy Dawson's body language now betrayed a deep and desperate purpose. But to what aim, he couldn't yet gauge. He remembered what Gifford had said about the Snake House.

'I've got to lock my car,' he stalled. 'The bloody keys are still in it.' Instead he reached into the glove box to pull out his mobile.

'You won't need that,' Dawson dissuaded him, before nudging Ivan into the off-roader, locking his rifle in the back.

Ivan perched uneasily amid a chaos of chocolate-bar wrappers, feed merchants' invoices, final fuel demands in red, old newspapers muddied and crumpled, and the stink of filthy dogs. No evidence of any crack habit here either, not that he knew much about sniffing and snorting. Resentment and fear were growing in him in equal measure. He wondered again where Dawson's handgun was. In that sort of baggy clothing, it could be tucked away anywhere.

'Strap yourself in,' the other man ordered. 'We don't want some local plod squeezing me for fifty quid.'

They lurched down the sodden gulley towards Welsh Way with the hedges scraping against the windows. Over the bridge now, and up towards Nether Wapford with the wipers spreading not clearing the mud which clung to their blades. Then, after the foresters' cottages Dawson swung left.

'Welcome home,' the driver announced, passing through the freshly painted white wooden gates, then rattling over a cattle grid. 'And happy days,' he muttered sourly.

The Land Rover crossed another, more solid little bridge, with the Wap flowing fast underneath, and on towards the main house and its numerous spotless outbuildings. In the near distance could be seen fields under water.

There was no dog this time but, like Wiseman's Farm, no sign of any other human life. The contrast between this so-called farm and the tip of a place they'd just left couldn't be greater. Here were signs of serious money. The driveway itself was a smooth dark Tarmac leading to a property rendered dazzlingly white, set on a wide ironstone terrace. The house looked as if it had been built only yesterday.

Ivan noted the dark leaded windows, while the roof bore purply shining slates with not one out of place. He sat in silence, puzzled and tense as the driver parked to one side of the house.

'Their blind side,' Dawson explained cryptically, getting out but leaving his rifle in the back. He closed the car door with barely a sound.

'Come on.' He waited until Ivan had climbed out and laid a finger across his lips. 'This is my anniversary surprise.'

Ivan remembered the man in the florist's and suspected, with a thudding heart, that this was going to be no ordinary celebration. He tried to hang back, but Andy Dawson pushed him ahead to the heavy studded door, and let the brass knocker drop four times. Ivan risked a glance at the expressionless face behind him, but the steely blue eyes were fixed firmly ahead.

The door was opened by a small woman, whose distinctive dark eyebrows immediately rose in alarm. She stared at Ivan.

'Who's this?' she asked.

'Just a friend, Mother.' He pushed the toe of his boot across the threshold. 'Aren't you going to ask us in? I've got a little something for your anniversary.'

She backed away, her black tracksuit and short black hair merging in colour inside the unlit entrance hall, but her face, like her son's, was white as a moon.

Ivan recognized the flowers from Friday in a vase on a nearby table.

'Roy?' she called out. 'It's Andy.' Then she set off to fetch her husband.

'Well, isn't that nice?' The farmer nudged Ivan farther into the house. They waited there in the semi-darkness, on a black-and-white-tiled floor.

Ivan desperately longed for any means of escape, but husband and wife were approaching down the far stairs.

Roy Dawson, dressed in perfectly creased slacks and a Coq Sportif sweater, glanced briefly at Ivan then ignored him.

'Look, son, is it more snow you need?'

Ivan blinked. This was getting weirder and weirder.

'Snow? Give me a fucking break.'

'Roy, you *know* what this is about.' His wife looked up at him. 'We've gone over it, God knows how many times. Now, if you two want to talk about that, maybe your friend could sit outside in the Land Rover. I'm sure he wouldn't want to listen to our dirty washing.'

'Is that all you can call it, you stupid witch?' shouted Andy Dawson.

Ivan watched her face tense up with fear.

'Roy,' she pleaded. 'Get him *out* of here.'

But Dawson senior had seemed to grow yet more impassive, his eyes unblinking behind his glasses, even when his son stepped forward aggressively.

'That's right,' Andy sneered, 'just push me out of the way. Bury me under the fucking carpet like you've done all these years. Well, not any more. For the first time in his miserable life, Andrew Walter Dawson is fighting back.' With the imperceptible movement of a trained soldier he whipped out the automatic from inside his camouflage jacket. As he stood poised, legs apart, Ivan held his breath, numb with terror.

'In there,' Andy Dawson barked at them, 'and

you, Mr Browning, stay in front of me.' The muzzle gestured at the first door to the right – a lounge with a huge hooded wood-burner blazing away behind its glass doors. Like the rest of this former farmhouse, the room had been professionally decorated, in blues and in greens: colours that fleetingly reminded Ivan of his intended urns.

But pottery was now the last thing on his mind. And death was the first.

'Sit down.' Andy ordered his parents towards a settee whose plump upholstered depths would make any quick escape impossible. It was also the farthest seat from the phone. The Dawsons were surprisingly acquiescent, as if this was a ritual they'd gone through many times before. They sat holding hands, their four feet pressed close together – his in those same immaculate shoes Ivan had noticed on Friday. Hers encased in black snakeskin.

Snakeskin? Remembering Gifford's strange little analogy, and the reptilian bodies wound round that tree in the forest, he wanted to be sick. This whole thing was bizarre and grotesque. He thought of Valerie. How much he missed her.

'Now, son, we've always been able to talk about things, haven't we?' Roy Dawson kept up a patronizing tone, which Ivan found incredible in this volatile situation. Obviously arrogance and confidence were in huge supply and his wife tilting towards him seemed to draw from this. Her expression slowly changed to one of mockery as her son grew visibly more agitated.

'I've had enough of bloody talking, can't you

see?' Andy countered. 'What are words? Easy and cheap? And that's just fine for both of you, isn't it? Just fob the annoying bastard off, then off you go, dear, back to your cold uninhabitable house, your clapped-out car, your fucked-up everything. Oh *do* try and make a go of it, Andy – a big strong lad like you.' The son's voice turned cold, cruel, as he stepped closer, teasing them with the weapon. He then pulled a tubular device from his breast pocket, and fitted it over the barrel of the handgun. The same as Jo Oakley had done.

O Jesus, Jesus... Ivan gasped as the son expertly fitted it. This cokehead had planned this all along.

Still neither of his targets made any sound, any protestation. Had they all been this far before? He couldn't tell.

But he was gripped by pure terror. What was he fucking *doing* here? What on earth could he fucking *do*? The last twelve days he'd become sucked into a world of totally depraved madness. He hoped that the pale girl whose face had recently haunted him would now extend herself to become his Guardian Angel – because, Christ, he was going to need *something...*

Andy Dawson pointed the gun between them again.

'It's not *that* poor little cow my dear relatives should have put a match to all those years ago, it should have been bastards like you. But you're both going to die because you've killed *me*, and any chance I might have had to make a go of my life... And you,' he turned to his still immobile father, 'expected me to stand by and watch Pikey get rich. Have him rubbing my nose in it. Well, all those clever fucking Oakleys are out of it now.'

Roy Dawson then leaned forwards to make his point. 'The police came round yesterday, but we insisted you'd never had anything much to do with Anthony Pike.' Paler now, yet still with irritating reason in his voice. 'Thank the Lord we caught up with his father in time and, for a not unreasonable sum, he handed back all your foolish messages.' His eyes were fixed on his son, whose skin had taken on the waxy sheen of marble. 'I also made your emails untraceable.'

Andy Dawson snorted contempt. 'What else have you done? Killed Pikey as well, you cruel cunt?'

'Now you're talking utter nonsense.'

'Don't kid yourself, Dad. Your only motive is to keep yourselves out of the shit. Still, I expect the plods'll soon be sniffing round again.' He gave a sick little laugh. 'But at least I can save them the trouble of having to listen to any more of your fucking lies.'

For the first time Roy Dawson made an attempt to rise, but his son kicked him in the shin and his father roared in pain.

'And let's not forget the one who's with me every time I have to write out my full fucking name.'

'Who's that then?' Doreen Dawson struggled to rise from the drowning cushions.

'You know bloody well who. Walter Dawson. He shot Graham Tripp, didn't he? Tortured the lad first then pop, pop, took both his eyes out. Only fifteen. Poor fucker.'

477

Ivan felt vomit rising. He felt the young man's hot beery breath on the back of his neck.

'Sick sick sick, the bloody lot of you, and you always have been!' Andy ranted. He lifted the gun level with their heads.

'Don't!' Ivan tried to yell, but not a sound emerged. He was quite suddenly mute, his voice completely gone. It was as if the one way he might save these two sitting ducks had been spirited away.

The farmer stared relentlessly into each pair of now-pleading eyes. And, after four dull thuds, he was checking the magazine for one last cartridge, while four fountains of blood gushed out from their eyes onto the best furniture, its occupants lolling together, their moans dying with them.

Ivan had watched the killer's every movement executed in tortuous slow-motion. *O Jesus help us.* He felt his knees give way, the vomit rising.

'Look at me.' Andy then forced him round to see the strange smile fixed on his lips. 'You make one move and you get this too, OK?' Ivan nodded, wanted to assure him, but what could he do with no voice? His own death was going to be a silent affair. Just like Tony Pike's.

To Ivan's bewilderment the man began to gabble in Latin, his eyes half closed as the words tumbled out from his crazed mouth.

Via lata gradior
more iuventutis,
implico me vitis
immemor virtutis,
volutatis avidus

magis quam salutis,
mortuus in anima
curam gero cutis.

When at last he'd finished, he calmly removed the gun's silencer and, to Ivan's horror, placed the muzzle between his lips and hauled back the trigger.

The sole survivor puked up even as he ran, bits of the dead man's brain still stuck to his hair, his jacket, the backs of his hands. He skidded on the hallway tiles, and almost fell – then along the Tarmac drive to the bridge, then the cattle grid, to the open gate. Not a soul around, just the bells of St Mary's church tolling through the rain.

He looked back. There must be several phones he could have used in that house, but no way, not in there. Not ever.

He snatched up some clumps of grass to wipe his hands, his mouth, then gathered enough strength for a final dash towards the foresters' cottages – and the door of number nine.

'Help!' he yelled, his voice suddenly working again, loud and awesomely clear. A middle-aged woman answered, looking aghast.

'Call the police. To Dawson's Farm,' he burbled. Then, just before he passed out, he saw that two chequered Mondeos were already sweeping by.

So how can I hope for any sleep now? I listen to Ben's dreaming, as he runs once more with the corgis along the River Teifi. But when at last the bolt is lifted, and the barn door pulled open, he won't move of his accord, just grips my hem with his teeth as we're pulled into the colder air. There's a hard frost, I can tell, but not whether it's night or day, because of my blindfold. My bones feel weak as dust.

I hear four shod hooves. Collen? Is that her being harnessed or another? Then two more weights climb aboard, making the cart I lie in unsteady, until a crack of the whip sets the animal to a faster pace. I wish I could judge from the rhythm if it's her or not.

Ben's still close to me as I try to turn over, so as maybe to loosen the ropes around my wrists and ankles. But there's nothing prominent I can rub them against, and how can I instruct him to chew them? My stomach's knotted tight and I hurl my head sideways to be sick. Even that doesn't make the hound move away.

I try to call out, as I fancy I hear other voices nearby which might hear me, but my lips have gone numb. Not even a whisper leaves my throat.

Now we stop. Three men now, two whose speech I recognize, but the other sounds older and in a hurry. Hurry for what? I can smell the forest again, hear the snap of branches, then swearing.

Who'll take me back now? Take me back! Jesus Christ, help me. But when I try to summon up His face, the same as in my Bible, there's nothing there, just those strangers I've seen before. My unknown friends.

Bless me... Bless me, I implore them... Because that's all you can do.

Thirty-Two

The wind outside Tripp's Cottage seemed to rock his never-ending nightmares back and forth like the tide delivering strange flotsam to the shore, then drawing it back out to sea. But these were no ordinary leavings. They were coffins open to the sky, tipping and tilting, letting in water, one minute grazing the shingle, the next slumping back into the waves – sinking, sinking – finally yielding their corpses to the surface, now adrift on a spreading shroud of blood ... the recently dead Dawsons, Gifford with his scorpion pendant glinting in the sun, and all the rest of them, bobbing towards the horizon, with their bleached bones kicking in protest on the current.

Ivan woke up, half expecting to look upon that same grisly ocean with its distinctive coppery smell of blood, but here he was in his bed, with trees and sky clearly visible beyond the window. It was a sky of torn grey rags, ever changing – bringing his dizziness back. He turned to see his wall mirror, his empty bookshelves. Then his watch. 2.30 p.m., Monday 26 November.

He coughed to clear his throat, then spoke a few words to himself – clear as a bloody bell. Like a miracle, his voice had returned, but how had *he* returned to Tripp's Cottage?

Half closing his eyes, everything was spinning like that Crazy Cottage he'd once stepped into as a kid in an amusement park, while visiting Dublin with his father and mother.

Father? Mother? Liam and Maeve, of course – not Roy and Doreen with mouths agape, covered with blood, as the fifth shot had brought fresh slaughter into that perfect room.

Someone must have cleaned him up, since he didn't recognize these striped pyjamas several sizes too big. He decided to keep them on under his clothes and found his green sweatshirt and jeans had also been washed and dried, and smelt of fabric conditioner, while his socks had been rolled up into a neat ball.

Who on bloody earth?

Ivan picked his way downstairs to the phone. Seeing there was one message, he touched play and held his breath.

'Robin Grimble here. Just to say we seem to have missed each other this morning, so I've left copies of the relevant material in an envelope with Mrs Jonas next door. No need for their return. If you want to meet up sometime, give me a call. I'd love to look round the cottage again. Bye.' Sunday 11.13 a.m., the machine indicated. Just as the carnage had been about to begin.

Ivan looked outside, saw the Saxo, and panicked. *The keys? Where are the bloody keys?* Not in his jeans, nor his jacket.

He tried the living room, and immediately saw the keys were on the table along with his mobile and an envelope. He gulped and opened it. The first piece of folded paper was obviously torn from Valerie's diary and underneath lay Jo's folded manila envelope.

Monday, 1p.m.

It was Mrs Clent you called on after your terrible ordeal – she cleans at the surgery and was kind enough to do your washing and give you her husband's old pyjamas, which you can keep. I arrived at her cottage just after you'd regained consciousness and given your statement to the police.

I'd warned them you'd be at Cymric Farm as I was naturally anxious for your safety. However, I can see my concern has been misplaced. (See note enclosed which I found under the bed after your last visit.)

When the Police found your car abandoned at Cymric, they went straight round to Dawson's Farm. I must say Detective Constable Marsh has been particularly efficient.

I won't be bothering you again, Ivan, though I have other news as well, for it's obvious you don't need me after all. You obviously relish danger more.

VR

That same sickness returned. Shit shit. He'd not even noticed that Jo Oakley's envelope was missing from his jacket pocket. Now the one little beacon of hope he needed most had been snuffed out.

He then switched the kettle on and was just making himself a coffee, wondering what to do next, when there was an insistent rap at the door.

Ivan opened it just enough to see Mrs Jonas holding out a large white envelope. Her new hairdo had been unravelled by the wind and now

483

framed her face like a cloud of Old Man's Beard.

'You was out but, oh Lord, fancy seeing that Grimble boy again yesterday after all these years. 'E's not changed one jot.'

'Cheers.' Ivan opened the door wider and took the envelope from her, noting its slightly buckled flap, but too weary either to confront the woman or to discuss Robin Grimble.

'Ye look peaky, if you don't mind me sayin'.' She peered at Ivan through her glasses.

'I'm fine, thanks.' He began to close the door.

'Well, just be thankful yer not some poor bloody cow.'

'Why's that?'

His neighbour turned round as she reached his gate. 'Foot-and-mouth's over at Red Barn. Not six miles away.'

Ivan sat down and slid a knife blade under the envelope flap. Then, holding his breath, drew out copies of two pen-and-ink sketches, together with a compliment slip.

GREY SNORTON LOCAL HISTORY SOCIETY.

In haste. I hope these are of interest,
Robin Grimble

Ivan stared at the two cross-hatched images, then switched on the light for a clearer view. Whoever had drawn the originals was quite an artist, he thought. The first sketch showed a stout fellow in a battered black hat standing in a field together with a better-dressed younger man, obviously striking a deal. Behind them a blur of cattle distinguished only by their long black-tipped horns.

He peered closer. There was something horribly familiar about the background: that same low farmhouse, the flatness of the view beyond. It was Dawson's Farm. With trembling fingers he turned the drawing over and read the inscription: *Llew Parry, Cardiganshire drover, with Noah Dawson. By Matthew Tripp. Artist. 20 March 1829.*

Ivan swallowed, the now cold coffee not tasting of much in his stale mouth. He scrutinized Noah Dawson again. Probably mid to late twenties, a handsome profile, obviously fairly well-heeled to be able to purchase an entire herd.

Little did that dapper figure know, Ivan mused, what was fairly soon to follow.

Ivan then turned his attention to the second of Robin Grimble's enclosures. This sketch showed a bedraggled young girl draped in a shawl, mounted bareback on a ribby pony, with a tired-looking dog alongside. At the front, holding the pony's rein proprietorially, was a small lad no more than five years of age.

He fetched a magnifying glass from his workshop drawer. The girl's straggly dark hair rested on her shoulders, and her face – Ivan focused on that pale oval, whose dark eyes he already recognized – it was her, the one he'd seen in his mind's eye, or was it *out* of his mind's eye? And the more he stared through the convex glass, the more it seemed the girl's lips were moving.

'Find me and bless me. Find me and bless me, if that is the only thing you do for me.'

He felt more than dizzy, the walls around him and their familiar pictures were beginning to shift. As if that photocopy were some holy relic, he carefully turned it over and read: *Eddie with our Welsh stranger. Tripp's Cottage. 11 March 1830.*

Eddie? That was a new name. Was he the Tripps' son or possibly a neighbour's child?

Just as Ivan was about to take the picture into the better light of the hall window, the telephone rang. He started, and the drawing slipped from his hand to lie face-up on the floor. Finally he lifted the receiver.

'Mr Browning?' He recognized DC Marsh. 'We'd like to call in for a chat, in, say, half an hour?'

'That's OK. I'm not going anywhere,' he muttered. His gaze strayed back to the upturned drawing; the girl's face seeming even more luminous against its shaded background. And even more desperate?

'Mr Browning?'

'I'll be here.'

'We're on our way.'

Ivan picked up the picture and set it prominently on the mantelpiece.

After rinsing out his mug, he went to the mirror and stood for a moment staring at his shocking pallor and two days' dark stubble. Suddenly he felt a strange sensation begin in his feet; a warm prickling as if he were standing on hot cinders rather than on cold tiles. As he rubbed one foot against the other, the friction only made things worse. It felt as if the soles of his feet were now roasting.

'*Jesus Christ!*' Tearing off his socks, he noticed that both his feet had turned the colour of dyed salmon.

Shit, he had to do something. He must talk to Valerie.

'It's me, Ivan.'

'Didn't you see my note?' Her voice seemed chilly and distant. Ivan tried to get his thoughts in order.

'For God's sake, Valerie. It's not what you think, and I can explain it all later. Thing is, I need to see you. Can you get over here quickly? Something really weird's going on. Bring your crucifix and do you have a prayer book?'

'Yes, of course. I was a convent girl. Are you all right, Ivan?'

Her query fell on deaf ears, as he grabbed his jacket and stuffed his burning feet into trainers.

He locked up the cottage and waited for her in the lane outside. After a ten-minute wait, suffering that same heat, he saw the familiar Lada approach round the bend, its engine making an alarming noise.

Valerie stepped out, lifted a pink file from the passenger seat then hurried over. In a new hacking jacket, black jeans and heeled boots, she looked wonderful.

'Where are we going?' she quizzed him, as they set off round the side of the workshop.

'You'll soon see.'

She tapped the folder. 'I did go to North-ampton this morning, after all. Getting hold of information wasn't a problem, and I had one amazing find...'

Ivan kissed her cold cheek. 'Thanks.'

Valerie blushed.

'Go on,' Ivan prompted.

'It's a long letter from Hannah Tripp herself, dated 21 March 1830.'

Matthew's wife, he recalled, as they jogged through the main riding, still heavily scored by tyre tracks, and past rotting tree stumps and stool-based oaks overtopped by beeches and elms, all conspiring to protect the gloomy quietude beneath. Ivan winced occasionally at the pain in his feet.

'I know you'll think I'm bats,' he panted, 'but that little Welsh girl is leading us there. Keep thinking of her. She needs us more than ever ... we need to put her to rest, *now*.'

Valerie pulled some hair out of her eyes which had a faraway look, as if she too were being drawn into that mysterious past.

'This is about it, I reckon.' They had reached a wide clearing, in the centre of which the ground seemed strangely bare of vegetation. 'Hang on a minute.' Ivan suddenly gripped her arm. 'Can you hear something? Like singing? Listen.'

They both stood as though rooted, still as their surroundings, ears tuned to the slightest nuance of sound. First the muffle of moving crowns overhead, the odd branch falling, then a faint, light song – a girl's voice – as if she were out on the hills somewhere and the air of that distant place was bearing it away.

But, as they concentrated, the sound grew

more distinct, her words more clear. The same ones he'd heard in that dark crowded tavern on his dream journey, except that this time a smell of woodsmoke and singed flesh accompanied it, and filled the clearing.

'Get a whiff of that,' Ivan said, feeling disorientated, needing to sit down.

'This is *so* weird.' Valerie's mouth stayed open in wonderment as he pulled his trainers off. The skin of his legs was also reddening.

'This is never where she wanted to be, I mean here in Nether Wapford. I know that, but what could I do? What can I do?'

Bless me ... bless me...

With trembling fingers, Valerie Rook pulled her small gold crucifix from her neck and over her head then thumbed through her prayer book till she found a page that might help.

'This is one poor soul who must find peace, and if she can't find it here, at the point where her soul departed, she'll never know it.'

'So what do we do?'

'Pray with me.' She knelt down, and he followed, closing his eyes as she read.

'O God, merciful Father, that despisest not the sighing of a contrite heart, nor the desire of such as be sorrowful, mercifully assist our prayers that we make before you in all our troubles and adversities, whensoever they oppress us; and graciously hear us, that those evils, which the craft and subtlety of the devil or man workest against us, be brought to nought.'

As Ivan followed her words, keeping his eyes tight shut on an infinite darkness, the singing faded and the ghostly sound of crackling fire finally dispersed into the stillness.

An utter peace descended. There were five minutes of total silence before Valerie gently tapped her folder. 'You know, if it hadn't been for the bravery of one woman living here, nothing of this tragedy would ever have come to light...'

'Who was that, then?'

'Sarah Hamer. The physician's wife. You must read it later.' She replaced the little crucifix around her neck. Ivan examined his feet and his shins and saw they were their normal colour.

Neither spoke as they left the site, but when Ivan turned round, knowing that he could never go into this forest again, he saw briefly what seemed like a patch of light grey ash in the middle of the clearing, luminous against the leafy soil.

Thirty-Three

The wind had dropped to an eerie calm and, feeling curiously lightened, Ivan and the doctor's wife reached his cottage and headed round the front. A police car was waiting next to her Lada and he recognized DC Marsh with Whitrow alongside.

Valerie now looked utterly drained.

'I'm really grateful for what you did out there,' said Ivan.

'It was for both of us, remember?' Keeping her back to the police car, the hint of a smile forming, she added, 'And so was Saturday.'

He wanted to reach out and touch her, but Marsh was looking their way.

'Hey, I've got something to show you. Hang on there.' With a backward glance at the two waiting officers he went indoors, deposited her file on the table and fetched the drawing. 'Arrived yesterday. Amazing, isn't it?'

Valerie studied it for a while. 'What a beautiful girl.' She looked at Ivan, her lips trembling. 'With everything else going on, I never even told you I found out her name.'

His breath tightened in anticipation. But then he heard the police car door slam with a vengeance, and both men were heading for the cottage.

The moment had gone.

Frustrated, Ivan indicated for them to go in and

491

he returned Matthew Tripp's handiwork to its new place of honour.

Both policemen seemed to fill the small living room and, with daylight from the single window falling on Marsh's cheek, Ivan was aware that something about his appearance had changed. He seemed very tense, very controlled. His regular features were strangely grey and the usually pristine brown suit bore unfamiliar creases. It also looked like he'd missed a morning's shave. Join the club, Ivan thought, feeling his own coarse chin.

Valerie produced a plastic wallet from her shoulder bag and handed it to the detective. 'I realize you've got the dreadful Pike and Dawson killings to deal with,' she began, 'but I think you should see these photos of my car tyres slashed and these letters sent to me. I suspect it's the Oakleys' doing.'

Ivan gasped in surprise. 'About bloody time, too.'

Valerie looked at both men. 'You may wonder why I didn't tell you about any of this earlier, about the letters, the threats, but I had a marriage to think about. I still *have* a marriage to think about.'

Ivan shot her a glance of concern as Marsh, having studied the photographs, then extracted the two manila envelopes, and scanned both enclosed messages. 'Mmm, very nice, I must say. Thank you, Mrs Rook.' He dangled them between his thumb and forefinger, then passed everything to his colleague. 'I should say you're not the only one to receive this kind of message or to be threatened.'

'Who else, then?' Ivan queried.

'That's not for me to say. However, it's all adding up. Bit by bit.' Marsh's eyes strayed to the mantelpiece where he spotted a note which Ivan had once scribbled to himself, almost hidden between two cards. *Jo. Try Pronto cabs.*

His sudden frown was reflected by the mirror, but thankfully no one had noticed.

'It doesn't matter to me now, anyway.' Valerie avoided Ivan's eyes. 'I've made a decision.'

'About what?' Ivan was immediately on alert.

'My husband's not keen about staying in this area. He'd like to move away as soon as possible.' Valerie still avoided Ivan's eyes. 'And me too.'

Shit, she couldn't leave him. Not now. She was the one decent thing that had happened to him in this evil place.

'What about Small Copse Farm? I thought restoring that was your dream?' When he really wanted to ask, *What about me?*

But Valerie didn't reply and Whitrow glanced again at the note in his hand. 'Well, I have to say that would be a great shame for all concerned – but I suppose it's par for the course.' He ignored Marsh's warning look. 'When you come to think of it, Cold Firton's never kept a doctor for much over three years. Even Dr Willis, your husband's predecessor, was hoping to keep going until his retirement, but then his wife ended up in St Andrews.'

'The mental hospital?'

Whitrow nodded.

Ivan suddenly felt very cold. The constable

493

hadn't finished. 'Well, that apart, all I can say about the spate of recent crime round here is that until *every single one* of our entrepreneurial friends is apprehended and questioned, nothing much is going to change, so people like your good selves will be driven away–'

Marsh interrupted, pulling rank. 'The less the Oakleys and the Dawsons think we know, the better. Now then, Mr Browning, the reason we're both here–'

'Tell me, why wasn't that firearms incident here followed up properly?' Ivan had begun to colour, needing answers fast. His frustration was near boiling point. 'I mean those two had weapons and tried to bloody top me.'

Marsh kept cool, his eyes roaming round the room. 'We couldn't proceed far because, as I'm sure Constable Whitrow's already explained, we've got no proof of those two person's identities.'

'No *proof?* I don't bloody believe this.'

'It's more than likely they were casual hoodlums,' the DC continued undeterred. 'God knows, we get enough round here who seem to think that forest is their private playground.'

'*What?*' Ivan looked in disbelief from one to the other. 'I told you it *was* her. I should know, for fuck's sake! *And* some guy in a deerstalker cap.' He banged his fist on the table.

Ivan was tempted to mention Jo's vicious assault on a nurse, but that would only land Valerie in trouble for disclosing confidential information.

'Look,' he growled instead, 'she told me it was

494

Stephen Oakley and that he'd shaved his head. Then she also let on that the rest of the Oakleys were holed up at the Sea View Hotel in Cromer. Now would I be making *that* up?' His voice rose. 'Would I?' It was nerves.

'We knew nothing about that.' Marsh now looked faintly uncomfortable under Valerie's stare.

'I've always reckoned that girl had big problems,' the stalwart constable mused. 'Still, what do you expect with the company she's been keeping in the past thirteen years?'

The detective's eyes narrowed. 'Why do you say thirteen?'

'Monica and Harold Oakley adopted the girl when she was eleven.'

A tiny furrow formed between Marsh's eyes. He pulled himself together and recommended that Mrs Rook should be getting on her way soon because of the worsening weather. Indeed, the sky had deepened to almost black in parts as if night was imminent.

'I'll go with her,' said Ivan, swallowing his pride. 'Make sure she's safe.'

But Marsh held him back with surprising strength. 'Look, none of our friends are likely to be showing their heads round here. We've completely secured Wiseman's Farm, unless one of them fancies kipping out in the fields.'

Valerie gave Ivan a brief wave then executed a nifty three-point turn and disappeared as oncoming rain began to darken the road. Ivan stared after her, feeling strangely alone now, his stomach like lead. He suddenly thought of Jo Oakley's damp and bloodied coat. Kipping in the fields was *exactly* what she might be doing – with or without her so-called Bird Dog.

With every second his unease in this place was growing. Why hadn't she just killed him outright in the cottage with her discreet little automatic? Or did she prefer a waiting game to totally wreck his life, just like hers? To make them quits?

He watched Marsh follow Whitrow towards the hallway.

'I'd say there's been a pretty bad falling-out among thieves.' The DC ducked a meat hook. 'Not that I'm surprised with that lot. We got a call just half an hour ago from our colleagues in Kent. They found someone who must be Stephen Oakley in a place called Pluckley. Been badly beaten up, and not expected to live.'

Ivan's frown deepened.

'Jo made out they were all really close. Him and her, almost like, you know, *lovers*.'

Whitrow was staring out at the rain.

'She'll say anything, that one,' he said suddenly.

My God. He's really letting it out, Ivan thought.

'Well, let's hope the rest of the Oakley dawn chorus will enlighten us sooner rather than later,' Marsh added flatly.

Ivan had a sudden thought.

'No way is Jo Oakley trotting about with the rest of them. I reckon she's a loner – operating in her own weird world. So you've *got* to find her. And if that wasn't Stephen Oakley with her here, then who the *fuck* was it?'

Marsh seemed unmoved. 'Given where Oakley was found, the lot of them may be aiming for one of the channel ports. They'll hide whatever car they're using, and head for the continent as foot passengers, along with the rest of the grey brigade. This time of year you can take pot luck with the ferries, no need to book. Bound to have plenty of cash on them.'

Suddenly the phone rang and Marsh stepped forward to pick it up.

'Belinda Pillock.' Another small smile touched his lips. He seemed almost relieved. 'The Auctioneers. For you, Mr Browning.' He passed over the receiver.

The niece apologized that they couldn't make it that afternoon after all, but would he like to fix something for the next day.

'Yeah, tomorrow morning if possible, please. When's the soonest you can get here... Nine-fifteen? OK.' He replaced the receiver, sensing a weight lifting off his shoulders.

'We might need you as a witness, Mr Browning. Oh, and while we're here...'

Still expecting to be quizzed about Gifford, Ivan tried to prepare his responses. Meanwhile Marsh extracted a small pad from his pocket and looked round for somewhere to rest it.

'May we sit down?' The DC indicated the living room again.

'I'd like to sort something else out first.'

They both looked at him in faint surprise.

'Don't Mrs Rook and I get any sort of protection meanwhile?' Ivan shivered, hearing the rain's constant bleak threnody against the window – battering against the whole outer fabric of his prison.

'It's a matter of resources. Always the bottom line, I'm afraid,' Marsh replied reasonably.

'We *could* push for it, though, boss.' Whitrow again probably overstepping the mark. 'He's got a good point.'

But the DC was getting impatient. This was taking too long, and he'd other more important things to do with his afternoon. His pen worked heavy black circles on the pad.

'I know your previous statement was given in rather traumatic circumstances,' he began, 'but was there anything in Andy Dawson's behaviour yesterday morning which hinted at his state of mind? Please think hard.'

Ivan sneaked a look at the grate, all harmless ash now. Then he glanced up at the girl on her pony. 'The rifle in his hall spooked me a bit,' he began. 'And I knew he had a handgun somewhere, but otherwise he seemed OK. Just very bitter about his family. Quite a bright guy, bit intense, I suppose. Knowledgeable too.'

'Why exactly did you go to Cymric Farm? Stir up a bit of aggro?'

'Course not.' Ivan glared. 'Well, I suppose I wanted to have a go at him about dumping that cow shit.'

Marsh rested his chin on a fist, his dark blue eyes formidable. 'Now, about Gifford's murder.'

Ivan reddened, his heart racing. The other man missed nothing.

'Forensics found a one-pound coin in the man's mouth, and another,' he coughed delicately, 'up his back end. Also, his genitals were removed. We know how vicious certain gay lovers can get when they fall out, but this was an appalling act of savagery.'

Ugh. Jesus. Ivan remembered Gifford lying on his stomach on that crimson bed. He suddenly felt ill. 'That's so bloody sick.'

'I think, given Stephen Oakley's recent circumstances, our late friend Mr Andrew Dawson has to be a major suspect here. We also heard from Mr Gifford's brother that someone was sending threatening emails, so we'll be examining both the deceaseds' PCs very closely.'

Ivan struggled to find words.

'I can't see Andy Dawson doing anything so extreme,' he argued, relieved the spotlight was off himself however briefly. 'He'd got enough other worries of his own to worry about the past or the family name.'

Then, remembering Jo's wired-up state when he had last seen her, a suspicion in Ivan began to grow. He thought of the dead man's ransacked bathroom and the chaos in that spare bedroom as if someone had been searching for hard drugs and trying to disguise it as a lover's quarrel. Was she really capable of such mutilation, though?

Ivan dug out Jo's envelope and, blushing slightly, straightened out her scrawled words under its flap. 'I wonder if she had a bit of a thing for me.'

Marsh's pen made a sudden violent zigzag on his pad. He quickly regained his composure. He was about to pocket the envelope when Whitrow intercepted him.

'I'll take that, sir, with the others, if you don't mind.'

'Thank you, Mr Browning,' Marsh said evenly, in control once more. 'By the way' – those ultramarine eyes were fixed on him in a way Ivan had never seen before, like it was let's-give-this-jerk-a-fright time – 'you *did* come straight home here on Friday night, didn't you?'

The silence felt solid as concrete. Ivan glanced at Whitrow.

'I'm not saying anything else without my solicitor,' he said firmly.

Marsh remained unperturbed. 'You realize we'll need to continue taking statements from everyone who encountered Gifford during last week. So we'd appreciate it if you remain available until the investigation is complete. It shouldn't take us long.'

Ivan felt like a fish with a hook sunk deep in its mouth.

Marsh closed his notebook, screwed the cap on his pen, every movement calm and irritatingly precise. He'd had some little revenge, but not enough. 'We'll leave you in peace now. Give you time to think things over.'

Peace? Joke of the decade. But Ivan wasn't finished. 'What about the inquest on Tony Pike?' he demanded.

'It will be covered in your local newspaper,' said Marsh wrily, getting up and picking at his softened trouser creases. 'That's the best.'

Ivan suddenly needed the cottage to himself to unscramble his head.

Marsh reached the front door and suddenly turned round. 'We've finally managed to investigate George Pike's workshop. Would you call it

500

that, Brian?'

The constable smiled. 'No, sir, more like a bloody operating theatre.'

'Well, whatever, a real Aladdin's cave. Some nice wheels, including three green trucks but we know two are still out there somewhere, five Pronto cabs, and a partridge in a pear tree.'

'Four cabs–' Whitrow interjected.

But Marsh quickly moved on, 'There were traces of heroin in the trucks' spare tyres. Very neat, I must say.' He paused. 'Also a few cars that would seem to be hot, including, wait for it, your missing Golf.'

Ivan gripped the back of the chair. His precious car, oh joy.

'New wing mirror, new wheel arch, all very smart, I must say. Nice shade of blue, too.'

'Blue?' Ivan gulped. He'd never choose a blue car in his life. His joy was fading fast. 'What about my gear that was in the boot?'

For a moment both officers stalled, unsure as to who would answer first. Eventually Marsh took over.

'I'm afraid it's not easy to say, but naturally once things are sorted out...'

'What d'you mean, sorted out?' Ivan's renewed hopes took a dive.

'It wasn't your *gear* we found in the boot. It was Ian Pike.'

Ivan forgot to breathe.

'Been there a couple of days at least. Since Friday, probably.'

He froze. This was unreal. Worse than unreal...

But Whitrow had cleared his throat for his turn.

501

'The old man must have got the wind up after Anthony's death,' he said, pleased to air his knowledge. 'His kid knew far too much about the whole shebang: lorries with fake loads – you know, footwear, clothing, even bloody marmalade – all coming in for servicing. I mean, he wasn't going to take him with him, was he? The boy was probably getting greedy like the rest of them–'

'No father would do that, surely?' Ivan interrupted. 'No way.'

'Well, as far as we know, George Pike was the only one with a key to that place, and the only one who knew its alarm code. Incidentally, we found some tidy key-cutting gear in there and a stack of false plates.' Whitrow followed Marsh to the front door. 'Anyhow, sir, we'll let you know when your car's ready for you.'

'I don't want it now,' Ivan said simply. And the unfolding vision of that strange boy with his horrible bulging eyes all crushed up in his boot like those nineteenth-century corpses in their hampers, made him rush through to the kitchen as the front door closed behind them.

He bent over the plughole. All he must think of now, was getting out of here. Trial or no trial. He'd helped Valerie lay the Dawsons' poor little victim to rest, he'd done all he could. In the uneasy silence that ensued after the police had roared away in a muddy spray, he checked that all doors were securely locked and bolted, then sat down and hurriedly opened up Valerie's pink file.

As he scanned its enclosures, he realized with a sinking heart that despite the intervening years, the births, the deaths of generations, the passing of kings and queens and the never-ending legislation to govern and control, human nature still bore the seed of evil and, like those once-coppiced and pollarded trees in the forest, no amount of felling would stop that evil growth.

The phone's ringing stabbed through his thoughts. He let the answerphone pick up Valerie's slightly nervy message. She'd arrived back home safely, but had been aware of strange blue headlights behind her all the way from Trappers' Lane. Then, on turning into her drive, she had seen a black taxi race on up Church Street.

Ivan thought for a moment, then dived to the phone. He dialled but the line was already engaged. Maybe the Rooks were just keeping the phone off the hook.

On impulse, he tried Constable Whitrow's number.

'How many Pronto cabs did John Oakley run in all?' he asked when the man finally answered.

'Five of them, why?'

'But I think you said you saw only four at the garage.'

'What are you getting at?' Whitrow sounded uncomfortable now.

'I'm not sure. Just thought you ought to know that Mrs Rook noticed a black cab following her home.'

'Plenty of other firms do that run,' Whitrow said too quickly, and Ivan suddenly had the distinct impression the man was no longer on his own. 'So let's not be getting too jumpy.'

The cottage grew cold as evening descended, bringing an intense bleakness to his heart at the prospect of Valerie being shut out of his life, now that Dr Rook's future was taking a different turn.

As Ivan tried to put Valerie out of his mind, he continued to pore over the photocopied sheets, while the girl rider stared down at him from the mantelpiece.

He dialled Church House every so often and still the line was engaged. By the time he'd read the Records material several times over, he knew exactly why he had felt that ghostly mouth on his hand, those urgent whisperings, why all those manifestations of things too terrible for the girl to bear had become fused into his and Valerie's lives.

For when you are powerless in *this* wicked world, what other option is there?

Tripp's Cottage,
Nether Wapford

Sunday, 21 March 1830

My dear Lizzie,
So much has happened since I last wrote before you went away and I can scarcely put pen to paper on account of events almost too terrible to recall. I ask if I am cursed and wonder if you have any notions as to why this might be. I must first mention a very strange occurrence indeed, which to this day leaves me unsettled the more I dwell on it.
On 11 March, just before our sickness struck, I was outside clearing the main drain when I looked up to

see a girl on a rough chestnut pony with a hound. They were halted by our gate, and I have never seen three such wretched creatures, soaked through and weary. But Eddie ran out to greet them and begged his father to make a drawing of them while they stood so still. Out of pity, we then invited her in and tethered the pony to graze out the back. But the girl seemed always frightened and kept trying to leave us. Only after two days did she seem to settle, and Matthew got Mr Dobbs to fit her pony with a new shoe. She barely spoke a word at first except to whisper her name, Siân Richards, and she could barely walk, poor girl. When she slept in the outhouse, that dog would not leave her side. She loved the twin boys and Matthew, and I thought she might stay and be a help to me with cooking and sewing and minding the boys. Then suddenly our fortunes changed for the worse.

We had all been unwell since the twelfth, especially little Eddie, with his poor blue hands, who was in and out of the privy day and night like many others in the village. (I have since learnt that the cholera took Arthur and Helen Dawson's only child on the thirteenth, and his brother's on the fourteenth. So my fears were not unfounded.)

On the Sunday, Eddie seemed recovered and fussed to play with his twin Jack on the open grass by the forest. Matthew and the Welsh girl stayed with them until they settled on building a house of twigs. Then later we suddenly heard a shot and Jack came running in. He swore it was one of the Dawsons with a pistol, but couldn't tell which as they'd fired at Eddie from the dark of the wood. Imagine, dear Lizzie, when your child dies before you. Folks have suggested it was the Dawsons because they had suffered with the

505

plague and us not, and Matthew was all for going over to their farm with the constable and facing them. I begged him not to. They'll kill you too, I said, but, oh Lizzie, when the girl came through early next day to lay the fire, she found him hanging up on the beam from a salting hook. I have never heard such a cry of pain from anyone, and will never forget it as long as I live.

Such woe.

When I'd got back from putting flowers on the graves at St Mary's after the burials, she had vanished, the poor dog and all, leaving two pence for her lodging and a letter for someone called Huw, which I cannot now pass on as there was no payment with it, and I now have no money to spare. It is all my fault that the girl went missing and then perished the way she did. I should have taken her with me to the graveyard. But how do we recognize the devil even when he is amongst us?

I return to this letter after lying down a while, but I shall never sleep deeply again until I die and join both Matthew and Eddie in heaven… I could not continue except for little Jack, I will write more tomorrow.

22nd March

The cholera here is worse than in Cold Firton, and you were more than wise to go to the coast. Even though the rain is still falling, the smell is bad enough to keep one inside one's own four walls, but I shall have to go soon and collect the eggs.

Mrs Hamer, the physician's wife, has been calling on every dwelling without fear for her own safety. She *is the one true Christian amongst our church-goers and all these quarrelsome dissenters.*

Oh Lizzie, write me soon, when you are back in Broom House.

Your loving friend,
Hannah

AN ACCOUNT OF THE CONDUCT AND EXECUTION OF
LUKE DAWSON, aged 50 years, NOAH DAWSON, aged 27 years, & ARTHUR DAWSON, aged 23 years, of Dawson's Farm, Nether Wapford.

Who underwent the awful Sentence of the Law, on the New Drop at Northampton, Friday 30 April 1830 for a murder committed on SIAN RICHARDS, aged fourteen years from Nant-y-Fedw in the county of Cardiganshire. The unfortunate culprits were tried at the Lent Assizes on 28 March 1830 for the wilful burning alive of the aforesaid in Wapford Forest by first light on the morning of Tuesday 16 March. The judicial procedure was hastened to rid this county of three such vile persons, namely the accused, without any alternative fate of transportation being offered by the Judge.

Sarah Hamer, aged forty years, wife of Benjamin Hamer, physician of Cold Firton, was a material witness to this appalling crime, and showed great courage in speaking out. She was fortunate to creep away alive and to instantly report to the constable how the girl was brought blindfolded to the forest by cart, already tied by the hands and feet. Knowing the victim to be mute, they felt no need to bind her mouth, yet, at the point of death, Mrs Hamer remarked upon a haunting Welsh song which rose from the victim's lips, and the terrible barking of her devoted hound. Afeared of anyone hearing this commotion, they flung the wretched creature onto the flames to perish with her.

In their defence the three villains, all prosperous farmers, had claimed that the said SIAN RICHARDS had first brought the cholera to their village and killed their children. They pleaded that to save their other children they were right in their actions, and they showed no remorse even at the moment of sentence. But today we witnessed a different scene, with all three begging to be spared. A piteous sight, with their three wives weeping noisily in the crowd. However, none of them wished for the chaplain or the chapel, and one by one were launched into that world from which no traveller returns, their bodies being taken away for burial at an undisclosed site.

Thirty-Four

With Oliver Pillock already mentally checking the fencing and assessing the garden, his niece Belinda rang the door bell of Tripp's Cottage and tried to disguise her shock at the state of the man who answered it. She couldn't believe this was the same person to whom she'd shown the cottage only last June. He'd clearly lost weight, his eyes were bloodshot, haggard and even afraid.

'Enter, why not?' he slurred. 'Look, go where you like, think what you like. I don't bloody care. You can put a fiver reserve on the dump, if you want, or better still put a bloody match to it.'

'Oh come on, Mr Browning, you don't have to be so negative. Someone else'll love it, just like you did.' Her yellow cagoule dripped rainwater onto the mat, and still the downpour hurled itself against the windows. 'Once the foot-and-mouth's under control, it'll be like the rush hour round here. I mean no one wants to think of all those lovely deer in the forest being shot, do they? Or see great mounds of burning animals all over the place while they're looking for somewhere to live. Well, no good worrying. I'm sure it'll all be all right in a week or so. So I don't think we'll have any trouble with this.'

'I'll believe it when I see it,' he said glumly, squatting to stack his John Clare library in a Safeway Toilet Tissue box, which now seemed wholly appropriate.

As Miss Pillock did her rounds with rather more obvious enthusiasm than Cartwright, Ivan placed his rubber-banded collection of cuttings on the minibus tragedy in a bin liner. The time was when he'd pored over them almost every night just to torture himself. But it seemed his penance had been exacted one hundred times over. As a final touch, he added his fags and lighter to the sorry pile and sealed up the bag with a twist tie.

'I may not be around much after tomorrow,' he called up the stairs to Miss Pillock. 'I'll be up here with a van on Thursday, then going back to London.'

'Well, don't forget to let me have a spare key.'

He thought of the kiln: that dead weight he'd so laboriously assembled. It could stay here. It was *meant* to stay here.

'I'm leaving the kiln in my workroom,' he informed her. 'You never know, someone else might fancy becoming a potter.'

'Great. We'll add it to the details and I'll phone through tonight about our suggested reserve, around eight if that's OK with you. We often get artistic types like yourself looking for somewhere quiet.' She peered at him down the narrow stairs. 'I've got some gossip you might be interested in.'

'Go on.' Even though he thought he'd heard enough to last a lifetime.

'Douglas Cartwright's estate agency is totally abandoned. No one knows where he's gone, nor his daughter, stupid cow. Just a notice on his door saying closed until further notice.'

Half of Stoneshanger must be folding up, Ivan mused, but he felt some satisfaction.

'Good riddance, we say. Hey,' she suddenly called from upstairs. 'These are nice.'

'What are?'

'The flowers.'

He hurried up and followed her into his bedroom, as the scent reached him first.

'Jesus.'

There on the bed lay six newly cut daffodils, their colour a pale straw yellow, more subtle, more delicate than he'd ever seen in his life, with a thin red line around each cup in the middle.

'Lenten Lilies. They're gorgeous, but best to put them in water, mind. They'll last for ages then.' Belinda Pillock exited to check the bathroom.

He was enough of a horticulturalist to know that these Welsh emblems had flowered impossibly early. With a shiver, he realized that they had literally come from another world. He gathered them up cautiously, letting their strange sweetness suffuse his whole being, bring fresh tears to his eyes, and hope to his embattled soul.

That evening, despite the rain's continuing racket, Tripp's Cottage felt eerily empty, as if Valerie's simple act of faith in the forest clearing had expunged all its previous unhappy associations. For the first time since moving in, Ivan felt freedom, and those daffodils, majestic even in an empty salad-cream jar, seemed to represent some sort of future.

Nevertheless, before he embarked on the

journey to Cold Firton for his final pottery session, he said a quick prayer, and he kept his foot down as he drove along the waterlogged road until he reached Wiseman's Farm. Sure enough, barbed wire was still looped around its gates, so it looked barricaded just like all the other diseased farms now in the area. But as he slowed down to peer through the passenger window, he could swear he saw an upstairs light suddenly flick off.

His heart began racing. *Jo? Who else could it be?*

No way was he hanging round to find out, though.

Just as he approached Small Copse Farm, he noticed a white sign jutting from the hedge.

OLIVER PILLOCK AUCTIONEERS
FOR SALE BY PUBLIC AUCTION
TUESDAY 19 DECEMBER
THE GATEHOUSE,
MARKET HARBOROUGH

So, everybody now leaves.

As he made his way to Cold Firton, he finally got Valerie on his mobile. She seemed relieved to hear his voice.

'Ivan, thank God. The line's been down, and I've been so scared.'

'Are you on your own there?'

'Yes. Michael's holding a late surgery tonight.'

'Just make sure everything's properly locked up. I may be along in ten minutes or so. I've just got to check no one's turned up for my class, OK?'

'OK.'

He then told her to alert Marsh about the mysterious light at Wiseman's Farm. Valerie promised she would, then told him there was something he ought to know.

'I've just spent half an hour on the new computer that Roy Dawson installed for Michael on Friday evening.'

'And?'

'I managed to find a website on Jo Oakley, but talk about weird...'

'Go on.'

'Its borders were made up of oak leaves, like some sort of forest close-up. No date or place of birth or any family mentioned, mind, but,' Valerie speeded up, 'lots on the various establishments she's lived in, particularly a place called Holmlea near Haslemere in Surrey.'

Ivan frowned. 'Not Essex then?'

'No, why?'

'Nothing. What kind of place, exactly?'

'Some secure unit for women: drug offenders, baby killers, all sorts of misfits really...'

'Keep going.'

'Apparently she was being kept in their high-security block, but one evening had managed to bind a young nurse's hands – then tried to cut off one of her breasts.'

Ivan was passing Church House now, his hand unsteady on the wheel. 'And?'

'There was an internal hearing, it seems, but it was all hushed up. Holmlea was private, of course, and funded by some pretty big players. So their psychiatrists conveniently declared her

513

unfit to plead. However, to appease the nurse's family, they holed her up for six months after an interim assessment under section 38 of Mental Health Act. Then, after a pay-off, hey presto, she was back here as if nothing had happened. But, Ivan, that's just the start—'

'Valerie?'

'Yes?'

'Do exactly as I tell you. Stay downstairs near the front door.'

'Why?' She recognized the fear in his voice.

'Because I love you.'

And, as he sped up the hill towards the village hall he prayed she was an obedient listener.

Thirty-Five

By eight o'clock, the Saxo was braving the worst of the rising flood waters. Ivan and his tense companion were passing Dawson's Farm but he couldn't bring himself to look at it. And the next time he was on this road would be his last.

His passenger's clothes smelt damp, full of rain. For when he'd called in at Church House on his way back from the village hall, Valerie had been wandering around in the driveway gathering up all her new clothes which had been flung from an upstairs window. They'd lain there like so much salvage, dirtied and sodden – Michael Rook's final gesture before closing the door on the wife who'd finally revealed some of the secrets of her past, her hopes for the future. The wife who had made up her mind to abandon him.

'I see you're getting rid of Small Copse,' he said, spotting the auction sign again.

'Woman's privilege,' she replied, but without any smile, for the weird orange light which bloomed over Cymric Farm seemed to touch them both even inside the car. The afterglow of death – of flocks and herds heaped up on their backs, still smoking in the rain.

Back at the cottage, despite his own sudden loss of appetite, Ivan made them cheese sandwiches and two coffees. While Valerie was upstairs, changing into a pair of his old jeans and his favourite red sweatshirt, he began doctoring his register. No one except Flora Deedes had turned up for his class at the village hall, but she'd kept him talking there for twenty excruciating minutes, comparing Open College of the Arts courses with others on offer. Twenty minutes in which Dr Rook had returned to Church House and briefly, savagely, reasserted his influence.

Ivan was about to cut the sandwiches into triangles when the phone rang, making him drop the knife in his haste to get to it. It was a man's voice, tired and strained. His breathing uneven.

'Who is it?' Ivan asked suspiciously.

'I must speak to Mrs Rook, please.'

'Who are you?'

'Kingsley Gilbert, her solicitor. It's urgent.'

Ivan signalled to Valerie, hovering at the top of the stairs, then listened intently as the conversation unfolded.

'My safe was forced open last Friday, around lunchtime,' the man wheezed. 'It happened while I was at a Law Society function in London.' Ivan knew what was coming next. 'Whoever did it was extremely skilled and accurate. And, oh dear, I'm very sorry, Valerie, but I'm afraid your gold cigarette lighter has been taken.'

A look of alarm spread over her face.

'So why tell me only now?' she protested. 'Why not earlier, for God's sake? I could have told the police.'

Silence, in which the tiniest click on the line could be heard.

'Mr Gilbert?'

'Valerie, this is extremely difficult. The *only* person apart from you and your friend Mr Browning who knew where that item was being kept *was* an officer of the law. An officer with excellent credentials and, so I believed, an impressive professional.'

Gilbert hesitated and Valerie gripped Ivan's arm.

'Now, either he's been indiscreet and made that fact common knowledge, or one of you–'

Valerie's neck began to redden. She held the receiver even more tightly.

'That's preposterous! Neither of us has breathed a word to anyone about that lighter. We're in enough danger already.'

Here she stopped, as Ivan prised the receiver from her hand. Charlie Gifford's unsettling words, *just a whisper in the breeze*, rang like a mantra in his brain.

'Mr Gilbert, it's Ivan Browning here. Who exactly are you referring to?'

'Detective Constable Marsh.'

'Holy shit.'

'Well, that does seem to tie in with what Constable Whitrow's suspected for some time.'

'Whitrow?' Valerie and Ivan exchanged surprised glances.

'Now he's got police protection, yes. He believes Marsh had been phone-tapping and very cleverly shielding the Oakleys' and the Dawsons' so-called "business" interests from the CID in Stoneshanger ever since he joined there, and from anyone else who was suspicious. Whitrow's convinced he masterminded the Oakleys' recent

517

escape after their bungled attempt on Valerie's life in Woolerton. I can only assume that this particular theft is to ensure that they never come up before a court of law for her brother's murder. Though heaven alone knows what the other terrible tragedies will reveal.'

'Have you confronted Marsh yet?' Ivan quizzed the solicitor.

'He's totally disappeared like the remaining four Oakleys. And there's a warrant for his arrest, but he's still armed.' Gilbert's voice trembled, and it seemed an effort for him to go on. 'How he got into my office so easily, I do not know. He must have had a key cut specially for the front door, as the back door into the yard can only be reached by going through the premises.'

'Pikes garage, over at Westhope,' Ivan said bluntly. 'They cut keys. I bet Marsh knew about that little outfit.'

Kingsley Gilbert's breathing grew more laboured. He wanted to speak to his client once more, but his voice had almost disappeared. 'What about you, Valerie? Are you all right?' he asked when she came to the phone again. 'Your husband told me where you might be.'

She hesitated, as if she could never trust him or anyone again. 'I'm fine, thank you.'

'My dear, I'm so sorry.'

She hung up and stared at the receiver, her thoughts and actions frozen on the implications of what the man had revealed.

'Storm or no bloody storm, we're bloody going now,' Ivan announced. For the deluge had notched up a gear, overlaid by that same growling wind that seemed to shake the cottage and flicker its lights.

They both made some final silent trips up and down the stairs, hefting luggage and sundry carrier bags. Then Ivan checked that the gas was turned off and the TV aerial unplugged, Valerie watching his every move as if in a dream. But just as he was about to go and call on Mrs Jonas, to let her know he was leaving, the phone rang again, this time with a frightening intensity.

Valerie jumped, letting out a cry. 'Don't answer it!' she yelled.

'I've got to.' But this was nothing to do with Belinda Pillock with a reserve price for the cottage.

The caller did not speak, but let him ask twice who was there. Finally a female voice responded, high and wild as the storm itself, veering back and forth, obviously speaking into a mobile, sounding as if she was drunk or stoned. Jo.

'Cut the crap, mate, and just listen,' she slurred.

'OK.' His hand sweated on the receiver. That dizziness again, that weakness in his legs, but he made himself hang on.

'I presume you've seen my CV?'

'What the hell are you talking about?' He beckoned to Valerie to stand close by so she could hear as well.

'Any server engine will do. Just type in www.Jo Oakley. It's all there. Every last fucking detail. I've a good guess who went to all the trouble, mind. The bastard. Then he's got the cheek to put fucking Happy Birthday at the end.' Her words grew ever less coherent and, to lessen the onslaught, Ivan angled the receiver away from his head and closed his eyes.

'Still, mustn't complain. I've done OK, what with one thing and another, I mean, thirty grand from M and H for my notes and stuff to your scruffy tart, plus sorting out Tom Coles and his stupid dog wasn't bad, eh?'

Ivan's mouth fell open as she went on.

'Same for the chef and a bit extra for his suicide note and the tree decorations. I thought those were pretty cool, didn't you?'

Ivan felt this unstoppable evil pervade his system. He reached out and slipped his arm round Valerie's comforting shoulders.

'Then there was the granny,' the voice went on. 'I got thirty-five out of the Os for wrapping my hands around her squidgy little throat, which is not a lot when you think what they'll scoop up with her cottage. I had to get that Dr Rook creep to look at her, though, making out I was the doting granddaughter.'

Valerie winced while Ivan recalled the lie about the old girl's death. All the lies, in fact...

'Was all this money to feed your habit?' Ivan managed to ask, barely above a whisper.

'Two-way thing, yeah. *They* kept themselves clean, *I* got the fixes.'

'You need help, Jo...'

'That's what they always said at Holmlea. Stupid fuckers...'

'What about Charlie Gifford?'

'Put that down to Dawson.'

'Andy?'

'Don't be dumb. *Roy* Dawson.'

Ivan gulped.

'My real dad, isn't he? And guess what?'

Silence followed as again the cottage lights wavered. 'M's my real mum. He poked her in the forest near you. Now *that* must have been worth a view...' She chuckled to herself. 'Then when she's up the duff, she dumps him for Harold.'

'You're making all this up.'

'I'm not. She's just phoned from Switzerland somewhere. Only got three months to live. Wanted to put me straight on a few things. Kind of her, wouldn't you say, after all this fucking time? Anyway, she hated Dawson's guts 'cos he tried to make her get rid of me, but I was too big at eighteen weeks, wasn't I? I clung on. The clinic couldn't do it. As it was, I was two months premature.'

Ivan felt sick. His hand gripped Valerie's shoulder more tightly.

'Still, she got quits when she had me back, making me an Oakley, giving me a posh home. You think, every time he saw her she reminded him of what he couldn't have, and me, well,' her voice grew suddenly conspiratorial, 'I could be *useful* to him.'

'Useful? What the hell do you mean?'

'His right-hand person, wasn't I? Just like I was with the Oakleys. Hell, I'm not fussy where the fucking money comes from, long as it comes. I've just made fifty grand for wasting Gifford. But nothing was as sucky as shoving that poor old queen's head up his arse. That's the lowest I've ever gone. Dad's idea, in case you're wondering.'

521

Her sick laugh curdled into Ivan's ear. 'I'm glad he's stiff. Nasty cunt, doing my CV like that. Him and his ugly wife and that la-di-da milk mouth of theirs. Just think, Mr Browning, that Andy was my half-brother... Yuk.'

Ivan realized he wasn't breathing. He saw the black trees over the other side of the lane swaying perilously in the gale.

'And the Pike brother?'

'No sweat there. I'd got Pikey on his own so my dad could start carving, then once we'd caught that pervy brother of his in that workshop, and kneed him where it hurt, we crammed him in your car boot. Though Christ knows where their old man's chickened off to in that truck of his. Me and my partner picked up fifty each for Pike's two kids. Keeps him interested in me, though, doesn't it?'

'Your partner? Who's that?'

'Hang on, hang on. Give me a chance.'

'This isn't real.' Ivan glanced at Valerie who was shaking her head while he wanted to throttle that weird mad voice for ever.

'Oh, but it *is*, Mr B. It is. And you and that short-ass doctor's wife you're shagging – you're *next*. By special request from my grass-eater 'cos he doesn't want you two spoiling our plans for our happy-ever-after. And after the last cock-up in that poky hole of yours, my services will be free, gratis and for nothing. For *lurve*, Mr B, for lurve. You know, you made him extremely jealous with those white rosebuds you bought me, and for showing him that crappy note I wrote you. And when my man gets jealous, hey, better watch out.'

'Rosebuds? Note? Who the hell are you talking about?' And then he realized.

'Philip Marsh. Detective Constable. You got a problem with that?'

Ivan gasped. Tried to collect his thoughts.

'Why steal Harold Oakley's lighter?'

A short sour laugh followed. 'So he'll never be short of a bob, stupid. Better than a measly police pension, that.'

Suddenly Ivan was aware of a man's voice trying to shut her up. But there was no stopping Jo Oakley. Her pulse was pumping, her mind on fire...

'He got the Os to shuffle off so he could cosy up to the *real* big money,' she rattled on proudly. 'That meant the Dawsons and Oak Leaf Distribution.com. Pity it's not worked out. Never mind, he's got me and my inheritance. That's the main thing, innit?'

'You're a crazy liar, Jo Oakley. The old girl left you *nothing*. I know that for a fact.'

Ivan slammed the phone down and yanked its connection from the wall. He grabbed the sketch from the mantelpiece, and locked the cottage door then hurled himself into the driver's seat with Valerie beside him.

'Would you fucking believe it?'

'Yes.' She shivered, then kissed his cheek and stroked his hair to calm him down. 'Come on. We'd better go.'

'For fuck's sake, where?' He revved the engine, set the wipers whirring frantically.

'Somewhere safe. Somewhere where there are more angels than devils.' She fastened her seat belt and checked all around that no one else was about.

'That may be more difficult than you think.'

Ivan floored the tiny throttle and roared off down Syke's Way, thinking west, like before, but not back to Ireland. Maybe Wales...

No lights, just turmoil overruling the sky, with the glow of flames scattered at random over the black sodden landscape – scorched carcasses and their cloven hooves striking into the air.

Epilogue

There's still too much rain. It swills through the narrow lane and slows up the small red hatchback on its escape across country towards Banbury. Neither fugitive speaks, because mere words cannot drive away fear.

Instead the woman toys with her crucifix, recalling that unearthly experience in Nether Wapford forest which finally brought them together, her unhappy marriage and the disease of greed which surrounded them here.

Suddenly, blue headlights loom up behind. The same ones maybe which followed her to Church House the previous evening.

Even through the spray she can see two silhouettes locked close together in the front seats. Not kissing – for Philip Marsh will never squander any gratitude on deceit. Instead, he and the girl who has lied to him are fighting to the death, until a single shot rings out. Their night-coloured taxi cab, now out of control, swerves from verge to verge then finally rears up off the Tarmac.

Of all the thunder trees lining the road, it hits the widest and the oldest. As heavy steel sears through the ancient trunk, flesh and living sapwood mingle, while screams of the dying fill the night, unheard.

Translation of drover's hymn

Lord, guide me in your hand
Don't let me wander here and there,

I am a pilgrim on my way
My road is long and far,

I am a pilgrim here
An alien on my way.

Dafydd Jones, drover, from Caeo
(late eighteenth century)

The publishers hope that this book has given you enjoyable reading. Large Print Books are especially designed to be as easy to see and hold as possible. If you wish a complete list of our books please ask at your local library or write directly to:

Magna Large Print Books
Magna House, Long Preston,
Skipton, North Yorkshire.
BD23 4ND

This Large Print Book for the partially sighted, who cannot read normal print, is published under the auspices of

THE ULVERSCROFT FOUNDATION